── THE FACE ──

...of innocence
...of fear
...of misery
THE FACE of vulnerable Emily Gorden.

── THE FACE ──

...of beauty
...of success
...of wealth
THE FACE of a woman whose past is over and whose future has just begun...

THE FACE

Marvin Werlin and
Mark Werlin

A
Pub

Cop

All
right
Book
multa
Toron

Library

ISBN: 0

All the c
to actual

Manufactu

First Editic

FAWCETT GOLD MEDAL

To my daughter, Andrea, whose love, understanding and humor gave me courage.
And to The Clan: Tim Custer, Jason Blume, Wayne Moore, Don Johnson, Neil Elliot, Dennis Safren, and most especially to Maureen Dubin.

—Marvin Werlin

To Judy—Qui comprend la règle du jeu, et aussi les mystères du coeur.

—Mark Werlin

THE FACE

Marvin Werlin and Mark Werlin

FAWCETT GOLD MEDAL • NEW YORK

ACKNOWLEDGMENTS

Many people helped to make this book possible. Our deepest gratitude to: Alec Cowan, Bill Thomas, Jay Allen, Peter Koehn, Helen Westcott, Alan Mage, Skip Ferderber, Blanche and Albert Nissim, Betty St. Clair, Dana Wynter, Brian Higby and Jim O'Daniel, Ed Morrison, Jane Rotrosen, and a very special thanks to John Saul and Michael Sack.

THE FACE

PART

I

1

IT WAS DARK AND RAINING. SHE WAS LYING ON THE street, face pressed against the rough concrete, her body wracked with pain. Her clothes were soaking wet, pasted to her arms and legs. There was an acrid smell of burning rubber in the air, and closer by, the odor of decaying garbage. People were running and screaming. She tried to call out, only to discover that her mouth was filled with blood. All she could see was a blur of distorted shadows racing past. She wanted to reach out to them, but her arms wouldn't move. Then she heard the sound of sirens, faint and tinny at first, as if coming from a great distance. They drew closer, getting louder and louder. Their piercing howls became ear-splitting, and despite the pain lashing through her, she cried out, her screams mingling with the sirens into one long continuous shriek that seemed to go on and on and...

Emily woke with a shock, still hearing the frightful clamor of the sirens. She stared wildly around the room, then, in a frenzied movement, her arm shot out and she slammed her hand down on the clock, silencing its jarring alarm. The abrupt quiet that followed was like a sudden cease-fire on a battlefield. She sat up in bed, trembling and sweaty, and clasped her arms tightly around her knees. Familiar objects and pieces of furniture swam into focus, and the pounding fear in her heart slowed down to the safe recognition of the beginning of another day. Grey morning light seeped through the slats of the venetian

3

blinds, and the terrifying nightmare began to fade like an unwelcome visitor making a slow departure.

"Emily, are you awake?" Nora called from the kitchen.

"Yes, Mom," she muttered. Then louder, so her mother could hear, "Yes—I'm going to shower."

"Well, hurry up, honey, I've got breakfast going." There was a clatter of dishes being set on the table, and then Sheila's petulant cry, "Hey, shut up—I'm still asleep!"

Emily got out of bed, slipped on a robe, and walked down the hall. It was seven o'clock in the morning, but it could have been midnight for all the light that came into the house that early. She went into the bathroom, flicked the light switch, and turned on the shower over the tub. When the water felt right to her hand, she took off the robe and her nightgown, stepped into the tub, and pulled the plastic shower curtain closed. The water ran over her like a warm, languorous caress, and she closed her eyes, imagining an elegant bathroom of marble and tile, with sliding glass doors that opened onto a terrace filled with plants and white wrought-iron furniture. She saw herself leaving the shower wrapped in a thick terry-cloth robe and stepping onto the terrace, where a tray of coffee and hot croissants would be waiting on a glass-topped table. The morning would be clear and brilliant; there would be a delicate scent of wildflowers in the air. . . .

Emily opened her eyes to the stained, yellowing vinyl wallboard surrounding the tub and the cracked, peeling plaster on the wall above. It won't be this way forever, she thought. Someday I'll have the marble and tile bathroom, and the house to go with it. It was a conviction that never failed to cheer her, a promise she had made to herself that she was determined to keep.

She finished showering and stepped out of the tub, then began to dry herself before the full-length mirror fastened to the back of the door. Her reflection was misted by steam, giving the effect of a quickly brushed watercolor. She liked seeing herself like this. At the age of twenty-

4

two, she was slender, with shapely legs and softly rounded hips. Her waist was thin and her breasts were small, pink-tipped, and firm. The mist began to clear and she saw her dark brown hair, long and thick, streaming wetly over her face.

Her face.

She turned and looked out of the corner of her eye at her right profile. She had her father's nose, longish and a bit thick, but not too awful. Her cheekbone was good, and her eye looked nice like this, long-lashed and deep blue. And her chin was strong, but not overbearing. It was the pretty profile of an attractive girl with a good figure. She turned and looked at herself full-face. The mirror was clear, and on an impulse, she lifted her hands to her long hair, swept it back off her face and pulled it tight.

No miracle had occurred while she had been asleep. It hadn't gone away overnight, or changed in size, color, or ugliness.

On the left side of her face, a jagged red scar ran from her temple down to the bottom of her jaw, disappeared under her chin, and continued down the side of her throat. Scar tissue tugged one side of her mouth into a slight grimace and pulled at the outer corner of her left eye, giving her the expression of a clown's look of despair.

Emily stared at her face, repressing a surge of rage and shame. The scar was the reality of her life. It was a constant reminder of a memory that time could never erase, the terrifying shock and pain of the accident that had occurred when she was a child. The substance of her recurring nightmares, it was burned into her mind with all the clarity of etched glass. The rain-slicked street, the sudden lurch of the car, and her father's fear-stricken cry, "Hold on, sweetheart!" Those were the last words she had ever heard him say, the last words he ever spoke. She didn't know that until days later. And it was months later that she began to wish she had died with him.

Now, standing before the mirror and examining her face with hard, critical eyes, she whispered, "I'm still holding on, Daddy. I'm still holding on."

Back in her room, Emily got dressed. She put on a navy-blue skirt and a blouse she had made herself. It was a pale grey, with a high ruffled collar that covered the scar on her neck. Then she carefully brushed her hair so that a thick fringe of bangs hid her temple, and its straight fall would cover as much of the left side of her face as possible. That and a pair of dark glasses she wore whenever she went out completed her efforts to hide the scar. It helped, somewhat. For years she had told herself that she was indifferent to the stares and whispers, the quickly averted eyes. But it wasn't true. She had never become used to the shock, embarrassment, and pity she saw in people's faces when they looked at her.

Before leaving, she glanced around her room. It was plain, but clean and neat, simply furnished with a bed and matching side table, a dresser, an old sewing machine, a bookcase, lamp, and side chair. Only one piece stood out in jarring contrast to the others: a large, modern tilt-top drawing table. Emily had saved for almost a year to buy it, and it was her pride and joy. The ambitions and dreams of success that filled her every waking hour were all focused on the work she did at that table.

She paused for a moment to look at a sketch that was taped to the table. It was for an assignment in the costume design class she was taking three nights a week at Los Angeles City College, a gown that might have been worn by one of the ladies-in-waiting to Marie Antoinette. Library books of research lay open around the sketch, and preliminary drawings were tacked alongside. She decided she wouldn't take it to class tonight—the drawing still needed work. But it was good, she thought. Someday her designs would enhance the beauty of an actress on the stage or the screen. That was the dream she cherished, to create beauty from behind the scenes, where it didn't make any difference about the scar. And perhaps one day, when she had achieved great success, she would be wealthy enough to afford the plastic surgery necessary to make her whole again. That was her ultimate goal, the ambition that sustained and nourished her.

Her reverie was interrupted by Nora's voice calling out for her to come to breakfast. Emily gathered up her purse and a small cardboard portfolio and hurried down the hallway toward the kitchen. Sheila's door was open, and she stopped for a few seconds to look into her sister's room. As usual, it was a shambles. Clothes were flung everywhere, record albums lay scattered on the floor, bottles of make-up were jammed on the top of the vanity. Posters of rock stars had been hastily tacked up on the walls, and photographs of teenage movie and TV heartthrobs were stuck into the frame of a mirror.

Sheila was sprawled across the bed on her stomach, her shortie nightgown twisted up around her waist. Her face was turned toward Emily, eyes closed, lips parted slightly. Her blond hair was a mass of bright gold on the pillows, and her slim, tanned legs and hips looked honey-colored against the white sheets.

Emily stared at her eighteen-year-old sister with mixed emotions of resentment and envy. Before the accident they had been real sisters, playing together, getting into fights, and making up. But in the years since, the scar had come between them. Sheila had been terrified of Emily's face and ashamed in front of her playmates that her big sister was so disfigured. As time passed and they grew older, they became even more distanced. Sheila enjoyed a popularity in school that Emily had never known, and showed little interest in Emily's steadfast pursuit of a career. Now they had almost nothing in common and were simply cordial to each other.

Emily closed Sheila's door and went into the kitchen. Nora was at the stove, frying bacon. She looked up at her daughter and said, "Coffee's ready. Pour me a cup, will you?"

Emily did as she asked and then sat down at the

Formica-topped table. The kitchen was small and cramped, like the rest of the house. Years of cooking had put a shiny, dirty-yellow patina on the painted cabinets and shelves. The flowered wallpaper was grease-stained and peeling in the corners. A few plants stood on the window sill, their leaves straining toward the light, brown and dry at the tips.

Nora filled two plates with bacon and eggs and set them on the table. She sat down opposite Emily and started to sugar her coffee. She was an attractive woman in her middle forties who worked in a neighborhood beauty shop. She used a little too much eyeshadow and mascara, but her skin was still smooth and didn't wrinkle up when she laughed, the way some women's faces did. Her dark hair was cut short, and a once-a-week rinse kept the grey from showing. But the strain of raising two daughters alone was evident in the tense line of her mouth, the somewhat fearful expression in her eyes.

She looked over at Emily and said, "Sheila got in late again last night."

Emily sighed to herself; she had heard this complaint before. "I know," she replied. "I heard you yelling at her."

"I'm really worried about her. She hangs out with such a bunch of creeps."

"Sheila can take care of herself," Emily murmured with disinterest.

Nora bristled at her dismissive tone and shot her an angry glance. "Are you kidding? She's just a kid!"

"Once you get her into cosmetology school, she'll be fine."

"I wish I could believe that."

Emily went on eating, aware of her mother's need for reassurance, but ignoring it. She was tired of discussing her sister's shortcomings, and a little resentful of Nora's incessant concern for Sheila.

A tense silence ensued between them. In an effort to change the subject, Emily asked: "Did you check the *TV Guide*?"

"Yes, *Mata Hari* with Garbo is on at ten."

"Oh, good. The costumes in that are terrific. I'll get home from class just in time to see it."

Old movies on television were the only thing they really shared. Nora had come to Hollywood from a small town in the mid-west when she was a teenager. Like thousands of girls before her, she had arrived with a dream of finding fame and fortune in the movies. She was pretty, but unsophisticated and inexperienced. All she found were empty promises and occasional work as an extra. Then she had met Nick Gorden and fallen in love. She had often told Emily: "I think that's one of the reasons I married him—we were Nick and Nora. You know, like in the 'Thin Man' movies. The perfect couple." Now Nora relived her dreams on the "Late Show" with a nostalgic regret for what she imagined her life might have been. But for Emily the films were a constant source of inspiration, an example of the goals she was determined to achieve.

Emily finished her breakfast and stood up. "I've got to go—"

"So early? The store doesn't open until nine. Have another cup of coffee with me." There was a shrill note of pleading in Nora's voice.

Emily was anxious to leave. "I can't. I left some paperwork on my desk that has to be finished this morning."

"Okay, okay," Nora muttered, pouring herself more coffee.

Emily opened her purse and took out her dark glasses. She went to a mirror hanging on the wall, put them on, and arranged her hair to cover more of the left side of her face. She caught a glimpse of Nora watching her, then quickly looking away. Her mother's face flamed with embarrassment, as if she had been caught in an illicit act.

Emily picked up her purse and portfolio, bent to kiss Nora's cheek, and said, "See you tonight, Mom."

"Sure, honey. Have a good day at work and a good class."

As she left the kitchen, Emily glanced back. Nora was

hunched over the table, staring into space, her eyes brimming with tears. Emily wanted to say something to comfort her, but couldn't. She remembered how it used to be, before the accident. Nora was happy then, a young woman with a bright, quick smile who fussed over her daughters and was proud of them.

Now Sheila was straying beyond Nora's reach, and Emily had the scar. It stood between them like a living presence, a barrier of welted scar tissue and bruised flesh, an insult stamped on the face of the child Nora had borne.

And Emily knew that despite her mother's efforts to ignore the scar, there were times when she found the sight of Emily's face unbearable.

2

Emily GOT INTO HER CAR AND LET IT WARM UP FOR A few minutes. It was an old Ford and a rattletrap, always on the verge of breaking down. But it was her one means of independence, and escape from the house. She backed out of the narrow driveway and started down the street. The early-morning light was already choked with smog layered in the air like a pile of dirty blankets, and the neighborhood looked bleak and desolate.

The lived in Silverlake, a community that bordered Hollywood and extended to the beginning of downtown Los Angeles. The area was a leftover from the past, a time of clear, sunny days and soft ocean-scented breezes. Once the small Spanish-styled stucco houses had gleamed fresh against neatly trimmed green lawns. Bougainvillea had splashed trails of scarlet over red-tiled roofs and whitewashed walls. And residents could harvest crates of oranges from trees in their backyards.

Now the red-tiled roofs were chipped and dull; the white stucco had mottled into a scabrous oatmeal color. Lawns were brown, ragged, stifled by clumps of weeds that spread like a disease into cracks in the sidewalks. And the orange trees had long since given up the struggle to survive in the polluted air.

Emily turned onto Sunset Boulevard and drove past dreary blocks of used-car lots, wrecking yards, dingy junk shops, and second-hand clothing stores. A sight-seeing tour bus passed her on its way into Hollywood, and she glanced at the array of faces peering out the dust-streaked windows. Tourists. How disappointed they must be, she thought. The Hollywood of the imagination was infinitely more glamorous and beautiful than the shabby reality through which they were driving.

As she approached the store, Emily looked at her watch; it was just a little after eight—still time to get her paperwork done before the Skolskys arrived to open. She parked in an unmetered zone a block away and began to walk. She liked this part of the boulevard. All the buildings had been erected in the twenties and thirties and still retained traces of art deco facades. Now they gently sagged together, supporting one another like elderly people unable to stand alone.

Emily passed Mr. Wineberg's used-books store, D'Angelo's Italian grocery, and Mrs. Riker's shop, "Curios and Collectibles," which featured mostly cheap wicker baskets and brass items made in Taiwan. They all knew her, and she felt comfortable being among them. No one had ever, by word or gesture, made a comment about her face. They were people who had known anguish in their own lives. They understood her.

She came to Skolsky's store and took out her keys. A hand-lettered wooden sign hung from a wrought-iron holder over the entrance. Painted in gilt and scarlet, it gaudily proclaimed, "NOB HILL ANTIQUES: Beauty is in the eye of the beholder, so come in and behold."

Emily unlocked the front door and went in, closing the door behind her. Furniture of every description, style, and period was jammed together, leaving only a narrow path from one end of the shop to the other. Hanging from the ceiling was a multitude of light fixtures, some dulled brass or wood, others dusty cut-glass crystal chandeliers. Along the walls a large assortment of straight-backed chairs hung on racks that ran the length of the store.

She made her way to the rear, turned a treacherous corner around a massive dining room table, passed before a pair of tall mirrors that reflected her in wavering, musty images, and arrived at an officelike corner containing a desk, some filing cabinets, and a typewriter on a small rolling table. The air was thick with odors of wood and furniture polish. She opened the back windows, switched on the overhead lights, then sat down at the desk and began to check through a stack of invoices. By the time she had finished and was filing them, the proprietors, Victor and Ethel Skolsky, arrived.

"Good morning," Emily called out to them.

"What, you're here so early again?" Victor said. His accent was thickly Russian, his voice tobacco-hoarse from an endless flow of cigars that were always clamped between his lips. "Whatsa matter, you don't get enough of this place in regular hours?" He looked at her through pale, rheumy brown eyes and smiled, creating an irregular grid of lines across his face.

Victor shrugged out of his jacket and hung it up on a coat rack. He was a short man with a large, balding head that seemed buried in massive, hunched shoulders. When he wasn't dealing with a customer or moving pieces of furniture, he was in a shed that was attached to the back of the store, where he did refinishing with the careful, delicate touch of an artisan.

Ethel Skolsky was a tall, formidable-looking woman with stern grey eyes, a long bony face, and rust-colored hair that was wound tightly into a bun. She took off her coat, methodically rolled up the sleeves of her black tailored blouse, and said to her husband, "Victor, open the front doors and put out the furniture while I make the tea." Her accent was similar to Victor's, and her voice almost as husky. She turned to Emily with a smile that suddenly rearranged her harsh features into a sunny expression of warmth. "It's nice you come in early to work," she told her. "We appreciate it. Now you'll have some tea, yes?"

Emily agreed; it was a morning ritual she always enjoyed. After Victor had set out various pieces of furniture on the sidewalk in front of the store, the three of them gathered at Ethel's desk, which stood on the other side of the store from Emily's office. Fragile china cups were filled with tea from a gleaming silver samovar, a delicate Meissen sugar bowl and thin slices of lemon on a Wedgwood saucer were set out, and while they drank, they discussed the work to be done during the day.

The shop was not just a neighborhood furniture store. Almost all the pieces were fine, genuine antiques from wealthy homes and estates. Ethel attended several auctions a week and had a sharp eye for furniture that was in demand by the decorators and interior designers who made up the body of their clientele. The Skolskys were very canny about their business operation. They maintained a low overhead because of their location, and operated on a cash-and-carry basis, accepting checks from only a few well-known customers. All the receipts were kept in an old-fashioned combination lock safe that stood near Ethel's desk. Twice a week she took them from the safe and deposited them in the bank.

Emily had been with the Skolskys for over a year. She kept the books, typed letters and invoices, checked out bills of lading, and notified customers when a new shipment came in. While doing this, she had learned a great deal about different periods and styles and had come to appreciate the beauty of French armoires, English breakfronts, Victorian side tables, and Belgian cabinets.

When she had first started working in the store, she had thought of it as a refuge, a place to hide from any contact with the public. For a month or two she had stayed at her desk, finding a variety of excuses not to mix with the customers. The Skolskys understood and said nothing. As time went by, however, Emily overcame her selfconciousness and began to enjoy chatting with the people who frequented the shop. Most of the men were gay, and she was entertained by their gossip about the stars they worked for, the homes they were doing, the social whirl of dinners, premieres, and elegant parties they attended. Some of them were friends with film costume designers, and she eagerly sought out information about the movies on which they worked, determined to learn as much as she could about the business.

As for the women who came into the store, many of them were the wives of men in the film or TV industry. Bored or unhappy, they had turned to decorating as a means of finding some recognition on their own, a desire with which Emily could sympathize. But she knew that despite the cheery exchanges she enjoyed with these people, they saw her only as the girl who worked for the Skolskys, the mousy one with the scar, who was so dependable. She didn't mind. She was positive that someday, scar or no scar, they would all know who she was.

Later that afternoon, Emily looked up from her desk to see Harriet Bradshaw enter the store. Harriet was a plump woman with a horsey face and a loud New York voice. She was a new customer, and Ethel Skolsky regarded her with some suspicion even though Harriet's husband was an executive at Universal Studios.

"You people are a godsend!" Harriet brayed. "That cabinet is exactly what I was looking for!" Her darting eyes glistened with triumph.

Ethel nodded. "It's a nice piece," she agreed.

They were standing beside an elegant Sheraton mahogany display cabinet that was crossbanded and inlaid in satinwood and ebony. Harriet ran a pudgy hand over the surface of the wood. Diamond and ruby rings sparkled on her fingers, and a ferocious smile of accomplishment revealed a gleaming row of perfectly capped teeth.

Emily chuckled to herself at the woman's appearance. Harriet was dressed in a beige pantsuit that emphasized every corpulent inch of her stocky figure. Oversized sunglasses were shoved back into a disarray of blond hair, completing the casually messy look so many women from Beverly Hills affected when they were "working."

Emily was about to return to her work when she noticed a young man carrying a package come into the store. For a moment she sat transfixed, unable to take her eyes from him. Tall and broad-shouldered, with a lithe, athletic build, he was more handsome than any man she had ever seen. A mass of tousled black hair fell over his wide forehead, and his face had the patrician beauty of a Renaissance nobleman: a finely sculpted nose, high cheekbones, large, darkly lashed green eyes, and a full, sensuously curved mouth the color of deep red wine.

He looked around for someone to help him, then began to walk toward Ethel and Harriet Bradshaw. As he approached them, Harriet was saying: "Really, Mrs. Skolsky, I hope we get to know each other well enough to let me pay by check. I hate to carry around this much in cash. Don't you think you're being a little *too* cautious?"

"It's cash and carry," Ethel replied stoically. "Maybe later we do checks. We had a lot of checks bounce from a lot of rich people. Getting the money from them was like pulling teeth with long roots—hard and painful." Then she saw the young man. "Yes? What can I help you with?" she asked him.

"I'm from the Ace Delivery Service," he replied, holding out the package. "Will you sign for this, please?"

Ethel looked over at Emily and said: "Would you take care of it?" She turned to the young man and gestured toward Emily's desk.

Harriet Bradshaw was clutching a thick wad of bills in her hand as he walked past her. She stared at him, her eyes raking over his body. He was dressed in a black windbreaker that accentuated his broad shoulders, and tight-fitting jeans that clearly defined his muscular legs and buttocks. Ethel reached out and gently pried the money from Harriet's hand. "I'll get you a receipt," she muttered.

Emily made a pretense of looking busy as he came up to her. "Will you sign on line twelve, please?" he asked, holding out the package, a clipboard, and a pen. His voice was deep and had a rough, impatient sound.

"Yes, of course," Emily murmured, keeping her head lowered. She took the parcel, signed the sheet on the clipboard, and gave it back without glancing up.

16

"Any chance of getting a glass of water?"

Emily hesitated, then forced herself to look up at him, instinctively tugging at her hair to cover the scar. His deep green eyes framed by sooty black lashes were staring directly at her. She felt her heart skip a beat, and her breath caught in her throat. Finally she managed to answer: "Yes, there's a water cooler near the back door."

"Thanks," he replied, giving her a quick, friendly smile. Then he stepped away. She watched him get the water, her eyes riveted to every move he made. As he lifted the cup to his lips, she saw him glance at Harriet, who was still staring at him. He grinned at the woman, and she smiled back, arching her body slightly so that her large breasts strained against her jacket. The silly cow, Emily thought. In another minute she'll start salivating!

Just then Ethel came up to her with the cash she had taken from Harriet and said, "Emily, put this in the safe, please—I have another customer."

Emily took the money and went to the safe. She dialed the combination, opened the door, and put the money in a tray inside. Then she closed the door, gave the dial a spin, and returned to her desk. He was waiting for her.

"I forgot my pen."

"Oh, yes—here it is." She took it from the desk and handed it to him. His fingers brushed against hers, and she jerked her hand away, feeling her face grow flushed. She sat down and nervously riffled through some papers, uncomfortably aware that he hadn't moved.

"Do you like working here?" he asked.

"Yes, I do...." There was an awkward moment of silence, and she searched for something else to say. "Do you like being a messenger?" she finally asked.

"Yeah, it's okay. I have to run all over town, but what the hell, it's a living." He paused, then added, "I just do this to get by. I'm really an actor."

"Oh? I'm interested in theater, too. I'm taking costume design classes at—"

Harriet suddenly appeared at the desk and interrupted bluntly. "Excuse me, young man, but did you say you were an actor?"

He turned to her. "Yes, I did. Why? Are you a talent scout?" he asked brashly.

Harriet drew herself up with a look of importance and loudly declared: "Well, no, but my husband is an executive at Universal Studios."

The young man said, "Oh, really?" He gave her a dazzling smile and Harriet's face began to glow. She took his arm and pulled him away from Emily's desk. They walked to the front of the store while Harriet talked excitedly. She reached into her purse and gave him a card. He nodded and smiled, and she patted his arm eagerly.

Emily watched them with narrowed eyes, furious at the woman's rudeness. It was typical of Harriet and of other women like her who came into the shop, to wield their status and wealth like a club to get what they wanted. And he was no better, toadying to her at the mention of her husband. Another hungry actor looking for a connection, she thought disdainfully. She tried to go back to work, but couldn't help staring at them until he had concluded his conversation with Harriet and was about to leave the store. He turned at the door, caught her eye, and waved, but Emily looked away, feigning indifference.

Harriet started for the back of the store, calling out, "I didn't get my receipt, Mrs. Skolsky."

Emily saw that Ethel was busy with a customer, and said, "I'll make it up for you, Mrs. Bradshaw. I just have to finish this letter."

"I really can't wait," Harriet said impatiently. "I'm running very late."

"It will only take a minute," Emily said tightly. She finished the letter, inserted a receipt form, and quickly typed it out. Then she handed it to Harriet with a forced smile and said, "Here you are, Mrs. Bradshaw."

Harriet took the receipt and stared at Emily coldly, her eyes fixed on the scar. The expression on her face was arrogant and contemptuous. Emily felt the weight of that intimidating look sink down on her, but she stared back, refusing to be shamed into looking away. Harriet stuffed the receipt into her purse and walked away with a thinly veiled attitude of disgust.

Raging with suppressed anger, Emily jammed a piece of paper into the typewriter and began a letter, trying to put the woman out of her mind. But frustration gripped her with unexpected force; after all these years she still had not yet succeeded at insulating herself from such scornful cruelty. She saw that the letter was full of errors and pulled it out of the machine, crumpled it up, and threw it in the wastebasket. Just then she heard Harriet say to Ethel, in a voice loud enough to carry across the store, "Aren't you worried about upsetting your customers by employing someone who is handicapped, like that girl?"

Ethel's face became a stern mask. "We've never gotten any complaints about Emily," she said coldly.

"Well, I can tell you, she certainly upsets me!" Harriet retorted sharply.

Ethel's grey eyes went hard as slate. "Then you should shop elsewhere," she replied, dropping every word like the thud of a drum. "I wouldn't want you to get sick."

Harriet turned a bright scarlet. "Well, I didn't mean . . . I was simply suggesting that you—"

"Thank you for your suggestion," Ethel said dryly. She turned and walked away with an air of supreme indifference.

Fuming, Harriet shot an outraged look at Ethel's retreating back, yanked her sunglasses down from where they were shoved into her hair, settled them on her nose, and stalked out of the store, her chunky body quivering with fury.

As Ethel went by her desk, Emily looked at her anxiously. "I wasn't trying to be rude to her, Mrs. Skolsky."

"The woman asks for it," Ethel replied. "All she has to say is 'hello' and she's in trouble. I had an aunt like that once, back in Russia. We all hated her. Don't worry,

Emily—if she doesn't come back, I wouldn't miss her."

Emily gave her a grateful smile and went back to work. But as the day wore on, her thoughts were dominated by the young actor. She couldn't forget the impact of his handsomeness, the touch of his fingers. Why had he taken the time to talk to her? Anyone that handsome could never be interested in her. He was just being polite. A romantic fantasy began to take over her; what would it be like to go out with him, have him hold her in his arms, make love to her? Then she grew angry at herself for thinking so foolishly. How could romance have any place in her life, with the way she looked? For now there was only one thing to be thought of, worked for; her goal to become a designer. Once that was achieved, her life would open up; she could become the woman she had always dreamed of being: accomplished, successful, and beautiful.

At the end of the day, Emily left the store and got into her car. It was a little after five o'clock and the streets were crowded with going-home traffic. The sky was going slate grey, and the early spring twilight threatened to evaporate into darkness at any moment. She headed for a small restaurant on Vermont Avenue where she usually had something to eat before going to class. Only after she had been driving for a few minutes did she realize that the image of the young man had lingered in her mind and that she was searching nearby cars and the sidewalks, vainly hoping to catch another glimpse of him.

3

THE CLASS SHIFTED RESTLESSLY, BUT EMILY LISTENED with rapt attention as Jerome Bradley, a distinguished-looking man in his late fifties, made his closing remarks.

"—and so, you must remember that to be effective, costumes designed for a play or a film should not only contribute to the theme of the drama but enhance it and the character of the roles being performed. And, in order to do that, the designer must have an extensive knowledge of theater, art, music, history, all the cultural arts, to be able to draw upon those resources when he needs them."

Mr. Bradley paused, glanced at the clock on the wall of the schoolroom, and waved his hand. "Okay, kids, that's it for tonight. See you next week."

A collective murmur of relief filled the room as the class gathered up their belongings and started to file out the door. Bradley caught sight of Emily leaving with the others, and called out to her, "Emily, may I speak to you for a minute?"

She came up to his desk and said, "Yes, what is it, Mr. Bradley?"

Bradley smiled up at her; Emily had been in his classes for a year, and he had watched her progress with satisfaction and a sense of his own accomplishment. She worked harder than anyone else, and her flair and imagination were evident in every sketch she did. He had great hopes for her.

"The cast of *Cyrano* has been working on their costumes from your sketches," he told her. "Tonight they're doing a walk-through to see how they feel. I thought we might drop by and take a look."

Emily hesitated; she wasn't sure she could face a stage full of people. It had taken every bit of her strength and willpower to enroll for this course, knowing that she would have to endure the same indignities she had gone through as a child in school. She had managed to ignore the stares and whispers that had greeted her first appearance, but even now, a year later, she never stayed after class to socialize with the other students over coffee. Nor had she ever been asked.

Bradley sensed what she was thinking and said, "We can just sneak in and sit in the back of the theater. No one will see us."

Emily nodded gratefully. "Yes, I'd love to go."

They left the classroom and crossed the campus to the building that housed a small theater where student productions were presented. Several weeks before, Bradley had offered his class the challenge of creating costumes the actors could put together themselves; there was no budget for anything elaborate. Emily had read the play in high school and had seen the film starring Jose Ferrer on television. The play took place in 1640 and she knew it would be impossible for the cast to try to duplicate the costumes of the period, so she had asked if she could improvise and work on a romantic impression that could be obtained by restructuring thrift shop clothes.

All the sketches had been shown to the director and he had seized upon hers; they were simple, had great style, and were easy to construct with a limited expenditure of money. When Emily heard the news, she was jubilant; it was her first success as a designer. Now she would see the results of her efforts.

Emily and Mr. Bradley entered the back of the theater and heard a chorus of angry voices coming from the stage. The actors were assembled before the director, a thin, tense young man with unruly red hair and nervous hands.

His name was Gary Johnson, and he and Emily had met a few times to discuss her ideas. He was sitting on a high stool in the center of the stage, yelling at several members of the cast. One, an anemic-looking girl dressed in a frilly pink nightgown, was in tears.

"This looks like shit!" she cried. "How can I play Roxane looking like this?"

"And what am I supposed to be?" a burly young man shouted. "A skid row bum?" He paraded around in an old black suit that had baggy trousers and a long jacket with wide lapels. The other young people were similarly attired in ill-fitting old clothes and looked like a band of rowdy children playing dress-up in their grandparent's wardrobe.

"Where's Maria?" Gary shouted, waving his hands. "Goddammit, Maria, where the hell are you?"

A short girl with dark frizzy hair, wearing jeans and a sweatshirt, flounced angrily to the front of the stage. "This ain't my fault, Gary! I did the best I could with this crap!" She dropped a large canvas bag she was holding on the floor and faced him defiantly.

"Your best?" He stared at her, incredulous. "This is your best? You saw the sketches—you said you knew what to do, that you've been sewing since you were ten!"

"Yeah, well I have! But there's a difference between sketches and this junk!"

Mr. Bradley leaned over to Emily and whispered, "I was afraid this might happen."

"But the sketches were so simple," Emily said, crestfallen. "And I wrote the instructions out very carefully."

"Ah, but you assumed they could read," Bradley chuckled. "Well, shall we go up there and help them?"

Emily shrank into her seat. The stage was bright with hot white lights; there were no shadows in which to hide.

"Okay," Bradley said sympathetically. "I'll go give them a hand—"

Emily sat up. "No, I can do it."

"Good girl! After all, you have to start learning to protect your ideas." They left their seats and started down the aisle. Mr. Bradley called out, "Gary, relax. The Marines have landed!"

Everyone crowded around them, all talking at once. Bradley held up his hands for silence, and said, "This is Emily Gorden. The costumes were her ideas, and she's going to help you with them."

All eyes turned to her. Emily felt a tight constriction in her chest, positive that they were all staring at the scar. But she knew that once and for all she would have to overcome her self-consciousness if she were ever going to have the success she wanted. And this was the first step. She took a deep breath, then asked Maria, "Do you have pins, scissors, and some ribbons?"

"Yeah, in my bag." Maria picked the canvas bag up from the floor and held it open. "Take whatever you need."

Emily approached the girl in the pink nightgown. "Hi," she said tentatively.

The girl's eyes darted over Emily's face. "Hi, I'm Shelly," she stammered nervously. "Can you do anything with this?"

The nightgown hung in a straight line fall to the floor. It had short, puffed sleeves and a limp edging of lace around the square neckline and the hem. Emily pulled the neckline out so that the girl's shoulders were revealed, and fluffed out the tiny sleeves. From Maria's bag, she took a long length of pale yellow ribbon and tied it around Shelly's waist, just under her small breasts, to create an Empire look. Then she said to Maria, "Tack the ribbon in place, and let the ends flow down her back." To Shelly, she said, "Spray-starch the lace and use a warm iron on it to give it some life. And get a piece of black velvet ribbon to wear around your neck like a choker. Fasten it in front with a small pin, or maybe your mother has one of those old cameo brooches you can wear. If you can't find any low-heeled dancing slippers in a thrift store, use a pair of ballet slippers that go with the gown. And put your hair up in long curls, then fasten them at the back of your head with a barette. It will add to the whole period look."

Mr. Bradley smiled at the authoritative sound of Emily's instructions. He patted her on the back approvingly and said, "I don't think you need me anymore." He waved to the group and left the stage.

The actors grew quiet and attentive as Emily went on to the boy in the baggy black suit. She tried to ignore that fact that she was now the center of attention and looked at the folds of dark cloth enveloping his body.

"I'm playing Cyrano," he said, glaring at her arrogantly. "I've asked two agents and a casting director to come see the play. I *have* to look good!"

"You will," Emily said quietly. "What's your name—or do you want me to call you 'Cy'?"

A ripple of laughter went through the group, and the boy gave Emily a sheepish grin. "I'm Bob. And listen, I really do have agents coming to the show—"

"I'll do everything I can to make you look terrific. Now turn around."

Bob turned his back, and Emily gathered up the excess cloth of the loose-fitting jacket until it was comfortably snug at his waist. She pinned it carefully, telling Maria, "Take out all the surplus from the inside so that it fits like this. Just make a seam down the back—no one will notice it."

She turned Bob around, took the scissors and started to cut away the lower part of the wide lapels, then trimmed away the sharp points of the upper lapels until they were rounded off. She told Maria, "Cover these cut edges with a black satin ribbon so that it creates a border for the collar." She looked back at Bob, and asked, "Do you have black boots?"

"Yes—"

"Cut the cuffs off the pants, and blouse them inside

the boots. Find a red vest and wear it under the jacket. You'll need a cravat—"

"A what?"

"It's a piece of white cloth tied in a loose, floppy bow and worn under your shirt collar. We can fasten the sleeves of the coat at the wrists to make the arms look fuller, and see if you can find an old top hat someplace."

"Will that be enough?" Bob demanded. "Cyrano was something of a dandy. . . . "

Emily smiled. "We'll put some red satin ribbon around the hat, okay?"

She turned back to Maria and said, "I can help you with the rest of the costumes in the evenings, if you like."

The girl nodded vigorously. "Terrific! I really appreciate it. You are very clever!"

Gary Johnson breathed a sigh of relief and exclaimed, "Emily, thank you! You're saving the play! Listen, before you leave, can you do something for the guy who's playing Christian? Do you have the time?"

Flushed with her success, Emily nodded happily. "Yes—I can stay for a while."

Gary looked around the stage and yelled, "Alec? Where's Alec?"

A young man stepped out from behind the group and came to the front of the stage. "I'm right here, Gary," he said quietly. He looked at Emily and gave her an impish grin. "Hi. Small world, isn't it?"

It was the young man from the messenger service who had been in the store that afternoon.

For a moment Emily was completely dumbfounded. She nodded to him and replied in a choked whisper, "Yes, it is. . . . "

Gary said, "Alec, why don't you and Emily go to the dressing room so she can work on your costume while we rehearse the first scene?"

"Sure, that's okay." He began to walk backstage.

Maria handed Emily the canvas bag and said, "Leave

it with Gary when you're finished. I gotta split. I got a date waiting."

Emily took the bag and hurried after the young man. He was waiting for her in the doorway of a room just off the stage.

"We can do it in here," he said.

She followed him into a brightly lit room crammed with props, tables spilling over with makeup, and the actors' street clothes. Emily put her things down on a chair and straightened up, flinching at the harsh light. He held out his hand and said, "I'm Alec Darcy."

She took his hand timidly and stared at the face she had been thinking about all day. His curly black hair lay in ringlets across his forehead; his green eyes seemed almost hooded by the long, heavy lashes. He held her hand a moment longer than necessary, and the warmth of his fingers traveled like a lick of flame along her arm and into her body.

"I'm Emily Gorden," she said, pulling away her hand.

"I know. I watched you out there. You were good. Can you do anything for me? I'm a lousy actor, but I can pull it off if I know I look good."

Flustered by the intensity of his eyes, she replied: "Yes, well, I can try." She stepped back, feeling uneasy; her hair had fallen back somewhat and most of her scar was visible. But there was nothing in his expression to suggest that seeing it made him uncomfortable.

Alec waited while she examined his costume. He was wearing a short black waiter's jacket, a white shirt, and a red sash around his waist. His trousers were ordinary black pants.

"The sash and the trousers are wrong, but the jacket and shirt are good," she said. "Christian is such a romantic character, he'd have more of a Byronic look...."

"Byronic?" Alec questioned.

"Yes, after Lord Byron, the poet. Would you object to wearing tights?"

"No—in fact I thought about that and brought a pair with me." He rummaged through a paper bag and brought them out. "They're black, okay?"

"Yes. Take off the jacket and the sash and put on the tights—"

He had the clothes off before she was finished, and started to unzip his fly. Emily moved toward the door, saying: "I'll wait outside. . . ."

"You don't have to," he said matter-of-factly. "Is there anything you can do to give the jacket more zing?" He began to take off his pants.

She turned away, only to find that she was facing the mirrors and could see him reflected behind her. He was wearing the shirt and a pair of white jockey shorts. His legs were tanned, smoothly muscled. As he got the tights up over his narrow hips, he jammed his hand down in front to arrange his genitalia, then pulled the black material up to his waist so that it stretched tight over his firm buttocks. He tucked in the shirt and turned to her. "Okay, now what?"

He saw her looking at him in the mirrors, and their eyes locked. For a few seconds she felt powerless to move. She blushed and lowered her head, nervously patting her hair into place to hide the scar.

"You don't have to do that for me," Alec said quietly. "I've already seen it. What happened—an accident?"

It was the first time anyone had addressed her about the scar so directly, and on a first meeting. Usually people were politely careful *not* to mention it and waited some time before asking about it. Most of the time they ignored it entirely, trying to act as if it didn't even exist. His blunt question, so casually asked, almost came as a relief.

"Yes, a car accident when I was nine," she answered. She turned away from the mirrors and faced him.

"You shouldn't worry about it so much; it's not that bad," he said nonchalantly. "So, now what, with this so-called costume? I feel like an extra in a high school operetta."

"Pull the shirt out and blouse it, then—"

He looked at her quizzically and she went up to him. "Like this," she said, tugging at his shirt. "We can tighten the cuffs, then if you push them up a little, they'll blouse, too, like a pirate's shirt."

She was very close to him and could feel the heat of his body. The shirt was open almost to the waist, and she saw a mat of black hair against the deep tan of his chest.

"Do I get a cravat, like Bob?" he asked softly. There was a subtle, insinuating tone in his voice that she found disconcerting.

She backed away, confused, "Yes, we can use the red sash. Is it all right if I cut it to make it shorter?"

"Sure, you're the costume designer."

Her hands trembled as she trimmed the sash. Everything about Alec—the way he talked, his indifference to her scar, and his overwhelming physical presence—unnerved her.

Emily put the scissors down and held out the red cloth. "You can tie it now."

"Do it for me, will you? I'm all thumbs when it comes to tying knots."

She hesitated, reluctant to approach him. But Alec stood, waiting. She went to him and slipped the cloth around his neck. He bowed his head, and his dark hair brushed lightly against her face. A jolt of excitement went through her. They were very close, as if at any moment they might embrace. She made a loose, floppy bow, then stepped back and said shakily, "Now put on the jacket."

He slipped it on and struck a relaxed pose. "Well, how do I look?"

There was beauty and arrogance in the dark intensity of his face, a flowing, sensual line to his body. Somehow the whole room seemed altered by his presence. The colorful jumble of props, clothes, tables, chairs, and mirrors became an exotic background that set off his splendid physique.

Emily's throat was dry, and she swallowed hard. "You

look very nice." The words sounded lame and stupid, but she was afraid to speak further.

He smiled and turned to examine himself in the mirrors. "What do you think about the jacket? Is it too plain?"

"A little. I'll take it home and trim it with some braid. You'll need shoes—maybe a pair of black patent leather. We have some old brass buckles at the store I could put on them. . . ."

He grinned excitedly. "Hey, that would be great! I have a pair of patent leather shoes—cheap but shiny. Could I drop them by the store tomorrow?"

Emily tried to contain her excitement at the thought of seeing him again. "Yes, that would be fine."

Suddenly they heard Gary's voice calling Alec onstage. He started for the door, then stopped and said to her. "Will you wait for me until the rehearsal's over? Tell me how I looked?"

"Yes, I'll wait for you," Emily answered in a whisper.

He stared at her for a long moment, then Gary called again. "I'm on," Alec said. "Let's hope I can do justice to the costume." He smiled, gave her a sly wink, and hurried out of the room.

Emily followed after him and stood in the wings as he walked onstage. There was a burst of applause, and some good-natured ribbing about the tights. Then Gary gestured wildly for attention, and the scene began. Emily couldn't take her eyes off Alec. She watched every move and gesture he made with the intensity of a jeweler examining a rare gem. Under the glare of the hot stage lights, his Italianate beauty was vivid: his black hair gleamed, spots of color bloomed on his cheeks, and his body had a supple, feline grace. She was only dimly aware that the scene was going badly, so fixed was her attention on him.

When Gary finally dismissed the company, Alec stormed offstage. He caught sight of her and said brusquely, "You're still here—good! Wait for me. I'll be out in a minute." He went into the dressing room. When he reappeared, he was still angry. He took her arm and muttered

"Let's get some coffee. If I don't talk to somebody, I'll start throwing things—"

A few minutes later they were seated in the back booth of a coffee shop across the street from the college. Emily was a little stunned to find herself there, especially with Alec. She looked at him furtively as he opened a pack of cigarettes and took one out. His thick dark eyebrows were drawn together in a scowl, and his mouth looked sulky. He lighted the cigarette and drew in deeply, letting the smoke out with a deep sigh. They ordered coffee, then Alec leaned back against the booth, the cigarette clenched in his lips. A thin curl of smoke drifted around his face, and his eyes were lost in dark shadows. Emily sipped her coffee, not sure of what to say.

"I don't know what the fuck I'm doing in this play!" he burst out. "I'm no actor!"

Emily spoke tentatively. "You need time, and training—this is just the beginning...."

"No, it's the end. I'm finished with trying to do something I'm no good at. I've been in this town for six years, and all I've been getting is a fast shuffle. Six years of people telling me I'm perfect for movies or TV!"

"Well, you are very handsome," Emily said in a low voice. "Maybe you need an agent, someone to help you get started."

Alec laughed harshly. "I've had an agent—he was more interested in my ass than he was in my talent. Nobody helps anybody in this town—they just get what *they* want." He leaned forward, cupping his chin in his hand. "I guess it really doesn't matter. I don't have any talent anyway—"

"That's not true," Emily protested. "You were very good. The others are just amateurs. Actors have to have someone to play off, to respond to; otherwise, they just flounder."

Alec looked at her with interest. "How do you know so much about it? Have you ever done any acting?"

"No, of course not. How could I?" she stammered.

31

Her hand moved automatically to push her hair across the scar.

Alec scowled and his voice was sharp. "Will you stop that shit? Stop tugging at your hair! You've had that scar since you were nine, and you're still here, in the world. You've got more balls than a lot of people I've known with less to complain about, so knock off the 'uglies' crap!"

Emily recoiled before his tirade, her face flaming with embarrassment.

Alec leaned across the table, concerned, and took her hand. "I'm sorry, I'm sorry—that was stupid of me. I'm just taking out my anger on you."

Emily started to get up. "I really should go. It's getting late...."

He shook his head and sighed, "Now you're mad at me. See, that's why I'm not a success. I do the same thing to agents, casting directors, and any party I walk into. I can clear a room faster than anybody I know. C'mon, drink your coffee," he urged softly. "You want some pie or cake, something?" He gave her a crooked, pleading smile and said imploringly, "Please stay and help me break my jinx."

Emily couldn't help smiling, and sat down. "Okay, I'll stay. And I think I'll take you up on the pie—I am a little hungry."

He gave a small groan. "Please don't. I'm not even sure I can pay for the coffee!"

They both began to laugh, and Emily said, "I can spring for the coffee, and something to eat. Are you hungry?"

"I'm starved!"

They ordered some sandwiches and pie, and Emily looked at him wonderingly. "I've never met anybody like you."

"You must not get out much. There are hundreds of me all over Hollywood. Thousands, probably, only some of them make it pay."

"Now you're the one who's putting himself down."

"Yeah," he said sadly. "But I just can't make it work onstage, or on the screen. I had a shot at a couple of TV things—just a few lines. But nothing happened—zilch! I can do it, here and now; you want charming? I'll give you charming."

He leaned back a little, tilted his head to one side, and gave her a warm smile followed by a conspiratorial wink. He was charming.

"You want sexy?" he asked. He lowered his head to his chest, then raised it slowly, looking at her from under the thick fringe of his black lashes. His green eyes smoldered for a few seconds, then suddenly glinted, like the spark of a match being struck. His full red lips parted slightly. "Am I sexy?" he asked in a hushed whisper.

Emily discovered that she had stopped breathing. Finally she managed a choked ". . . yes."

Alec sat up abruptly and ground out his cigarette. "See what I mean? But I can't make it work in front of a camera."

He shoved his coffee cup aside, centered the ashtray before him, and lit another cigarette. Emily listened quietly as he went on talking. He was twenty-four and had come to Hollywood from a small town in Idaho when he was eighteen. To keep himself going, he had worked at whatever he could find: telephone sales, waiting tables, bartending, and now messenger boy. Someone had suggested he get into a play that would act as a showcase for him, and he had ended up in the drama department at the college.

An hour passed, and Emily finally told him that she had to get home. He broke off, apologizing for talking about himself so much. "You're a good listener. Most people in this town are like me." He grinned. "They just talk about themselves. Next time you'll do all the talking and I'll listen."

Next time? Emily wondered.

She paid the bill, waving aside his thanks, and they left the coffee shop. "Where do you live?" she asked.

33

"Just a few miles from here, down near Sunset and Alvarado. I have what is laughingly called a bachelor—that's a room and bath with full complement of roaches. But it's cheap. And the bus stops at my front door. Among other things that I don't have is a car."

"I can give you a lift—it's on my way."

Alec smiled broadly. "I thought you'd never ask."

In the car they were silent until he directed her to a shabby side street off Sunset. She pulled up in front of his apartment building and turned to say good night.

"Don't go yet," he said softly. He reached out and turned the key in the ignition, shutting off the motor. The street was quiet, almost unnaturally still. He sat back, his face darkly shadowed. "I really enjoyed talking with you tonight. Are you coming to the rest of the rehearsals?"

"Yes, I told Maria I would help her with the costumes," Emily replied in a small voice. She felt nervous and unsure, alone with him like this. He made no move to leave, and she murmured, "I'd better get home, it's very late."

"I know. But . . . listen, I like you. I feel like we share something; we have something in common. I know this will sound crazy to you, but in my own way I've been going through a lot of shit because of how *I* look. Do you understand?"

"I think so."

"I've been with a lot of girls, but they never listened to me or cared about anything except my looks. Like that crazy broad in the store this afternoon who gave me her card. She wants a lap dog to play with, but she doesn't give a damn about *me*. I think you like me, the guy underneath the face. And I've been honest with you, and I like the feeling it gave me."

"Thank you," Emily said faintly.

He grew quiet. Emily sat, unable to speak. The silence between them was almost unbearable, filled with a frightening intimacy of secret thoughts and unspoken desires. Yet she had no wish to make a single move that would end it. Then Alec put his hand on her arm. She felt the pressure of his fingers, and her heart began to race. He started to pull her toward him.

"Now listen," he said huskily. "Don't argue or get hysterical. I'm going to kiss you good night."

A sudden panic shot through her. "No, you can't," she pleaded. "Please, nobody ever—my mouth, it's . . ."

"There's nothing wrong with your mouth." His voice was low, caressing.

She tried to turn away, but he wouldn't let her go. He pulled her close to him, and his lips touched her cheek. They were warm, gentle, but insistent as he sought to reach her lips.

"No, please, please," Emily moaned. Tears filled her eyes and spilled down her face. She felt the tip of his tongue capture one, and her body quivered at the sensation. He cupped her chin with his hands and forced her to face him. Then his lips were on hers.

For a few seconds she was numb with fear. Alec made no move to touch her body, no effort to open her mouth with his tongue. Their lips were simply pressed together in a kiss that was chaste, almost reverent. Her fear began to subside, and she slowly became aware of the touch of his mouth, the feel of his lips as living flesh. A heat swept through her, touching secret parts of her body, overwhelming her with emotions so new they were shocking.

Alec let her go and sat back. She remained still, her eyes tightly closed. Then she opened them and bowed her head, afraid to look at him.

"That was your first kiss, wasn't it?" he asked.

She nodded.

"I'm glad it was me." He opened the door and began to get out.

"Alec, wait. . . . " she said. He paused and looked at her. "Would you like me to pick you up tomorrow, give you a lift to the college?" she asked timidly.

He smiled. "I'd like that very much, if it's not too much trouble."

"Oh, no. It's no trouble. I get off work at five-thirty. I'll be here a few minutes later."

"I'll be waiting out front. Until tomorrow, then."

"Yes," she whispered. She heard his footsteps go up the walk and waited for the sound of the apartment house door being closed. Then she let her breath out in a deep sigh, started the car, and drove away.

Nora was waiting up for her, anxious and concerned. Emily explained about the rehearsal, pleaded being tired, and went to her room. She closed the door, took off her clothes and slipped into bed. There was no thought of sleeping, only a wish to stay awake for as long as possible to relive every single minute of what had happened. Her mind was filled with fragmented images, like frames of a film that had been spliced together with no cohesion: her first glimpse of Alec in the store, onstage, in the dressing room, his black hair and green eyes, the shape of his tanned legs, the firm flesh of his hips, the sensuous curve of his lips when he asked, "Am I sexy?" She remembered his fervent sincerity in the car, the touch of his mouth on her cheek, her lips.

A sharp, searing pain of sexual desire burned in her loins, and she curled up like a child, clutching the blanket around her. It's a dream, she thought. I just imagined it. But she could still taste his lips. She put her fingertips to her mouth and traced its shape. Then she felt the ridge of scar tissue at the corner of her lips and she pulled her fingers away with a jerk, as if they had accidently touched fire.

4

THE NEXT DAY SEEMED ENDLESS. EMILY MADE A CON-
centrated effort to keep her mind on her work, but all she
could think about was seeing Alec again. She chatted with
customers and answered their questions, typed letters,
and filed papers, all in a hazy blur of doing business just
to get through the hours. Several times she escaped to
the bathroom and examined herself in the mirror over the
sink. Would Alec like her clothes? She had gone through
her entire wardrobe before choosing a slim black skirt
that molded her hips, and a rose-colored blouse with a
high, artfully draped cowl that covered her throat. Her
hair gleamed from brushing, and she had tried using a
little makeup to hide the scar. But nothing could disguise
the welts of ridged flesh. If anything, the makeup seemed
to make the scar more obvious, and she finally washed
it off.

As the afternoon wore on, she grew more anxious. Did
Alec really like her? Or had he just been kind because
she was so sympathetic? Was that why he had kissed her?
She chided herself for behaving like a schoolgirl, for taking it all so seriously. Yet she couldn't stop her heart from
racing at the thought of him.

A few hours before closing time, Emily went to a glass
counter standing near the front of the store and looked
through a tray of small pieces of brass: rings, neckbands,
hinges, knobs, and other assorted items. She found two
corner squares, fittings that had come off a French cabinet. They were perfect for the buckles on Alec's shoes.

She took them to Ethel Skolsky and asked her to deduct them from her paycheck, explaining that she was going to use them on a costume she was designing. Ethel waved aside her offer to pay for them and gave them to her. Emily was aware of the woman studying her curiously and blushed, as if Ethel could read her mind and see the image of Alec pictured there.

When the store finally closed, Emily flew to her car. Traffic was heavier than usual, and she worried about being late. Impatience made her daring, and she began to dodge quickly around sluggish lines of cars, ignoring the angry honking of horns and irritated cries of other drivers.

She turned into his street and slowed down. It was a shabby neighborhood, inhabited by transients, blacks, and Hispanics. Children played listlessly on the trash-littered sidewalks, and men huddled in groups on the steps of old apartment houses, drinking beer from cans and gazing with unseeing eyes at the poverty around them. She drove along, searching the grimy, pitted buildings, trying to remember which one was Alec's. A fear that he might not be there, that he had forgotten about her picking him up, suddenly overtook her, and a sick feeling began to grow in the pit of her stomach.

Then she saw him waiting on the curb, and at the sight of him all her fears vanished. He was wearing a white tee shirt that stretched across his broad chest and emphasized his strong arms. Faded jeans clung like a second skin to his long muscular legs, and a newsboy's cap on his dark head gave him a roguish look. He was holding a jacket and a paper bag in one hand and waving to her with the other as she pulled up in front of him.

Alec opened the door and swung himself into the car. "Hi, how are you?" Before she could answer, he leaned over and gave her a quick kiss on the cheek. "I brought the shoes," he said, holding up the paper bag.

Flustered by his easy show of affection, Emily nervously replied, "I have the buckles in my purse. And I found a couple of yards of red velvet at home—I thought

38

I'd make you a cape for the second act." That was a lie; she had gone out on her lunch hour and bought the red velvet.

"A cape! That's terrific!" He threw his head back and laughed delightedly. "I'll knock 'em out on stage!" He put his arm around her shoulders and hugged her. Emily almost ran a red light.

"Are you hungry?" she asked, a little breathless. "We have time for something to eat before the rehearsal starts."

Alec got a serious look on his face. "Emily, I'm not going to lie to you—I can't afford to buy us dinner."

"But I can—"

"No, I don't feel right about that. I'm still embarrassed about you paying the bill at the coffee shop last night."

"Then we'll go dutch," she insisted.

Alec sighed and looked away from her. "I'll have some coffee while you eat. I can't afford dinner."

Emily heard the note of shame in his voice and was moved by an overwhelming urge to help him, take care of him. But she knew she had to be careful not to injure his pride. "Alec," she began tentatively. "You can't go through a long rehearsal on an empty stomach. Please have dinner with me, and let's not worry about who pays the bill."

He turned back to her, his eyes filled with gratitude. "You know, you really are wonderful," he said quietly.

Emily smiled, almost lightheaded with happiness.

In the days that followed, her bliss continued unabated. Each night, after work, she picked Alec up, they had supper together, then went to the rehearsals of the play. She worked with Maria at a sewing machine backstage, often stopping to watch him do a scene. Afterward they had coffee and talked for hours.

Emily was shy at first, hesitant to confide in him about herself. "I'm really not that interesting," she told him.

"You're the most interesting girl I've ever met," he said impatiently. "Don't give me that ca-ca-lottsa."

"Ca-ca-lottsa? What does that mean?" Emily asked, laughing.

Alec grinned. "It's an expression I made up—it means a lotta ca-ca. Now stop playing timid and tell me about yourself. How did you get started in costume designing?"

Encouraged by his interest, Emily told him about the long, lonely months after the accident and her father's death, how she had kept Nora company sitting up late at night and watching old movies on television. Fascinated by the elaborate gowns and dresses in the films of the thirties and forties, she had begun to fill sketch pads with drawings of the costumes. She was only nine years old, but the idea of becoming a designer began to take root. Her mother taught her how to sew, and by the time she was in her teens, she was making all of her own clothes.

"Did you make that outfit you're wearing?" Alec interrupted.

"Yes—" She paused, then shyly asked, "Do you like it?"

"It's sensational! But you're always wearing high-necked blouses and sweaters. I'd like to see you in something a little more low-cut." He gave her a Groucho Marx leer and wiggled his eyebrows.

Emily flushed and lowered her head. "Well, they help to cover the scar on my neck," she said in a low voice.

He stopped joking, reached across the table, and put his hand against her cheek. "If it makes you feel better, okay. But don't do it for me—it doesn't matter."

His words brought a lump to her throat, and she swallowed hard; it seemed inconceivable, even ludicrous, to her that he could mean what he said, that he cared for *who* she was, not what she looked like. But every time they saw each other, she wanted more and more to believe what he told her.

Two weeks went by, and as the opening of the play drew closer, rehearsals were extended into the weekends, allowing them to see each other every day. Each night, when she took him home, they would sit and talk for a while, then Alec would kiss her good night before leaving the car. Innocent at first, their embraces soon grew more passionate. Alec was always tender and considerate, but she could sense his growing frustration with her fear and inhibitions. Where sex was concerned, Emily was a complete novice; she had never experienced the necking and petting that was part of the ritual of growing up, that other girls her age simply took for granted. But at the same time, a fierce longing to make love with him took possession of her every time he held her in his arms.

One evening, after rehearsal, they skipped having coffee and drove up Laurel Canyon to Mulholland Drive, cruising along the twisting road until they found a secluded turnout off the highway. Emily parked the car and they stared at the view of the city spread out beneath them. It was one of those rare, clear evenings when the sky looked like a bolt of black velvet that had been unrolled and tossed across the top of Los Angeles. Stars gleamed in the inky darkness, and the lights of the city twinkled in a multitude of jewellike colors, an abstract mosaic made of precious gems.

"This is perfect," Alec sighed. "What a gorgeous hunk of real estate. And what I wouldn't give to own a small piece of it."

Emily smiled. "Someday you will. Someday you'll be a famous actor and you'll own a big piece of it."

Alec shook his head. "That's not the way it's going to happen—not to me. I'll never make it as an actor, Em. I just don't have it."

"Don't say that," she protested. "You're wonderful in the play. Someone will see you and realize that. I know they will."

"That's just ca-ca-lottsa." He laughed. "But I love it. C'mere, girl—I want to kiss you for being so prejudiced."

He pulled her into his lap, cradling her in his arms. His lips moved over her eyes and nose, and when they reached her lips, she opened her mouth. He moaned deep

41

in his throat as their tongues touched. He began to caress her, his hands moving over her breasts, down to her thighs. Emily trembled and stiffened with fear. At the touch of his fingers on her bare flesh, she grew weak, almost faint.

"Don't be frightened," he whispered.

She buried her face in his neck. "Please wait," she pleaded.

"I will, baby, I will. We have time. . . ." He kissed her again, filling her mouth with his tongue.

She gave herself up to his lips, dazed by his ardor. Her fingers curled into his thick hair, then slipped down the column of his throat, exploring the satiny texture of his skin. She encountered the buttons of his shirt and tentatively undid one.

Alec released her and asked huskily, "Do you want to touch me? Feel me?"

A ragged sigh escaped her lips. "Yes. . . ."

He leaned his head back against the seat, eyes closed, lips parted, and offered himself to her. She cautiously unbuttoned his shirt and slid her hand under the cloth. His flesh was warm, smooth. When her fingertips grazed his nipples, they peaked under her touch and his body quivered. She opened the shirt completely and pressed her face against his chest, tasting him with her lips and tongue. Alec gave a small gasp of excitement, arched his back, then spread his legs wide. Emily felt the rigid length of his erection straining against the thin fabric of his jeans. Terrified of the hunger for him that raged through her entire being, yet lost in waves of fiery sensations, she moved her hand down his body and let it settle timidly over the bulge between his legs. He shoved himself into her palm, sighing deeply as her fingers tightened around him.

"Squeeze it," he whispered thickly, and she did. He began to move against her hand, urging her to stroke him. She had never touched a man so intimately, never experienced the power of giving sexual pleasure. At once elated and afraid, she blindly did as he urged.

Suddenly Alec pulled her tight against him. His hand moved under her skirt, fingers reaching to get inside her panties. "Oh, Em—I want you, I want you," he muttered hoarsely.

For a moment, Emily froze. Tears filled her eyes. "Alec, I can't—not yet, not here, like this. . . ."

"Okay, baby, okay—" He clamped his hand over hers, his hips working frantically. His breath came in short gasps. "But you do want me, don't you? Say it! Say you want me!"

"Yes!" she whimpered. "I want you—I want you."

He shook convulsively, then stiffened. Deep, guttural sounds came from the back of his throat. "Emily, hold me!" he cried. His fingers dug into her flesh. "Hold me, Em, I'm going to . . ." He uttered a final choked cry and plunged his mouth down to hers, his body jerking violently under her hand.

When at last he grew still, they sat clinging to each other for what seemed an eternity. Finally Alec loosened his hold on her and gave a deep sigh. "Christ, I haven't come in my pants like that since I was a kid in high school."

Still dazed by the ferocity of emotions that had been unleashed within her, Emily began to cry softly. "Oh, Alec, I'm sorry. I didn't mean to—"

"Sorry? Are you kidding? It was great!" He laughed and began to rock her in his arms like a child. "It was terrific! And it was all your fault! Your fault," he chanted, "your fault, you sweet, sexy thing." He put his cheek against hers, murmuring, "Sweet Emily, sweet, sweet Em . . ."

She held him close, wanting to stay in his arms forever. He had made the past vanish, and for the moment there was no thought of the future. There was only the immediate present and the wonder of being with him.

5

Throughout her adolescence, Emily had been isolated by the scar from the special friendships and popularity enjoyed by other girls. While they went through the teenage ritual of discovering sex, sharing secrets, and teaching each other the centuries-old rules in the game of how to attract boys, her romantic imagination had been fired by the films she had watched on television. Besides stimulating her desire to become a costume designer, they had provided an almost mythic depiction of love. The larger-than-life figures on the screen became her idols, and their stories an escape from the harsh reality of her own life.

She had often imagined herself as the heroine of the films she loved, like the homely spinster played by Bette Davis in *Now, Voyager*, who finally emerged as a svelte and beautiful woman of the world. Even more to the point was *A Woman's Face*, in which Joan Crawford suffered the agony of a disfiguring scar until she was made beautiful by plastic surgery and found true love. And she never failed to weep at the discovery of beauty and truth made by Dorothy McGuire and Robert Young, who played the drab girl and scarred soldier in *The Enchanted Cottage*. Romance, as expressed in films, became the core of her inner life.

Now, in the few short weeks that she had known Alec, Emily felt as if they were reenacting one of those movie love stories. He was the embodiment of all her romantic fantasies, the man who saw her beauty where no one else could. When she was with him, she thought of the two of them as being cloaked in a kind of poetic enchantment where all reality disappeared.

She was reluctant to tell Nora and Sheila about him, afraid that they would never understand how this miracle had happened. Although she hardly dared admit it to herself, she was in love with Alec and desperately wanted to keep her secret from any possibility of ridicule or suspicion.

But keeping Alec a secret proved to be more difficult than she had expected. For the first time in her life, Emily lied to her mother. To cover the hours she spent with him, she told Nora that she was working at late-night rehearsals doing fittings and sewing. At first she felt somewhat guilty about the deception, but soon the lies were told with shocking ease, and she was astonished at her own ability to be so devious.

The only thing that marred Emily's happiness was the constant bickering and arguments between Nora and Sheila. To Nora's way of thinking, the only successful women in the world were beautiful women. She had little faith in Emily's ambition to be a designer, not because she didn't think Emily was talented but because of the scar. And so she had pinned her hopes on Sheila, determined that the girl would make something of her life. What she refused to recognize was that Sheila had no interest in her mother's plans for her.

Emily did her best to avoid their quarrels, but very often she was drawn into them against her will. One night, after leaving Alec, she came home and heard them yelling at each other in the front room. Nora's voice was raised in a shrill, angry cry, "You're turning into a little tramp!"

"That's not true!" Sheila cried. "All we did was listen to some records!"

Emily tried to go directly to her room, but Nora heard her coming into the house and called out, "Emily, get in here!"

With a sigh of resignation, Emily went into the living room. Like the rest of the house, it was small, cramped by a low ceiling, and in dire need of fresh paint. The furniture had been bought at Sears years ago, and now it looked worn, threadbare. A few dime-store prints hung on the walls, and the drapes at the windows had faded from their original sky blue to a musty grey color. On the mantel over the fake fireplace stood a number of family pictures in cheap wooden frames: a wedding photograph of Nora and Nick, snapshots of Emily and Sheila as children, a recent high school graduation portrait of Sheila smiling full-face into the camera, and an older one of Emily, with the scarred side of her face turned away. Shoved into a corner was the most important piece of furniture in the entire room—a television set on a rollaway stand.

Nora glared at Emily as she came into the room. "Where the hell have you been?" she snapped. "It's after midnight!"

Emily calmly replied, "At rehearsal. I told you I'd be late." She looked over at Sheila, who was flopped on the couch like a rag doll. The girl's face was tear-streaked, her makeup smeared, mouth set in a sullen pout. "What happened?" Emily asked her.

"Nothing happened," Sheila muttered. "Mike Garcia came over to listen to some records with me, and we—"

"They were necking and getting stoned!" Nora broke in furiously. "I got home late from work and found them in her room, on the bed, blasting the whole goddamned street with that lousy rock music and getting stoned!"

"Oh, for Christ's sake," Sheila whined. "So we were a little high—so what?"

Nora rushed across the room and slapped the girl on the face. "I don't want that bum in my house ever again!"

Sheila fell back against the couch, her cheek flaming with the imprint of Nora's hand. She stared at her mother with eyes hard as stones. "What the hell do you want me to do—sit home alone every night and watch television like you?"

Nora lifted her hand to deliver another slap, but Emily stepped in and grabbed her mother's arm. "Okay, that's enough," she said quietly. "Mom, go make some coffee and calm down. Sheila, go to bed."

Nora pulled away from Emily and left the room, head bowed, weeping softly. Sheila stood up somewhat unsteadily, and Emily went to help her. Once they were in her room, Sheila flung herself on the bed. She sat up against the pillows, hugging her knees to her chest. Under the tangled mess of blond hair, her face was pale, eyes puffy from crying.

Emily sat down beside her. She couldn't help feeling a stab of envy; even in her disheveled state, Sheila still looked beautiful. She also looked very young and vulnerable, and Emily was reminded of the little sister she had played with and loved so many years ago.

"Why can't Mom leave me alone?" Sheila said miserably. "She's at me all the time."

"She's just worried about you. And I can't blame her for not liking Mike—he was always pretty wild, even when we went to school together."

Sheila's eyes grew defensive. "Yeah, so what? He makes me laugh, feel good. Besides, he's just somebody I hang out with; I'm not going to marry him, for Christ's sake." She took a cigarette from a pack on the night table, lighted it, and drew deeply. "God, I wish I had some money." She let the smoke out through her lips, a thoughtful expression on her face. "I'd be out of here in a minute, live in my own place where I could do anything I wanted."

"You don't mean that."

"The hell I don't! I'm sick of this place," she said bitterly. "And I'm sick of her. All she wants me to do is go to cosmetology school and be a fucking hairdresser like she is! I don't want to go to another school. Shit! I just got out of high school!"

"Mom's concerned about your future."

"My future! That's all I hear—what am I going to do with my life. I'm fed up with all of it!"

"Sheila, I know how you feel—"

"No you don't!" she exploded. "She's always telling me how grateful I should be." Sheila mimicked Nora's voice. "You should thank God every day for what you have. Look at poor Emily, and what she had to endure. But at least she's doing something with her life, working and taking classes, trying to make something of herself, even with the way she looks!"

Sheila's voice was ugly with rage, and the words continued to pour forth in a rush. "Yes, I want to get away! From Mom, and from you! Every time I look at you I feel guilty! Why the hell should I feel guilty because I'm pretty and you're not?"

The torrent of invective lashed at Emily like a series of violent blows. Her face drained of all color, and she was unable to move or speak, as if she had been turned to stone by some dreadful curse.

Suddenly aware of what she was saying, Sheila stopped. She grew frightened at the expression on Emily's face, and in a voice quivering with shame, she cried, "Emily, I'm sorry—I didn't mean..." Her eyes filled with tears and she began to cry.

Emily reached out stiffly and put her arms around the girl. She stroked Sheila's hair and patted her shoulder. "It's all right," she said dully. "Don't cry—it's not your fault. It's nobody's fault, not yours or Mom's or mine. It's just the way things are."

The two sisters clung to each other, but each of them knew that not even this close moment would help bridge the gap that had separated them since childhood; the damage that had been done over the years was irreparable. Emily remembered the months of torment she had gone through, swathed in bandages like a mummy, while Sheila had hovered near her room, too young to understand what had happened; she had only been four years old. After the bandages had been removed, the sister she had known was gone, and there was a stranger in her place. Emily could still hear Sheila crying out in terror the first time she had seen the scar.

When Sheila finally went to sleep, Emily crept into her room, exhausted but unable to close her eyes. She lay awake for hours, thinking of what had happened to her family. The scar had made victims of them all: Nora was afraid of it and had unwittingly given Sheila a sense of shame about her own unblemished beauty. They were all ensnared in a tangle of guilt, repressed anger, and hidden fears.

But now she had Alec, and everything had changed; he had released the beauty locked within her and made the scar less important. Would knowing that make a difference to her mother and sister? Emily wondered. She tried to imagine what would happen if they met him. Would they understand his feelings for her? No, they would think it impossible for a handsome man to be attracted to her. How could they think otherwise, when all they saw was the scar?

But Alec had seen more, he had seen into her heart and soul. And all he asked of her was that she do the same—see him as a man, not an image. Could they understand that kind of sensitivity? No, she decided, it was best that they didn't meet him—not yet. Besides, for the moment, she really didn't want to share him with anyone.

He was her secret love, her refuge.

6

THE FIRST DRESS REHEARSAL OF THE PLAY WAS CHA-
otic. Emily worked furiously to repair burst seams, replace
lost buttons, mend ripped skirts, cover torn bodices with
pieces of ribbon and lace. Maria had abandoned the play
a week earlier, and Emily had to contend with all the last-
minute emergencies alone. As the cast lurched through
each scene, she waited in the wings, ready with needle
and thread for the next calamity.

Even though it was a rag-tag production done on skimpy
sets with improvised costumes, Emily was enthralled by
the fervor and magic of the play, thrilled at being involved
in its creation. This was the beginning of what she had
yearned for, dreamed of—to be part of the noisy excitement, the rush and bustle, the terrors and joys of working
in theater. And all of it was heightened by her feelings
for Alec, the fact that they were sharing in it together.

During the famous third-act balcony scene, her heart
leaped at the sight of his flinging off the red cape she had
made and preparing to climb up the balcony to claim his
kiss from the girl playing Roxane. For a moment, she
herself was Roxane standing there with outstretched arms,
glowingly beautiful, ready to give herself to her lover. In
a low whisper, she murmured Cyrano's lines:

"Yes, that is love—that wind of terrible and jealous
    beauty,
  blowing over me—that dark fire, that music..."

50

When the last scene was finally played and the curtains swept closed, a tired cheer went up from the bedraggled cast. Mistakes had been made in the lighting cues, lines had been flubbed, costumes torn and repaired, props had been misplaced, and some of the furniture had been stumbled into, but they had gotten through the first dress rehearsal.

While Gary Johnson kept everyone on stage for critical notes, Emily went to the small room off the hallway behind the stage that had been given over to wardrobe and began to clean it up for the night. A half-hour later the actors were dismissed and they headed for the dressing rooms. Emily finished straightening up and went to wait for Alec in the hallway. The door to the men's dressing room was open, and she could hear the voice of Wally Clark, one of the actors, saying, "Hey, Alec, we're all going over to Larry's for pizza and beer—why don't you join us?"

"Thanks, Wally," Alec replied, "but I can't—I'm busy."

"Emily Gorden again? We've all seen you two over at the coffee shop." Wally gave a lewd laugh. "What's with you, man—you into scars?"

There was a sudden sound of scuffling, then a shout from one of the other boys as a fight broke out. Emily heard Alec shout, "You son of a bitch! Don't you ever say anything like that again!"

Emily stood frozen, pale with shame and humiliation. Tears stung her eyes, and she started to move away when Wally burst out of the room with Alec in hot pursuit. Wally saw her and blanched with embarrassment.

"Oh, shit! Emily—I'm sorry—"

"Get the hell out of here!" Alec yelled.

Wally ran off and Alec went to Emily, took her in his arms. Behind them a few other boys stood watching from the doorway of the dressing room. Alec turned around, glaring, and went back to slam the door in their faces. He returned to Emily and said, "Let's get out of here."

They walked to her car in the parking lot. Emily handed him the keys, and he opened the door for her, then got in on the driver's side. He put his arm around her shoulders and held her close.

"I'm all right," Emily said.

"Well, I'm not!" Alec exploded. "That stupid shithead! Next time I see him, I'll break his goddamned—"

"No, don't, Alec—it's really all right." She turned her face up to his and smiled. "I never had anyone fight for me before."

He gave her a lingering kiss, then sat back. "Are you hungry?"

"No, not really."

"Want to drive up to Mullholland?"

"No—" She paused, then said, "I want to go to your place."

Alec looked at her, surprised. His eyes searched hers anxiously. "Em, are you sure?"

"Yes, I'm sure," she answered softly.

"But it's late, and—" He hesitated, then turned away glumly. "I don't want to spend just an hour or two with you."

Emily was silent for a moment. Then, in a low but confident voice, she said, "I'll call my mother from your place and tell that I'm spending the night with Maria, that we're going to work late redoing some of the costumes for tomorrow night's rehearsal."

Alec stared at her wonderingly. "The whole night? You'll spend the whole night with me?"

"Is that all right? I mean, do you want me to?"

He broke into a wide smile, then laughed out loud. "Do I want you to? Christ, what a question!" He pulled her to him and kissed her, his tongue teasing inside her mouth, hands moving over her breasts. "Yes, I want you to— yes, yes!" he whispered against her lips.

He started the car and drove out of the parking lot, one arm tight around her shoulders. Emily put her head on his chest and closed her eyes. Deep inside her she was a little fearful about what lay ahead. But sleeping with Alec was what she had dreamed of, wanted, since their first evening together. In the few short weeks that they had known each other, he had given her validation as a woman. He cared for her and she trusted him, and now she would give him proof of that trust. She saw herself, once more, as the heroine of all her favorite films, giving herself to the man she loved.

A few minutes later Alec turned the car into his street and parked. Emily followed him into the building and up the stairs to the second floor. The hallway was narrow and had a damp, stale odor of age and decay. Somewhere a fretful baby cried and a man's voice was raised in anger. The overhead lights were dim and cast an ugly yellow glow over a threadbare carpet and enameled walls that were thick with layers of dust.

Emily grew apprehensive; the atmosphere was oppressive and a little frightening. She began to wonder if she had made a mistake coming here. She could still leave, she thought nervously; she didn't have to stay. But what would Alec think? She had promised to spend the night with him. She couldn't turn back now, like a frightened schoolgirl. Alec stopped at a door, opened it, and turned to her with a smile. In the pale light his face looked shadowy and romantic, and for a moment she remembered him on the balcony, holding Roxane in his arms; only it was she he was embracing and kissing. All her fears vanished and she followed him into the room.

Alec turned on some table lamps and said, "Welcome to my hovel. Excuse the mess, but I wasn't expecting company." He grinned, and hurried to pick up pieces of clothing that were scattered all over the room.

Emily looked around, feeling a little uncertain. The room was small, shabbily furnished, but it was clean and comfortable. There were a couple of easy chairs, a dinette set, a desk, and an old brass bed covered with a dark blue chenille spread. On a bookcase to the right of the bed stood a small television set, an inexpensive record player and some albums, and a stack of paperback novels. In the shelves were books on theater. Half-opened folding doors revealed a galley kitchen, and she noticed some barbells and a set of weights on the floor. Then she saw a group of photographs of Alec hanging on the wall over the desk. They were theatrical pictures in a variety of poses and clothes: the young executive in a business suit, a college boy in a pullover tennis sweater, a workman in tee shirt and jeans holding a bottle of beer, and several pictures in brief swim trunks taken on the beach.

He came up to her and said sheepishly, "A little gallery of me. I'm all ego, just like any other actor."

"I think they're beautiful," Emily said. "May I have one? A little one I can keep in my wallet?"

He opened up an album that was lying on the desk and pulled out a picture of himself in the tennis sweater. "How's this one?"

"That's perfect, thank you." Emily tucked it into her purse and glanced at him nervously, unsure of what to do next.

"Would you like to hear some music?" Alec asked. "I have a great Roberta Flack album."

Emily nodded and he went to the record player. A moment later the Bob Dylan song "Just Like a Woman" filled the room. Alec came back to her and said, "Are you hungry? Want me to call out for a pizza?"

"No, maybe later..." Emily hesitated, then said, "I'd better call my mother."

"Right. I'll turn the music down so she doesn't think you're at a party."

Emily went to the phone and called Nora. She tried not to sound flustered, but she couldn't keep her voice from trembling a little. When she was finished and hung up, Alec took her in his arms and said, "You're pale and shaking like a leaf. Don't be frightened." He grinned and kissed her lightly. "How 'bout a glass of wine—Gallo, 1974—a vintage year?"

Emily smiled and shook her head.

"Then how about a dance?"

"Oh, I don't dance—I never learned how."

"C'mon, I'll teach you. It's easy, but we have to take off our shoes, or the people downstairs will start banging on the walls."

They slipped off their shoes and Alec pulled her close to him. "Just relax and follow me. Listen to the music and let your body move with mine."

The started slowly at first. Emily held herself back a little, but he tightened his arms around her and she yielded, letting herself feel the pressure of his body against hers. She touched the soft curl of hair on the nape of his neck, and the skin beneath her fingertips felt smooth and tense. They began to sway in time to the languorous beat of the song, their hands gliding over one another in slow, delicate caresses, speaking wordlessly, by touch alone, of their excitement.

Alec bent his head and kissed her. His tongue licked softly at her lips, and she opened her mouth in response. Her sense of time and place began to blur; she was aware only of his kisses, infinitely varied, following one on the other in swift succession. She locked her arms around his neck, and he slipped his hands down to her buttocks, gripping her tightly. She felt his erection pressing against her, and for a moment she grew almost faint from the heat of his body. Drawing her lips away from his for a moment, she threw her head back to catch her breath, then kissed him more passionately, sliding her fingers into his thick curly hair. Their mouths ground against each other, and he slid his leg between hers so that they were locked together.

The music stopped, and for a few seconds the needle dragged in the end grooves. Then there was silence. Alec took his lips from hers and she looked up at him. His face was flushed; his green eyes were flecked with gold, his lips wet and glistening. In the dim light he looked feverish with desire. "Are you sure?" he asked in a thick, husky whisper.

Emily felt as she were floating through a vast, warm space. She sensed a subtle, anxious tremor in his legs and moved her hands dreamily over his back, as if to soothe him "... Yes," she replied.

He began to undress her, pausing to caress each part of her body as it was exposed. Despite her need for him, she began to feel increasingly vulnerable, and panic rose up to displace passion. He tugged at her panties, and she suddenly pulled away from him, ashamed of her fear.

"What is it? What's the matter, Em?" he asked.

"I'm afraid," she confessed tearfully.

He reached out and took her arms, holding her carefully, as he would a fragile work of art. "Don't be afraid, baby. I won't hurt you. I promise. You do want me, don't you?"

"Yes, of course I do," she cried brokenly. "I've wanted you since the first time I saw you. But how can you want *me*?" Instinct made her lift her hand to her cheek. The scar seemed to draw her whole face into its jagged, tormented line.

"So that's what you're afraid of," Alec said quietly. "The scar. But you know that's not what I see when I look at you. Emily, you're beautiful. Any man would want you if he could see you the way I do."

He turned her around so that she was facing a full-length mirror on the door of the closet. Standing behind her, he looked into the mirror with her. "See how beautiful you are," he said in a low, mesmerizing voice. His hands traced the line of her shoulders to her breasts, and he cupped them, touching the nipples lightly. "Beautiful, firm, they just fill my hands," he crooned softly. His fingers grazed over her skin, causing small shudders of delight. "Your body really turns me on...." He moved in front of her and sank to his knees, slowly pushing down her panties and lifting her feet a little to help her step out of them. Then he slid his hands around her hips and pressed his face against her thighs. "Beautiful legs, and a small, sweet ass..." He looked up at her imploringly. "Shall I go on, or do you believe me?"

She bent to him as he rose and lifted her in his arms. "Do you believe me?" he asked again, and she answered with a kiss that was passionate and filled with gratitude.

He carried her to the bed, put her down, and began to take off his clothes. She watched him through glazed eyes, boldly examining every part of his smooth, supple body. When he lay down beside her, she reached out for him, eager to touch his flesh. They kissed deeply for a long time. Her lips sought out the hollow of his throat, the firm swell of his chest, the small tips of his flat nipples. A ray of light fell across her face, and she realized that the lamp was still on. The illumination felt harsh and threatening.

"Alec, please turn off the light."

He leaned over her and said, "No. I want to see you while I make love to you. And I want you to see me, to see what you do to me."

Before she could protest, his lips were on hers once more, his hands playing along the inside of her thighs. She slid her hands down his back to his buttocks, and he groaned as her fingers began to explore between his legs. He covered her body with his, and Emily slipped into a world of pure sensation, feeling at once drugged, yet more alive than she had ever known.

Alec spread her legs a little, touching her lightly, then his fingers slipped inside her. She gasped and her body tensed, refusing him further entry. He moved down the bed and put his lips on the curve of her loins. His tongue teased over the skin, licking delicately into the soft tuft of pubic hair until his mouth was fastened on her vagina. She moaned, shocked at what he was doing, but gripped his head with her hands, greedy for more. She tightened her thighs around his face and gave herself up to the fiery sensations that rocketed through her body.

Alec lifted himself up and began to ease into her. She waited, breathless, crying out a little at his size. There was a sudden sharp pain and she gasped. He paused, waiting for the pain to pass, then entered her more fully, waited again until her quick breaths had subsided, and finally filled her completely.

She murmured his name over and over as he rested, unmoving, inside her. She kissed him feverishly and he began to move his hips, slowly at first, then more quickly, with long smooth strokes. Emily caught his rhythm and they began to move together. He whispered to her, urging her on, and she locked her legs around his waist. Suddenly Alec sat up, pulling her with him so that she was sitting on his lap, impaled on him. He kissed and licked her breasts, kneaded her buttocks, moving her with impatient, urgent thrusts. Her head whipped from side to side and she began to whimper. Choked cries came from the back of his throat as he approached his climax. He kissed her fiercely, then moved so that she was lying on her back once more. His body hammered at her with increasing speed and she felt herself on the verge of a huge, swelling wave of excitement that was about to break. They cried out together in hoarse groans that rose to shrieks as he gave a final lunge and came, pushing her over the edge into a drowning shock of turbulence that shook every fiber of her being.

Emily held him close as he remained deep inside her until he was spent. She uttered broken sobs of endearment, stroked his damp hair, and gave him soft, sweet kisses, knowing that not a single part of her life would ever be the same again.

7

DURING THE FOLLOWING WEEK, EMILY SPENT AS MUCH time as she could with Alec. As soon as rehearsals were over, they would go to his apartment for a few ecstatic hours. Gone was the hesitancy of their first night together; as soon as the door was closed behind them, they were in each other's arms. Emily was astonished at the wild, raging passions he unleashed in her. She was like a starved child, hungry to experience everything she could. Alec was a superb lover and expert teacher, driving her to heights of frenzy that made her scream or expressing moments of such tenderness that she wept. His room became a citadel where nothing else in the world existed but the two of them, and she began to measure her life by the exact number of minutes and hours they were together.

Emily became more adept than ever at keeping her affair with Alec a secret. She slipped into a dual existence with the ease of an international spy. There was no suspicion, either at home or at work, of the extraordinary change that had occurred in her life. The lies she continued to tell Nora to cover the time she spent with Alec no longer troubled her; if anything they heightened her sense of being involved in a clandestine romance. It was a touch of movie melodrama that delighted her, a silver-screen fantasy that made her feel somehow mysterious and alluring.

She wanted to do everything she could to show her love for him. She stocked his small refrigerator with food so they wouldn't have to stop at the coffee shop to eat after rehearsals. Late at night, when she came home, she worked on his costumes, embroidering the cape she had made him, trimming his jacket with braid and making him a new shirt. As the cloth moved under her hands, it became his flesh, and she would close her eyes for a moment, remembering the sculpture-like perfection of his body.

The opening night of the play drew closer, and Alec became nervous and irritable, worried about his performance. Each night, at dinner before rehearsals, she comforted and encouraged him; later, in his apartment, she would run lines with him until he felt secure. One night, after they had made love, he seemed unusually quiet. When Emily asked him what was wrong, he told her that he had lost his job with the messenger service.

"Oh, Alec, I'm so sorry. What happened?" she asked.

"Somebody at dispatch fucked up, I made a couple of wrong deliveries, and the manager chewed me out. I told him to shove the job up his ass—and walked out. Well, what the hell," he sighed. "It's happened before. I'll find something else."

Emily took him in her arms. "Of course you will. And I'll do everything I can to help you."

He smiled and kissed her, then said, "You don't know what it means to me to have somebody like you, someone who believes in me, cares about what happens to me."

"I feel the same way about you," she murmured. "Oh, Alec, we're so lucky to have each other. We can do anything as long as we're together."

She hugged him tightly, only vaguely aware that what she had just said had the faint echo of some movie love story she had seen. But the words came from her heart with all the passion and fervor of a brand-new emotion. She thought of them as two lovers made strong by their feelings for each other, united against the harsh demands of an uncaring world.

* * *

Emily began to help Alec with small loans, but he told her he couldn't go on taking money from her. She protested, of course, yet was privately pleased by his sense of independence, his strength. He started looking for a job as a waiter, and the evenings they spent together were abruptly interrupted. Alec explained that the best time to apply for these positions was late at night, when the managers were in. Several nights a week all they had time for was a quick cup of coffee after the rehearsal before he took off to search for a job. Those nights she spent alone were agony. She worried about him and missed him, longed for the feel of his hard body against her, the touch of his hands and lips.

To take her mind off her need for him, Emily began to work on a special dress for the opening night of the play. She was particularly concerned about the cast party Gary Johnson was giving after the first performance. She had expressed some reluctance about attending, but Alec had insisted that they go.

She searched through all of her fashion magazines and books on movie costumes and finally found her inspiration in some of the gowns created for the MGM films of the thirties by her favorite designer, Adrian. More than anything, she wanted to look as beautiful as she could for Alec, and so she worked up several sketches of a low-cut dress that would show off her smooth shoulders and firm breasts. She redesigned and modified a gown that had been worn by Joan Crawford in *Sadie McKee*, a film made in 1934. The finished drawing was of a simply cut, black crepe sheath with a halter neckline trimmed in drapes of grey chiffon that left her arms and shoulders bare and ended in a deep vee-cut at the small of her back. It was an elegant and glamorous dress with only one flaw; it had to be worn by a woman with a beautiful, unmarred throat.

Emily stared at the sketch for a long time. Alec had said that she didn't have to cover her neck with high collars to hide the scar, that it didn't make any difference

61

to him. She thought about that as she picked up a pencil and sketched the scar on the drawing. When she was finished, a surge of despair brought tears to her eyes; she couldn't wear the dress, no matter how beautiful it was. Alec might not pay any attention to the scar, but everyone else would see it. If anything, the beauty of the dress would only heighten the ugliness of the scar.

In a gesture filled with helplessness and rage, she snatched the drawing up to throw it away. Then suddenly she remembered something Mr. Bradley had said about designing costumes that would compensate for an actress with a problem figure, or to disguise signs of age. She erased the scar and began sketching furiously. An hour later she sat back, satisfied with what she had accomplished. She had added a length of darker grey chiffon that wound around her throat from collar bone to chin, clasped at the back of her neck and floated down behind her like a long, trailing scarf. And for a touch of color, she put a flaming lipstick-red rose in beads and sequins at the point of the low-cut decolletage.

Emily knew that the dress had little in common with the current fashions, but that meant nothing to her; she had decided years before that she could never look like other girls, no matter what new designs she wore. In her eyes, the scar made that impossible, and so she felt compelled to create an image of her own. All the clothes she had designed for herself were created to draw attention away from the scar and give her a feeling of self-confidence. And now that Alec was in her life, she was even more concerned about how she looked. Despite everything he said and did to prove how little he cared about the scar, she couldn't help feeling that his own remarkable beauty deserved equal perfection in the girl he cared for. She couldn't give him that perfection, but she could use her talent to present as striking and attractive an appearance as possible. In her own mind, it was a way of making it up to him for her disfigurement.

* * *

The play was scheduled to open on a Saturday night, and when the day arrived, it was filled with a rush of frantic activity. A dress rehearsal took up most of the morning and afternoon. When it was over, Emily drove Alec back to his apartment so he could get some rest, then she hurried home to prepare for the opening-night performance. Sheila was out shopping and Nora was at work, which gave her a few hours alone to bathe and change her clothes. She decided to take the dress she had designed with her and put it on before she and Alec went to the cast party. There were bound to be some emergencies during the performance that she would have to take care of, and she didn't want to risk anything happening to the dress.

A few minutes before Emily was ready to leave to pick up Alec, Nora came home. She was ill with a cold that had been lingering all week and told Emily that she didn't think she was up to going to the play.

"I'm sorry, honey, but I feel just awful. Can I see it another night?"

"Sure, Mom. Don't worry about it. Just take care of yourself. The play is running weekends for a month. Maybe you can go next Saturday, if you're feeling better." Emily began wrapping her dress in tissue paper and put it into a large box.

"Christ, I hope so," Nora replied. She started to cough and took out a handkerchief. "I'd better go to bed." She was about to leave Emily's room when she asked, "What about Sheila? Since I can't take her, can she go with you?"

Emily froze. How could she take Sheila? She was picking Alec up in a few minutes, and later they were going to the party, then back to his place. She turned to Nora and said, "She can't come with me. I have to leave in a few minutes—we're doing a run-through before the performance. And after the play, I'm going to a cast party."

"Well, I suppose she could take the bus. Then she could meet you after the play and go to the party with you."

"No, she can't do that," Emily said quickly. "The party

is for cast members only. And it may run very late. You'll have to give her your car."

"Are you kidding?" Nora objected. "The way she drives?"

Emily gathered up her purse and the dress box. "Mom, please, don't give me a hard time," she said brusquely. "This is an important night for me, and I don't want to have to worry about Sheila. Give her a break and let her drive your car. If you start treating her like an adult, maybe she'll begin to act like one."

Before Nora could reply, Emily started out of the house. She called back over her shoulder, "I'll leave her ticket at the box office—and don't wait up for me."

Nora went after her, saying, "Okay, okay—I'll give her the car. And good luck, baby. I know the costumes are going to be terrific."

Emily flashed her a smile from the car, then drove off, breathing a sigh of relief. For a moment she had been afraid that all her plans for the evening had gone down the drain. Alec had told her that they would leave the party early so they could go back to his place and make love. For the last couple of weeks, while he had been job hunting, they had seen very little of each other. Tonight they were going to make up for it, and the last thing she needed was to have Sheila around to spoil everything.

For the last week Emily had been worried about Alec meeting her mother and sister. She had gone over the scene many times in her mind and had it all planned. When they came backstage to see her after the play, she would introduce them casually, as if he were just another member of the cast. Then she would hurry them out, and go off to the party with Alec.

Now all she had to worry about was Sheila meeting him.

An icy fear suddenly gripped her. How would Alec react to meeting Sheila? And Sheila—what would she do? Emily had seen her sister flirt with boys, and knew the effect she had on them. One look at Alec and Sheila would light up like a torch. Would Alec respond? But how could she think that of him? she admonished herself. There were several pretty girls in the cast who had tried to capture his attention and had gotten nowhere. He had even told her about all the girls he had known and how little they had meant to him. She had to trust him, trust that he really loved her.

Alec was waiting outside his apartment house when she pulled up. He got into the car and kissed her. "Ready for the big night?" he asked.

Emily smiled and replied, "I have an extra supply of safety pins in my purse to cover all emergencies. Did you get some sleep?"

"A little." He looked out the window thoughtfully.

"Are you worried about tonight?"

"I'm worried, period. I haven't found a job, my rent's due in a couple of weeks, and I can't go on taking money from you."

Emily took his hand and held it tightly. "Don't worry about it now, darling. You're so wonderful in the play, somebody is bound to notice you. Agents will be there, and a casting director from Univeral promised to come tonight. I just know something terrific will happen for you."

Alec laughed and hugged her. "God, you're good for me. Okay, coach, I'll get out there tonight and give it everything I've got."

"Not everything—" She glanced at him slyly. "Save some for later—for me." She reached over and stroked his thigh.

"Hey, stop that! I'll have a hard-on for the whole performance, and I'm wearing tights! How would that look?"

"Just wonderful," Emily sighed. "And every woman in America would agree with me."

"What happened to the sweet little innocent girl I met just a few short weeks ago?" Alec cried in mock despair.

"I've traded her in for a new model." She glanced at

the dress box on the back seat. "A new and more dazzling Emily Gorden will be seen later tonight."

When the curtains finally rose on the opening-night performance, no one sitting in the audience would have guessed at the pandemonium that had raged backstage an hour before. Emily was everywhere at once, helping with makeup, needle and thread flying to repair tears and rips, soothing frantic actors, attaching ribbons that had come loose, and improvising on articles of clothing that had been stained or damaged. Onstage a table collapsed and had to be repaired, several lights went out and were replaced, a member of the crew slipped and fell, spraining his ankle, and the sound effects man frantically worked at adjusting a jammed tape machine.

The audience of friends, parents, and relatives shifted uneasily in their seats at the late curtain, but when it finally rose, there was a burst of applause for the set, then everyone settled back to watch the play. First-night nerves produced a number of false moves, garbled lines, and missed cues. But by the third act the actors had everything under control, and the final scenes were smoothly performed. A wave of applause broke as the curtains swept closed and opened again for the company to take their bows.

Emily stood in the wings, her eyes glistening with tears as Alec and the other leads stepped forward to bow. Attractively disheveled from his death scene, he appeared to her like a living masterpiece by an artist's brush: young, radiant, and more beautiful than she had ever seen him. She was swept by a feeling of love so deep and compelling that it made her weak. She looked from Alec to the program gripped tightly in her hand. Instead of being listed with the other members of the crew and staff, she had been given a separate credit: "Costumes Designed by EMILY GORDEN."

She glanced back at Alec and thought of this as a moment she would cherish in her heart forever.

As the cast began to leave the stage, Emily went to the wardrobe room to collect the costumes and store them for the next performance. When Alec came by, flushed and excited by his success, he closed the door and swept her into his arms.

"Was I good?" he cried.

"You were marvelous!" She held his face and kissed him deeply.

"How did I look?"

"Sensational! Like a star!"

He hugged her to him. "I owe that to you, baby," he whispered. "All that work you did on my costumes."

"You're worth every minute, and more—much more. Now get out of here before the others come in."

"I'll come get you as soon as I'm changed. Then it's party time!"

"Give me a few minutes to get the costumes put away and change into my dress."

Excitement buzzed through her as the cast came by to give her their costumes and congratulate her. Gary Johnson burst through the door, hugged her hard, and said, "I could never have done it without you!" A few minutes later Mr. Bradley appeared, smiling broadly. "I'm astonished, my dear, at what you accomplished. You have a wonderful talent, and I know that one day you will be a very important designer."

Emily felt lightheaded with happiness as the babble of compliments and enthusiasm went on. Finally, she managed to close and lock the door and started changing into her dress. A few minutes later, while she was brushing her hair, Alec knocked loudly and called, "Emily, your sister is out here to see you. Are you ready yet?"

She paused and looked toward the door. Sheila was there—and she had already managed to meet Alec. For a moment her spirits sank, then she took a deep breath and answered, "I'll be out in a minute."

Emily turned to look at herself in the full-length mirror. The dress clung to her figure, and the tiny appliquéd rose in beads and sequins glittered at the low-cut neckline, emphasizing the shape of her breasts. She adjusted the chiffon scarf so that it covered her neck, and turned to see how it floated down her back. Even though she had tried the dress on several times at home, she was a little startled by how she looked. It was more sophisticated than anything she had ever worn, and for the first time in her life, she saw herself as being beautiful. Except for the scar. It almost seemed to separate itself from the rest of her appearance, as if to mock the effort she had made to disguise it. A familiar despair began to shrivel her feeling of happiness, when suddenly she remembered a line from an old Bette Davis movie that made her smile: "A woman is only beautiful when she is loved." And she was loved—by Alec. And that made all the difference.

She picked up the evening purse she had bought to match the dress and opened the door to see Alec and Sheila waiting for her down the hall. Sheila was wearing a new dress that she hadn't seen before, a tight-fitting mini in vivid red jersey that accentuated every curve of her body. Her blond hair was loose and casual, like a hood of gold around her face, and her lips were made up in the same color as her dress. Alec was leaning against the wall, staring at her while she spoke to him, a smile playing at the corners of his lips. He looked up as Emily approached them, and his eyes widened for a moment.

"Hi, sorry to keep you waiting," Emily said, looking at Alec to see his reaction to the dress.

"It was worth it," he said softly, his eyes sweeping over her. "You look wonderful."

Sheila gave her a big smile and said, "Oh, yes, Em, you look terrific. I was just telling Alec how great he was in the play." She flashed a sidelong glance at Alec and added, "It must have been fun doing costumes for him."

"It was, and for the rest of the cast, too," Emily replied pointedly.

"Oh sure, and they all looked great," Sheila said quickly. "I was very proud of you."

"Thank you," Emily said dryly. For a moment she was uncomfortably aware that for the first time in their lives, she and Sheila were vying for the attention of the same man. Or were they? Alec seemed to be regarding Sheila with the same cool indifference he had shown some of the more aggressive girls in the cast. Even so, the confidence she had felt moments before was suddenly shaken.

Just then several members of the cast came hurrying down the hall. One of the girls stopped briefly and said, "Emily, what a supper dress! Did you make it?" The others yelled at her to hurry, and she went after them, calling out over her shoulder, "Hurry up, you two—it's party time!"

Emily looked at Sheila and said, "We have to go. Thanks for coming, and tell Mom I hope she feel's better."

Sheila gave her a sad smile. "I will. Have a good time at the party. I wish I could join you, but I know it's only for the cast."

She gave Alec a meaningful look, as if challenging him to invite her. He started to say something, but Emily spoke up first, "Yes, it is. Besides, you know how Mom worries if you stay out late."

Sheila's eyes narrowed for a few seconds, then she smiled brightly and said to Alec, "Well, good night. You were really terrific. Someday I bet you'll be a big star."

Alec laughed and replied, "Thanks—nice meeting you, Sheila."

She gave them both a little wave and walked away, her hips moving provocatively under the red jersey.

Alec took Emily's arm and they started down the hall to the exit that led to the parking lot. "I didn't know you could be so tough," he said with a sly grin.

"What do you mean?" Emily asked stiffly.

"The way you got rid of your sister—very neat."

Emily flushed. "Well, I just didn't think she'd enjoy—"

"Ca-ca-lottsa!" He laughed. "You just didn't want her

around me. Afraid the pretty sister would turn me on, right?"

"I can't hide anything from you, can I?" Emily said, blushing furiously.

"Not a whole hell of a lot." Alec chuckled.

Emily remained silent as they got into the car and turned onto Vermont Avenue in the direction of the Hollywood hills where Gary lived. Alec looked over at her and grinned. "They don't know anything about me, do they—your mom and sister? You've been keeping me a secret, haven't you?"

"Yes," Emily confessed in a low voice. "Do you mind? It's not really because I was worried about your meeting Sheila. I just wanted to keep it secret for a while, something private, just between the two of us. . . . I didn't want to share you, not yet. Are you angry?"

"No, of course not. I feel the same way about you. What we have is very special—and speaking of special, that dress is a knockout!" He took one hand off the steering wheel and slipped his fingers into her decolletage. "I like this," he said huskily. "You designed it like this for me, didn't you?" Then he touched the chiffon at her throat. "And this was for you—to make you feel more secure."

Emily took his hand and held it to her breasts. "Yes. Is it all right?"

"I've never seen you look so beautiful. You're the one who's going to be a big star someday. A famous designer. It feels good, doesn't it, having some success."

Emily sat back, sighing contentedly. "Yes, it's wonderful."

Alec put his hand back on the wheel and stared ahead. "Yeah, the applause, and all the compliments and congratulations—it's a terrific feeling. It sets you up inside, makes you feel like you're in control, like you could make the whole world do whatever you wanted it to." His voice grew more intense as he went on. "There's nothing like it, that feeling of power. It's what everybody wants, to make the world dance on your string. And someday I'm going to have it." His hands gripped the wheel and his eyes burned with an odd excitement. "I'm going to get success and all the power that goes with it."

Emily felt herself caught up in his fervor and said breathlessly, "Of course you are. And I'll be right there, cheering you on."

He turned to her, his face vivid in the reflection of street lights, his eyes glittering. "You'd help me, too, wouldn't you? You'd be there for me whenever I needed you."

She moved closer to him. "You know I would."

He put his arm around her shoulder and pulled her to him roughly. "Let's not stay too long at the party," he said, his voice suddenly ragged. "We'll take a couple of bows, let everybody see your dress, then beat it back to my place. Okay?"

They stopped for a red light, and he leaned over and kissed her, his lips hard, demanding. A horn behind them honked; the light had changed. Alec started up again, still holding her in a tight, almost bruising embrace.

Emily pressed her face against his chest, her heart beating wildly, dazed by a sudden, overwhelming sexual hunger. "Let's skip the party," she muttered.

Alec's lips spread in a wide, tight smile. "That's my girl," he whispered softly.

8

FOR THE FIRST TIME IN HER LIFE, EMILY AWOKE TO EACH new day with a feeling of anticipation and excitement. *Cyrano* was playing to full houses every weekend. Gary Johnson had talked to her about doing the costumes for the next production, a revival of the thirties musical *The Boys from Syracuse*. Alec had found a job as a driver and messenger for the director of an export company and not only repaid the money she had lent him but even took her out to some expensive restaurants for dinner and to see a few new plays. He also told her that his performance had attracted the attention of an agent who promised to bring some casting directors to see him in the play.

Nora came to see the production. Afterward, she was a little bewildered, but very pleased to meet all of Emily's friends, including Alec. But Emily made sure that he was introduced as merely one of the members of the cast. Later, when she told her mother that she was staying overnight with one of the girls, Nora took it for granted that Emily was beginning to come out of her self-imposed isolation and enjoying a long-overdue social life.

But, of course, Emily was with Alec. On Saturdays, they would drive down the coast to a secluded beach near Malibu and lie in the sun. Emily wore a wide-brimmed straw hat that tied under her chin and shaded her face. Alec told her it made her look mysterious and aloof, like Garbo. "Garbo with tits." He laughed, bending his head to nuzzle her breasts. Then he would stretch out beside her and let her rub suntan lotion into the firm muscles of his back and legs. She would tease his flesh with her fingertips until he groaned and swore that he would embarrass both of them by standing up and letting everyone see how she had aroused him.

They would get back to his place a few hours before the performance and shower off the sand together, standing under the water in a tight embrace that ended with him making love to her there, pressed up against the tiled wall.

After the performance, they would go back to his place for a midnight snack, take off their clothes, and dance naked to his records until they fell into bed, clasped in each other's arms.

On Sunday mornings, Emily made breakfast, and afterward they'd read the Sunday *Times*, commenting to each other on the new plays that were opening, the films they wanted to see. The afternoon would drift lazily away and then it was time to go to the college for that evening's performance.

These were golden days for Emily. Her entire life revolved around Alec; he was all she could think of, no matter where she was or what she was doing. Sometimes, while she was working at her desk, the thought of him aroused rich and vibrant fantasies. She imagined herself and Alec as a wealthy, successful couple, being creative together in plays or films. She saw the two of them as the darlings of the theater world, sought after by famous celebrities for exclusive, intimate dinners and parties or entertaining in their own palatial, beautifully furnished home. She daydreamed of them flying to London or Paris to work on a play or standing at the rail of a ship cruising the Mediterranean or making love on the moonlit sands of a beach in Tahiti.

There were moments when Emily was sure that this happiness was all a dream, that her euphoria couldn't last. Then she would take Alec's picture out of her purse and devour it with her eyes, recalling the passion and fury of his lovemaking, the heights of ecstasy to which he drove her, and the warm, quiet times when they simply lay together, close and loving. More than anything else in the world, she wanted this joy never to end, and she vowed to herself that she would do everything she could to preserve it.

The first challenge to that vow occurred a week before the play closed.

One Friday night after work, Emily picked him up at his place and they went to dinner, as they usually did, before the performance. Alec was quiet and somewhat moody. She asked if anything was wrong, and he told her that he was tired, that he hadn't slept well. Later that night, he seemed distracted and preoccupied, even as they made love. Again she questioned him. Was there something wrong? Had she said or done something to upset him? He took her in his arms and reassured her that nothing she did was wrong. And then he said, with a sudden, almost desperate urgency, that she was the only right thing in his life.

The following evening, Emily grew more concerned. Alec was tense and irritable. He flared up at one of the crew backstage, froze during a scene and blew his lines, and later angrily blamed another actor for the mishap. When Emily drove him home, he told her that he wanted to be alone, that he was tired and needed to get a good night's sleep. They had made plans to drive up into the mountains near Lake Arrowhead the next morning, but he asked if they could do that another time.

"Alec, what is it?" Emily asked anxiously. "Please tell me. If there's something wrong, let me help you."

"I told you, there's nothing wrong!" he snapped.

Emily shrank back against the seat and Alec looked at her guiltily. "Baby, I'm sorry," he said more softly. "Didn't mean to take your head off." He smiled and leaned over to kiss her. "Don't worry—just be patient with me...."

"Alec, please," she whispered. "Let me help."

He touched her lips with his fingertips, silencing her, and said, "Come over tomorrow around two—that'll give us a couple of hours together, and I'll make up to you for being such a bastard tonight."

Before she could say anything else, he got out of the car and hurried into the apartment house.

The following evening Emily stood in the wings while the cast took their curtain calls. She watched Alec step to the front of the stage and bow to the audience. Even though he seemed more relaxed, she sensed that something was still troubling him. He was smiling, acknowledging the applause, when suddenly she saw the smile fade from his lips and his face go pale. He came offstage, hurried past her with a quick "See you in a few minutes," and disappeared into the dressing room. Later, after she had collected and stored the costumes, Emily went to find him.

Alec was waiting for her at the end of the hall by the exit door to the parking lot. His face was tense and his eyes were cloudy with apprehension. He grabbed her arm and muttered, "Let's get out of here." As they hurried to the car, he kept looking around the lot anxiously, as if expecting to see someone following them. When they were on the street, he hunched over the wheel, glancing repeatedly into the rearview mirror.

"Alec, what's wrong? Are you in some kind of trouble?" Emily asked.

"Nothing I can't take care of," he replied grimly. "But right now I need a drink, okay?"

They stopped at a small bar just off Vermont Avenue and sat down at a table in the back. Emily glanced around nervously; she had never been in a bar before. The place was dimly lit and shabby. A few rough-looking workmen stood at the bar, and a woman's raucous laughter came from one of the booths. The air was stale, thick with the odors of cigarette smoke and whiskey. A tired-looking waitress came over and Alec ordered scotch on the rocks. Emily asked for some ginger ale, and a few minutes later the drinks were set before them. Alec dropped some money on the tray, and the waitress ambled off to another table. Emily waited for Alec to say something. He took a deep swallow of the scotch and finally looked up at her, his face drawn. "I am in trouble, Em—" he said, his voice trembling a little. "I lied to you about the job as a driver. I don't have a job."

"I don't understand—what about the money you repaid me, the money you've been living on?..."

"I've been gambling," he admitted despairingly. "I borrowed some money from a couple of guys I know, and for a while I was doing really well. Then I lost what I had and borrowed some more. I lost that, too, and now..." He looked away from her, ashamed. "They want their money and I haven't got it."

"Oh, Alec... I would have gone on helping you until you found a job." She reached over the table and took his hand. "Something would have turned up."

He pulled away from her and ran his fingers nervously through his hair. "Nothing was happening for me," he cried desperately. "Nothing! And I couldn't stand taking money from you anymore. Oh, shit!" He buried his head in his hands. When he looked up at her, his eyes were glistening with tears. "I did it for us. I wanted to make a bundle so we could—I thought that if I had enough money, a nest egg, we could get married.... Christ, Em—I love you!"

She stared at him, her heart racing wildly. For a few seconds she couldn't speak. He leaned over and took her face in his hands and kissed her gently. "I'm sorry, baby— I didn't mean to spring it on you like this. I had something else all worked out in my mind—candlelight, soft music, a beautiful diamond ring—everything you deserve. Not this, some lousy bar, and me up to my ass in trouble."

Emily put her hands over his and held them pressed against her face. "I love you, too—you know that. And we can work this out, I know we can...."

Just then Alec glanced up over her shoulder. He stiffened slightly and his eyes went wide. "Oh, shit—" He dropped his hands and clenched them into fists.

"What is it?"

"A guy I know. I thought I saw him in the audience tonight. . . ."

"Is he one of the men who—?"

"Yeah, he sure as hell is. . . ." He pushed his chair back and rose from the table. "Stay here—I'll be right back." He gulped down the rest of his drink, then started toward the front door.

Emily watched him make his way through the bar and approach the shadowy figure of a man standing near the entrance. They spoke for a few minutes, and she saw Alec make a pleading gesture with his hands. The man shook his head, then put his hand on Alec's shoulder and roughly pushed him outside.

Emily sat frozen, not sure what to do. Fear gripped at her stomach, and her hands were shaking. A blast of music startled her, and the bar became more crowded. She glanced at her watch and waited, her eyes fixed on the entrance. A few minutes went by and there was no sign of Alec. Finally she stood up and hurried out to the street. Alec and the man were nowhere in sight. She looked up and down the sidewalk. There was no one around. Terrified, she called out tentatively, "Alec?" She took a few steps down the street. Long dark shadows made threatening shapes along the pavement. She called out once more, louder, "Alec?"

Then she heard it. A faint cry. "Em—over here..."

She ran toward the sound and came to a narrow alley a few doors down from the bar. "Alec, where are you?" she cried, peering into the inky darkness.

"Over here—" came a weak response.

She rushed into the alley and saw him lying on the ground near some trash barrels. A thin trickle of blood ran from his lips, and he was clutching his stomach.

"Oh, God! Alec, you're hurt!" She bent down to him

and he took her arm and struggled to his feet. "We must call the police," she said.

"No! No police!" Alec gasped. "I'll be all right—he just roughed me up a little. Get me to the car." He drew a deep breath and leaned on her heavily. "I'll be okay, baby. Just get me home."

Alec lay back against the pillows while Emily soaked a cloth in cold water. She squeezed it out, folded it, then placed it gently against the swelling bruise on his cheek. He put his hand over hers and held it, gazing deeply into her eyes. When he spoke, his voice was thick with emotion. "What the hell would I do without you?"

"I love you," Emily said simply. "And whatever trouble you're in, we'll work it out together."

Alec took her in his arms and folded her against his chest. "Thank you, sweetheart," he said softly.

Emily pressed herself closer to him, trying to calm the fear that still coursed through her. "Alec, how bad is it?" she asked. "How much money do you owe these men?"

He hesitated for a few seconds, then replied, "Five thousand dollars."

Emily was stunned; the figure seemed enormous to her. She straightened up and looked at him aghast. "Five thousand! But how could you have—?"

"Baby, please, I don't want to talk about it. I must have been crazy. I just wanted so badly to get enough money together so we could have something to get married on." He sat up and faced her. "Christ! I never even asked you—I never made a proper proposal—" He took her hands and held them tightly. "Em, like I said back in the bar, this isn't the way I planned it. But I love you very much. Will you marry me?"

The cloth had slipped off his face, and there was a slight puffiness around his lips. High spots of color flamed on his cheeks, and a tangled mass of black hair fell over his forehead. His large green eyes stared at her pleadingly, and she thought he looked like a beautiful child who had gotten into a scrape and needed comforting.

Emily choked back a sob, and her face was wet with tears as she gathered him into her arms and whispered fervently, "Yes. Oh, yes...."

"That's what I wanted to hear," he sighed. "Now nothing can hurt me, not as long as I have you."

Emily lifted her face and, as gently as possible, kissed his bruised lips. Even though she was frightened by what was happening, all that really mattered was that he loved her, wanted her for his wife. Knowing that gave her strength, and more than ever she wanted to help him, to take care of him.

Whatever happened, she thought, they would face it together.

9

THE FINAL PERFORMANCE OF THE PLAY WAS GIVEN THE following Sunday night. As the curtains closed for the last time and the cast took their bows, Emily stood in her accustomed place in the wings, her attention fixed on Alec. He looked tense and drawn, and she could see his eyes sweeping through the theater. When he straightened up, he glanced to where she stood and gave her a quick smile; the man wasn't there.

There was a closing party onstage after the audience left. Alec and Emily stayed long enough to have some wine and chat with the other members of the cast, then they left to go back to his apartment. During the drive home, he was quiet, reflective. As soon as they were in his place, Emily went to make some coffee and Alec sat down on the edge of the bed, his head bowed, hands hanging limply between his knees.

"I'm boxed in, Em," he said wearily. "I've tried to borrow the money, but it's impossible. I don't know where else to turn."

She brought him a cup of coffee and sat down next to him. "Won't they let you pay it off when you find a job?"

Alec shook his head. "That's not the way they operate. The bastards want all of it now, or else. . . ."

"Or else what? You simply haven't got it. What are they going to do—kill you?" She started to smile, but it died at the expression on his face. "Alec, no—they wouldn't. . . ."

Alec stood up and began to pace the room. "They

might. It's happened before. They might just beat the shit out of me until I'm crippled. The other night was just a warning." He stopped pacing and stared out the window, hands jammed in his pockets, his back stiff with tension. "Or they could make me work for them...."

"Work for them? How?"

"Dealing—pushing dope to high school kids," he replied bitterly. "Or pimping. They've already suggested that." He turned and gave her a rueful smile. "I've got the looks to attract girls, teenagers getting off the bus, runaways...."

Emily stared at him, shocked. "Alec, they couldn't...."

"Sure they could! That's their business!" He slammed his fist against the wall. "Christ! A lousy five thousand bucks! That's all I need to be free of them!"

Emily's voice quivered with fear. "There must be something we can do."

Alec went to her and took her in his arms. "Baby, I'm sorry. I'm so sorry," he murmured. "I didn't mean to get into this mess, or make you part of it. You've been so good to me." He gave her a lingering kiss, then pulled away. "There's really only one thing I can do," he said in a hard voice. "I've got to leave, get out of town, get away from them—"

"No! You can't do that!"

"What else can I do? I can't involve you in this, and I can't go on being afraid every time I go out. I'll go someplace, get a job, and maybe someday—"

"No, you can't leave! Alec, please!" Emily's voice broke and she began to cry. "We'll think of something. We'll do something—I can't lose you, not now—"

"Oh, God," he groaned, holding her close. "I don't want to leave, Em. I love you so."

She clung to him with all her strength. Her whole world was suddenly crumbling away, and the taste of fear was in her throat. She fiercely sought his lips, and Alec held her close. They lay back on the bed and began to make love, desperately seeking a refuge from the panic that threatened to engulf them.

The next day at work, Emily was in a daze. All she could think about was Alec. The store was unusually busy, and even though she made an effort to keep her mind on what she was doing, Ethel and Victor Skolsky couldn't help noticing how upset she was. A few minutes before they closed the store, Ethel approached her and asked, "Emily, are you not feeling well?"

"No, Mrs. Skolsky, I'm fine," Emily replied. "Just a little tired. I didn't sleep too well."

"Maybe you're coming down with a cold." Ethel sniffled and held a handkerchief to her nose. "I'm feeling a bit under the weather myself. Must be something going around."

"Yes, I think so. My mother's had a cold for a few weeks," Emily said.

"Well, take care of yourself—get plenty of rest and take vitamins." Ethel smiled sympathetically. "We don't want you getting sick. It's going to be a busy week. A new shipment is coming in tomorrow."

"I'll be all right. Thank you, Mrs. Skolsky."

Victor came up to them after seeing a customer to the door. He had a thick wad of bills in his hand. "Here," he said, giving them to Ethel. "Mr. Gilmore bought the big French armoire. We'll move it out tomorrow and have a little more space for the new shipment."

Emily caught herself staring at the money as Ethel took it and went to put it away in the safe. Victor settled himself heavily in the chair by her desk and sighed deeply. "A busy day," he said to Emily. He gave her a tired smile. "You look a little peaked, too."

Emily returned her glance to him, the image of the money still lingering in her mind. "What? Oh, yes, I am a little tired." She reached for her purse and stood up. "I just need a good night's rest. See you in the morning."

She left the store and started for Alec's place. The

evening was warm and humid. Traffic was sluggish, and the air was thick with exhaust fumes and smog. People walked slowly along the pavement or stood and stared with no apparent intent or direction, as if a kind of paralysis had settled over them. Emily sat behind the wheel, her nerves on edge. Alec had called her earlier in the afternoon; they had planned on meeting later that night, but he'd said he had to see her as soon as she got off work.

Traffic broke a little, and Emily impatiently edged the car forward. Her mind was in a turmoil; Alec had sounded terribly frightened on the phone. She'd been busy with a customer and hadn't had the time to find out what was wrong. Now her imagination raced with nightmarish fantasies of walking in and finding him bruised and bleeding from another beating.

When she finally reached his street, she parked the car and rushed up the stairs to the apartment. Alec opened the door and pulled her into his arms. His face was pale and there were dark circles under his eyes.

"They called," he said tensely. "I've got a week to pay up."

Emily sat curled up in the chair, her face buried in her hands, while Alec paced back and forth, nervously chain-smoking.

"I've got to get out of town," he said harshly. "It's the only thing I can do."

"No, please—" Emily moaned. She looked up at him. Her eyes were red from crying, and her face was streaked with tears.

Alec knelt beside her and took her hands. "Baby, don't make this any harder for me than it already is. I don't have any choice. They've got me by the balls."

"There must be something we can do," she cried weakly.

"Let's face it, Em—neither of us can lay our hands on that kind of money, not in a week, a month, or a year."

"I know. I've been thinking about it all day," Emily

said dully. "I began to hate every customer who came into the store. God! When I think of all the money they spend on furniture..."

Alec suddenly grew quiet. His eyes narrowed slightly, and he stared at her for a few minutes without speaking. Then he asked slowly, "Em, do they take in a lot of cash?"

"Yes, mostly. The Skolskys have had some trouble with bad checks, so they keep to a policy of cash and carry, except for customers they know...." The words trailed off as she realized what he was getting at. No, he couldn't be thinking that; it was absurd. She gave a nervous giggle, then stopped as he kept his eyes fixed on her.

"Where do they keep the money?" he asked.

"Alec, you can't be thinking of..."

"Em, where do they keep the money?" he asked again, more sharply.

"Alec, for God's sake—!" She saw that he was serious, and her voice sank. "In a safe at the back of the store."

"Do you know the combination?"

"Yes."

Their voices had dropped to whispers, as if they were already plotting the details of the crime. Alec stopped asking questions for a moment. A look of hope and excitement burned on his face. Then he said, "Are they covered by insurance for theft and break-in?"

She nodded her head miserably. "Yes. I've handled the papers myself."

"Then they wouldn't suffer any losses, would they?"

Emily took a deep, shuddering breath. "Alec, I can't do this—they've been good to me. They trust me!"

Alec remained kneeling in front of her. He put his arms around her hips and rested his head in her lap. "I know what I did was wrong," he began softly. "But I did it for us, because I love you so much. Now I'm trapped. I don't want to lose you, Em—I don't want to have to run away, maybe never see you again. I don't think I could handle that...." The words caught in his throat in a choked sob.

Emily leaned forward and he came into her arms and pressed his face against her breasts. A terrible struggle raged within her, a struggle that pitted years of loneliness against the possibility of a lifetime of happiness. If she didn't stand by him now, she might lose him, and what would her life be then? How could she face the empty days and lonely nights? Not to see him, hear his voice, his laughter; feel the touch of his lips, his hands; his body moving against hers.

The thought was unbearable.

10

THE NEXT DAY, TUESDAY, VICTOR CAME INTO WORK alone; Ethel's cold had gotten worse, and she was in bed nursing a fever. The new shipment arrived; large, expensive pieces that customers were waiting for. Emily was on the phone all morning and afternoon, notifying the decorators and interior designers. When she wasn't on the phone, she was typing out receipts and letters or helping Victor. She handled the payment on every sale that was made, stacking checks from trusted customers in the desk drawer, and putting the cash into the safe.

She tried not to think about anything except what she was doing. But the constant flow of money made that impossible. Every time she handled the cash her hands burned, as if they were being branded. By the end of the day she was exhausted from work, and drained by the emotional turmoil she was going through.

Before going home, she called Alec from a public phone to make sure he was all right. They had agreed that she should spend more time at home; now it was imperative that they keep their affair a secret. Once *it* was over—she couldn't bring herself to say the word *robbery*—everything would be all right. Then they could begin to think about the future.

The future. Being married to Alec. Mrs. Alec Darcy. Those were the words she repeated to herself again and again. Whenever her strength faltered at the thought of

86

what they were going to do, she told herself that loving Alec—and knowing how much he loved her—was all that really mattered.

"Honey, you didn't eat very much of your dinner," Nora said.

"I'm really not hungry." Emily pushed her chair back from the kitchen table and stood up. "We had a rough day at the store, and I'm tired. I'm going to lie down for a while."

"Don't you have meetings this week about the new show at the college?"

"No, they've been postponed until the cast is set," Emily answered. She had told Nora that the drama department was going right into a new production. It was another lie, so she could spend more time with Alec. But now she couldn't even do that. "I'll just take a little nap," Emily said. "Any good movies on tonight?"

Nora beamed. "One of the best—*Wuthering Heights*!"

Emily almost laughed aloud at the irony; the tormented passions of Cathy and Heathcliff, the star-crossed lovers, wasn't what she needed to see right now. Still, some of the gowns were beautiful. "Call me when it comes on, and I'll watch it with you," she told Nora.

"I don't believe you guys," Sheila said, shaking her head. "You must have seen that movie a hundred times!"

Nora gave her younger daughter a glance filled with scorn. "It's a very romantic story," she said.

"Yeah? Well, I guess so," Sheila mumbled, picking delicately at a chicken leg with her teeth. She put it down and wiped her mouth with a napkin. "I'll give you a hand with the dishes, Ma, before I go out."

"Where are you off to?" Nora demanded.

Sheila gave her a bright, artificial smile, and said quickly, "I'm meeting a couple of the girls down on Sunset. We're going into Hollywood to see *The Towering Inferno*."

"Oh? I hear the special effects in that are terrific. And

Paul Newman is in it, isn't he? God, that man gets better looking every year!"

Emily went into her room and lay down on the bed. Through the open door she could hear Nora and Sheila discussing Paul Newman's blue eyes and the duration of his marriage to Joanne Woodward. She smiled to herself, and for a few minutes imagined her own marriage to Alec. In years to come, perhaps that's how they would be talked about and admired: a loving couple working together in the film industry, with the respect of the whole country. She sighed deeply and closed her eyes, wanting the fantasy to go on, to obliterate all thoughts of what they were going to do, the crime they were going to commit. No, I can't think of it that way, she told herself. I love Alec, and I have to help him.

Sheila suddenly appeared in the doorway. She had changed her clothes and was dressed in a tight-fitting sweater and a mini-skirt that made the most of her lissome figure. She was brushing her hair, and she grinned down at Emily as she continued the languid fluid strokes.

"What's happening with the new show?" she asked.

"Not much, yet," Emily replied. "They're reading actors for the cast."

"Oh, yeah? Will that guy be in it? The cute one I was talking to—what's his name?"

"Which one do you mean?" Emily said, deliberately feigning ignorance.

Sheila laughed, and patted her hair. "Come on, Em—there was only one really cute guy in the show—you know, the dark-haired one with the green eyes."

"Oh, him. Alec. I don't know. Probably not. It's a musical, and I don't think he can sing or dance."

Sheila walked over to the mirror and idly gave her blond hair a few more strokes of the brush. "Gee, that's too bad. . . . You see him much?"

Emily stared at her sister, suddenly on guard. "No, of course not. Why would I?"

"Oh, I just thought—you know, working together like that on the play—"

"I doubt that he even noticed me," Emily replied, trying to sound casual. Then she added dryly, "I don't attract a lot of boys."

Sheila turned to her with a look of concern. "Gee, Em, I didn't mean to make you feel bad...."

"I know, I know," Emily said wearily. "Don't apologize." She turned her face to the wall and looked as if she were going to sleep.

Sheila hesitated for a moment, then said, "Well, I'd better get going—the girls will be waiting."

Emily made no reply, and she heard Sheila leave the room. She lay very still for a few minutes, her heart pounding. Tears began to gather in her eyes, and she stuffed her hand in her mouth to keep from crying aloud. Someday, she thought, I won't have to lie, not to Sheila or Nora or anyone.

Wednesday morning Victor told Emily that Ethel was too sick to come in, that she was staying home for the rest of the week. They would have to handle the heavy business they were doing alone. All the customers who had been notified about the new shipment came in to claim the pieces they had ordered, and business was brisk. Victor was kept so busy that he didn't have time for the usual mid-week deposit at the bank, and the cash box in the safe was getting thick with money.

Emily's nerves were stretched raw with apprehension. Alec's deadline was Saturday. Victor had told her he would go to the bank on Friday. She and Alec would have to commit the robbery on Thursday. Tomorrow night.

During the afternoon, while she was on her lunch break, she called Alec.

"We have to do it tomorrow night," she told him.

Alec sucked his breath in sharply. "Okay. Make an excuse to get out tonight, and come here. We'll go over the details."

Emily's voice began to quiver. "I'm not sure I can do it. . . ."

"Just remember that I love you," he said softly. "Like you said, together we can do anything."

Emily nodded her head and swallowed hard. "Yes. I'll see you tonight."

The rest of the day was a blur. Emily moved with automatic determination. Her mind was numb; there were no more arguments or choices to make. The decision was final. Alec had given her every proof of his love and devotion. Now she had to stand by him.

That night Emily told Nora she was going out with one of the girls from the college. Nora, drowsing in front of the television set, smiled and told her to have a good time. She trusts me so completely, Emily thought as she left the house. But then, how could she possibly suspect me of anything? Like everybody else, she believes that I'm exactly as I appear. Emily touched her fingertips to the scar, tracing the ridges and welts of crimped flesh. This is what she sees, what she and everyone else thinks I am. The scar is my protection against suspicion. Only Alec knows the truth.

As she drove through the streets, Emily slipped once more into a sense of being a player in a film. The sounds of traffic, the flashing neon of store signs and illuminated billboards, grey shapes of people wandering along the pavements, all were romanticized into screen images. And she was at the center of the drama, driving through the night to a rendezvous with her desperate lover, the man to whom she had committed herself.

Alec looked up from the notes he was making and saw Emily standing by the windows. She was staring out at the city, arms clasped tightly across her chest, her head tilted to one side, like a wistful child.

"Are you all right?" he asked.

She turned to face him and nodded.

"Okay—let's take it from the top," he said.

"You make it sound like the rehearsal of a play," she said with a wan smile.

"Like Shakespeare said, 'All the world's a stage, and all the men and women merely players,'" Alec replied grimly.

He made room for her beside him on the bed, and she sat down. "I think this will work," he said, looking through his notes. "We get there around eleven, park in the back alley, and get in through the rear entrance. You have the key to turn off the alarm for the back door, which we leave open slightly. I wait by the door and cover the alley while you open the safe and get the money. Then you close the safe, lock the door, turn the alarm back on, and we leave."

"It sounds too easy. Shouldn't we try to make it look like a break-in? Cut the wires to the alarm or break the lock on the door?"

"We don't have to do all that. Professionals can pick a lock and turn off alarms. And any good safe-cracker could open that old safe in seconds. All you have to do is walk in Friday morning and wait for the old man to discover that the money is missing."

Emily stood up and began moving nervously around the room. "But what if they suspect me? What if the police begin to question me?"

"Why should they suspect you? Think of all the people who come into the shop who know they do a cash-and-carry business. The customers, the delivery men, the people in the other stores on that block. Any one of them could have cased the store for weeks. I tell you it's a perfect set-up."

Emily stopped pacing and looked at him with apprehension. "Oh, Alec—I'm scared, really scared...."

He put his notes aside and went to her. "I know you are, baby," he said, taking her in his arms. "But it's going to be all right. I'll be there with you."

She put her arms around him. "Keep telling me that," she whispered. "Keep telling me we'll be together. It's the only thing that gives me courage."

He put his hand under her chin and lifted her face to his. "You know, I'm a little scared, too. I've never done anything like this before, either."

Emily couldn't help smiling at the earnest expression on his face. He looked so beautiful and at the same time so young and vulnerable, like a little boy. She opened his shirt and put her arms around his body. Her hands moved over the smooth muscles of his back.

Alec sighed deeply and buried his face in her hair. "I don't ever want to lose you, Em," he murmured. "I need you—" He brought his mouth down to hers and kissed her tenderly. A sweet rush of excitement went through her, and the kiss lengthened, grew more passionate. His tongue began to tease the inside of her lips, and she shuddered with pleasure.

Alec suddenly pulled away and swept her up into his arms, his hands under her skirt, fingers bruising the flesh of her thighs. She flung her head back, and his lips were on her throat. She tore open her blouse, and his mouth fastened on a nipple, biting delicately, then licking it with his tongue. She gasped and stifled a moan. Alec looked up at her, his eyes gleaming, lips parted and moist. "Oh, Christ, I love you, Em—" he muttered, carrying her to the bed.

In moments they were both naked and he was kneeling above her, breathing hoarsely. "Look at me," he said raggedly. "Don't take your eyes away from mine."

Emily stared up at him as he slowly moved into her. She took a sharp breath at the moment of entry, then cried out softly as he took her completely and fully. Her eyes never left his, and for a moment she felt as if he had penetrated her very soul, not only with his body but with his whole being.

"We'll always be part of each other," he said in a hushed whisper. "I want you to remember that."

Emily stared into the depths of his eyes, intensely moved by an overwhelming joy. It was as if they were consummating a union more sacred than marriage.

11

LATE THE FOLLOWING AFTERNOON, EMILY WAS AT HER desk, finishing up some letters. Victor was with a customer at the front of the store, and when he finished, he came back and sat down on a nearby armchair. His heavy shoulders sagged and he let out a deep sigh.

"Make a note to hold that French commode for Mr. Kramer until next Monday," he told Emily. "He wants to bring his wife in to see it."

Emily nodded, finished the letter she was typing, and put it into an addressed envelope and sealed it. She looked up at Victor and said, "Mrs. Skolsky called a few minutes ago. She wants you to bring home the ledger of this week's sales so she can go over it. I put it on your desk."

"Thank you, Emily." He pulled a cigar out of his shirt pocket, put it in his mouth, and lit it, rolling it slowly between his fingers.

She glanced at her watch. It was almost closing time.

"You look tired," Victor said sympathetically. "It's been a hard week. You deserve a bonus for all the extra work you've done."

"It wasn't so bad—I didn't mind." Emily stammered, feeling a rush of shame at his concern. "You did all the work. You should get some rest tonight."

Victor laughed and heaved himself out of the chair. "No, not tonight." He took his jacket from the coat rack and began to pull it on. "Tonight is my poker night. A good hot game and I'll feel as fresh as a daisy. A neighbor of ours is going to stay with Ethel, so I won't have to miss it."

Emily reached for her purse and stood up. She could barely bring herself to look at Victor as she said good night and left the store. Once in her car, she let out a deep, ragged sigh and started to drive, her hands trembling against the wheel. The time-plan she and Alec had decided on was beginning now. First she would attend her class at the college. She had missed several of them during the run of the play, and it was perfectly normal for her to return, now that the play was over. The class let out at ten o'clock, and she would go to pick up Alec. They'd drive to the store, and when they were finished she would take him back to his place and then go home, just in time to watch the late show with Nora. All perfectly normal. A choked sob tore out of her throat at the thought. There was nothing *normal* in what she was about to do. A voice within her cried out, "You've never committed a crime in your life!"

But Emily knew that after tonight, it would never again be true.

At ten o'clock, she was on her way out of the class when Mr. Bradley approached her with a look of concern on his face. "Emily, are you all right?" he asked.

"What? Oh—yes, I'm fine—"

"I was worried about you. You seemed very distracted tonight. Is there anything wrong?"

"No—no, there's nothing wrong. I'm just a little tired, that's all. Thank you, Mr. Bradley."

Before he could question her further, she fled from the classroom and went out to her car. Sweat beaded across her brow, and her hands felt moist, clammy.

All she could think was that once Alec was with her, she would be all right. She kept reassuring herself that in an hour or so it would all be over. And years from now they would look back on this night as a bad dream that they had shared.

* * *

He was waiting for her on the street outside his building. Emily slid over and let him get behind the wheel. He pulled her to him and kissed her.

"Are you okay?"

"Yes, I am—now."

They drove in silence until they approached the store. Alec slowed down, searching the street and the flow of traffic for any sign of a police car. Then he turned the corner and pulled into the alley and stopped by the back door. The narrow lane was thick with shadows and dark, impenetrable corners that appeared filled with danger. The sounds of street traffic were muted, and only the faint barking of a dog broke the stillness. Garbage bins stood behind each store in an uneven row, like a straggling line of tired soldiers.

Alec peered into the darkness for a few seconds, then spoke in a hoarse, urgent whisper. "Okay—here we go. Now remember, don't rush. Take your time. Be deliberate, and it'll be over in minutes."

He leaned over and gave her a quick, hard kiss. "I love you, Em, and don't forget what I said last night; we'll always be part of each other."

Emily nodded, pressed his palm to her cheek, and then she was out of the car. She went to the back door, the keys in her hand. First the alarm had to be turned off. Then the two deadbolts unlocked. Her fingers felt stiff, and the simple movements were labored, awkward. She pulled the door open and stepped inside, breathing the familiar scents of dust and furniture polish.

For a moment she stood absolutely still. The headlights of passing cars threw quick beams of light across the front of the store, momentarily illuminating the bulky shapes of furniture and casting eerie shadows on the walls. She held her breath and tried not to think about anything except Alec and how much she loved him. Then, using a small flashlight, she made her way past Ethel's desk to the safe and knelt in front of it.

Emily knew the combination well enough to use it every day without hesitation, but now the numbers themselves seemed to elude her, resist her efforts. She made a mistake in the sequence and anxiously spun the dial to begin again. This time it worked, and the door swung open. She reached into the cash box and began to stuff the money into her purse.

Suddenly there was a noise at the front door. Startled, Emily dropped the flashlight. Her head shot up and she saw the figures of two men silhouetted through the glass. One of them was opening the door and coming into the store. It was Victor.

Paralyzed by fear, Emily crouched by the safe, unable to move.

"Sam, I'll just be a minute," she heard Victor say to the other man. "I forgot the sales book, and you know Ethel—" The rest was lost in a burst of laughter as the two men started for the back of the store.

Emily's breath caught in her throat. The sales book! It was still there, on the desk, only a few feet away! Then she realized that the flashlight had rolled out of reach. And it was still on.

She heard the footsteps of the two men stop. They had seen the flashlight.

There was a hushed whispering between them, then silence. Suddenly Victor cried out, "Who's there? Don't move—I've got a gun!"

Emily felt the blood drain from her face. The gun. Victor kept a loaded revolver hidden under a shelf on the side wall of the store.

She wanted to cry out, not only to stop him but to warn Alec. She opened her mouth, but only a hiss of air escaped her lips.

He was coming toward her. She would be caught. And so would Alec.

There was a sudden flash of light as Victor reached out and turned on a desk lamp. Emily stared at him wildly, saw the shocked look on his face, the gun pointing at her.

A kind of madness came over her, a hysteria of terror and panic. A crazed shriek tore out of her throat, and she lunged forward, arms flailing, trying to get the gun. Victor fell back against the desk, gasping in surprise. Like figures in a nightmare, they struggled clumsily for a few seconds, and then the gun went off with a deafening roar. There was an explosion of shattering glass, and Emily reared back, watching in horror as Victor clutched his chest, his face contorted in pain. Then he fell heavily to the floor.

Shock rooted her to where she stood, her mind and body turned to stone. She heard the other man run screaming from the store, and moments later the sound of a siren. Police were suddenly around her. Someone was on the phone, calling for an ambulance, and someone else was kneeling over Victor. There was a babble of voices and the cold grip of handcuffs. Then a voice said to the man on the phone, "They don't have to rush—the old man is dead. No, not a gunshot wound—he had a heart attack."

A policeman loomed up in front of her, his lips moving quickly, reading her rights. But all she could hear was "The old man is dead. . . . The old man is dead."

She looked down at the body and saw Victor's face staring up at her, his eyes still open in a shocked look of disbelief. Then, like a door slamming shut, her mind went blank and everything dissolved into darkness.

12

Emily lay on her narrow bed and stared into space. She was in the Sybil Brand Institute for Women, a detention center for adult female offenders that was located in East Los Angeles. Most of the women there were under arrest for prostitution, others on charges of theft, violent crimes, or crimes related to narcotics and alcohol. The institute had twelve dormitories, six cell-blocks, and an infirmary, and it was here, in a state of shock, that she had spent her first night after being booked on charges of burglary and first-degree murder.

Now she was in one of the dormitories, only dimly aware of the other women around her who were talking, laughing raucously, gossiping or complaining. They were no more than grey phantoms in the barren landscape that her life had become. In the last few days she had moved through the drab, colorless surroundings like a sleepwalker, barely aware of what she was doing. Orders were given and she obeyed them, and the days passed.

But her nights were filled with agonizing thoughts and hideous images. Victor Skolsky's lifeless eyes haunted her. She would never forget the look of disbelief on his face when he discovered her at the safe, or the grimace of pain that contorted his features before he died. She had killed him, as surely as if she had fired a bullet into him. Nothing could ever alleviate the burden of guilt she would carry for the rest of her life.

Then a picture of Alec's face would rise up in her mind, juxtaposed over Victor's. And he, too, was dead. Beaten

99

and bloody, lying in an alley somewhere or in a ditch in one of the canyons.

Or had he gotten away? The police had found her car in the alley with no one inside. He had heard the shot and had run. She prayed that somehow he had escaped, had left town and was out of reach of the men who were after him.

As for herself, she felt only a sense of complete desolation. For the second time in her life, fate had struck her down. Nightmares of the accident that had scarred her face began to recur, and in them were mingled images of Victor lying dead and Alec being beaten. Sometimes she could hear her father's cry, just before they crashed: "Hold on, sweetheart!" But when she woke, surrounded by the harsh faces of women who were thieves and prostitutes, his voice would fade, and she was left without even a faint glimmer of hope.

Chester Anderson mopped his brow with a large white handkerchief, tucked it back into his coat pocket, and lit another cigarette. He was a short, stocky man in his late thirties, with a wide, sincere face and thinning blond hair. A pair of thick horn-rimmed glasses sat precariously on the high bridge of his nose. He adjusted them carefully, then looked across the table at Emily.

She sat quietly, her hands folded in her lap, seemingly unaware of the warm, humid day. The mid-morning light in the visitor's room of the institute was glaringly bright and harshly illuminated the deep circles under her eyes and the vivid line of the scar.

Chester winced inwardly at the sight; the girl had troubled him since he had been given her case. Not so much because of the scar—as a public defender, he had seen a lot of kids who had been cut up or maimed—but because of her manner and attitude. Every time he had visited her, she presented a facade of quiet resignation. Yet he sensed that beneath this exterior was another girl, someone who would not have committed such a foolish crime. He was sure that her story about wanting the money for an operation on her face was a blatant lie. All the material he had gathered on her background pointed to her being hard-working, resolute in her career goals, and well-adjusted to being scarred. Still, he thought, you could never tell; a scar that bad would be tough to live with every day of your life. Maybe she had cracked, as she claimed.

Chester tapped the cigarette on the ashtray in front of him and said, "Emily, do you understand why I want you to plead not guilty?"

"But I am guilty," she murmured in reply. "Mr. Skolsky is dead."

"Yes, but he died of a heart attack, not from a gunshot wound. The law states that in the commission of a violent felony—in your case, the burglary—if someone is killed, the person who provoked the violence that led to the death is held to be culpable. This is also known as 'transferred intent,' which means that the intent was to burglarize, but is transferred to the killing. That's why you're being charged with burglary *and* first-degree murder. Do you understand that?"

"Yes, I think so—"

Chester continued, "Now, we don't know how the prosecution will proceed, and in your case there are mitigating circumstances. If you plead guilty, you could wind up in prison for life. But if you plead not guilty, we have a chance to reduce the charges by plea bargaining."

Emily shook her head wearily. "Mr. Anderson, I don't understand all of what you're saying, but I'll do whatever you tell me to."

Chester smiled encouragingly. "Good girl. Trust me, and I'll do the best I can. I'm arranging an examination for you with one of the psychiatrists here at the institute. I think her report could help us."

He began to gather up his papers and put them into a briefcase. "Just one more question before I leave. I know

I asked you this before, but let's go over it again anyway. Did you do this all alone? Was there anyone else involved in the burglary?"

Emily stood up, her back stiff, her face set in an expressionless mask. "There wasn't anyone else involved, Mr. Anderson. I told you that."

He gazed at her steadily for a few seconds, then sighed and stood up. "Okay, Emily, whatever you say." He went to the door and opened it. A matron stepped into the room, and the three of them walked out into the hallway. Chester took Emily's hand and pressed it warmly. "I'll be back in a few days. You look tired; try to get some rest."

"Thank you, Mr. Anderson. You've been very kind."

Chester watched the two women disappear through a doorway that led to the dormitories. She's lying, he thought to himself. She's covering up for someone. And there's not a damned thing I can do about it.

Dr. Ellen Wilson, one of the resident psychiatrists at the Institute, looked up from the file on her desk and saw Emily standing hesitantly by the door.

"Emily Gorden? Come in and sit down," she said crisply.

Emily walked into the small, sparsely furnished office and took a chair near the desk. She was nervous; Dr. Wilson's report might be crucial to getting the charges against her reduced, but even more important to Emily was that it could substantiate her story of wanting the money for an operation. She was determined to keep Alec out of it.

"I just want to finish reading these depositions, and then we'll talk," Dr. Wilson said, flashing a quick, businesslike smile.

Emily nodded, and studied the psychiatrist. Ellen Wilson was in her early forties, she guessed, and had a long, thin face. She wore little makeup, and her red hair was cut in a short, simple style that suggested she had no time or inclination for fussing with her appearance. She wore a doctor's white jacket over a plain, crisply tailored blue blouse, and no jewelry. Emily began to feel uneasy; there was little in Dr. Wilson's appearance or manner to suggest she might be sympathetic to Emily's story.

Dr. Wilson put aside the papers, arranged a pad in front of her, and picked up a pencil. She gave Emily a cool, level glance, and said, "Unfortunately, we don't have a great deal of time; I have a lot of girls to see, and the state doesn't provide for lengthy examinations. So let's get right to the point. Mr. Anderson has given me statements from your mother and sister, Mr. Jerome Bradley, your costume design teacher, and Mrs. Ethel Skolsky. All of them agree that you're hard-working and honest but that you've always been unhappy about being scarred. Is that true?"

"Yes."

"How long have you been scarred?"

"Since I was nine. I was in an automobile accident with my father. He was killed."

"Did you have a difficult time in school because of your appearance?"

"Yes. The other kids treated me like a . . . freak." Emily searched the woman's face for some sign of sympathy, but Dr. Wilson simply regarded her with cold, professional interest.

"Tell me how you feel about being scarred."

Emily tried to think quickly, to find the right words to make her story sound credible. "People don't understand—I think I frighten them." Emily paused, then went on nervously. "My sister is very beautiful, and I can't help being jealous of her. And my mother—she's a beautician, and all she does is help make women look more attractive. But she can't do anything for me. . . ." Emily's voice trailed off.

"Go on, please," Dr. Wilson said.

"Well—when I was a kid, I got interested in costume design from watching old movies on TV. All those women were so beautiful and glamorous. I wanted to be like them."

Dr. Wilson watched Emily's face for a sign of dissimulation. She'd heard all the lies in her work at the institute. Emily was not the first disfigured girl to commit a crime out of bitterness at being rejected by society. But the others had a hardness that Emily seemed to lack, and they had suffered abuses within their families. And that was clearly not the case here. Still, there were some recent incidents mentioned in the statements that might have triggered a breakdown. She rifled through the papers, then pulled one out and said to Emily, "In Mrs. Skolsky's statement to Mr. Anderson, she mentioned some trouble you had with one of her customers, a Mrs. Harriet Bradshaw—"

"Yes, she complained to Mrs. Skolsky about my upsetting the customers because of my face."

"And your sister admitted that she had said some very harsh things to you a few weeks ago, that she had hurt you—"

Tears began to fill Emily's eyes. "Yes—but she was very upset at my mother...."

"But you were angry and hurt?"

Emily nodded, feeling somewhat relieved; Dr. Wilson sounded more sympathetic now.

Ellen Wilson made a few notes on her pad, then looked up at Emily and asked with calculated bluntness, "Have you ever had a boyfriend?"

Emily was instantly on her guard. "Most boys look the other way when they see me. That's why I wanted the money—that's why I—"

"You didn't answer my question," Dr. Wilson said sharply.

Emily felt a rush of confusion. Did the woman know something about Alec? But how could she? "No—no, I've never had a boyfriend," she stammered.

Leaning back in her chair, the psychiatrist gestured to the pages of depositions on her desk. "From these statements, it appears that you are self-sufficient, well-motivated, talented, and intelligent. Surely you must have believed that someone would eventually recognize those qualities and see past the surface." Her voice was deliberately hard and unsympathetic. She could see the effect her statement was having on Emily, but that was her job: to separate real criminals from the truly disturbed.

Bewildered and frightened, Emily tried to collect her thoughts. She had to say something, do something to convince the doctor. If she even suspected a lie, how could anyone else be persuaded to believe her?

"Answer me, Emily," Dr. Wilson said sternly. "Didn't you think it was possible for someone to see past the scar and care for who you are, not what you look like?"

Emily suddenly heard Alec's voice saying almost the identical words, "Baby, I don't give a damn about the scar—I love who you are, not what you look like." For a moment she wanted to scream the truth, to tell this cold, unfeeling woman that she had been loved, and by a man who was more beautiful in body and spirit than the doctor could possibly imagine.

She began to cry as she struggled to tell the lie. "No, I didn't!" Emily sobbed helplessly. She leaned across the desk and swept her hair back off her face. "Look at me, Dr. Wilson! How could any man see past *this*?"

Ellen Wilson instinctively recoiled; overhead fluorescent lights bathed the scar in a harsh white glare, revealing every inch of mutilated flesh. She caught her breath and replied in a choked voice, "Yes, Emily. You've made your point."

On the morning of the day set for the trial, Chester Anderson and the assistant district attorney met the judge in his chambers to discuss the equities of Emily's case. Chester Anderson had done his job well. He presented his depositions and Dr. Wilson's report. He pleaded leniency on the basis of these statements and on the fact that Emily had no previous offenses. And he recounted the mental anguish Emily had suffered since childhood because of the scar.

The resolution of this session was a reduced charge of attempted burglary and involuntary manslaughter. The new plea was entered, and Emily pleaded guilty to the reduced charges. Then a date was set for sentencing.

Emily awoke with a feeling of dread. The waiting was over. Today she would be sentenced. Chester Anderson had tried to reassure her that the judge would be fair. She might even be put on probation or, at the very least, receive a reasonable sentence. A reasonable sentence. What exactly did that mean? How long would she be shut away from the world? From any possibility of ever seeing Alec again? If he was still alive. Almost three months had elapsed, and she had not heard from him. She made every excuse she could think of: he was hiding out somewhere and was waiting until he was sure it was safe to write her, or perhaps he was in another part of the country and didn't know where she was being kept.

She thought, too, about Nora and Sheila. They had visited her a few times, but each meeting was a painful time of awkward conversation, anguished silences and tears. And each time, as they prepared to leave Emily sensed in them a feeling of relief, as if they had performed a distasteful obligation. Not that she could blame them; the story had been carried in all the newspapers and briefly on television, bringing a tabloidlike notoriety into their lives. They couldn't help expressing more shock and dismay than sympathy. Nora admitted that she had taken some time off from work at the beauty shop because of all the gossip among the women. And Sheila complained that she was whispered about wherever she went.

After they had gone, Emily was left with the feeling that whatever happened to her, she would have to face it entirely alone.

"Okay, girls, let's move it! This is the big day!" a police officer sang out cheerfully.

Emily and a group of other young women who were going to be sentenced boarded the police van that would take them to the Criminal Courts Building in downtown Los Angeles. A couple of hookers took seats near the front and teased the driver, offering him sex if he would stop the bus en route and let them out. The other girls were quiet and tense; one began to cry and was ignored.

Emily sat alone at the back of the van. In the past months many girls had passed through the Sybil Brand Institute, most of them for a couple of days or weeks. Few, if any, had tried to make friends with her or approached her to join them for coffee and conversation. Emily didn't mind; it was a little like being in school again, where she was stared at, whispered about. Some things didn't change no matter where you were. But what would it be like in prison?

She peered through the barred windows, thinking about the people she saw on the streets, the people who were free. Or were they? There were small signs of vitality: a youngster tugging at his mother's elbow to get her attention; a group of Chicano boys laughing together and shoving each other in tough gestures of youthful machismo. But the prevailing mood was one of defeat, embodied in the flat, dull faces of people hurrying to work and ignoring the drunks, the lost men lying sprawled in doorways or walking unsteadily toward no apparent destination.

Emily turned away from the scene and closed her eyes. Her hand went to her scarred cheek and she thought: All of us are in prisons of one sort or another.

Sentence was about to be pronounced. Emily stood up and Chester Anderson rose with her, his hand on her arm. Out of the corner of her eye, she saw Nora and Sheila sitting in the visitor's area, their faces white and strained. She hadn't realized how frightened she was until she had stood up. Now her legs felt weak; her hands trembled. The courtroom looked distorted, unreal, and the judge's voice was an indistinct drone of sound. Emily blinked her eyes to clear her vision, and made an effort to hear the words that would determine the rest of her life.

"... and it is the sentence of this court that Emily Gorden be remanded to the California Institution for Women for the term prescribed by law of not more than four and not less than two years...."

The words echoed and re-echoed in her mind like the clanging of gates being closed, one after the other.

PART

II

13

THE CALIFORNIA INSTITUTION FOR WOMEN SPRAWLED across 120 acres of sun-baked earth in San Bernardino County, some fifty miles east of Los Angeles. To Emily it was like being in a foreign country where she didn't know the language or the customs.

She went through the first days of processing in a semi-dazed state, numbly doing whatever she was told. Clothes were issued: underwear, Levi's, shoes, a coat, and pajamas. Personal garments could be sent to her, but they were subject to a rigid dress code that stated when and where she could wear them.

She was taken to one of the housing units. They consisted of adjoining complexes of single rooms that accommodated 120 women. The door to each room had a window in it, depriving the women of any privacy.

The room Emily was assigned was not the cell with bars she had expected. But it wasn't much better. The cramped nine-by-seven-foot space contained an iron cot with a paper-thin mattress that was stained and worn from years of use, a dirt-encrusted sink, a toilet, and a closet area. She stared at the stark walls and bare floor in utter despair, reeling from the stench of urine and feces that had been left in the toilet bowl. She spent her first evening on her hands and knees, scrubbing the room clean.

She had been told to think of the prison as a kind of college for women, and, indeed, the grounds were referred to as the "campus," and the housing units as "cottages." But the barbed-wire fence and armed guards in watchtowers gave the lie to those euphemisms. And no college was ever subject to the "count." Five or six times a day, a horn would blast shrilly throughout the buildings, demanding a mad scramble and run by the inmates to their rooms. It was the security check against escape. Minutes later, when each woman was sitting on her own bed, the doors were automatically closed and locked. Then a guard walked by, looked in each window, and checked the number off her list. Counts were made in each living unit, the hospital, work areas, and administration. When the "count clear" call came over the P.A. system, the doors were opened and normal activity was resumed.

This was not a college. It was a prison. And the women in it bore little resemblance to schoolgirls. Many of them were prostitutes, drug dealers, forgers, thieves, or murderers. They were a bitter, sullen group whose faces bore the imprint of lives that had been cruelly spent.

Emily was frankly afraid of them. For the first few weeks, she made every effort to be inconspicuous. But she was aware that they were watching every move she made. No one spoke to her; they simply watched in silence or looked away if she happened to catch their eye.

One evening she had just finished showering and turned to find the woman next to her staring at her face with a look of disgust. The piercing gaze was more direct and brutal than any she had ever encountered. Panicked, she threw her hand up to cover the scar and hurried to get back to her room.

While waiting for a work assignment, Emily learned the meaning of "doing time." She spent hours sitting in her room or wandering silently around the compound with other inmates under the watchful eyes of the guards. She kept to herself, afraid to talk to anyone, afraid to be approached. The women gossiped, argued, or whispered together with the seriousness of children sharing secrets. They traded "goods"—cigarettes for cosmetics, cosmetics for perfume, perfume for clothes—an endless exchange of things for things that provided them with a brief activity, a fleeting moment of pleasure.

Sometimes a fight would suddenly break out, and a stir of excitement rippled through the women. Voices were raised in shrill encouragement, sides were taken, bets were made. Then the guards would break it up, the excitement would dissipate, and they were left once more to their hollow wandering.

One evening, when dinner call was announced, Emily joined a group of women on their way to the dining room. As before, no one spoke to her. She tugged her hair over the scar and kept her head down. Inside the cafeteria-style facility, she picked up a tray and waited in line. Suddenly she was pushed from behind and shoved out of her place. The woman who had pushed her moved up, leaving no room. Bewildered by the sudden action, and frightened, Emily tried to get in line behind her. But the next woman roughly elbowed her aside. No one seemed to notice what was happening. The line of women continued to move forward, ignoring Emily as if she didn't exist. She stood watching them with mounting fear and confusion.

Just then, a tall, thin black girl was opposite her. Emily glanced up, trying to keep back the tears. The girl stared at her hard, then reached out, grabbed Emily's arm, and pulled her into the line.

"Thank you—I didn't know what—"

"Don't talk," the girl said in a low voice. "Just walk in front of me and get your food."

After she was served, Emily moved out into the dining room and looked back to thank her benefactor. But the girl walked past her without a glance and joined a group of women at a table. They all looked over at Emily for a moment, then started whispering to one another.

Emily found an empty seat at a table on the far side of the room. The women around her moved their chairs closer together, tacitly excluding her from their company.

A few minutes later they stood up to leave. As they walked past her, one of the women made a quick gesture with her hand and knocked a steaming cup of coffee into Emily's lap. The hot liquid burned through her thin Levi's, and she cried out.

A sudden silence fell over the room. One of the guards hurried over and asked, "What happened?"

Emily's eyes darted around the room; everyone was watching her, waiting to hear what she would say. Ignoring the fiery pain spreading across her thighs, she looked up at the guard apologetically and stammered, "I'm sorry—I spilled my coffee."

The woman stared at her for a minute, then glanced at the others. She knew what was going on. It had happened before to new inmates. She looked back at Emily and muttered, "Next time be careful."

The guard moved away, and everyone in the room resumed her meal. Emily pressed a napkin to her legs and the burn began to subside. She tried to go on eating, but couldn't control the trembling of her hands. Now she was really frightened. In the past she had been able to cope with or ignore the way people responded to her scar. But here she was facing something far more terrifying—the threat of physical violence.

A few weeks later, Emily was put on one of the many work programs in the prison. She was assigned to a garment-manufacturing enterprise called Correctional Industries. It was a sewing factory where the women made clothing that was sold to tax-exempt agencies like state and veterans' hospitals and orphanages. The hours were long, and the working conditions unpleasant. There was no air conditioning in any of the work buildings, and when the temperature rose, the heat was almost unbearable. Tempers flared and fights broke out. Sometimes a few of the older women would collapse and have to be taken to the infirmary.

Emily learned the mechanics of pattern grading, marking, spreading, cutting, and bundling. It was mindless, uncreative work. She toiled over an outdated sewing machine, finding a certain irony in the fact that once she had thought of herself as a costume designer. Now she was making crude institutional clothes for a wage of six dollars a month.

The women she worked with were little more than cordial. A few of them chatted with her during breaks, but conversation was limited to complaints about working conditions. There were no overtures of friendship. But neither were there any incidents like the one that had taken place in the dining room a few weeks before. For the most part, Emily was left alone, quietly ostracized, just as she had been as a child in school. She knew it was because of the scar. During work hours, the heat was so intense that she wore her hair pinned back and a sweatband around her head. At first, leaving her face so exposed made her feel almost naked. But as the days passed, she realized there was no reason to hide the scar. She became resigned to the fact that even in a prison society, it made her an outsider.

One night, after dinner, Emily went to the prison library, checked out a couple of paperback novels, and returned to her room. A movie was being shown in the recreation hall, but she was too tired to go. And she was still wary of being in a crowd of inmates. Even though she yearned for some company, she felt more secure when she was alone.

Making herself as comfortable as possible on the narrow bed, she began to read one of the novels. The book had been through many hands; the binding was split, and some of the pages were loose. It was a romance, and obviously popular. Someone had even underlined the sexier passages. As she continued to read, Emily felt a sharp tug of sexual need; the words conjured up images of Alec and the hours of lovemaking they had shared. Memories of the two of them in bed together began to blur the pages, and finally she put the book aside and closed her eyes, trying to fight off the sexual frustration that was overtaking her. She wondered, as she had so many times during the past months, if he was safe. Where was he now? What was he doing? God, if only she knew that he was all right, she could more easily endure what she was going through. The real hell of her existence was not knowing what had happened to him. She turned over and buried her face in her arms as tears began to seep through her closed eyes.

"Hey, girl—you asleep?"

The question brought Emily to her feet, and she blinked at the figure standing in the doorway. It was the girl who had helped her in the dining room.

"No—no, I wasn't sleeping," she replied, wiping away the tears with the back of her hand.

"Well? You gonna keep me standing out here in the hall?" the girl demanded.

"Oh—no, please come in," Emily answered hurriedly.

The girl walked into the room with a studied nonchalance. She had a thin, supple body, and moved with the easy grace of a dancer. A neatly shaped Afro crowned her head, and her skin was the color of teak. She had high, sharply defined cheekbones, a small nose, and a fine, softly rounded jawline that might have been shaped by a diamond cutter's precise hand. Dark, flashing eyes were accented by eyeliner, and her full lips were a startling shade of bright red.

"I wanted to thank you for helping me, but I haven't seen you around—" Emily started to say.

"Yeah, well—I been kinda busy," the girl responded brusquely. She looked around the drab room and scowled. "Christ, this is a shitty hole—no pictures on the wall, or TV or anything."

"My mother is sending me a few things," Emily said faintly. The girl's arrogant manner made her uneasy.

Suddenly the girl turned to face her and held out her hand. "I'm Rina. That's R-I-N-A. Rina Lavalle," she announced defiantly.

Emily took her hand. "I'm Emily—"

"I know, Gorden—right?" She sat down on the bed and pulled out a pack of cigarettes. "Wanna smoke?"

It was more a command than a question. Emily hesitated before saying, "You're supposed to take them, even if you don't smoke, aren't you?" At Rina's puzzled look, she went on quickly, "I mean, I heard that you can trade them. . . ."

Rina's look of confusion deepened. "Don't explain it to me, girl!" she said sharply. "I been here a long time, and I know all about it. God, are you that *green*? Here, take the fuckin' cigarette and do what you want with it!"

"I'm sorry," Emily mumbled nervously. "There's a lot of things I don't know yet—" She took the cigarette and held it awkwardly.

"I can see that, but I still don't believe it." Rina watched her fumble with the cigarette, then said in a softer tone, "Why don't you smoke it? It's kind of a friendly thing, sharing a cigarette. Breaks the tension."

Emily smiled a little, aware that Rina was trying to help her. She nodded, and lit the cigarette.

"Just drag on it easy, and let it out slow," the girl said encouragingly. Then she suddenly burst out laughing, a rich, whooping sound. "Goddamn, I can't believe I'm teaching you how to smoke—and you such a bad girl!"

"A bad girl? What do you mean?" Emily began to cough as smoke went up her nostrils and brought tears to her eyes. Rina's laughter filled the room, and Emily couldn't help giggling. "I'm getting it," she said, taking another drag. "See—?"

Rina smiled approvingly, and the two women smoked in silence for a few minutes. Emily began to relax and observed her visitor's clothes. Rina was wearing designer jeans that clung to her long, sleek thighs, and a short-sleeved batik-print blouse that fitted tightly to her small breasts. A pair of white sandals added a note of summery fashion to the ensemble. Some of the inmates, particularly those with special privileges, were allowed to receive clothes from home. Rina was obviously one of them, Emily thought.

"What did you mean when you called me a 'bad girl'?" she asked.

"You kidding me?" Rina stared at the scar, and Emily instinctively began to tug at her hair to cover it.

"What the hell you doing, girl?" Rina abruptly demanded. "Why you covering up your mark?"

"My what?"

"You playin' some kind of game with me? Your *mark*, where your old man cut you. I never seen one that bad. What the hell did he use—a butcher knife?"

"Nobody cut me. I was in a car accident when I was nine years old. My father was killed, and I went through the windshield and got scarred."

Rina's eyes went wide. "You're not lyin', are you? No, I can see that. You ain't no working girl, are you?"

"You mean a prostitute?" Emily asked, dumbfounded.

Rina started to laugh wildly, shaking her head from side to side. "Oh, shit!" she gasped. "I just don't believe it!"

"What's so funny? I don't understand."

"Funny? Girl, it's a scream!" Rina cried. "Everybody in this joint who seen that scar thinks: 'That's a bad girl. Look how her old man cut her—she must've been real bad.' So everybody's afraid to mess with you. They all waiting or testing you, like that bitch in the dining room. They all thought you some mean fucker off the streets. And you ain't never done the streets or done time or anything! Girl, that's funny!"

"Well, what should I do? Should I tell them the truth about my scar?"

"You crazy? The truth don't have no place in this institution," Rina sneered. "You go on letting them think you one tough hooker, that your pimp put his mark on you. Then they leave you alone. You only tell the truth to your friends, and you choose them carefully. Or—"

She smiled broadly, revealing sparkling rows of perfect teeth. "They choose you." She paused for a moment, then went on, "I knew there was somethin' different about you, first time I saw you. That's why I come here tonight." Then she asked quietly, "You want to tell me what you in for?"

Rina's declaration of friendship was clear. Emily felt a sense of relief and gratitude; after so many weeks of aching loneliness, she finally had someone she could talk to. She would tell her everything—except about Alec. Never about Alec. No one could know about him, or possibly endanger him in any way. Not even another prisoner.

"Yes, I'll tell you," Emily said to Rina. "But first, could I have another cigarette?"

Rina smiled and took out the pack. The next hour passed quickly as Emily told her story—the same lie she had told to everyone. It was so practiced by now, it almost sounded like the truth, even to her.

When she was finished, Rina shook her head sympathetically. "I can't blame you, girl. That's one mean scar. Too bad the old man kicked. On a first offense, attempted burglary, you'da got off for sure."

"What about you?" Emily asked. "Why are you here?"

Rina leaned back against the wall and sighed. "I was just fuckin' stupid. A dumb little black girl tryin' to make her way to the big time by peddling her ass. I been hookin' since I was fourteen. Cops and jail ain't new to me. Hassled, busted, in and out of the tank, probation, I had it all. And I still didn't learn. Then I met this honky stud who really knew how to do it. Honey, he was *hot*, let me tell you! When that boy fuck, I sing like an opera star! He became my old man, and we really got into it, livin' together like some old married couple. Then I find out he's dealin'. Well, what the hell—I done a little pushin' myself, from time to time, makin' a little easy money. So—I help him. For a while we really had a high old time.

Until we get caught. He jumped bail and took off. And here I am, just coolin' it till my parole come up in a few months."

Emily was quiet for a few moments, thinking about what Rina had told her. Then she asked, "What about your folks? Have they been doing anything to help you?"

Rina frowned and took a deep drag on her cigarette. "I ain't got no folks on the outside. My family is here. You'll find out about them, later—" she replied somewhat vaguely.

Emily didn't question her further; she knew that there were boundaries that had to be observed. For the moment it was enough to know that she had found someone with whom she felt safe.

Rina stood up. "It's late—I gotta split."

"Oh, please don't go, yet. There're so many things I want to ask you—it's been so long since I've talked with anyone. . . ."

"Hey, girl, take it easy." Rina chuckled. She touched Emily's cheek with long, elegantly tapered fingers. "You really hungry. I know the feelin', but in this place you can't show what you feel too much, or those bitches eat you alive. Put a lid on it; walk tough, and act tough. Lord knows you already *look* tough. . . . Now, you didn't mind my sayin' that, did you—about lookin' tough? 'Cause if you did, I'll never say anything like that again."

"No, I didn't mind," Emily said with a smile.

"Good. We'll talk again real soon." Rina gave her a broad wink. "And don't you worry. I'll teach you everything you need to know about this place. Now, watch me. This is your first lesson."

As she approached the door, the warm, good-natured look on her face suddenly disappeared and was replaced by a bored, insolent expression. It was a look that Emily had seen on all the women's faces at one time or another. It fell into place over Rina's features like a mask.

"See you soon, girl," Rina whispered. Then she was out the door and gone.

Emily undressed and got into bed, thinking how, for a little while, visiting with Rina had given her the illusion of freedom, of spending some time with a friend. Then the lights went out and the doors were automatically closed and locked all over the unit.

14

As THE WEEKS WENT BY, EMILY LEARNED THE TRICKS of surviving in prison. Rina gave her tips on which guards to avoid and which could be cultivated as "friends"; how to get extra food and hide it in her room for snacks; how to play sick and get a day off work; and how to make her way up the graded scale for privileges.

Following Rina's advice, Emily openly displayed her scar at all times and adopted a testy, somewhat hostile manner to go with her image. In an apparent reversal of their former attitude, the other women began to give her a grudging respect, as if now they recognized her as one of their own.

In a strange and unexpected way, the experience gave Emily a freedom she had never known. No longer feeling compelled to hide the scar, she moved among the inmates with a new confidence and authority. This was a world much different from the one in which she had lived. Completely self-contained, and rigid in its own peculiar codes and demands, it allowed only the strong to survive. And Emily was determined to be one of the survivors.

She began to revive her dream of becoming a costume designer. Nora sent her some art materials and a few of her books on fashion designing, and Emily started to sketch again. The drawings were like a periscope through which she could see out of her submerged world into another reality. The harsh days momentarily dissolved, replaced by fantasies of opulent gowns made of dazzling fabrics, furs, and jewels.

But there was no escaping the monotony of prison life. The drab procession of minutes, hours, days, and weeks took its toll in nights without sleep and days of despair. The only place she could hide was in her sketches and her thoughts of Alec. In one notebook, which she kept well hidden, she did drawings of him from memory, lingering over the details of his eyes and lips, the fine soft wave of his hair. But in time, this only brought her more frustration and became too painful to bear.

Being with Rina helped, somewhat. They saw each other frequently, played cards in the recreation room, or visited in Emily's room and talked about their lives. But when Emily asked about her other prison friends, Rina grew vague and changed the subject. Emily understood; everyone had a right to their personal privacy, and respecting it was part of the prison code. Besides, her friendship with Rina was helping her learn how to do what the inmates called "easy time"—making the term of one's sentence as comfortable as possible. But one night an incident occurred that gave Emily a surprising insight into Rina's life.

They were on their way to the rec hall to see a movie when Emily noticed a woman following them from a distance. She had seen her before, watching them in the dining room or in the library when they went to look at the new magazines.

Emily leaned close to Rina and said, "We're being followed."

"I know. Just ignore her."

"Who is she? I've seen her around a lot. She's always watching us."

"She ain't watching us. She's watching me," Rina said evenly. "Don't pay her any attention, and maybe she go away, like a bad pimple."

"But who is she? And why does she keep watching you?"

"Her name is Hook—Louise Hook, but we call her 'Lou.' And she's really bad, so be careful...."

Emily gave a quick glance over her shoulder; the woman was still there. She was of medium height, in her early forties, Emily guessed, and had a square, strongly built figure. Her dark hair was cut short, and she wore no makeup to hide a complexion that was pitted and sallow. She was wearing the same clothes Emily had seen her in before: a white tee shirt, jeans that stretched tight over her thick legs, and a dark blue windbreaker.

"What's she in for?" Emily asked Rina.

"You name it. That fat ass been in and out since she had her first period. She's one mean mother."

As they approached the entrance to the rec hall, the woman suddenly called out, "Rina! I want to talk to you."

Rina paused, took a deep breath, and said to Emily, "You wait here. I be right back." She jammed her hands into her jeans pockets and strolled over to Lou with an insolent smile on her lips.

Emily watched them. Rina said something, and Lou scowled, drawing her thick eyebrows into a straight line over a short, pugnacious nose. Then she made a threatening gesture with a fist, but Rina laughed, caught the fist in her hand and put it against her own cheek. Lou seemed to relax. A thin smile spread across her face like a crack in a pane of glass. She stroked Rina's face, then abruptly slapped it hard. Rina didn't move, but continued to smile as if nothing had happened. Lou stepped back, glanced over at Emily with narrowed eyes, then turned and joined three women who were standing nearby, waiting for her.

Rina returned to Emily with a worried look on her face. "Okay, I think she's had her fun for the time being. Let's go see the movie."

"What was it all about? She hit you."

"Yeah, but not too hard," Rina said, trying to smile.

Emily glanced back and saw Lou and her friends standing together in a tight group, watching them. Inside the building, Rina suddenly said, "I hate to fink out on you, girl, but I gotta split. I got some business to take care of. I'll catch you later and tell you what's goin' down, okay?"

Emily watched uncertainly as the girl ran down the corridor and went out through one of the side doors. She felt a little apprehensive for a few minutes, then shrugged it off; intrigues among the women were not unusual, nor were irrational outbursts of temper. When Rina was ready, she would tell her what was going on.

In the rec hall, a screen was set up and there were rows of folding chairs for the inmates. Emily spotted a few empty seats against the back wall and took one. Just before the lights went down, she noticed Lou and her friends come in. They looked around, saw the empty chairs next to Emily, and walked toward them. Emily was tempted to get up and move before they reached her, but the hall was filled; there were no other empty seats. The women sat down as the lights went off. Lou was three chairs away, to Emily's left. The fourth woman took the seat next to her on the right.

"Would you like to change places with me so you can sit with your friends?" Emily asked her.

"No, that's okay," came the reply. "Just stay where you are."

The film began. Emily tried to relax and watch it, but all her senses were alert to the women sitting on either side of her. She felt surrounded by their menacing presence and wanted desperately to get up and leave.

Suddenly Lou changed seats with the woman on her left and sat down next to her. Emily's heart began to thud dully in her chest, and her palms grew sweaty. She sneaked a glance at Lou; the woman was staring at the screen, her heavy face expressionless.

The film was a raucous, noisy comedy, and the audience responded with roars of laughter. Even Lou seemed to get caught up in the frantic action on the screen; her eyes squeezed shut, and her thick body shook with mirth.

She looked over at Emily and gasped: "It's great, isn't it?"

"Oh, yes, it's a riot," Emily replied with a strained smile.

Still laughing, Lou tilted her chair back to rest against the wall and casually put her arm on the back of Emily's chair. Emily's shoulders tensed at the contact. Then she felt Lou's fingers playing idly with her hair. Fear knifed through her like an electric current. She sat paralyzed, every nerve in her body taut. Lou's fingers became more insistent, stroking her hair, twining through the thick strands, tugging at them playfully. Unable to bear the woman's touch any longer, Emily began to lean forward in an unobtrusive move to free herself. Lou suddenly jerked her head back by the hair, snapped her arm around Emily's neck in a hammerlock, and clamped a hand over her mouth. At the same instant, the woman sitting on Emily's right grabbed her arms and held them in a viselike grip.

It all happened so quickly that for a few seconds Emily was immobilized by shock. Then a scream of terror rose in her throat, choked off by the grimy hand across her mouth. She writhed and twisted in fear, moaning deep in her chest. But no one heard her; the noisy soundtrack of the film and gales of laughter from the audience obliterated any sound of struggle. She tried to kick, but Lou increased the pressure around her neck, almost choking her, and seized Emily's left knee with her free hand to hold her still. Then Lou brought the leg of her chair down on Emily's foot with all her weight.

A bolt of pain shot through Emily's body. Her eyes rolled wildly in her head. She worked her mouth against the hand clamped over it, trying to get her teeth into the fleshy palm. Lou shifted her body, raising the chair for a second. Then she brought it down again hard, grinding it into Emily's foot. There was a feeling of small bones breaking and blood seeping through torn flesh. The pain was so intense that Emily's head snapped from side to side, despite Lou's hold on her.

Still holding Emily's head in a crushing grip, Lou whispered, "You tell anybody what happened and you're dead. Got that?"

Emily's eyes blinked agreement, and suddenly the two women released her. She slumped in the seat, trying to catch her breath. Her face was running with sweat and tears, and pain raced through her leg like a fire.

A few minutes later she was dimly aware that Lou and her friends were gone. She braced her hands against the seat and tried to stand. A low, agonized moan escaped her lips. Holding on to the back wall for support, she began to hobble out of the hall. In the corridor, she looked at her foot; it was beginning to swell, and blood was oozing through the thin cloth of her tennis shoe. She leaned against the wall, closed her eyes, and took deep breaths, trying to keep from passing out. Then a hand was on her shoulder, shaking her. She started up, terrified, and saw Rina looking at her anxiously. With a ragged sob of relief, she collapsed in the girl's arms.

"It wasn't as bad as it looked—or felt," the nurse said. "One small broken toe, and a hell of a bruise. How did it happen?"

"I was leaning back in my seat—and when I straightened up, the metal leg came down on my foot," Emily said. "It was just a stupid accident."

The nurse gave her a level, disbelieving stare. "Okay, if you say so. We won't have to plaster it, but the bandage should stay on for a couple of weeks until it heals. You'll have to keep your weight off it." She went to a cabinet and took out a pair of crutches. "Here, use these to help you get around. And come back to see me in a couple of days so I can change the bandage."

Emily slipped the crutches under her arms, and she and Rina left the infirmary.

"It's a good thing I came back to get you for a cup of coffee," Rina said. "You were really a mess. Lucky none of the guards saw you. Now tell me. Who did it?"

"You heard what I told the nurse. It was an accident."

"Bullshit! It was Lou, wasn't it? She and her buddies followed you into the movie, and she did it. Then she tells you if you talk, you're dead, right? Jesus! That's her line, girl! And she only did it to get back at me."

"To get back at you? Why?"

Rina gave her a sly grin. "So, Lou did do it, huh? Goddamn, I was dumb to leave you alone with that bitch around!"

"Why did she want to get back at you?" Emily asked.

"'Cause I won't let her be my pop."

"Your 'pop'? What does that mean?"

They had come to Emily's room. Rina took the crutches and helped Emily lie down on the bed. "You want me to undress you?" she asked.

"No, I can manage," Emily answered. "Tell me what 'pop' means."

Rina hesitated, looking uncomfortable. "I think I'll let Claudia explain all that to you. She can do it better than me."

"Who's Claudia?" Emily asked, slipping off her clothes and getting under the covers.

"She's a friend of mine. I been meaning to introduce you to her—she is some woman, let me tell you, girl. You'll like her. I'll come get you tomorrow and take you to her. We'll have a little party to cheer you up."

"A party? I don't understand...."

"You will. I gotta go now. You get some rest, and I'll see you tomorrow."

Emily nodded sleepily; the nurse had given her a sedative, and it was beginning to take effect. "Okay, tomorrow." As Rina stood up to leave, Emily reached for her hand and grasped it tightly. "Thanks for helping me—"

Rina's large dark eyes grew moist with tears. "It was

really all my fault, and I'm sorry; I should've known better. You go to sleep, now, and tomorrow you'll meet Claudia."

"Claudia—" Emily repeated, closing her eyes. "Yes—she's your friend...."

"Yeah, that's right. She's my friend. And my 'pop.'"

The next evening, Rina and Emily walked across the grounds to another one of the housing units. An officer looked up from her desk as they walked in, and said in a stern voice, "Where are you girls going?"

"I'm taking Gorden to meet Claudia. Where do you think we going, to a night club?" Rina said.

Emily was a little apprehensive about the guard's reaction to Rina's tone. But the woman simply nodded and went back to the magazine she was reading.

"I thought you had to have a special pass to visit someone in another unit," Emily said.

Rina smiled. "Most people do. But Claudia's got influence. She looks after her children."

"I don't understand."

"You will," Rina said cheerfully.

They walked down a corridor past opened rooms very much like Emily's: sparsely furnished, the walls bare but for a few photographs that were tacked up. Some of the women were playing lonely games of solitaire, others were reading or listening to a radio. They seemed wrapped in an air of helplessness, mute figures caught in a desperate silence. But within that silence ran an undercurrent of suppressed hysteria that threatened to explode at any moment like a gale force.

Emily limped along on her crutches, trying to keep up with Rina. "Hey, slow down," she said. "I'm not used to these things yet."

"We almost there," Rina said. "Claudia's room is just around the next corner."

Emily swung herself around the corner and saw Rina

standing by a doorway. "Here it is, girl," she announced. Then, looking into the room, she called, "Hey, Pop, I brought you a new orphan."

Emily moved up to the doorway, glanced inside, and gave a small gasp. Beautiful macramé hangings disguised the drab walls; a deep yellow shag rug covered the floor. Soft light was cast by a brass lamp; a wall shelf supported a table radio and a color television set. Seated on the bed, propped up by plush decorator pillows, was a striking blonde who, she guessed, was about thirty-five. The woman looked as though she had just stepped out of a Beverly Hills salon; her hair was beautifully cut and fell in soft waves around her face; lightly applied makeup made the most of a smooth complexion, large hazel eyes, a generous mouth, and a small, slightly tilted nose. She was wearing a red velvet wrapper and low-heeled gold sandals.

Emily slowly followed Rina into the room. She noticed a small table near the bed, on which there was an electric coffee pot, some cups and saucers, and a tray of pastries.

"I told you we was gonna have a party." Rina chuckled, delighted by the look of astonishment on Emily's face. Then she said, "This is Claudia—Claudia Sherwood, the classiest broad this joint has ever had the privilege to incarcerate."

A deep, throaty laugh came from Claudia. "Very nicely done, Rina. Hello, Emily. I'm delighted to meet you at last." With a graceful gesture of her hand, she waved at the two girls to make themselves comfortable. "Emily, why don't you take the chair—Rina, help her with the crutches. Would you both like some coffee?"

Emily sat down, almost speechless. She felt as if she had wandered into another world by mistake; Claudia had the appearance and manner of a gracious hostess presiding at an intimate gathering of old friends.

Coffee was served and cigarettes passed around. Rina took a pastry and curled up on the bed next to Claudia, a contented smile on her face.

"I'm terribly sorry about the incident with Lou," Claudia said to Emily. "Are you in any pain?"

"No, thank you," Emily murmured.

"I'll do my best to see that doesn't happen to you again," Claudia said, with an edge of authority in her voice. She sipped her coffee for a few minutes, studying Emily's face and figure. "Rina told me about the accident you were in as a child," she went on. "It must be very difficult for you, having that scar. You're really a very pretty girl. And I understand that you're interested in costume designing. Please tell me about it—I'm fascinated by people with creative talent." She pointed to the macramé wall hangings. "Those were made for me by a very talented girl who left us a few months ago. Some friends of mine helped her to set up a little shop, and she's doing quite well now."

Under Claudia's gentle questioning, Emily began to talk, and for the next half hour she told the woman about her ambitions. Claudia listened to her intently, her eyes never leaving Emily's face. When she was finished, Claudia leaned forward and took her hand. "You're going to do it. I know you will. Just listening to you talk about it with such fervor convinces me that you will accomplish your goals."

Claudia spoke with such conviction that tears welled up in Emily's eyes. "Thank you, Claudia. I really needed to hear that."

Claudia sat back and sighed deeply. "I know how awful this must be for you, being in a place like this. But don't let it get to you—continue to work on your sketches, and please, do let me see them sometime soon."

Rina sat up and said to Claudia, "I told Emily that you'd explain to her about Lou...."

Claudia frowned, and a dark look came over her attractive features. "She's really a very unhappy woman. But she's dangerous. She's a threat to the only security we have in this place—our caring for one another, our families. Lou is like people I've known on the outside. They dominate with brute force and reach out to grab whatever they want, no matter who gets hurt."

Emily listened carefully while Claudia explained about the social structure of the prison. Women clustered together in what they called "playing family." Older women became "grandmas," the tougher, more masculine types called themselves "pops," and their lovers were "moms." Friends who protected one another were called "sisters."

"Is that why Rina calls you 'pop'? Because you're lovers?" Emily asked faintly.

"You don't know very much about lesbians, do you?" Claudia said, smiling at Emily.

"Not really. But I have noticed a lot of the women here behaving—well, affectionately toward each other."

"Very discreetly put," Claudia said dryly. "The truth is, that's all most of them have the chance or inclination to do. As for Rina and myself—I *am* a lesbian, and, for the moment, Rina is my—shall we say 'close friend'? It's not her way of life, just as it isn't for many of the women here. But we all need some form of love and affection to help us remember that we're human. There are women who have been here a long time, women with boyfriends or husbands and children. The men can't, or won't, visit them very often, and many of the children are in foster homes. That's why we have our 'families.'"

"Yeah, that's the way it is," Rina chimed in. "It's how we say 'fuck you' to the authorities. They can tell us when to get up, when to eat, when to shit, but they can't stop us from having family."

"Crudely put, but to the point," Claudia said, smiling at Rina fondly.

"But what about Lou?" Emily asked. "Why did she want to hurt me?"

Claudia's eyes narrowed. She lit another cigarette and puffed on it slowly before answering. "Lou is a very stupid, cruel woman who happens to be a lesbian. She wants Rina to be her lover. She saw that you and Rina had become friends, and that's why she attacked you. To threaten Rina—a form of coercion. But I don't think it will happen again. She has me to contend with, and as you can see"—she gestured to the comfort of the room— "I'm not without some influence in this institution."

She paused, then smiled broadly. "I know what you're thinking, Emily. You're wondering what *I'm* doing here, what crime I committed. That's a long and not terribly interesting story. Why don't we save it for another time? We'll see each other again. And we will be friends, won't we?"

"Oh, yes—of course we will," Emily replied eagerly. "Being with you and Rina makes me feel like a real person again."

"You are a real person, and a very important one. We're your family now, and we'll take care of you." Claudia stood up and helped Emily to her feet. "You're a sweet, sensitive girl, and I'm very glad I know you. We'll see each other very soon. I promise."

Rina helped Emily back to her room. After the girl had left, Emily lay on her bed, thinking about everything that had transpired in the last few hours. The sympathy that Claudia and Rina had expressed seemed like a gift sent to lighten her despair. Even more heartwarming was the feeling of being accepted by the two women despite her scar. In that way, she thought, they were like Alec, caring about her because of who she was, not how she looked.

Alec. The thought of him brought a flood of memories so intense that she almost wept. But at least she had those memories, and the hope that he would be there for her when she was released. If he was safe. Oh, God, she prayed, let him be safe. Please let him be safe.

The lights in the unit were turned off, and there was the sound of the doors being closed and locked—a sharp, staccato noise, like muffled bursts of gunfire going off, one after the other. They seemed to echo through the long, still corridors, from building to building and across the grounds, only to fade at last into the thin air of the night.

15

LIKE EVERY WOMAN IN THE PRISON, EMILY KEPT A CAL-
endar, marking off each passing day. Including the three
months she had spent at the Sybil Brand Institute, she
had been imprisoned for almost seven months. Aside from
this record, time had little meaning; days and nights followed each other with monotonous regularity. The only
thing she looked forward to were her visits with Rina and
Claudia. They became close friends, and Claudia finally
confided the reason for her imprisonment. She had been
the bookkeeper for a successful Beverly Hills investment
company. When the tax laws changed, and loopholes
tightened, her employer began to make increasingly risky
investments on behalf of his clients. As these schemes
failed, he was forced to dip into other investors' monies
to pay off his best clients. Claudia remained loyal to him
and helped adjust the books to conceal the manipulations.
Eventually the fraud was uncovered, and both of them
were tried and convicted.

"I'm a very good businesswoman, and I should have
known better," Claudia told Emily. "It was a lesson I will
never forget. Fortunately, I made some very close polit-
ical friends while I was in business, and they've been able
to help me here."

She paused and smiled grimly. "Some of them might,
at this very moment, be in prison themselves, but for their
wealth and power. And they know that *I* know all about
them. But they also know I can keep my mouth shut. So

they'll be there to help me when I get out. Being trusted by people with power can give you power."

"Perhaps you're right," Emily said thoughtfully. "But I don't want to depend on other people. I want to make my own way, and do it so well that I'm in control, so that I have the power."

Claudia raised her eyebrows in mock surprise. "Well, listen to the girl, as Rina would say. You're getting stronger every day, aren't you?"

"Yes, I am," Emily stated quietly. Then she smiled and added, "With a lot of help from my friends."

"Speaking of friends, has my little group done their job? Has Lou given you any more trouble?"

"No. I haven't even seen her around lately."

"Good. But be careful. She's not easily put off. I suspect she's just biding her time. If she makes a move, let me know, and I'll take care of her."

One morning Emily received a letter from Nora telling her that she was coming to see her the following Sunday. Emily was overjoyed; it had been almost two months since Nora's last visit. The letter was filled with apologies and explanations; Nora had started working at a new beauty salon, and her schedule had been so rough, she was too tired to make the drive. But now she had everything under control; they would have a long visit and catch up on all the news.

Emily counted the days, and finally it was Sunday. She went to the recreation center, where a small crowd of inmates and their relatives had already begun to fill the visitors' room. Nora was waving to her from a table in the corner.

Emily had hoped that Sheila would be with her. She hadn't seen her sister since the day she was sentenced. There had been a few hastily written notes, but no visits. Nora always made excuses for the girl, but Emily understood; Sheila couldn't handle the embarrassment of coming to see her in prison. A lot of inmates complained about the same thing. Emily couldn't help missing her; even though they weren't close, she and Nora were all the real family she had. Concealing her disappointment with a smile, she went to her mother and they embraced.

Nora was shocked at Emily's appearance. The girl's face was pale and there deep circles under her eyes. Her hair was pinned back, and the scar was more visible and livid than ever. They sat down at the table, and Nora's eyes filled with tears.

"Mom, please don't cry," Emily said.

Nora dabbed at her eyes with a handkerchief. "I'm sorry, honey. I just can't get used to seeing you in this place. Are you getting any rest? You look so tired."

Emily gave her a wry smile. "Some nights it's hard to fall asleep. But I'm okay. Really I am. I've made some friends, and they help me a lot. But let's not talk about me—you look wonderful. I love the new hairstyle, and that color! It's just great."

"It's called 'champagne'—you don't think it's too much?"

"No, not at all. I like the dress, too. You've lost some weight."

"Yeah. Well, like I wrote you, I'm working at a new place in one of those shopping centers on Wilshire, and it's very classy. So I had to overhaul the old bag. One of the girls helped me." Nora patted her hair self-consciously. "I think she did a good job."

Emily beamed at her mother. "Some old bag! You never looked better. One of these days you'll be telling me you've met some wonderful man who wants to make an honest woman of you."

Nora blushed and lowered her eyes. "Well, as a matter of fact, I have been seeing someone. Oh, it's nothing serious—just a few dates...."

Emily's smile froze. She had a sudden sense of her mother's life going on without her, a feeling that events were happening, would continue to happen, in which she had no part. Recovering herself, she said with forced enthusiasm, "Mom, that's great news! I want to hear all about him. How 'bout I get us some coffee—then you can tell me everything."

"Sure, baby. Here. I brought some change."

Emily took the money and went to one of the vending machines that lined the wall. Waiting for the coffee, she took advantage of the moment to collect her thoughts. Nora was seeing someone. She might even marry again, build a new life for herself. If she did, would it include her? Had she told the man that one of her daughters was in prison? Her hands shook a little as she returned to the table with the coffee and sat down.

"Now, tell me all about him," Emily said brightly.

"His name is Sam Jeffries, and he's a widower, about my age, and very nice-looking." Nora gave her an embarrassed smile. "I think he likes me. Anyway, we've only been out together a couple of times, so who can tell?"

"Has Sheila met him? What does she think?"

Nora got a serious look on her face. She toyed with her coffee cup for a few seconds, then said slowly, "Well, to tell you the truth, Sheila hasn't met him. That's really why I wanted to see you today—I didn't want to write it in a letter."

"What's wrong? Has something happened to her?"

Nora's expression turned to one of disgust. "Yes, something happened, all right. She eloped. Sheila's married."

Emily stared in disbelief. "Sheila is married? When did it happen? Who is he?"

"It happened almost two months ago. I didn't want to write you about it—I was that upset. I don't even know who he is—I never met him," Nora said bitterly. "I didn't even know how long they'd been seeing each other, but I think it started soon after you were arrested. You know Sheila; she never confided in me. I suspected something was going on—she was out almost every night, and being very secretive. Then I came home from work one day and found a note telling me she had gone off to Las Vegas to get married. I was worried sick until she finally called. She told me she was happy and not to worry, that they were going to stay in Vegas because he had a job there. And that's it—that's all I know. She hasn't even written."

"God, I just can't believe it," Emily said. "Don't you even know his name?"

"Oh, yes—I forgot to tell you. His name is Alec Darcy."

Emily looked at Nora for a few seconds, then smiled, as if her mother had made a joke. "What did you say?"

"Alec Darcy. Sheila is now Mrs. Alec Darcy. It's kind of a romantic name. Don't you think so?" Nora sipped her coffee, then looked up at Emily with a puzzled frown. "I thought it sounded a little familiar—didn't you introduce me to one of the kids in the play at the college whose name was Alec?"

Emily sat absolutely still, trying to control the cold waves of shock rushing through her. Nora repeated her question, and Emily said, "What? Oh, no—there wasn't anybody in the cast named Alec."

Nora went on talking, and Emily tried to concentrate on what she was saying. But all she could hear was "His name is Alec Darcy. Sheila is now Mrs. Alec Darcy. . . . Mrs. Alec Darcy . . ."

A dull pounding began in her head, and she looked around the room angrily, as if blaming the noise on the visitors. Their voices seemed to grow louder, their laughter more frenetic.

"Honey, what's wrong?" Nora asked anxiously. "You look so pale. Are you sick?"

Her mother's voice seemed to recede. Emily wondered why she sounded so distant, and the others so loud. She saw Nora's lips moving and strained to hear her.

"Emily, what's the matter? Are you upset because Sheila got married?"

"Where did they meet?" Emily asked dully.

"I told you, I don't know. I didn't even know they were seeing each other. They kept it a secret."

A secret. They had kept it a secret the way she and Alec had kept it a secret, Emily thought. The pain in her head increased; a sick feeling began to churn in her stomach. The taste of bile rose in her throat, and she swallowed hard.

"Mom, I've got to go. . . . I've had a little cold, and I'm not feeling too well—" The words were hard to say. She stopped and stood up, weaving slightly.

Nora half rose from her chair. "Should I call somebody? Do you need any help?"

"No, no—I just need to lie down for a while. . . ." Emily leaned over stiffly and kissed her mother's cheek. "Thanks for coming, Mom—I'm sorry—I'll write you."

Nora's face began to blur before her eyes, and she turned away. The noise in the room was deafening; her head felt ready to burst. Emily staggered through the crowd to the door and went outside. Gulping deep breaths of air, she started for her unit. The ground seemed to tilt under her feet. She stumbled, then righted herself and went on. Some women who were sitting with their families on the benches along the walk called out to her. But she ignored them, blindly pushing herself forward, setting one leg in front of the other like a child just learning how to walk.

At her unit, she reeled past the guard in the control room. The woman looked up from the paperback she was reading and called out, "Gorden, are you sick?"

Emily began to run. The hallway seemed endless until she reached her room. Once inside, she stopped and stood in the middle of the cramped, narrow space, her mouth open, gasping for air. She clutched her head, trying to stop the pain. Then something deep inside her snapped and she began to tremble violently.

It was a lie! All of it, from the very beginning, she

thought. A low moan escaped her lips, became uncontrollable, and grew into a cry. A convulsion shuddered in her stomach, and she bent over the sink to vomit. But nothing came up. Her throat constricted, then cleared, and the cry rose to a shriek.

A guard came running down the hall and stopped at the doorway. "What's the matter, Gorden—you sick?"

Emily looked at her wildly. "It was a lie!" she gasped. "He told me he loved me, that the scar didn't matter." She turned and thrust her face to the mirror over the sink and pulled her hair back tight. A grotesque image stared at her: mad eyes, mouth opened and twisted, the scar streaming over face and neck like a fresh, ugly wound. She began to scream.

The guard, a stocky woman named Harrison, rushed into the room and took Emily roughly by the shoulders. "Calm down, Gorden—they all lie. . . ."

"But he told me that he loved me," Emily cried savagely. "That I was beautiful!"

"And you believed him?" Harrison laughed. "Christ, Gorden, look at yourself. How could you fall for that shit? Now, just take it easy and—"

Emily let out a howl of anguish and smashed her fists into Harrison's face. The woman fell back, then scrambled to get a grip on Emily's arms. The two women struggled. Emily clawed at the guard's face. The woman reared back and punched her hard in the stomach. Emily doubled over in pain. She could hear other women running in the hall, shouting and jeering. She made another lunge at Harrison and felt a searing blow land on her face. There was sudden gush of blood from her nose and mouth. A final scream ripped out of her, and she fell to the floor. Then blackness descended like a shroud, and she saw and felt nothing.

Emily opened her eyes. Everything was black. Then it gradually became soft and filmy, like grey gauze. A blurred pattern of pale light and dark shadows came into focus. Moving her head cautiously, she looked around and saw that she was in the infirmary. In the beds around her, women lay sleeping, their bodies oddly shaped lumps under white sheets. A desk lamp illuminated the figure of a night nurse sitting at the end of the aisle.

Emily struggled to sit up, only to discover that she was strapped to the bed. Her head fell back against the pillow, and she winced; every part of her body ached. A bandage was stretched over her right cheek, and under it was a dull, insistent throbbing. Her throat felt raw, and her mouth dry as cotton. She licked her lips; they were cracked and parched.

"Water—" she croaked in a whisper. Then, making an effort, she said louder, "Please, give me some water. . . ."

The night nurse came down the aisle to Emily's bed. She was the same woman who had taken care of her foot. She poured a glass of water from a pitcher and held it to Emily's lips. "What's with you, Gorden? First your foot, and now this." When Emily had finished, she asked, "How do you feel?"

"I hurt."

"I'll bet you do. Harrison really worked you over. I'll give you some pain killers in a few minutes, and you'll sleep like a baby."

"What happened to my face? Why is it bandaged?"

"Harrison cut your right cheek open when she hit you. It's okay—just needed a couple of stitches, nothing serious. You're a real tiger, aren't you—you almost broke Harrison's jaw. You're lucky they didn't throw you into solitary."

"You took stitches? Will there be a scar?" Emily asked.

"Nothing like the one you've already got," the nurse replied. "A little makeup should cover it." She saw Emily shifting painfully under the straps and began to unbuckle them. "I don't think we'll need these anymore. We were afraid that when you came to, you'd give us a bad time. You were pretty wild. What happened?"

Emily stretched her arms and legs, feeling shots of pain

in the muscles. "I got some bad news and flipped out," she answered. "Is Harrison okay?"

"A little banged up, but on her what difference does it make?" the nurse replied, laughing. "Be careful, though— she's mad as hell at you."

A woman on the other side of the room cried out. The nurse said, "I'd better go see if she's okay. I'll be back in a minute with some pills for the pain."

"I won't need them," Emily told her. "It's not so bad now." She didn't want to be sedated. She wanted to stay awake, to think.

"Well, if you do, just holler." The nurse moved away from the bed.

For a long time Emily lay very still. The throbbing in her cheek began to subside, and she wondered what it would look like when they removed the bandages. Another scar on my face, she thought calmly. And then, They'll punish me for hitting Harrison; they'll take away my privileges. Or worse. But none of that mattered—not what they would do to her, or how she looked.

Finally she made herself think of him, even whisper his name into the dark: "Alec." She forced herself to relive everything that had happened, everything he had said and done from the first day he had walked into the store, and into her life.

He must have seen Harriet Bradshaw pay for her cabinet with cash. And he had seen Emily at the safe, putting the money away. That's why he had stopped at her desk to talk with her; he had started to plan the whole thing then. If she hadn't met him that night at the rehearsal, he probably would have found an excuse to come back to the store, see her, take her out, make her love him.

Oh, Alec, she thought grimly, you were a much better actor than I realized. Every word and gesture had been a carefully planned performance, every romantic moment beautifully staged. And she'd been so easy, so willing. So foolish! She had believed every word he had said.

And the sex. Emily felt a crushing weight of humiliation, and tears flooded her eyes. Had he cringed inside when she had clung to him, given herself to him? Or had he laughed to himself afterward? She moaned silently, berating herself; she had played out every one of his scenes like a puppet! Taking care of him, terrified when he had been beaten—and that had been staged for her benefit, too, hadn't it?

Had it all been done just for the money? Or was it something else, some cruelty in him that made him use her that way, enslave her? It was a thing she had to understand, even if it took the rest of her life. Was he really that perverse? Or was he just a criminal, a petty thief who didn't have the guts to commit his own crime?

And now he had Sheila. And she had introduced them, the opening night of the play. Sheila must have known what he was doing. Perhaps they had even planned it together! The idea so staggered her that she almost cried out. Was it possible that her own sister could have betrayed her? Yes, it was possible. For someone as fascinating and sexy as Alec, Sheila would have done anything—just as she herself had done everything he had asked.

A fierce anger came over her. She would confess, see the superintendent and tell the truth. She would betray Alec and Sheila as they betrayed her. But she couldn't do that to Nora, she thought wildly. She couldn't put her mother through all that anguish again, not now, just when she was beginning to find some happiness of her own.

As for Sheila, sooner or later she'd find out what kind of man Alec was. He'd use her, lie to her. He must have already involved her in some crime to get the money to run away. And she probably thought it was the most exciting thing ever to happen to her. But in time, Sheila too would suffer. Emily was sure of that.

As the long hours of the night crawled by, Emily began to formulate a plan. By dawn, she knew exactly what she had to do. Her state of mind was calm, her determination resolute. She would survive being in prison. And when she was free, she would work hard, find a way to achieve success and power. What was it Alec had said about power? "It's what everybody wants—to make the world dance on your string...." Yes, she would get that kind of power.

And then she would get Alec. Her hatred was icy, implacable. Someday she would find him and make him pay for what he had done. It was just a matter of time. And she had a lot of time to plan her vengeance.

She would get that son of a bitch.

16

As PUNISHMENT FOR ATTACKING OFFICER HARRISON, Emily was stripped of all privileges and restricted to her room every night after work for a period of one month. No movies, visitors, playing cards in the rec room, going to the library, or any of the other amenities that made life bearable.

Emily didn't mind; there wasn't anything they could do to hurt her. Not now. And besides, it gave her time to think about her plan. Other than that, time had no meaning, except for the fact that it was passing. Prison life clanged around her with its rules and restrictions, bad food, the daily unnerving scream of the horn calling for "count," the fear of sudden, uncontrollable outbreaks among the women. But she attacked each day with one thought: Make it pass quickly.

The nights were more difficult. She was plagued by insomnia, and when sleep finally came, it was filled with nightmares that left her exhausted the next day. But she went on doggedly, working in the factory, eating her meals, and going to her room to fall across the bed, drained of all strength.

Rina managed to get past the guards one night and bring her some candy from Claudia. They both wanted to know what had happened, but all Emily told her was that after visiting with her mother, she had broken down, flipped out. It was an acceptable lie; many women did the same thing after visits with their families. That brief contact with the outside world often left them in anguish.

Emily had no intention of sharing the truth with Rina and Claudia or anyone else. Everyone sensed the change in her. The role she had been playing according to Rina's instructions was no longer a performance. There was a hard, steely glint in her eyes, a challenge in the set of her shoulders. The new scar on her right cheek was still fresh and raw, and she made no effort to cover it.

One evening she took out the drawings she had done of Alec with the intention of shredding them, flushing the scraps down the toilet. But seeing his face brought a fresh wave of rage and contempt, and she kept them. Night after night, she would take them out and study them, imagining what she would do when she found him. Her hatred and desire for vengeance grew, became the cornerstone of strength she needed to get through each day.

And with every passing hour, she cherished that hatred and nourished it until it was all-consuming.

When the restrictions were lifted, Emily was told that she was required to see a counselor in the Psychiatric Treatment Unit. One morning she was excused from her job and went to the Administration building. There she encountered Claudia, who was working in one of the offices. She saw Emily walking down the corridor, called her name, and hurried out to greet her.

The two women embraced, and Claudia said, "Rina told me what happened. Are you all right? I've been terribly worried."

"Yes, I'm fine now," Emily replied. "I'm on my way to see one of the counselors. Is this where you work?"

"Yes. I supervise the bookkeeping department." She smiled slyly. "Before I got here, the bookkeeping was a model of inefficiency. There was terrible graft and waste. Now that I'm in charge, there's no more waste—just the graft."

Emily laughed. "No wonder they're so good to you."

Claudia widened her blue eyes in an expression of innocence. "Oh, it's all very legal, of course."

"Of course," Emily agreed dryly.

One of the guards called out to her, and Claudia said quickly, "Come and see me tonight. I've missed you." Then she went back into the office.

Emily continued down the hallway to a small office at the rear of the building. She knocked on the door, then walked in. A big-bosomed, motherly-looking black woman was sitting behind a desk stacked with papers and folders. Greying hair was softly waved around a big, strong face, and she was wearing a neatly tailored dark blue suit and a crisp white blouse.

She looked up at Emily from behind rimless glasses and said, "Emily Gorden? Please sit down. I'm Martha Kane. I've got your folder here somewhere. . . ." She rummaged through the papers covering the top of her desk. "Ah, here it is." She opened the folder and thumbed through the pages quickly, then looked at Emily. "Do you want to tell me about the reason you attacked Officer Harrison?"

"Not particularly," Emily answered calmly.

Martha Kane put the folder down and clasped her hands together on the desk. "Emily, don't let's be difficult about this. Believe it or not, I'm here to help you. I've read the file on you and know that you're not like so many of the girls who come through here. You have no previous record, you're not into prostitution or drugs, and you've had a good education." She glanced at the file. "I also see that you were attending Los Angeles City College and taking classes in costume designing. Is that the same as fashion designing?"

"No, it's designing for the stage or screen, not retail or ready-to-wear."

"Oh, dear—and I was hoping you might give me some tips on how to dress." She gave Emily a wide smile that revealed even white teeth. "As you can see, I have something of a problem figure, which is polite way of saying that I'm a big woman."

"What you're wearing is fine," Emily said. "Tailored suits are good on large women. You might consider a thin pinstripe, though. They help give an illusion of being slimmer."

"Thank you. I'll remember that," Martha said. "Do you plan to continue your studies when you leave here?"

"Yes, I do, Mrs. Kane. Or is it Miss?"

"It's Miss, but please call me Martha—I hate being reminded that I'm not married at my age," the woman said, laughing. She opened a pack of cigarettes and offered one to Emily. "Would you like some coffee? There's a pot over there on the table. And would you bring me one?"

Emily went to the table and poured two cups. "Cream and sugar?" she asked Martha.

The big woman sighed deeply and replied, "Just sugar—three lumps. I'm cursed with a sweet tooth."

Emily smiled and returned to her seat and handed Martha her coffee. The two women sipped from the cups and smoked in silence for a few minutes. Then Martha said softly, "Tell me about the scar, and how it's affected your life. Is that why you attacked Officer Harrison? Did she say something about it to upset you?"

"You're very shrewd, aren't you?" Emily said coolly. "Coffee and cigarettes, a few jokes about your figure, some interest in my creative ability, and now you want my life story."

"Very clever of you to see through my little ploy," Martha responded evenly. "But you're right. I want to be your friend, if you'll let me."

"Will it help me when my parole comes up?" Emily demanded.

"It could. I might even be able to help you while you're here. I have a feeling that you're just acting tough to protect yourself. You don't have to do that with me."

"I have to protect myself from everyone," Emily said curtly. "No one is going to protect me but me."

"Perhaps that's true, when you're with the other inmates. But not here in this office," Martha insisted.

The phone on her desk suddenly rang. Martha picked it up and answered. She listened for a moment, glanced at her watch, gave a reply, and hung up. "I'm sorry—I have to attend a meeting with the superintendent. I'd hoped we could talk longer. I wish you'd think about what I said—I do want to be your friend, and I do want to help, if you'll let me."

She stood up and held out her hand. Emily rose from her chair, hesitated for a moment, then took Martha's hand and said with studied indifference, "I'll think about it. Thanks for the coffee and cigarettes."

Martha Kane watched her walk out the door and down the hallway. Then she picked up the phone and dialed the switchboard. "Lillian? It's Martha Kane. Would you call the Riverside Hospital and leave a message for Dr. Matthew Sheridan? Tell him to call me as soon as he can, please? Thanks, dear. Yes, that's right—Dr. Matthew Sheridan."

It was August, and a furnace heat pressed down on the grounds of the prison. The air was dry as smoke, and the lack of air conditioning in the living units and work areas made life completely unbearable. There were many cases of heat prostration, and the atmosphere was thick with tension. All the guards were alerted to keep an eye out for trouble; it was a dangerous season.

One afternoon, Emily was sent to the supply room to get bolts of material for an order of clothes from a state-run home for the aged. She left the work area, grateful for the opportunity to escape even for a few minutes from the noise of the machines and the complaints of the women. She stopped to wipe the sweat from her face with a wad of tissues, then made her way down to the hall to the supply room. When she entered, she recognized the trustee in charge as one of Louise Hook's cronies: a thin, bony young woman who had straw-colored hair and hard grey eyes and was called Bobby. She gave Emily a thin smile and said, "How's your foot?"

Emily ignored the question and handed her the order form. Bobby shrugged and turned to the shelves. She pulled bolts of cloth and loaded them into a deep, canvas-sided cart, pausing only to wipe the sweat from her face and neck.

"Give me a hand with these," she said irritably.

"It's your job, not mine," Emily replied flatly.

Bobby clenched her hands into fists. "You looking for trouble, cunt?"

"Yes, I am," Emily said without flinching.

The woman stared at her for a minute, then continued to load the cart. "Lou wants to talk to you," she muttered.

"Yeah? Well, she knows where to find me—this place isn't that big."

"I wouldn't fuck with Lou if I were you—she's a mean stud."

Emily remained silent. When the cart was full, she reached for the handle. Bobby's arm shot out and her hands fastened in a cruel grip around Emily's upper arms. "Did you hear me, bitch?" she hissed.

Emily tried not to wince at the pain. "I heard you," she said quietly. "Now let go of me."

Bobby grinned, showing a mouthful of bad teeth, and dropped her arms. She stepped back, making room for Emily to leave.

Late that afternoon, before she left work, Emily stole a pair of scissors.

A few days later the inmates were given a special recreational hour after the evening meal to enjoy a little respite from the heat and get some fresh air. They filed slowly out of their units and drifted lethargically across the grounds. It was a barren twilight, and waves of heat still rose from the dry earth.

Emily looked for Rina and Claudia, but couldn't find them. She strolled to the edge of the softball field and found a secluded bench to sit on. In the distance, outside the prison boundaries, she could see an expanse of flat, arid farmland and a lone tractor moving slowly along the horizon. She saw it turn and go back the length of the field, then turn once more and go forward. Back and forth in a measured pace, seemingly trapped in a prison made of earth as she was in one made of concrete. Bemused by the thought, she continued to watch the tractor, unaware of the figure approaching her.

"Gorden, I want to talk to you."

Emily whirled around and saw Lou Hook standing by the bench. She stared coldly at the woman for a few seconds, then said, "I don't want to talk to you."

"I know, I know—I don't blame you. . . ." Lou appeared nervous and ill at ease. She took a heavy drag on the cigarette she was smoking and looked away rather than return Emily's glare. "Just gimme a couple of minutes to explain something."

The words came haltingly, and Emily sensed that Lou was making an effort to appeal to her as an equal, an idea she found grimly ironic. "Explain what?" she asked harshly. "Why you broke my toe? Or why your goon, Bobby, threatened me the other day?"

"Okay, okay—I know you got a beef. I'm sorry about your foot; that was wrong of me. And forget about Bobby. She won't bother you again. She's just a dumb slut who's kissing up to me for some goodies. It's Rina I want to talk about."

Lou paused and ground out her cigarette, then lit another one. She was wearing a sleeveless grey work uniform that made her stocky figure look shapeless. There were damp stains under the arms, and she kept pulling at the skirt to free it from her heavy thighs.

"What about Rina?" Emily asked warily.

"Well . . ." Lou began hesitantly. "I thought you should know the whole story, about me and Rina, I mean. See, before Claudia came in, I was Rina's 'pop,' and everything was okay. But then Claudia showed up and took her away from me." She shifted uncomfortably and pulled at her uniform.

"So? Why come to me? Why don't you go after Claudia?"

"I can't. With her looks and clout, Claudia can get anything she wants. She got more power in this prison the first month she was here than I did in five years. If I went after her, they'd put me in solitary and throw away the key. But you know Claudia—you're her friend. You could talk to her about how I feel."

Lou looked at Emily imploringly. Her short dark hair was limp and fell over the square plane of her forehead like dribbles of spilled ink. In the quickly fading light, her face became shadowed, and the pitted complexion gave the appearance of a mass of tiny craters.

Emily suddenly understood why the woman had sought her out. Lou saw them as having something in common— she with her graceless body and eroded face, and Emily with her scar. A kinship of outsiders. The thought enraged her.

"I don't want to get involved," Emily said flatly. "You're trouble, and I'm trying to do easy time. You want Rina, that's your problem, not mine."

She got up and started to walk away. Lou caught up with her and grabbed her arm, forcing Emily to face her. "I love Rina and I want her back," she said. Her eyes narrowed to slits, and there was a desperate urgency in her voice. "Claudia's got her sewn up so tight, I can't even get near her. You've got to help me! I need that little black bitch, you understand? I *need* her!"

Emily pulled free of her grasp. "I don't give a fuck what you need," she snapped.

Lou's voice became a threatening growl. "Gorden, if you don't help me, I'll make your life a living hell."

Emily gave her a short, humorless laugh. "In this place that would be an improvement." Then she turned on her heel and strode away.

"Girl, I'm sorry you're being dragged into this mess," Rina said after hearing Emily recount her meeting with Lou. They were sitting in Claudia's room, hunched over coffee, and sharing cigarettes.

Claudia made a languid gesture and patted her silky blond hair. "It's really idiotic," she said. "But then, given the level of Lou's intelligence, I'm not too surprised. She's like a schoolyard bully, beating up on the little kids to get what she wants."

"Well, she'd better not come after this little kid," Emily said darkly.

"Maybe I should talk to her, get her off your back. . . ." Rina's offer was made tentatively, and she looked at Claudia like a child seeking protection from an adult.

Claudia reached out and stroked Rina's face lovingly. "You're such an amoral little cat." She laughed. "Always playing the angles to get what you want. That's one of the things I love about you." She turned to Emily. "Don't worry about Lou. I have a small band of stalwarts who listen and obey. They'll make sure that she keeps her distance."

Emily smiled. "I like your style, Claudia. I've learned a lot from you in the last few months."

"I'm not sure that I'm responsible for everything you've learned," Claudia responded shrewdly. "You're a lot tougher now than when I first met you, and I don't think that's any of my doing. I must admit, I rather miss the innocent little girl you used to be. What happened to her?"

"She went to prison and found out that life isn't a fairy tale," Emily replied. Then she added more thoughtfully, "Or an old movie." Seeing Claudia's puzzled look, she said, "That's a private joke."

Emily stood up. "I have to go. I need all the sleep I can get. We're doing men's jackets tomorrow for a veteran's home, and they're killers. See you guys later."

* * *

Emily got back to her unit a few minutes before the lock-up and went to her room. She took off her clothes and soaked a washcloth in the sink, waiting for the tepid water to run cooler before sponging off her body. When she was dry, she looked through a stack of paperbacks for something to read until lights out. Then she pulled the covers off her bed and let out a strangled cry of shock.

A dead rat, its body sliced open from neck to tail, lay across the pillow, soaking the white cloth with blood.

At that moment the lights went out and the doors began to close and lock. Emily fell back against the wall, terrified. In the dim light from the hall, she could still see the loathsome, mutilated rodent. She rushed to the door and began to pound on it, screaming for a guard. Several minutes went by while the sound of the doors being locked went off like gunfire in the hallway. Then a face appeared in the window. It was the guard Emily had attacked: Officer Harrison.

"What's all the noise for, Gorden?" she demanded.

"Open the door!" Emily screamed. "Goddammit, open the fucking door!"

"Now, Gorden, you know we can't do—"

"Somebody put a dead rat on my bed," Emily sobbed. "Please, get it out of here. Open the door and get it out!"

The guard held up her flashlight and shined it through the window. Emily stepped back and the beam swung around the room and stopped on the pillow. Harrison laughed and said, "Shit, Gorden, all that fuss for a little rat? It must have been a joke one of your friends played on you. Just flush it down the toilet."

"No, please, please," Emily wept.

"Don't be so chicken." The officer sneered. "You can handle it."

A terrible rage came over Emily and she smashed her fists against the door again and again. Harrison made a menacing gesture with her hand and said, "You keep that up and I'll throw you in the hole, you ugly bitch!"

Emily stopped, catching her breath, and stared at the

woman through the glass. "You were in on it, weren't you?" she asked hoarsely. "You had to be. That's how it was done—you did it to get back at me."

Officer Harrison grinned, then turned and walked away.

Emily leaned against the door weakly, grabbing deep gulps of air. She turned around and looked at her bed. She saw a tee shirt lying on the floor and picked it up. Then, drawing her breath in sharply, she went to the bed, dropped it over the rat, and quickly carried it to the toilet.

She spent the rest of the night on the floor, crouched in a corner.

17

A FEW DAYS LATER EMILY WAS WORKING AT HER SEW-
ing machine in the garment factory. She was tired and
edgy, drained of all energy from nights without sleep. The
horror of finding the rat still haunted her. She was sure
that Lou or one of her gang had done it, but there was
nothing she could do. Inmates tormented one another all
the time, and it was usually overlooked by the guards and
ignored by the authorities. They were considered private
wars, left to the women to settle among themselves. She
spent as much of her free time as she could with Rina and
Claudia, but during those moments when she was alone,
she felt a constant threat of danger close by and kept a
wary lookout for Lou and her friends.

During the afternoon, Emily was busily absorbed in
work and didn't notice Bobby enter the workroom pushing a cart loaded with bolts of fabric. The two officers in
charge were off in a corner, engaged in conversation.
Bobby stopped at several machines to deliver some fabric,
then proceeded down the aisle toward Emily. She suddenly quickened her pace, gave a loud groan as if she
were ill, then stumbled and fell heavily against the back
of Emily's chair.

Emily felt herself shoved violently forward. The material she had been working with ripped off the plate and
her hand slid under the needle. She let out a scream as
it ran through the top joint of her index finger, pinning
her to the machine. Then she fainted.

When she came to, she was lying on the floor and one of the guards was holding a cup of water to her lips.

"Are you all right, Gorden? Can you walk?" the guard asked.

"Yes—I think so. . . ." Emily looked up and saw Bobby standing in the ring of women who had gathered around her.

"Jesus, I'm so sorry," Bobby wailed. "It was an accident. I got dizzy from the heat and stumbled." She stared down at Emily with wide, innocent eyes.

"Okay, okay—the rest of you get back to work," the guard called out, helping Emily to her feet. "Go to the infirmary and get that taken care of," she said to her. "Can you make it alone? Or do you want somebody to go with you?"

"No, I can manage," Emily said, clenching her jaws against the throbbing pain in her hand.

Bobby shoved the cart aside to let Emily pass. "I'm really sorry, Gorden," she said loudly. "It was just an accident."

Emily looked straight at her with a savage expression. Bobby glanced quickly around to see if the guards were watching, then looked back at Emily, grinned, and gave her the finger.

Emily began to feel as if she were living in a prison within a prison. Fear dogged her every step. No one could help her. Even though Claudia had marshaled her own group to protect Emily, they couldn't predict or attempt to thwart the intricate machinations of Lou's reign of terror.

I have to take care of myself, Emily thought. No one can help me or do it for me. I have to be responsible for my own life.

She stole a needle and thread and sewed a clasp inside her prison jacket. Then she hooked the scissors she had stolen inside the clasp so that they were within instant reach, and began to wear the jacket wherever she went.

Days went by. A week went by. And Emily waited, knowing that at any moment Lou might confront her. She no longer sought help from Claudia and didn't expect any from Rina. A battle was on, and she was the target. Claudia was too powerful in prison politics to be directly attacked by Lou. And Rina was simply a pawn. Lou would never do anything to mar the girl's beauty.

Emily was sure that she had become the focus of Lou's rage because of her scar. She knew that people often attacked in others the thing they hated in themselves. And Lou, with her pitted face and lumpy body, couldn't bear the idea of Emily enjoying a close friendship with Rina and Claudia, two beautiful women. And that, she decided, was the real reason why Lou was terrorizing her.

At night, lying in the darkness of her room, Emily wondered how long she would have to go on defending herself because of her face.

Another week went by, and nothing happened. But Emily knew that Lou was playing a war of nerves to break her down, that eventually she would make her move. In the meantime, Emily began a series of sketches that she planned to use as a portfolio of her work, in the hope of finding a job with a costume house once she was released. Nora had sent her more art materials, including sketchpads, watercolors, inks, and pencils. Every night after the evening meal, Emily worked to produce striking designs that might attract the attention of a future employer. When she was finished, she put the drawings in a cardboard box that was kept at the back of her closet.

One night, while Rina was watching television, Claudia asked if she could see the sketches. Emily agreed, eager to get her response to the work she had done. As the two of them crossed the grounds to Emily's unit, Claudia said, "I think what you're doing is wonderful, giving yourself something to work for, to look forward to when you get out. I have a great deal of respect for you. And who knows? Perhaps someday we may work together. Famous designers need business managers, and I'm a damned good businesswoman."

"I think I'd like that," Emily said. Then she laughed and added, "As long as you don't juggle *my* books."

Claudia pulled a face and rejoined, "I've learned from my mistakes. I never want to be in a place like this again."

As soon as they entered the unit, Emily sensed that something was wrong. Officer Harrison didn't even look up as they walked by her desk. Several women were standing in the corridor, whispering to one another, but when they saw Emily and Claudia, they stopped and looked away guiltily.

"Something's up," Claudia said in a low voice. "I can feel it."

"So can I." Emily's heart began to race a little.

The two women hurried to Emily's room. At the doorway they stopped and stared in horror.

"Oh, God!" Emily cried out. "That bitch! That rotten bitch!"

The room was completely wrecked. The bed had been torn apart, sheets ripped and smeared with feces. Emily's few articles of clothing were in shreds and lay soaking in a puddle of urine. Some of them were stuffed into the toilet. Her art materials had been thrown all over the room. Smashed bottles of poster paint ran in vivid streams of color on the floor; pencils and crayons had been snapped in two, and all of her sketchbooks destroyed. And scattered over the debris, like handfuls of confetti, were her finished drawings.

White-faced and shaking with anger, Emily turned and raced to one of the women in the hallway. "Did you see Lou do this?" she demanded.

The woman shrank back, afraid to answer. Emily grabbed her by the front of her dress. "Tell me if Lou did this! Answer me, or I'll kill you!"

"Yeah—it was Lou and her gang," the woman muttered.

Officer Harrison started down the hall toward Emily,

but Claudia stepped in front of her and said, "Stay out of it, Harrison. You're responsible for this, and I'll have your ass for it!"

"Where is she?" Emily cried, staring wild-eyed at the other women. "Where's Lou?"

One of them called out gleefully, "She's in the rec room with her buddies. Go get the bitch, Gorden!"

Emily ran down the hall. Officer Harrison shoved Claudia aside and went after her. "Stop her!" Claudia yelled. "Don't let her get near the control room to sound the alarm!"

With a shout of defiance, the women surged around the guard, grabbing her arms and holding her fast. Other inmates began to pour out of their rooms. Caught in the fever of revolt, they joined the melee. Claudia raced after Emily, calling to the women she knew to join her.

Emily burst into the large common room that connected the two living units, and saw Lou and her friends gathered around the television set. She pulled out the scissors, screaming, "You bitch!"

Lou looked around, caught unaware, as Emily lunged at her. The two women fell to the floor and grappled with each other while the others scrambled out of the way. In a mindless frenzy, Emily raised the scissors to slash Lou's face. "I'll give you a scar to match mine!" she shrieked.

Lou's arm shot out to protect her face, and her knee came up sharply into Emily's stomach. The other women got into the fight, and one of them ripped the scissors out of Emily's hand. She felt blows raining down on her head and shoulders, but she kept her grip on Lou, savagely punching at her face and body. She was dimly aware that Claudia and some other women were trying to help her. Someone fell against the television set and it crashed to the floor. Tables were overturned, and there were screams of rage and pain. Lou managed to get away from Emily for a moment, blood gushing from her nose and mouth. "Kill her!" she howled.

Emily threw herself at the woman, bringing her down

once more. Kicking and punching, Lou fought back, crying out for help. Emily grabbed a handful of her hair and slammed her fist into Lou's face again and again. Suddenly she heard Claudia scream, "Emily, watch out!"

Emily looked up and saw one of Lou's gang with a chair raised above her head. Before she could move, the woman brought it down with all her strength across Emily's face.

She slipped in and out of consciousness. She felt herself being lifted onto a stretcher, heard voices of men speaking with urgency, the sound of sirens. It was the accident; Daddy had lost control of the car and she had gone through the windshield. No—that was the other nightmare. What nightmare was this?

Lights flashed past; she was being rushed along a corridor. Faces peering down at her swam in and out of focus, voices whispered around her. Was she dying? A man leaned close and he looked like Alec. Alec! She tried to scream, but there was no sound. She tried again, straining every muscle in her body. Someone said, "Take it easy—you'll be okay; just take it easy...." Then a needle was jabbed into her arm, and after that there was oblivion.

Sunlight streamed through the windows of a room in Riverside General Hospital. A nurse had just taken away her breakfast tray, and Emily lay quietly, staring at dust motes dancing in shafts of light. She had been there for two days, being treated for mild concussion, a broken nose, two broken ribs, and other minor injuries and bruises. Her rib cage was taped, and there were bandages across her nose and along her jaw, where stitches had been taken. One eye was swollen shut and discolored; the rest of her face was darkly bruised. She had caught a glimpse of herself in the bathroom mirror and had turned away quickly, sickened by the grotesque sight. But the doctors had assured her that eventually the bruises would heal and disappear, that she'd be as good as new. Whatever that meant, she thought wryly. For the moment, she was content to be here; it was clean and quiet, and she was being treated like a human being.

The morning hours passed fitfully, and she slept. Later, in the middle of the afternoon, the door opened and the nurse peeked in. "Emily, are you awake? You have a visitor."

Nora came into the room carrying a bouquet of flowers and a box of candy. She rushed to Emily's bedside, crying, "Oh, baby, I came as soon as I could!"

"Mom! Oh, Mom, I'm so glad to see you! How did you know I was here?"

"I got a call from a Miss Kane, and she told me what had happened." At the sight of Emily's face, Nora broke down and began to weep. "God, what have they done to you?"

Emily comforted her mother while the nurse brought a vase and put the flowers on the night table. After she had left, Nora pulled herself together and asked, "Are you in any pain, honey?"

"It's not too bad now. And they give me something when it gets too uncomfortable." Emily stared at her mother. Nora looked more beautiful than she had ever seen her: slim and tanned, wearing a smartly cut red dress and only a little makeup. "You look absolutely marvelous. What's been happening? Are you still seeing that man?"

Nora gave her a radiant smile. "Sam Jeffries—yes, I'm still seeing him." She paused for a few seconds, then blurted out, "I'm going to marry him!"

Emily felt herself go pale. "You're getting married?"

"Yes! Oh, Em—I'm so happy. He's a good man, and I really care for him. And we're moving to Canada—can you believe it? He grew up there, and his folks left him a place near Toronto. He told me it's just beautiful—"

She stopped, suddenly aware of the stricken look in Emily's eyes. "Baby, I'm not leaving you behind," she cried gaily. "I told Sam all about you, and he wants you to come and live with us when you're released. You'll love him. I know you will. In fact, he wanted to come with me today to meet you, but I told him I thought it was better if I saw you alone." She looked at Emily anxiously. "Please say it's all right. I want you to be happy for me."

Emily forced a note of gaiety in her voice. "I am happy for you, Mom. If I could, I'd be grinning from ear to ear."

Nora laughed and took a deep, satisfied breath. "I still can't believe it. It's like a dream come true, like one of those old movies we used to watch together. Would you believe it, Sam enjoys them, too? He's a real movie buff, and we have such good times together."

Emily listened as Nora chattered on about the plans for the wedding. They were going to be married in Toronto, where Sam had relatives, and then renovate the house that had been left to him. There was more than enough room for her, Nora kept insisting, and wouldn't it be exciting to come to a new country, live in a new city?

Her voice droned on, but now Emily was only half listening. She was thinking about something else, something her mother hadn't mentioned. Finally she interrupted the flow of words and asked, "Does Sheila know? Have you heard from her?" She held her breath, waiting for the answer.

A look of deep sadness settled over Nora's features, and she shook her head. "No, she doesn't know," she replied. "I wrote to her, but the letter came back stamped 'address unknown.' God only knows where she is or what happened to her." Tears filled her eyes, and she fumbled in her purse for a handkerchief.

So they've left Las Vegas, Emily thought. Or maybe Alec had just left Sheila, abandoned her for someone else. She was surprised at how calmly she could think about them.

She reached out and took her mother's hand. "Don't worry about Sheila. I always told you she could take care of herself. Besides, you have Sam now, and a whole new life to look forward to."

Nora brightened up a little. "You're right. Sheila always was an independent girl; I guess she'll be okay. And you will come to stay with us, won't you? Sam really meant it—about you coming to live with us."

Emily knew that it wasn't possible; she'd realized that from the moment Nora had told her about marrying Sam. Too many things had happened to her, things that Nora would never understand, that she could never even be told. And besides, Emily had to make a life of her own, achieve the success she had dreamed of. And find Alec. That was the future she had planned for herself, and nothing could change her mind or stand in her way.

Emily took her mother's hand and said, "Thank you for wanting me—and thank Sam for being so terrific. I'll certainly plan on coming to see you as soon as I get out, and then we can talk about my living with you." Then, trying to sound offhand about it, she asked, "Do you still have Sheila's old address in Vegas? When I get released, I may get a chance to go there and find out what happened—maybe while I'm on my way to see you."

"I think I do—" Nora looked through her purse. "Yes, here it is. I'll write it down for you." She took out a pencil and scribbled on a piece of paper, then handed it to Emily. "I'll probably hear from her soon, and when I do, I'll let you know."

Emily slipped the paper under her pillow. "Yes, do— I'd like to know where she is."

Nora looked at her watch, then back at Emily. "Baby, I have to leave—there're so many things to do...." Her eyes began to glisten with tears.

This was the moment Emily had dreaded. She clung to her mother, wondering how long it would be before she saw her again. A flood of memories rippled through her mind in quick images, like snapshots in a family album. Tears stung her eyes, and she felt like a little girl on her first day at school, being left to face the world alone.

After Nora had gone, she cried quietly for a while, then stared into the empty room thinking about the past and what had been changed or destroyed. And all because of a chance meeting with a man whose ruthlessness had left a wake of shattered lives behind him. She took the piece of paper Nora had given her from under her pillow and studied it. An address on a street in Las Vegas, with an apartment number. That's where Sheila and Alec had lived. Emily wondered if her sister had talked with other people in the building about herself and Alec. Maybe she had made a friend and confided where they were going. . . .

It wasn't much. But it was a beginning.

18

A FEW DAYS LATER, MARTHA KANE CAME TO VISIT Emily with news. Claudia and Rina and other women in the unit had made statements on Emily's behalf. As a result, Louise Hook was up on charges and Officer Harrison had been severely disciplined. Martha had personally investigated the case and had seen to it that Emily was completely exonerated.

Emily told Martha how grateful she was. "And thank you for calling my mother," she added. "You've been very kind. I'm sorry I was so rude to you that day in your office."

"I'm sorry I didn't have more time to get to know you better," Martha said. "But perhaps we can make up for that, now. Oh, by the way, I took your advice...." She stepped back from the bed and did a model's turn. She was wearing a dark grey pinstripe jacket over a white blouse and dark skirt. "What do you think? Do the pinstripes make a difference?"

"Yes, they do. Of course, it's just an illusion, but that's what good designing is all about—utilizing color, line, and cut to help improve how we look."

Martha came back and sat down on a chair by the bedside. "You'll have to give me more advice on what to wear. I've always had a problem finding clothes that didn't make me look like a bus. And I'm not just saying that to gain your confidence," she added with mock seriousness. "I really mean it!"

Emily couldn't help laughing. "I believe you. And you do have my confidence."

"Good. Now we can really talk." Martha adjusted her glasses and was about to say something when she spotted the box of candy Nora had brought. She gave a groan. "That's the trouble with visiting friends in a hospital— they always have candy around. Either offer me some or hide it!"

"For a psychologist, you have very little self-control," Emily joked, opening the box and handing it to her.

"Don't remind me," Martha mumbled. She popped a chocolate buttercream into her mouth, closed the box, and handed it back to Emily. Then she folded her arms across her wide bosom and smiled happily. "Now that I've had my fix, let's talk about you."

As much as she liked the woman and appreciated what she had done for her, Emily couldn't help begin to feel a little uncomfortable. "What do you want to talk about?" she asked uneasily.

"Well, to begin with, your career. You seem pretty determined to make it as a costume designer."

"Yes, I am. I wish I could show you a portfolio of sketches I was working on. But Lou destroyed them."

"She didn't get all of them. When your room was cleaned, a sketchpad was found under the bed with most of the pages intact. Claudia brought it to me, and I took the liberty of keeping it. I think you're very talented."

Emily's eyes lit up. "That is good news. May I have it back? I'd love to do some work—I get so bored just lying here."

Martha frowned. "I don't have it at the moment; I gave it to someone to look at. But I should get it back soon, maybe even this afternoon. . . ." She glanced down at her watch, then looked back at Emily. "In the meantime, let's go on. Do you think the scar will stand in the way of your career?"

The bluntness of the question took Emily by surprise. "I don't know," she admitted.

"But certainly you've thought about it."

"Of course I have," Emily replied sharply. She touched the bandages on her nose and along the side of her jaw. "I may look even worse when these come off." Her voice broke a little, and she remained silent for a few seconds. Then: "This is hard for me to discuss right now—it's not my favorite subject. Can we talk about it later?"

"No, let's talk about it now. I think you've buried your feelings about being scarred for too long. Apparently the only time you broke down was when you tried to steal the money for plastic surgery."

"And you think that I may do it again?"

"I don't know what you may do again. That's why I want to know how you feel, what you think about yourself."

Emily felt her defenses slipping away under Martha's persistence. The pose of nonchalance she had perfected among the inmates began to crack, giving way to a rush of anger. "What the hell should I think about myself?" she said scornfully. "At the prison, they think I'm a whore marked by her pimp, and they actually respect me for that! In the real world, I had to hide so people wouldn't look at me like some kind of freak!"

"How did you hide?" Martha asked quietly.

"Behind my hair, dark glasses, high-necked clothes— anything to keep people from staring at me with pity or revulsion! The only thing that kept me going was the idea of being a designer for the stage or films. They aren't public figures—most people never see them, just their creations."

"So, you intend to go on hiding behind your work, too? But what about your own life? Your personal life?"

Emily laughed harshly. "What personal life? Until I can afford to get my face fixed, I don't expect to have a personal life!"

"But it takes time to achieve that kind of success and wealth," Martha went on doggedly. "How will you keep from breaking down again, working around beautiful women, designing clothes for them, seeing them all the time?"

"I've learned how to be strong," Emily replied in a hard voice. "I've had some very good teachers."

Martha looked at her thoughtfully. "That's what worries me. I think you've learned how to be tough, but I'm not sure that you've learned how to be strong."

Just then a man's voice said from the doorway, "Martha, forgive me, but I think you may be playing with semantics. Instead of using words like 'tough' or 'strong,' I'd say that Miss Gorden is a very *determined* young woman."

There was a hint of amusement in the rebuke, and Martha smiled as she stood up and turned to him. "Matthew, how long have you been eavesdropping?"

"Long enough to learn that Miss Gorden has a mind of her own, has made a fair assessment of her problem, and seems prepared to deal with it."

Martha threw her hands up in a gesture of defeat. "So much for the work of a trained psychologist," she said, laughing. She went to the man and took his arm. "Come in. I've been waiting for you. Emily, this audacious man is a very dear friend of mine and a wonderful doctor— Matthew Sheridan."

Emily looked at him as they approached the bed. He was a tall, slender man in his middle forties, elegantly dressed in a finely tailored brown suit, white linen shirt, and a silk rust-colored tie. He had thick dark hair greying at the temples, strongly arched eyebrows, and grey eyes that contained the searching gaze of a man who was curious about the world. His features were sharply chiseled; a thin aquiline nose, high cheekbones, and a strong jaw with a small cleft in the chin. Full, sensitive lips turned up a little at the corners, giving the impression that he was thinking about a private joke. Altogether, he exuded an aura of confidence, dignity, and wealth.

"How do you do," Emily said. Then she noticed that he was carrying her sketchpad. "Oh, you're the one Martha gave it to."

"Yes, I hope you don't mind." He handed it to her. "I was very impressed by your work. I think you are very gifted.

His voice was resonant and had the professional, soothing sound of someone used to calming the fears of others. Emily gave him a grateful smile and thanked him. He pulled up a chair alongside Martha's, and the two of them sat down. Martha said, "Dr. Sheridan is something of an artist himself." There was a sound in her voice that suggested she was making a joke.

"Oh? Do you paint, doctor?" Emily asked, faintly puzzled.

"Well, I'm a Sunday painter—you know, bad landscapes and awkward still-lifes." He smiled, setting a fine network of lines around his eyes. "But I do quite a bit of drawing—faces, mostly. You see, I'm a plastic surgeon. It was I who set your nose, and I don't think you have to worry about how it will look—I'm fairly competent at what I do."

"Stop being so modest," Martha admonished him. "You're the best man in the field, and you know it."

Matthew Sheridan made her a small, graceful bow and winked at Emily, as if to say, She's a friend, and exaggerates.

Martha turned to Emily and said, "I called Matthew a few weeks ago, after our interview, but he was out of the country. Fortunately, he got back a few days ago."

A spark of hope leapt in Emily's breast: Was Dr. Sheridan going to help her? Was that why Martha had called him? "Are you on the staff here?" she asked tentatively.

"No, I have my own practice. But the director and I are old friends, and I come in occasionally to lend a hand. When I returned Martha's call, she told me what had happened to you and asked me to help."

"Oh, I see." Emily's voice sank. "Well, thank you for setting my nose—"

"My dear, I didn't come in just to set your nose. Martha told me about your scar, and I wanted to see it."

Martha said to Emily, "For some time, now, I've been trying to get a rehabilitation project started to help women who have been disfigured, like you, in an accident, or who were born with some malformation. Women who, because of how they look, have been rejected by society and, as a consequence of that rejection, turned to crime. Dr. Sheridan agrees with my idea, and that's why he consented to come and see you."

"Does that mean it's possible that you could do something to help me?" Emily asked, trying to contain her excitement.

Dr. Sheridan nodded his head slowly. "It's possible. Aside from the problem of all the legalities, which I leave in Martha's capable hands, I'm not yet sure what *I* can do; I only had a few minutes to examine you before the bandages went on. So don't get too excited. These things take time, and we must get to know each other."

Emily turned to Martha, her eyes shining. "Do you think it can be done? Will they let me have the surgery if Dr. Sheridan can do it? Will I have to go back to the prison, or can I just stay here—?"

Martha held up her hand to interrupt the torrent of questions. "Emily, I don't have any answers for you yet. We'll both have to be patient for a while."

Dr. Sheridan added gravely, "And you must be prepared for the possibility that even my best efforts may not be sufficient to help you." He leaned forward and took Emily's hands in his. "But let's not worry about that just now. You must rest and get strong. If I *can* do the surgery, you're going to need all your strength."

His hands were warm and comforting, and there was something about the way he looked into her eyes that filled her with confidence. She saw that she might have a future as a whole human being because of this man, that her life could have a new beginning, a new meaning.

Matthew Sheridan held her hands a moment longer, and said, "I'll be back to see you in a day or so. Is there anything you need that I can bring you?"

Almost too excited to speak, Emily shook her head and murmured, "No—you've already brought me what I needed most. You've brought me hope."

19

EMILY FINISHED BRUSHING HER HAIR, PUT THE BRUSH down on the ledge of the sink, and studied her face. The bandages had been removed, and the bruises had almost faded completely. Her nose, though still swollen, looked much as it had before. There was a fine red line of a scar along her jaw where the stitches had been taken, and the small scar on her right cheek where Officer Harrison had hit her. *My face has become a living record of my life,* she thought grimly. *I'm beginning to look like a boxer who stayed in the ring too long.*

She returned to her room and went to stand by the windows. She had been in the hospital for almost two weeks and knew that she was well enough to be returned to prison. The thought pressed down on her like a weight, and she began to pace nervously. Martha Kane hadn't been to see her since the first visit over a week before and she hadn't heard from Dr. Sheridan, either. Her hopes for surgery were beginning to fade, and she felt a little angry for allowing herself to believe that they wanted to help her. After all, why should they? She was just another inmate. There was no one she could really depend on except herself.

She sat down in a chair and thought about the one person in whom she had placed her trust. Alec. There was no pain in thinking about him now. If anything, she had purposely begun to relive moments they had shared to give her the strength she needed for the future. Hatred and ambition were the two powerful forces she intended to use to get what she wanted: success, power, and beauty.

She began a daydream in which she found Alec and confronted him with the fact that she had survived so that she could destroy him. Embellishing the fantasy, she imagined the look on his face when he realized who she was, the terror in his eyes when he saw what she was going to do. . . .

Emily didn't hear the knock on the door or see it opened by Matthew Sheridan until he called out, "Good morning. I knocked, but you didn't answer—"

She looked at him blankly. "Oh, Dr. Sheridan. I'm sorry. I was thinking about something and didn't hear you."

For a moment she hadn't even recognized him. The distinguished, well-tailored man she had met was now dressed in tennis shoes, dark blue jeans, a red and white striped sportshirt, and a white cotton windbreaker. He was tanned, and his dark hair was wind-tossed, as if he had just come in from a game of tennis.

Sheridan put several large packages he was carrying down on the bed and said, "Forgive me for not getting back to you sooner. I had to visit a patient in Palm Springs for a few days, and my schedule got a bit tangled."

"I understand," Emily said quietly. Of course he was busy, taking care of wealthy people who could afford his services. Palm Springs—that accounted for the tan. She remained sitting in the chair, determined not to ask any questions about her surgery. She was done with pleading and depending on others.

"Aren't you curious about the packages?" Matthew Sheridan asked. A mischievous gleam sparkled in his eyes.

"Are they for me?"

"Yes. I thought you might like them."

She rose and walked slowly to the bed. Why had he brought her gifts? Was it to ease the disappointment? He had decided not to try and help her, and this was his way of kissing her off. Claudia had once said to her, "You have to be careful of powerful men. They make empty promises

174

to feed their own egos—then they do what's best for them, not for you. That's what makes them powerful...." Dr. Sheridan had probably decided that it wasn't in his best interests to get involved with a convict.

She opened the packages and found sketch pads, a large set of expensive water-colors, brushes, a drawing board, pencils, pastels, poster paints, and colored inks. Emily stared at the array of art materials, then glanced up at Dr. Sheridan. He was looking at her with a half-smile, waiting for an exclamation of surprise and pleasure. When none came, the smile turned to a puzzled frown.

"Don't you like them?" he asked. "Did I get the wrong things?"

"Oh, no. They're wonderful. Thank you," Emily replied politely. "I'll be able to start a new portfolio now. And you've given me so much; there's enough here to last until I come up for parole. You've been very generous, and I'm grateful. All of this will help make the time go so much faster."

He stared at her quizzically. "Make the time go faster...?"

"Yes. Life in prison goes by very slowly," she said with a trace of sarcasm.

"But, my dear girl, you're not going back to prison."

"What? I don't understand. When I didn't hear from Martha or you, I assumed..."

"—that we had decided not to try to help you," he finished for her. He smiled and shook his head. "And you thought I brought you these things to let you down easy. But that's not the case at all. Martha left it to me to tell you, only I got caught up with my patient and couldn't get back to you."

"You mean that I'm staying here, in the hospital? That you're going to do the surgery?" As she said the words, her legs suddenly went weak, and she sank to the bed.

"I mean that I'm going to do the surgery, if I can. But you're not staying here."

Emily stared up at him, bewildered. Dr. Sheridan sat

down beside her and began to explain. "Martha has been very persistent on your behalf, and I called in a few favors from several state officials I know. We've been able to circumvent the normal procedures, and you've been remanded to my custody for examination and possible treatment. In a day or so, Martha will bring you some papers to sign, and then we can make arrangements to move you to my clinic."

Emily was almost too stunned to speak. "Your clinic—?" she asked weakly.

"Yes, I have a private clinic in Laguna Beach. It's fully staffed and equipped and it provides a comfortable place for my patients to stay while they're recuperating from surgery." He gave her a charming smile and added, "It also gives them the opportunity to come back and stun their friends with how they look. Most of the people I've worked on hate to be seen still wearing bandages. I brought you the art materials to keep you busy until you leave and to occupy your time while my staff and I examine you and evaluate what we can do for you."

Emily listened to him, feeling dazed and a little frightened; it was all happening so quickly. She wanted to let down her guard and weep for joy, throw her arms around him, and cry out her gratitude. But she was torn by conflicting emotions and felt a need somehow to protect herself. She tried to collect her thoughts and finally managed to ask, "Why are you doing this for me?"

He put his hand under her chin and tipped her face up to examine it. "That's a good, honest question, and I'll try to answer it honestly," he murmured, studying the scar. "Martha gave me your file, and I have some idea of what your life has been like since the accident when you were a child. But then, there are a lot of people in the world who are maimed or deformed and have lived hard lives. I can't help all of them; I may not even be able to help you. But I've been given the opportunity to try, and I consider it a challenge to my skill."

He withdrew his hand and looked at her soberly. "I

don't think of myself as a benefactor of mankind. I'm good at what I do, and, practically speaking, it's made me very wealthy. But I do think of myself as an artist. And I regard you the same way. So—as one artist to another, I feel you deserve whatever help I can give you."

Emily remained silent for a few seconds, her confidence somewhat restored by his sincerity. Then she asked, "How soon after I come to your clinic will you know if you can do the surgery?"

"A few days. We'll make tests, study the scar, determine the state of your health. This is not just a cosmetic face-lift."

"And if you find you can't help me?"

The question was coldly direct, and Sheridan knew that he had to tell her the truth. He shrugged and replied, "Then you will have had a pleasant vacation and be returned to the prison."

Emily took a deep, shaky breath and let it out slowly. "Thank you for being so honest. I had to know exactly what the possibilities were."

"And now that you do—?"

"I'm prepared for whatever happens."

20

THE ARRANGEMENTS TO MOVE EMILY TO DR. SHERI-
dan's clinic were made with a swiftness that was almost
dizzying. Martha came the next morning with papers for
her to sign and some clothes she had rescued from Emily's
room at the prison. Later that afternoon, Emily was
released from the hospital and found herself being driven
to Laguna Beach in a car that Sheridan had sent up from
the clinic. She sat in the back of the limousine, dazed by
how quickly it had all been accomplished. The advantages
of power, she thought: a magic wand of influence had
been waved, and she was being spirited away like the
heroine of a fairy tale. A heroine who had only the clothes
on her back, and a shoulder bag stuffed with art materials.

The driver, a middle-aged black man in a dark blue
chauffeur's uniform, glanced over his shoulder and said,
"Dr. Sheridan put some things he thought you might need
in that box on the floor, Miss Gorden."

"Thank you," Emily said. She lifted the box onto her
lap and saw an envelope with her name on it taped to the
cover. The paper was a thick, creamy vellum, and
embossed in the upper left-hand corner of it were the
words THE SHERIDAN CLINIC. She opened the envelope
and took out a typewritten note that read:

Dear Emily,
I thought you might prefer to be wearing these when
you arrived at the clinic. I'll be there to greet you,

and if we should meet any of the other patients, I will simply introduce you as Miss Gorden, the daughter of a friend of mine. Under the circumstances, I think appearing incognito will be helpful. I hope you approve.

Until I see you,
Matthew Sheridan

The signature was scrawled in a wide, generous hand with a flourish on the last letter.

Emily opened the box and found a dark red, wide-brimmed hat, a pair of oversized dark glasses, and a lightweight wool cape the same color as the hat. Surprised, and pleased by his thoughtfulness, she shrugged out of her denim jacket and put the cape on over her blouse and skirt. Then she put on the dark glasses and finally the hat, pulling the brim low over her face. She looked at her reflection in the darkly tinted closed window and saw a vague, shadowy image of a young woman she barely recognized.

A few minutes later the car swung off the Santa Ana Freeway and onto Laguna Canyon Road. It wound through a pleasant vista of rolling meadows, and she saw cattle grazing peacefully and a few small farms in the distance. The terrain gradually became more hilly, covered with trees and dark green brush. They passed a number of cottages nestled at the foot of the hills, a pony farm, a lumberyard, and a number of other small businesses. The area had a quiet, rural feeling; the road was shaded by leafy trees and wildflowers splashed a profusion of riotous colors over the landscape.

They entered the town and turned into the busy flow of traffic on Pacific Coast Highway, the main street of Laguna. It was lined with shops, boutiques, art galleries, and restaurants. The sidewalks were thronged with people in sports clothes and swimwear. Long known as an art colony and famed for its French Riviera–like setting, the town had become a popular resort for tourists from all over the country.

Even though Emily had grown up in Los Angeles, only eighty miles to the north, this was the first time she had ever been in Laguna Beach. On the inland side of the highway she saw steep hills dotted with expensive houses that overlooked the picturesque village, long stretches of white beaches, and the vast expanse of the ocean. The coast side was crowded with hotels, colorful arcades, and patio cafés. At each intersection, she peered down sun-dappled lanes and saw the sparkling water and crowds of people, their tanned bodies glistening in the sunlight. Everyone seemed to be bursting with health and good looks. Emily couldn't help thinking of the tired, anxious faces and pale bodies of the women in prison, and she drew back from the window, feeling at once resentful and envious of how casually these people seemed to accept their blessings.

The car turned off the highway and began a steep ascent into the hills, leaving the bustling little town behind. They made their way along sharply curved hillsides, each turn offering another panoramic view of the coastline. Finally they emerged onto a long, flat plateau and a few minutes later swung into a black-topped circular driveway. Lush green lawns lay like an expensive carpet in the center of the drive. On the sides were groves of trees stretching back into woods that surrounded the entire area. At the apex of the circle drive stood the Sheridan Clinic. Emily's eyes widened; it was not at all what she had expected.

"Is that the clinic?" she asked the driver, incredulous.

He smiled and replied, "Yes, Miss Gorden. Beautiful, isn't it?"

Set in a bower of tall trees, the building was a gleaming white two-story Spanish Colonial mansion with low, sloping red-tiled roofs. As the car turned to approach the house, Emily caught a glimpse of a tennis court, and behind it, the large blue rectangle of a swimming pool. Off to the side, almost hidden in the shade of trees, were several cottages built in the same architectural style as the main house. A crew of gardeners were out on the grounds, going about the task of clipping and shaping hedges and weeding large beds of flowers.

The car drew up alongside the broad steps that led to the front entrance, and the driver got out to open the door for Emily. She looked up at the house, drew the cape around her somewhat apprehensively, and clutched the shoulder bag under her arm. As she started up the steps, the front doors opened and Matthew Sheridan appeared.

"Hello!" he called out, coming toward her. "Did you have a nice drive?"

"Yes, I did."

He took the shoulder bag from her and they walked up the steps. "You look very chic," he said with a smile.

"Thanks to you." She touched the brim of her hat self-consciously. "It was very thoughtful of you to send these along. I wasn't exactly dressed for a place like this. I thought it was going to look like a small hospital, not an estate."

Dr. Sheridan chuckled. "Everyone has the same reaction the first time they arrive. This used to be the home of a very old and titled family, one of the first Spanish settlers in California. I bought the place a few years ago and had it restored as close to the original as possible, allowing, of course, for the needs of my work. Later I'll give you a tour—it's really quite beautiful."

He led her into the foyer. It was a huge affair, with a floor of deep red, highly polished tiles, white textured stucco walls, and a high, timbered ceiling. Large arched windows looked out over the grounds, and an enormous glass and wrought-iron chandelier hung suspended from the dark beams. Capacious easy chairs, walnut and mahogany tables, hammered brass lamps, and thick, soft area rugs made up the furnishings. A wide, curving staircase with an intricately designed wrought-iron railing led to the second floor. Through several broad archways, Emily could see a number of other rooms, each beautifully furnished to go with the style of the house.

"You look a little pale," Dr. Sheridan said to Emily. "Are you nervous?"

"I'm terrified! I feel so out of place and—"

A man came out of one of the rooms and crossed the foyer to the front door. He was dressed in close-fitting jeans and a tee shirt that strained across his broad chest and shoulders. A bandage was wound under his chin and around his head, leaving a thatch of reddish blond hair to fall over his forehead. He waved cheerily to Dr. Sheridan, nodded to Emily, and went out the front doors.

Emily gasped. "Was that who I think it was?"

"Yes—Dirk Rodgers. Did you see his last film?"

"No, we didn't get it at the prison."

Matthew turned to face her directly. "Why don't we forget about the prison for the next few days? No one here knows anything about you except me and my assistant, Mrs. Travers. And she is a veritable Sphinx when it comes to secrets. Give yourself a chance to relax and enjoy yourself—at least, as much as you can while we're doing the tests and examinations. We have only a few patients right now, and they all respect one another's privacy, so I don't think you'll encounter any problems."

Emily nodded in agreement, but she couldn't quiet her feelings of uneasiness and doubt.

Matthew glanced at his watch. "I'd take you to your room myself, but I have a staff meeting in a few minutes, and Mrs. Travers said she'd—"

At that moment a woman came into the foyer and approached them, a smile of welcome on her face. Her matronly figure was disguised by a well-designed beige knit suit. Short blond hair framed a round, pleasant face, and her hazel eyes twinkled with warmth and good humor.

"Sorry I'm late, Matthew—I was going over the dinner menus. This must be Miss Gorden." She extended her hand and Emily took it. "I'm so glad you're going to be with us. I hope you enjoy your stay." She looked at Dr. Sheridan. "You'd better hurry; you're already fifteen minutes late for the staff meeting."

Matthew made a wry face. "Yes, Mother." To Emily, he said, "Travers is the real boss of this place. If we don't do as we're told, we get no supper."

"Oh, stop being charming and go act like a doctor," Mrs. Travers said with mock severity. "I'll see to it that Miss Gorden is settled in and made comfortable."

Before he could answer, she turned Emily toward the staircase and marched her away. "I'll come to see you later, Emily," he called out. Then he hurried off toward the back of the house.

Emily followed Mrs. Travers up the stairs. At the second-floor landing, they turned down a wide carpeted hallway. The woman said, "I put you in a very nice room with a lovely view of the ocean." She stopped at a door at the end of the hall and opened it. "Here we are. I hope you like it."

The room was large and filled with sunlight. A deep, sand-colored carpet stretched from wall to wall, and paintings of landscapes in gilt frames hung on the walls. A king-sized bed was covered with a down comforter, and the rest of the furniture—easy chairs, desk, tables, and lamps—were all fine pieces that blended perfectly with the decor.

"The bathroom is through that door," Mrs. Travers said. "And there's a television hidden away in the armoire." She opened a pair of French doors and stepped out onto a small balcony. "Come take a look at the view—it's really quite wonderful." When there was no response, she looked back into the room. Emily was standing still with an expression of bewilderment on her face.

"Is something wrong?" Mrs. Travers asked, coming back into the room. "Are you feeling ill?"

Emily shook her head, but when she spoke, her voice shook. "I wasn't prepared for all this. It's—it's a little overwhelming...."

"Oh, my dear, of course it is." Mrs. Travers took Emily's hand and patted it. "Don't be frightened," she said gently. "I know what you're going through; Matthew told me a little about you. But I'm the only one who knows, so don't worry about that. As for this very grand and somewhat ostentatious place—" She drew back and gave Emily a sly grin. "Relax and enjoy it as much as possible. It would cost a fortune if you had to pay for it."

Emily managed a little smile. "I can imagine. But I still don't understand why Dr. Sheridan is doing all of this for me."

"Why don't you get comfortable while I have some coffee sent up? Then perhaps I can explain it to you."

Mrs. Travers went to phone the kitchen, and Emily slipped off the cape, and dark glasses. She took her purse from the shoulder bag and went into the bathroom. It was large and gleamingly tiled, with a deep old-fashioned, clawfoot tub and a separate shower. Emily splashed cold water on her face, ran a brush through her hair, and returned to the bedroom. Mrs. Travers was waiting for her on the balcony, where there was a small white wrought-iron table and two chairs. She joined her, and the two women gazed out at the splendid view of the long, curving coastline.

"Isn't it spectacular?" Mrs. Travers asked. "I can never get enough of it."

Emily nodded, smiling wryly. "I used to imagine having a room like this with a balcony overlooking a view. But I never expected to get it under these circumstances."

There was a knock on the door, and a young man came in carrying a tray of coffee and pastries. Mrs. Travers introduced him as Steven, one of the staff attendants. He was young and blond and reminded Emily of the boys she had seen on the beach while driving up to the clinic. Instinctively, she turned her face away from him until he had put the tray down on the table and left. Then she sat down across from Mrs. Travers and said, "You were going to tell me about Dr. Sheridan."

The woman poured the coffee, handed Emily a cup, and sat back. "Matt Sheridan is one of the last great gentlemen in the world. He's also a bit of a romantic about his work, which is something you can't say for too many doctors. And he loves a challenge. Sometimes he reminds me of those kids who go surfing every day, looking for a bigger wave to conquer." She smiled, and an expression of pride and respect glowed in her eyes as she went on: "Oh, he's practical enough when it comes to business. But facelifts, nose jobs, and chin-tucks don't really satisfy his more—what shall we call them—creative urges? And so he tries to help people like you."

She paused and glanced briefly at Emily's scar, then continued. "You're not the only one he's done this for. The man has given freely of his time and talent all over the country. We have great respect for him here at the clinic. And needless to say, his patients adore him."

"I can understand why. He's one of the kindest men I've ever met. Is he married?" Emily asked.

Mrs. Travers frowned and looked away, her eyes gazing vaguely into space. "He was married, but she died several years ago. Her name was Lisa, and he adored her. I never got to meet her—it happened before I came to work for him. But I know how difficult it's been for him without her. That's one of the reasons he's so dedicated to his work. Loneliness can weaken the spirit or destroy the soul. Or it can produce a remarkable man like Matt Sheridan. He's channeled his loneliness into a kind of quest, an intensely personal effort to use his skill to help others, to create beauty where it didn't exist."

Mrs. Travers paused, and then, sensing the question that was uppermost in Emily's mind, she added, "If there is anything that can be done to help you, rest assured that Matt Sheridan is the man who can do it."

"Thank you," Emily said with a grateful smile. "That's really what I wanted to hear."

Mrs. Travers finished her coffee and stood up. "I must

leave now—I have a thousand things to do before dinner. We serve at seven in the main dining room, but if you prefer, we can send it up."

"Perhaps that would be better—I'm afraid I'm wearing all the clothes that I own. . . ."

"Oh, I forgot to tell you. Martha Kane explained what happened to your clothes and we picked up a few things for you in town. She gave us your sizes from your file; I do hope everything fits. But even so, this being your first night here, we can send dinner up if you wish. Just call me on the house phone and let me know."

Emily walked with her to the door. "Thank you for taking the time to talk with me, Mrs. Travers. It helped more that I can say."

"I'm very glad, my dear. Now get some rest, and perhaps I'll see you later this evening." With a cheery wave, she left, closing the door behind her.

Emily turned and slowly looked around the large, quiet room. She was alone; for the first time in over a year, she had real privacy. The realization left her feeling a little bewildered. But she was only a guest, she reminded herself, the privacy and luxury just temporary.

She went to the closet and pushed back the sliding doors. There were skirts and blouses, a pair of slacks, a dark blue dress, and a long, wine-colored robe. In the bureau she found a few sweaters, some underwear, and nightgowns, all neatly wrapped in tissue. All the clothes were beautiful and expensive. Were they temporary, too? Or could she take them with her when she went back to prison? She tried not to think about that. Dr. Sheridan had told her to relax and enjoy herself, and that's exactly what she intended to do.

Emily spent the remainder of the afternoon enjoying her newfound solitude. She took a long, hot bath, and then a nap in the wide, comfortable bed. When she awoke, it was almost six-thirty. She decided to remain in her room, and called Mrs. Travers and asked for her dinner to be sent up. Then she went to the closet, took out the robe, and put it on, delighting in the feel of the soft velour against her skin. In the bathroom, she brushed her hair vigorously until it gleamed, and let it fall across her face, just as she had worn it before going into prison. Her reflection in the mirror surprised her: she looked less innocent and vulnerable than she had remembered. There was a new expression of maturity in her face, a kind of aloof, guarded look she had seen on the faces of the women in the prison. And the robe made a difference, too—its soft folds clung to her body, giving her a sleek, sensuous appearance. She wondered who had picked it out: Mrs. Travers? Or Dr. Sheridan?

A few minutes later dinner was brought in on a serving cart by another attendant, a young woman this time, who said her name was Terry. A bright, vivacious girl, about nineteen, Terry had short dark curly hair, sparkling brown eyes, and was given to gossiping about the famous people in the house. As she set the plates out on the balcony table, she told Emily that besides Dirk Rodgers, the other guests included a famous actress of the screen and stage, a state senator, a well-known TV journalist, and the author of several best-selling romance novels—a woman who had claimed in all her interviews that she owed her youthful appearance to health foods and clean living.

"I guess they all do that," Terry said. "Lie about why they look so good, I mean. Especially people in show business; they have to maintain their image. Except that it's usually Dr. Sheridan who does the maintaining. You'd be amazed at some of the stars he's done."

"You sound like a real fan of his," Emily said, amused by the girl's breathless delivery.

"Oh, I am," she sighed. "I think he's wonderful, and so attractive. I guess I have a thing for older men. Don't you think he's good-looking?"

"I hadn't really thought about it," Emily replied. "But yes—he is handsome, very distinguished-looking."

"Yeah, that's the word—distinguished," Terry said with a dreamy smile. Then she lowered her voice to a confidential tone. "I'm not really supposed to talk about the other people here, so don't let on I told you, okay?"

"I'll keep quiet. I promise," Emily said.

"Great. Listen, when you've finished your dinner, just put the plates back on the cart and leave it outside your door—I'll come get it later." She paused and gave Emily's face a swift, searching look, then said, "And don't worry—by the time Dr. Sheridan is finished with you, you'll look terrific."

Emily was touched by the girl's sympathy. "Thanks, Terry—I must admit, I'm a little frightened about the whole thing."

"I know. Everybody is the first time."

After Terry left, Emily sat down to her dinner: a small Caesar salad, beef Bourguignon simmering in a light wine sauce, small new potatoes, homemade hot rolls, and for dessert, chocolate mousse in a tall, delicate parfait glass, and coffee. Emily couldn't remember ever having had such a delicious meal. This isn't a clinic, she thought; it's a four-star hotel! She poured a second cup of coffee from a finely crafted sterling silver pot, lit a cigarette, and reveled in a luxury she had seen only in the movies. The night sky was alive with stars, and in the distance twinkling lights threaded along the coastline and wound throughout Laguna like a tangled strand of jewels. The sound of the surf beating against the shore floated on the air, and somewhere nearby night-blooming jasmine added a sweet perfume to the tranquillity of the evening.

Lulled by comfort and a sense of well-being, Emily felt a renewed faith in what Dr. Sheridan could do for her. Everyone—Martha Kane, Mrs. Travers, even Terry—seemed so positive that he could help her. She began to think about what might happen in the next few days, when the sound of footsteps and the vague murmur of voices caught her attention. She peered over the balcony railing and made out the figures of a man and a woman walking on the path just below her room. They were illuminated by some light spilling from one of the ground-floor windows, and Emily saw that the woman was crying, a hand pressed to her face. The man had one arm around her shoulders, supporting her. When he spoke, she realized it was Matthew Sheridan.

"I've done everything I can," he was saying in an apologetic tone. "But I warned you about the dangers of repeated surgery at your age. You'll just have to learn to accept the effects of age."

The woman pulled away from him in anger, and for a few seconds Emily could see her face. It was Melinda Edwards, whose sultry beauty had endured on the screen for the last thirty years. Emily had seen many of her films. In the forties, the actress had played sex kitten opposite some of Hollywood's most famous leading men. She had matured into a fine dramatic actress, and Emily had read about her sensational performance a year before in a Broadway musical comedy.

"You're supposed to be the best!" Melinda Edwards cried out in her famous husky voice. "And now you say you can't do any more for me!"

Sheridan's reply was tinged with weariness, as if he'd been through this argument many times before. "Melinda, I'd be doing you a terrible disservice if I said otherwise. I'm just a surgeon, not a miracle worker. I can hold time back, but I can't stop it."

The actress said fiercely, "I'll go to that man in Rio—he'll be able to help me!"

"I don't think so, my dear," Sheridan said quietly. "But of course you're free to do as you wish."

Their voices faded as they drew further away. Emily sat back, feeling a cold chill sweep over her. She had always been a fan of Melinda Edwards and through the years had watched the actress grow more striking and vibrant with age. It came as something of a shock to learn that she was so fearful of growing old.

But even more upsetting was what Dr. Sheridan had said. "I'm just a surgeon, not a miracle worker. . . ."

The night no longer seemed as peaceful and reassuring as before. She went into her room, closed the French doors, and drew the drapes, muffling the sounds of the waves beating against the coast. An abrupt silence engulfed her, and she suddenly felt very alone and afraid. She walked slowly into the bathroom, turned on the lights, and stood before the mirror, staring at the scar for a long time.

21

EMILY WAS AWAKENED BY A PHONE CALL FROM MATthew Sheridan asking her to have breakfast with him. She scrambled out of bed and went to shower, trying to shake off the fears that still lingered from the night before. Before coming to the clinic she had told herself that she was prepared for whatever might happen. But now she wasn't so sure. The dream she had cherished for so long suddenly seemed like a tantalizing reality that was just out of reach, like the stroke of good fortune that seemed to elude some people all of their lives.

Finished with her shower, Emily went to dress. She put on a white, fitted blouse with a small crisp ruffle at the neck, and a pair of slim, dark-blue slacks. At the bottom of the closet, she found a pair of white sandals and slipped them on. She glanced in the mirror, and once again the image she saw there surprised her. What had happened to the girl who, for the last year or so, had seen herself only in the drab clothes of a convict? And how soon would she see that girl again? Emily put the thought out of her mind, grabbed up the pair of dark glasses, and left the room.

She hurried down the hallway to the stairs and went down to the foyer. Mrs. Travers came out of a corridor and saw her. "Good morning, Emily," she called gaily. "Dr. Sheridan is waiting for you on the south patio. Go out the front door, turn left, and follow the path. You can't miss it."

"Thanks, Mrs. Travers. Will I see you later?"

"Oh, yes, I'm making up a schedule of examinations for you, so I'll see you this afternoon."

It's beginning, Emily thought a little anxiously. She took a deep breath and went outside, where she paused for a moment, dazzled by the beauty of the day. Sunshine washed over the landscape with a warm, stunning intensity, and the sea shimmered in the distance, stretching to touch a never-ending sky. Emily drank the view in greedily, wondering what it would be like to wake each morning to such splendor. She smiled to herself, thinking: That's the difference between being rich and being poor—the rich can afford a great view.

She took the path to the left and followed it around the house to a large flagstone patio that was enclosed by low hedges and shaded by a grove of trees. Matthew Sheridan was sitting at a round, glass-topped table waiting for her. He was dressed in a white pullover sweater, beige linen slacks and loafers, and looked very casual and relaxed. He reminded her of the famous men she had seen profiled in magazines, men who were confident and at ease on the grounds of their estate, usually with a beautiful woman by their side.

Sheridan smiled and stood up as she approached. "Good morning. Isn't it a glorious day?" He held a chair for her, and she sat down. "Did you sleep well?" he asked, taking the seat opposite her.

"Yes, I did, thank you," Emily replied.

He poured each of them a cup of coffee from a pot sitting on the table, and glanced over at her approvingly. "You look very nice this morning."

"Thank you." Emily fingered the ruffle on her blouse nervously, a little flustered by the compliment. "All the clothes you got for me are beautiful...." She hesitated, than asked bluntly, "Did you pick them out?"

He looked a little surprised by the question, then smiled and said, "Yes, I did. How did you know?"

"I didn't—I just guessed," Emily murmured. "Do you always play fairy godfather for your less fortunate patients?" The question was asked more sharply than she had intended, and she was dismayed to see the smile fade from his lips.

"No, not always," he answered in an even tone of voice. "But Martha told me what happened to your clothes, and I thought you might like some new ones. Besides, I haven't shopped for a woman in some time, and I rather enjoyed it."

Emily's face colored with embarrassment. She said quickly, "I'm sorry. I didn't mean to sound ungrateful. It's just that I still can't believe this is happening to me."

"I know how difficult this must be for you," he said gently. "But please, enjoy it as much as you can. Now, are you hungry? There's a lot of breakfast here."

A serving cart of covered silver chafing dishes on candle-warmers stood by the table. He took Emily's plate, uncovered the dishes and served her slices of French toast, lightly scrambled eggs, and tiny sausages. She began to eat, trying not to betray her uneasiness with him. She found the man intimidating and at the same time felt an inexplicable need to win his approval, like a child wanting to impress a respected teacher.

"Do you live here all the time?" she asked.

"No, I have a house in Bel Air and an office in Beverly Hills. But I keep an apartment here as a kind of retreat—especially when there are no patients about. And this is where I do my Sunday painting. I even have a small studio you might enjoy seeing."

"Will you show me some of your work?"

"Only if you promise not to criticize," he replied, laughing. "I have a very fragile ego where my painting is concerned."

He began to talk about an art exhibit he had seen in New York a few months before. Emily's interest was sparked by his enthusiasm for the subject, and soon they were discussing artists whose work they both admired. At one point Emily held forth on how famous paintings had influenced comtemporary fashions and had provided the basis of costume designs for many films. Sheridan listened quietly, his eyes fixed on her face, moving only to refill her cup with coffee or light her cigarettes.

Suddenly aware that she had been talking steadily, Emily stopped, flushing with embarrassment. "I've been rattling on like a teacher giving a lecture—I'm sorry."

"Don't be. This is the most delightful conversation I've had in some time."

"Dr. Sheridan, your professional charm is showing; you're just being polite. Why, you must know some of the most famous and talented people in the world."

"I do. And let me tell you that they usually spend most of their time talking about themselves." They both laughed, and he went on. "It's astonishing how many famous people are boring. They've seen too much and done too much to be excited or curious about anything except the very small space they occupy on earth." He leaned forward and took her hand, his tone suddenly serious. "But you still have that curiosity and excitement. Please, don't ever lose it. It's very rare."

Emily was a little taken aback by the intensity of his voice. It was as if for a moment he had revealed some deeper, more compelling concern for her, something that had more meaning for him than simply a doctor-patient relationship. She withdrew her hand slowly and stammered, "No—I'll try not to."

After breakfast, Sheridan took her on a tour of the estate. He explained that the small cottages were quarters for the household staff and private apartments for his assistants. Then he showed her an old carriage house that he had converted into a residence for himself. It was spacious, with rough-hewn wood walls, a high, timbered ceiling, and a large, stone fireplace. A living room, kitchen, bedroom, and bath made up the ground floor, and a staircase led to a large loft he used as his studio. When he shyly showed her his paintings, Emily exclaimed over them. The graceful landscapes and still-lifes were done in fluent strokes of pastel colors and seemed to her a reflection of Sheridan himself—quiet and controlled, yet lyrically romantic.

They left the carriage house and started for the clinic. As they strolled past the swimming pool, Emily saw Dirk Rodgers stretched out on a chaise lounge shaded by an umbrella. A curvaceous blonde was lying next to him, her sleek body barely covered by a red bikini. Rodgers had his arm around her, and she was trailing her fingertips lightly over his massive chest.

"Dirk always brings a friend to keep him company when he comes here," Sheridan said humorously.

"Always? Has he been here before?" Emily asked.

"Oh, many times."

"But I thought he was so young. How old is he?"

"My lips are sealed," Sheridan replied solemnly, steering her into an arcade that led to the clinic. Once inside, he showed her the examining rooms, the small but completely equipped operating room, and a cheerfully decorated recovery room. Then he took her through a large dining room, a social room complete with comfortable chairs and couches and game tables. "Bridge is a favorite pastime here," Sheridan told her. "But the stakes rival those at the Las Vegas casinos."

Emily's favorite room was the library. It had floor-to-ceiling bookcases, a cozy arrangement of chairs around a brick fireplace, and French doors that led to a terrace and the gardens. While she was looking at the books, Mrs. Travers walked in, slightly out of breath. "Oh, here you are. I've been looking everywhere for you. Matt, you're wanted in your office, and Emily, you have your first examination in fifteen minutes."

"I told you she was the boss of the place," Sheridan said to Emily. He saw the look of concern on her face and patted her hand. "Don't worry. One of my assistants is just going to give you a physical. Part of my procedure is to do a complete medical workup."

"What happens after that?"

"I'll examine the scar, determine the stress ability of your skin, and take some photographs." He smiled reassuringly. "That's when I get to do the drawings I told you about—the faces I like to draw."

"You'll make sketches of my face? May I see them?"

Dr. Sheridan laughed and shook his head. "No—and not because I want to hide them from you. They're doodles really, like a painter's thumbnail sketches. They wouldn't have any meaning for you."

He took her arm, and they followed Mrs. Travers out to the hallway. "I'll see you in a few hours," he said. "In the meantime, you'll be in very good hands."

"How soon will you know if you can do the surgery?" Emily asked in a tremulous voice.

He hesitated for a few seconds. Emily's eyes pleaded for an answer, and he finally replied, "This evening. I'll tell you tonight. I promise."

Emily spent the rest of the afternoon undergoing a complete physical examination. When it was finished, Dr. Sheridan came into the examining room and studied her scar under a high-intensity magnifying lamp. He touched her face very gently, peering at the ridges of scar tissue tugging at the corner of her left eye and the side of her mouth. His fingertips were warm as they traced over the scar, and he was so close she could smell the light scent of his cologne. Her eyes wandered from the deep brow down the sharp line of his nose to his full, sensitively shaped lips, the square jaw, and the small cleft in his chin. Terry was right, she thought; he is attractive. His eyes suddenly connected with hers and he held her gaze for a few seconds with a grave, sober expression. Then he smiled and stepped away, made some notes on his clipboard, and said, "Now you're going to have some pictures taken. In a few hours, after I've had a chance to go over all the reports, I'll see you in my office."

Dr. Sheridan left her alone and then a nurse came in carrying a camera with a flash attachment. She drew the blinds, directed Emily to push her hair back off her face and sit very still. As the flashes went off, Emily couldn't help thinking of the mug shots that were taken of her when she was arrested.

Mrs. Travers came by and suggested that she rest until Dr. Sheridan wanted to see her. Emily went to her room and tried to nap, but sleep was impossible. She took out some of the art materials Sheridan had given her and began to sketch, losing herself for a few hours in creating designs.

At five o'clock, he called her on the house phone; he would see her now. A few minutes later she was ushered into his waiting room and told that he would be with her directly. Too excited to sit down, Emily paced nervously, examining the room. It was simply furnished with a few pieces that she recognized as fine English antiques. The walls were paneled in rosewood, and one featured a large watercolor by Turner. Another wall drew her attention; it contained two framed certificates, testifying that Dr. Sheridan was a member of the American Society of Plastic and Reconstructive Surgery and certified by the American Board of Plastic Surgery. Under these was an arrangement of photographs of Sheridan with some of his famous patients, international celebrities whose faces she recognized at once.

She was studying the pictures when Dr. Sheridan came out of his office. "How do you like my rogues gallery?" he asked, grinning at her. "I put those up to reassure my new patients. You can't imagine the shocked expressions when they see how many of their friends have been here. I've had to swear a blood oath that those pictures would never be made public. Someday, however, I will write my memoirs and name names!"

She had to smile at the mischievous twinkle in his eyes.

"Perhaps one day I'll be part of your gallery," she said lightly, trying to disguise her anxiety.

They went into his office and Emily took a chair by the desk. He sat down across from her and smiled broadly. "There's no perhaps about it."

Emily felt herself go pale. "You mean you're going to—?"

"Yes."

She closed her eyes, her body suddenly trembling uncontrollably.

"Are you all right?" Sheridan asked, leaning forward anxiously. "Shall I get you some brandy?"

Emily shook her head. When she opened her eyes they were filled with tears. "You're really going to do it?" she whispered.

"Tomorrow morning. You're a very healthy young woman, despite everything you've been through recently. I've examined all the reports, and the surgery should go very smoothly. You have what we call a hypertrophic scar, and it can be excised. If you're concerned about the details of the operation, I can tell you exactly what we're going to do."

"No—not right now," she replied, barely able to speak. She stared at him, dazed. "I can't believe it's actually going to happen, what I've dreamed of for so many years. . . ." She lowered her head and began to cry quietly.

Sheridan came around the desk and pulled her into his arms. She buried her face in his shoulder and all the fear and tension that had mounted during the past months poured out in wrenching sobs. He held her tenderly until she became quiet. Suddenly aware of his arms around her, she pulled away self-consciously, smiling up at him through her tears. Then a feeling of exhilaration came over her and she began to laugh, wiping her face with the back of her hand.

"Here, let me," Sheridan said softly. He took a handkerchief from his jacket and wiped away her tears. "Shall we celebrate?" he asked. "Would you like to have dinner with me?"

"No—yes—I mean, thank you, but..."

He laughed and gave her a quick hug. Then he put his arm around her shoulders and began to walk with her out of the office. "I understand, Emily. You'd rather be alone this evening. Many of my patients have responded the same way. In a manner of speaking, it's like saying a final farewell to who you've been."

"Yes, that's it exactly," Emily said.

But she was thinking of something else. And it wasn't a farewell to her past.

It was almost midnight, and Emily was still awake. She had written to Rina and Claudia and had just finished a letter to Nora, who was now in Toronto. A few days before leaving the hospital, she had received a long letter from her mother, filled with news of the wedding, her new home with Sam Jeffries, and how exciting it was to live in Canada. But there had been no mention of Sheila. Or Alec.

Emily lit a cigarette and walked out to the balcony. A full moon floated in the black sky, casting a silvery glow over the ocean, and the only noise that broke the stillness of the night was the rhythmic pounding of the surf. She felt as if she were suspended in a frozen moment of time that allowed her thoughts to swing freely between the past and the future.

Memories stirred within her, recollections of the countless ways in which her life had been shaped by the scar. Her relationship with her mother and sister had pivoted on a delicate balance between resentment and pity. The job she had chosen had been a means of escape from the world, of shielding herself from people's reactions to her face.

And Alec. It was painfully clear, now, that the scar had attracted his perverse attention, that their love affair had been based on his belief that her disfigurement would allow him to control her. And he *had* controlled her—at a terrible price: the death of a gentle old man, and the hellish months she had spent in prison. Rage coursed through her like an icy stream, and she shuddered, her eyes stinging with tears of regret and guilt. She walked unsteadily to the bathroom and washed her face, then stared at herself in the mirror. A cold resolve took the place of anger; fate had suddenly offered her a chance for a new life, and she was determined to use it to accomplish what she wanted. She brushed her fingers over the length of the scar, and it was as if she were following a familiar path, a well-marked trail connecting the past to the present. After tomorrow, she knew that she would not travel that path again.

But she also knew that she would not bury the past, not completely. Not until she had found Alec.

Matthew Sheridan stood on the shadowy terrace of his own apartment and stared up at Emily, watching until she left the balcony and disappeared into her room. He waited for a few minutes, hoping that she might return. When she didn't, he went back into his living room and poured himself a glass of Dom Perignon. Sipping it slowly, he walked over to a long, ornately carved Spanish table that he used as a desk and stared down at a blow-up print of Emily's photograph. Beside it lay sheets of tracing paper and some pencils.

He sat down, lit a cigarette, and continued to examine the picture thoughtfully. Then he opened the center drawer of the table and took out a photograph of a woman and put it down next to the picture of Emily. The woman had long dark hair and wide, beautiful blue eyes. She was wearing a white blouse with a ruffle at the throat.

For a long time he gazed at the two pictures lying side by side. His face was expressionless, reflecting none of the conflicts that troubled him. An hour passed as he continued to go over in his mind the possible ramifications of what he was thinking. Finally, he made his decision. He slipped a piece of tracing paper over the photograph of Emily and picked up a pencil. Then, glancing every once in a while at the photograph of the woman, he began to draw the outline of Emily's face.

22

"EMILY, ARE YOU AWAKE?"

The voice seemed to come from a great distance. She didn't respond, and soon it was lost in the hollow murmuring of other voices. She was moving slowly toward a shimmering glow that suddenly blazed up into a great light revealing a sumptuous ballroom. There were marble floors and gigantic crystal chandeliers and hundreds of people dancing. They were all clothed in elaborate period costumes, men in dark suits with braid and sashes, and women in gowns of silk, crinoline, velvet, and lace, emblazoned with rubies, pearls, and diamonds. Emily realized she was one of them, dressed in an exquisite gown of crushed velvet and silk. Her partner was a tall, shadowy figure who gently guided her through the intricacies of the dance. But there was no music, only the echoing whispers of the guests.

The dancers circled the floor in lazy arcs. Emily kept turning her head to look at them, gasping at the beauty of the gowns. She glanced up and saw that the walls were lined with mirrors, reflecting the dancers in endless multitudes. Then she saw herself, her gorgeous gown, her hair a mass of curls entwined with tiny flowers and jewels.

But she had no face, only a blank, featureless space where her face should have been!

As the dance grew more animated, she was whirled through the surging mass of movement. She struggled to see herself once more and caught another glimpse. But this time it was Nora's face who looked back at her, with an expression of helpless incomprehension. Emily was turned again and again, and each time she saw someone else. There was Sheila, her eyes fierce with resentment; Mrs. Skolsky, stoic in the depths of her sorrow; Harriet Bradshaw, her horsey mouth opened wide with laughter. And then she saw Alec. His lips were twisted into a sadistic grin that widened and grew into an evil yet seductive smile.

The hollow murmuring became louder, the dance more frantic. Emily was afraid and wanted to escape. She fought against her partner's grasp, but he refused to let her go. She began to beat her fists against his chest, pleading with him. He only drew her closer, whispering that as long as she was in his arms, she was safe. She looked at him and saw that it was Matthew Sheridan smiling down at her, reassuring her that she was safe, she was safe, she was safe....

"Emily, are you awake?"

She opened her eyes, and Dr. Sheridan's face swam into focus. He smiled and took her hand. The warmth of his fingers coursed through her, dispelling the last vestiges of the dance. The murmuring voices faded, and she saw that she was in the recovery room.

"How do you feel?" Sheridan asked.

Emily's throat was dry, her lips parched. She swallowed hard and answered in a croaking whisper, "Thirsty."

He poured some water into a glass, put a flexible straw in it, and held it to her lips. When she was finished, he put the glass down and said, "You'll feel much better soon, and we'll take you back to your room."

She touched the bandages covering her face. "Am I all right?"

"You're fine. We'll keep you on liquids for a day or so, and you may have some pain, but it should be minimal. We'll give you some codeine if you get too uncomfortable."

A nurse came into the room, and he stood up to leave. Emily reached out and took his hand again. "I had a dream," she said groggily. "And you were in it—"

"Was it a nice dream?" he asked softly.

"Yes, at first. Then I became frightened—but you were there, telling me I'd be safe...."

His fingers tightened on hers and he looked at her with an expression of deep tenderness. "And you are safe, my dear," he whispered.

"Will I see you later, when I wake up?" she asked, clinging to his hand.

He nodded his head, his eyes never leaving hers. "Yes."

Under Matthew Sheridan's care, Emily's recovery from surgery progressed in a succession of dreamlike days. Fresh bouquets of flowers were brought to her room every morning, Mrs. Travers and Terry were in constant attendance, taking care of her every need, and Dr. Sheridan stopped by several times a day and visited with her in the evenings.

Five days after the operation the sutures were removed, and Dr. Sheridan applied some bits of adhesive to compress the wound area. While he was doing this, Emily asked tensely, "Can I see my face?"

"I'd rather you didn't just yet," he replied.

A spark of fear leapt in her breast. "Is something wrong? Isn't it healing properly?"

"It's healing beautifully," he reassured her. "It's just that I'm a bit vain where my work is concerned—like an artist who doesn't want anyone to see his painting until it's completely finished." He lifted a dressing stretched across the base of her nose, examined the area for a moment, then put on a new bandage.

"Why is there a bandage on my nose?"

"There was some bruising on the nostrils and the tip as a result of the break in the bone. I just made a few revisions."

Before she could question him further, a nurse came

in with some reports for him to read. He finished applying new bandages and sent her off, promising to see her that evening.

The next few days passed more slowly for Emily. Aware of the strain she was under, Dr. Sheridan did everything he could to distract her. They spent the afternoons together in the library, poring over art books, and in the evenings, they played games of gin rummy or watched old films on television. They discovered a mutual love of books they had read as children, and when she was tired, he would sit by her bed and read aloud from *The Wind in the Willows* or poetry by Emily Dickinson.

On the night before the bandages were to be removed, he glanced up from the book he was reading to her and saw that she had closed her eyes. "Are you tired?" he asked softly. "Shall I leave?"

"No, not yet," she murmured. "I was just resting my eyes. I like hearing you read to me. It's very comforting. I feel like I did when I was a child getting over an illness, all tucked up in bed, with my father reading to me."

"Do I remind you of your father?" he asked.

There was an edge of sadness in his voice that made her open her eyes and look at him. He was leaning forward, peering at her intently, his thick, dark eyebrows drawn together in a frown.

"No, not at all," she replied. "I meant that you made me feel safe and protected. It's been a long time since I've felt so—so cared for."

He smiled and sat back, obviously relieved by her answer. "Good. I'm glad you feel that way; it's what I'd hoped for."

Emily stared at him curiously. "Why?" she asked quietly. "Why have you shown so much concern for me? You know how grateful I am for everything you've done, the care you've lavished on me since I came here. But I can't help feeling..."

"—a little suspicious?" he finished for her.

"Yes, I suppose that's it," she admitted, "I guess it's the result of being in prison—it can give you a very distorted picture of the world. Convicts believe that if somebody does something for you, it's because they expect something in return."

"But you're not a criminal, my dear. I knew that the first day I met you. I heard what you said to Martha Kane about your ambitions, your goals, and how you were prepared to deal with your life. I have great respect for that kind of strength. And I must admit that I felt sorry for you. I understood what drove you to attempt the burglary, the terrible need you felt to be like other people. I wanted to do what I could to help." His voice grew soft and reflective, as if he were thinking about something out of his past. "There have been times in my life when someone has pulled me back from the edge of the abyss. I simply wanted to return the favor."

For a few moments she was overcome with shame; like everyone else, he believed the lie she had told about the burglary, a lie she would never be able to confess. She tried to put the thought aside, and said, "Dr. Sheridan, how can I ever thank you, repay you for all—"

He moved from the chair to sit by her side and took her hands in his. "You've already repaid me in many ways. I've enjoyed the time we've spent together more than I can say. But there is one thing you can do for me...."

"Yes?"

He smiled. "I feel that we're friends now. And my friends call me Matthew."

Emily took one of his hands and brought it to her face, holding it gently. "Thank you—Matthew," she said in a faint whisper.

"And now you must get some sleep. Tomorrow's a big day—for both of us. The bandages will come off for good, and we'll have a proper unveiling of the new you."

After he was gone, Emily lay staring into the darkness. The new me, she thought. I'm not sure if I'm prepared to handle another new me—there've been so many in the last few years....

A series of images fluttered through her mind. She remembered herself as a child in school, facing down the stares and whispers of her classmates. And later, the shy, lonely girl dealing with her unhappiness by working at her design classes and dreaming of a career. Then she had met Alec, and another Emily had emerged—joyous and passionate, filled with new sensations of being loved. And finally the Emily in prison, masking her thoughts and feelings under the tough veneer of a convict.

And now? What would she see tomorrow, when the bandages came off? Whom would she recognize?

The next morning, just after breakfast, Mrs. Travers accompanied Emily to a large room adjacent to Dr. Sheridan's office where the bandages would be removed. Soft lighting, rose-colored walls, deep plush carpeting, and a vanity with a lighted mirror, like an actor's makeup table, gave the room the appearance of a luxurious beauty salon.

"This room was my idea," Mrs. Travers said. "It gives all our patients an opportunity to see themselves when the bandages come off under the best possible conditions." She had Emily sit in a swivel chair facing away from the mirrored vanity. "Dr. Sheridan will be along in a moment. Would you like some coffee while we're waiting?"

"No, thank you," Emily replied nervously.

A few minutes later Matthew Sheridan came into the room, followed by a nurse carrying a small tray. He greeted Emily with a warm smile and said, "The big day at last. Now, don't be nervous, just sit back and relax."

Emily nodded, almost immobilized by fear and anxiety. The nurse handed Sheridan a pair of scissors and he cut away the tape holding the bandages in place. Then he carefully unwrapped them until all that was left was the dressing on the left side of her face and across the base of her nose. When that was removed, he took off the strips of adhesive and wiped her face gently with several small moistened pads.

Emily's heart was pounding like a trip-hammer. She glanced anxiously from Mrs. Travers to the nurse to see their reactions. Mrs. Travers began to smile, and the nurse beamed, nodding her head in approval. Dr. Sheridan stepped back and stared at her. For a fleeting instant, there was a curious expression of pain and sadness in his eyes. Then a look of satisfaction spread across his face. He turned to Mrs. Travers and said, "The finishing touches, please?"

She took some makeup from the vanity and began to apply it to Emily's face. "This is when I get to make my contribution," she murmured. "A little pancake—and now some powder . . ." She paused, then moved away and said, "Now, look at yourself, Emily."

Emily turned slowly to face the mirror, gripping the arms of the chair, her heart in her throat. The moment she had waited for was suddenly at hand and she was terrified. She raised her eyes and looked into the mirror. And in that instant, the dream of her life was realized.

She saw the face of a beautiful woman.

The ragged welts of scar tissue that had pulled at the corner of her left eye and tugged one side of her mouth into a grimace were gone. Her blue eyes were now wide and expressive, her lips mobile and beautifully shaped. She turned her head with elaborate caution to see fully the side of her face where the scar had been. There was nothing there but a fine, threadlike line that was barely visible.

Tears began to fill her eyes, but she kept them fixed on the image in the mirror. "It's like looking at someone else," she whispered. Her face seemed thinner, the cheek-bones were more sharply defined, and her nose looked different.

"You've changed my nose," Emily murmured, surprised.

"Just a little," Dr. Sheridan replied. "Do you like it?"

The tip was less fleshy, and the nostrils had been tightened a little. Now the bridge had an absolutely perfect sweep and the base was small and delicate.

"Yes," she breathed in a long sigh. "Oh, yes—" She glanced up at him in the mirror and saw an anxious, worried look on his face. Rising unsteadily from the chair, she turned, arms extended, and embraced him, dissolving into unashamed tears. "You've made me beautiful. Thank you, Matthew. Thank you for giving me a new life."

His arms tightened around her and he held her close. Then, noticing Mrs. Travers and the nurse watching them, he let Emily go and stepped away with a flush of embarrassment.

Mrs. Travers came forward and gave Emily a big hug. "You look beautiful, dear, just beautiful." She turned to Sheridan and patted his face like an approving mother. "Congratulations, Matt. It's an extraordinary piece of work."

The nurse added her congratulations, then she and Mrs. Travers left the room. Emily gazed into the mirror, her fingertips tracing over the smooth skin as she wanted to make certain that what she saw wasn't an illusion. Sheridan came up behind her and stared at the two of them in the mirror.

"I never imagined I could look like this," Emily said with a tone of awe in her voice.

"You'll look even better when it's completely healed. There's still some swelling and puffiness, but that will disappear in time."

"In time...oh, Matthew, I'd almost forgotten." She swung around to face him. "I'll have to leave here now, won't I? I'll have to go back to prison—"

He smiled to calm her fears. "No, not yet. Not for a week at least. But let's not talk about that now. This is a time for celebrating. Shall we have dinner together? There's a restaurant in town called Victor Hugo's that serves marvelous French food. We can have drinks on the terrace, watch the sunset, and then, after dinner, take a walk in the moonlight."

"You mean go into town? Oh, I'm not sure that I..." Without thinking, Emily raised a hand to her hair and tugged it over the left side of her face. She stopped in mid-gesture and began to laugh, then whirled to face the mirror and swept her hair back off her face, crying exultantly, "I'll never have to do that again!"

When she returned to her room, Emily found that a free-standing, full-length mirror had been brought in. Taped to the frame was a red rose and a note from Matthew: "May you never fear to look into a mirror again." Emily smiled and unfastened the rose, then stared at her reflection. A woman she barely recognized was watching her, and for a moment, she experienced a sharp stab of fear. The face she had known was gone, and a part of herself that she had come to depend on was lost. The scar. Even though she had despised it, it had been a means of protection; it had insulated her from the world. And it had given her rage, out of which had come purpose and ambition. Now she was faced with a beautiful stranger, someone she would have to learn to live with and allow to become part of her breathing and thinking, her very being. And there was no longer an excuse for rage. She would never again have to fear the struggle to achieve success *in spite* of her face. All the despair and anguish she had known now belonged to the past. The thought was at once exhilarating and frightening.

23

Early that evening, while Emily was trying to decide on a dress to wear for her dinner date with Matthew, Terry came by to see her.

"My God, you're beautiful!" she exclaimed. "Don't you love it! Isn't it making you just crazy to see yourself like this?"

Emily laughed at the girl's enthusiasm. "Yes, I love it. And you're right—I feel a little crazy, and a little scared."

"Scared? If I thought I could look like you, I'd have my whole face done over! Are you going to celebrate? I'd go out and party for a week!"

"As a matter of fact, Dr. Sheridan is taking me to Victor Hugo's for dinner."

"Oh, that's the most romantic restaurant in town." Terry sighed. "What are you going to wear?"

Emily held up one of the dresses that Sheridan had bought for her. It was dark blue jersey, with a low-cut fitted bodice and a full skirt.

"That's a little old-fashioned for my taste," Terry said. "But you'll probably look like a million in it." She paused, and smiled slyly. "So—Sheridan is taking you out to dinner. He's never done that before—at least, not since I've been working here. You're the first."

Emily looked at her with a puzzled frown. "Am I?"

Terry nodded her head. "I've seen a lot of women come through this place, but he never took any of them out to dinner. Or sent flowers to their room while they were recovering from surgery."

"You mean *he* sent the flowers? I thought that was something the clinic did for everyone who came here."

"No, that's not part of the regular service," Terry replied, her eyes sparkling with mischief. "I think he's interested in you—if you know what I mean."

"Terry, I think you've been watching too many TV movies," Emily commented dryly. "Dr. Sheridan couldn't possibly be interested in me except as his patient."

Terry gave her an impish grin. "Yeah? Well, maybe— anyway, have a great time tonight." She started for the door. "The way you look, I think you're going to have a great time for the rest of your life."

Emily laughed gaily. "Thank you, Terry—I hope so."

After she was gone, Emily thought about what the girl had said, and decided that she was just indulging in a romantic fantasy. Matthew's other patients had the concern of relatives or friends, but she was alone. That's why he had been so thoughtful about sending flowers and was taking her out to dinner; she had no one else with whom she could celebrate this momentous occasion.

Emily slipped on the dress and brushed her hair. The fringe of bangs she had worn for so many years had grown out, and now she no longer needed them; her temple was smooth and clear. She applied some makeup that Mrs. Travers had given her, then stepped back from the mirror to see the total effect. She stared, still not accepting what she saw. In the past, no matter what she wore, the scar had always dominated her appearance, ruining her efforts to dress with some style. But not now. Her face was unblemished, and the line of her throat curved smoothly into her shoulders and breasts. She would never have to wear a high-necked blouse or sweater again!

Laughing delightedly, she began to move in quick dance steps, like a model being photographed for a fashion layout. She turned to make the skirt swirl, then paused to catch an elegant gesture, captivated by the girl in the mirror. A knock at the door interrupted her, and she called out, "Come in!"

Matthew opened the door, stepped into the room, and stopped, an expression of wonder on his face.

Emily whirled to face him and cried breathlessly, "Is it all right? I mean—do I look all right?"

His eyes swept over her face and figure. For a few seconds his face clouded over as if he had been seized by some painful memory. Then he smiled and said in a husky whisper, "You're perfect. Absolutely perfect."

Emily felt herself blush and she lowered her eyes, suddenly nervous under his searching gaze. "The dress is so beautiful," she said haltingly. "I'd almost forgotten what it feels like to wear good clothes."

"You look beautiful in it, but there is one thing missing...." He came toward her slowly and pulled a slim black case out of his jacket pocket. "A little gift to mark the occasion and complete your costume." He handed her the case.

"A gift? But you've already given me so much—" She opened the case and her eyes grew wide. A pair of diamond and ruby clips and a matching pendant lay gleaming against black velvet. "Oh, Matthew, they're exquisite," Emily whispered. "But I can't take them—"

"It would make me very happy if you did," he replied softly. "I really want you to have them."

"Matthew, I can't—they're so valuable, and I—"

"—and you must listen to your doctor," he said, overriding her objections with a smile. "Now, do as your told and put the clips in your hair, one on each side, and I'll fasten the pendant."

Too stunned to argue, Emily took the clips and turned to the mirror. She fastened them in her hair, just above each ear. "Like that?" she asked, glancing up at him as he stood behind her.

"Yes, that's right—it's a rather old-fashioned way to wear them, but they look so charming. Now the pendant..."

He put it around her neck and fixed the clasp. The pendant lay at the base of her throat and sparkled as it caught the light. He stared at her in the mirror for a few moments, his hands resting on her shoulders. "I was right," he said quietly. "They were meant for you."

Emily turned to face him. "Matthew, I don't know what to say—"

"You don't have to say anything. Your eyes say it all." He took her hands, lifted them to his lips, and kissed each one lightly.

The gesture took her by surprise, and she stiffened a little, suddenly wondering if what Terry had said was true. But before she could think about it, he released her and said, "Now, put on your cape—it's a bit chilly out—and let's go show you off to the world."

Matthew guided his Mercedes sports car smoothly over the hilly roads and down into Laguna. The night seemed touched by magic; stars gleamed in a velvety sky, and the air was perfumed with the scent of wildflowers. Streetlights cast an amber glow over the highway, and the beaches were like pale shadows reaching out to meet the dark waters of the ocean.

When they drew up to the restaurant, a parking-lot attendant took the car. Inside, the maitre d' greeted them with effusive charm. He and Matthew exchanged a few words like old friends, then the man took Emily's cape and led them into the dining room. The decor was rich and tasteful, with parquet floors, white walls hung with paintings, and tall, leaded windows that overlooked the sea. The tables were covered with heavy linen cloths and gleamed with crystal glasses, fine china, and silverwear. Emily felt as if she were in a dream that she wanted never to end.

As they were seated, she became aware of the attention they were attracting. Instinctively, she put her hand to her face, and whispered to Matthew, "Why are they looking at us?"

He reached out and drew her hand down. "They are

not looking at 'us'—they're looking at you."

To her delight, she saw that it was true; several men at nearby tables were giving her covert glances, and a few women eyed her with undisguised envy.

Matthew heaved a deep sigh. "I suppose it's something I'll just have to get used to—you being stared at every time we go out."

"It's not me; it's the jewelry," Emily said, her face coloring with embarrassment.

Matthew ordered dinner: salade Niçoise, coquilles St. Jacques, and a bottle of vintage champagne. Later, as they lingered over coffee and a dessert of creamy pastries, he asked her what she planned to do with her future.

"My parole hearing comes up in a few months, and if I'm released, I'd like to visit my mother for a little while— she's living in Canada now, with her new husband. After that, I want to come back to Los Angeles and begin to work as a designer. I'd like to find a job with a costume builder and really learn my craft."

"Is your mother the only family you have?" Matthew asked.

Emily hesitated and sipped her coffee. Then she replied, "No, I have a sister. She's . . . married. But I'm not sure where she's living right now."

"So, you're pretty much on your own, aren't you?"

"I'm used to it—I was never really close to my family."

After dinner, they left the restaurant and walked down a pathway that led to the beach. The ocean was dark and still, and wisps of clouds like a lace veil drifted past the moon. Once they were on the sand, Emily bent to take off her shoes. Matthew took her hand to steady her, and when she straightened up, he continued to hold it. They wandered silently along the edge of the beach and watched the surf rush over the hard-packed sand in a lather of white foam. Emily was acutely conscious of the warmth and pressure of his hand and grew a little uneasy. She couldn't help thinking about what Terry had said, especially in light of the extravagant gift he had given to her.

"You seem very pensive," Matthew said, breaking the silence. "What are you thinking about?"

"I was just thinking about everything you've done for me," she admitted. "And I'm trying to understand why. Oh, I know you explained it to me before, but even so . . ." She stopped walking and looked up at him. "Matthew, why did you bring me here? You could have done the surgery at Riverside, couldn't you?"

He was silent for a moment, and stared at her thoughtfully, trying to decide how to answer. When he spoke, his tone was guarded. "Yes, you're right—I could have done the surgery at Riverside Hospital. But I wanted to do more for you than just the surgery."

"Why?" she asked softly.

He took a deep breath and replied, "I was deeply touched by your strength and courage. I thought you had gotten a raw deal in your prison sentence, and in your life. And I wanted to make some of that up to you—" He broke off with a shy laugh. "This is a bit difficult for me— I'm not used to talking about my own feelings. I've spent the last fifteen years of my life listening to other people's problems and trying to help them: people who feared aging or being abandoned by husbands and lovers, or who desperately need to compete in a world that emphasizes the desirability of beauty and youth. But I must admit that I've felt little sense of accomplishment, as compared, let's say, to a researcher whose new cure for an illness relieves the suffering of thousands of people."

"But your work *is* important," Emily said. "You've given many people a second chance at life—like me."

"Yes, I know that in some cases my skill made a difference. And when I met you, I knew that you were one of them. . . ." He stopped, struggling to find the words to go on. "But—there was more to it with you. For reasons I can't explain, perhaps because I don't fully understand them myself, I felt an overwhelming need to do whatever

I could to make you happy." His voice sank to a whisper. "I felt drawn to you, and I wanted you to be near me. That's why I brought you here."

Matthew grew silent, and they continued to walk along the beach. The night air was soft and balmy, like a caress, and the ocean rippled a line of swells that steadily rose and fell, gleaming almost white in the moonlight. Emily searched for something to say. Matthew's admission had not taken her entirely by surprise. From the moment he had given her the clips and the pendant, she had begun to suspect that what Terry had told her was true. She glanced up at him. He was looking away from her, staring out at the ocean, as if he were afraid to see her response to what he had said. A light breeze had tousled his hair, and it fell across his forehead, softening the strong, resolute line of his profile. He sensed that she was looking at him, and his eyes flickered to her nervously, then quickly away. She couldn't help smiling; he appeared more like an anxious, vulnerable young boy than a famous and wealthy man. She took his arm and turned him to face her.

"Are you angry with me?" he asked in a choked whisper.

"Angry with you? Oh, Matthew, I could never be angry with you. It's just that—I don't know what to say...."

"You don't have to say anything. These last few days have been the happiest I've known in a very long time. All I ask is that you allow me to go on doing what I can for you. Will you let me do that?"

She gazed up at him and replied in a faint voice, "It doesn't seem fair—I don't know what I feel for you. I can't make you any promises—"

"I don't want you to, not now. I wasn't going to tell you any of this until much later, but I just couldn't wait any longer." He reached out in a tentative gesture and took her in his arms. "I was afraid if I didn't say something, I'd lose you."

Before she could make a reply, he kissed her, lightly

brushing her lips with his. Emily drew back for a moment. She saw in his eyes the same look of tenderness she had seen once before, when she had awakened from the surgery. But beneath that expression, she sensed an urgency and desire that both frightened and excited her. It had been so long since a man had held her in his arms. An image rose up in her mind of Alec naked, holding her close, kissing and caressing her body. She grew tense, remembering the touch of his lips, the satiny feel of his skin.

Suddenly she wanted to obliterate that memory, burn it out of her mind so that all that was left was the cold rage, the hatred she had nourished for so many months. And Matthew could help her do that. From the moment they had met, he had shown her only kindness and consideration; he cared for her as Alec never had. She put her hands to his face and said, "I'm glad you told me how you feel. Just be patient and give me a little time...."

Matthew's arms tightened around her protectively. "Oh, my dear Emily," he murmured against her hair. "All the time you need—all the time in the world."

24

A WEEK WENT BY IN A SUCCESSION OF LOVELY LAZY days. While Matthew spent the mornings examining patients or performing surgery, Emily devoted herself to preparing a new portfolio of designs. She worked at a drawing board in Matthew's loft studio, happily surrounded by his painting equipment and canvases. Whenever she grew tired of drawing, she would go through his collection of art books that filled a long, low bookcase that ran the length of the room. In many books there were inscriptions on the flyleafs from his wife, Lisa. She remembered what Mrs. Travers had told her about their devotion to each other, and wondered what kind of woman Lisa had been, what she looked like.

In the afternoons, they walked through Laguna, visiting the many art galleries and stopping at crafts shops and various boutiques. Everywhere they went, he bought her gifts—clothes, perfume, books—silencing her protests with a boyish eagerness to please.

In the evenings, they would drive to a restaurant in Newport Beach or Balboa or down the coast to La Jolla. Over dinner they talked, getting to know more about each other. Matthew spoke of his struggles to become a surgeon and of his fascination with reconstruction work—rebuilding faces that had been deformed at birth or destroyed in accidents. Emily discussed the work of famous costume designers, the contribution they had made to films and plays, the place they had in the history of the theater. She and Matthew listened to each other intently, each fascinated with the other's work and finding a mutual ground in their desire to create beauty.

Neither of them was inclined to talk about their personal lives. Emily described her childhood, her life with Nora and Sheila, and her studies at college. And Matthew told her briefly about his wife and how she had died of injuries from a skiing accident a few years after they were married. It was as if they had, without voicing it, mutually agreed not to let the past intrude on the happiness of the present.

One afternoon Matthew came to Emily with news. He had talked to his lawyer about her and had learned that there was an indeterminate sentence law in California, which meant that her parole hearing could be advanced sixty days. The lawyer had already put in a request for the advance, and it had been granted.

Matthew went on excitedly: "I called Martha Kane, and she went over your records. Including the time you spent in Sybil Brand Institute, you've served almost two years of your sentence."

Emily's heart was racing. "I don't understand—what does it all mean?" she asked in a shaky voice.

"It means that you'll be given a hearing at the next convening of the parole board. It's a special privilege based on your records, good behavior, and Martha's reports. She'll be there to testify on your behalf and to certify that you deserve a parole." He paused, then went on somewhat hesitantly: "There's just one thing—they'll want to know if you have a means of supporting yourself or if there is someone to vouch for your support. . . ."

"But there isn't. I mean, I don't have a job to go to, and my mother is living in Canada. . . ."

Matthew took a deep breath before replying: "Well, I took the liberty of telling Martha how I feel about you— and she asked if we were going to be married. I told her that as far as the board was concerned, she could say that we were engaged and that I'd take care of you."

Emily stared at him, stunned. He took her in his arms and held her close. "I know that this is all very unexpected. But I had to say something. You know how much I care for you, but you don't have to make any commitment to me because of this. The important thing is to get you released from prison. After that, we can let time take its course."

Emily threw her a arms around his neck, her eyes brimming with tears. "No one has ever been as good to me as you," she whispered. Then she kissed him softly on the lips. She felt his arms tighten around her, and she put her head against his chest, overcome with gratitude. Beyond everything else he had done, he had given her something she thought she had lost forever—the precious gift of trust.

Matthew put his hand under her chin and lifted her face to kiss her once more. His lips were warm, undemanding, yet passionate. She drew away from him and saw in his eyes the love he felt for her. "You do care for me, don't you?" he asked hoarsely.

"Yes, I do, in my own way," she replied softly. "But I need time to put my life back together...."

"I can wait, my dear. You're worth waiting for."

She smiled, kissed him again, lightly. Then she said, "In all the excitement, I forgot to ask—when is the hearing?"

"At the end of this week. In four days."

That night Emily tried to call Nora to tell her the good news. She couldn't get through to Toronto for a couple of hours because of a severe storm that had been raging in the area for several days. Finally she connected with the number Nora had given her. It was Sam's family, where they were staying until their house was ready. A man's voice answered, and Emily had to shout over the crackle of static on the line. When he finally understood who she was, he broke off and gave her someone else to talk to. Suddenly the line cleared and she heard a woman's voice saying, "Hello, this is Sam's sister, Elisabeth. Are you Emily, Nora's daughter?"

"Yes, I am," Emily replied. "Is my mother there, please?"

There was a long pause before the woman answered: "No—she's not...."

"Well, can you reach her? It's very important that I speak to her as soon as possible. I'll give you the number here, and she can call me back when she gets in."

The woman didn't answer for a moment, and Emily thought the line had gone dead. "Hello, hello—are you still there?"

"Yes, Emily—" Elisabeth Jeffries's voice broke, and suddenly she began to cry. "Oh, my dear, I'm so sorry—"

Emily felt herself go cold. "What is it? Has something happened to my mother?"

"Yes, a few days ago," the woman replied, weeping. "They were on their way to the house. They got caught in the storm, and the car skidded, went over an embankment." She paused, trying to regain control of herself.

"Were they badly hurt?" Emily cried. "Is my mother all right?" There was no answer. Emily's voice sank to a terrified whisper. "Is she dead?"

A ragged sob tore from Elisabeth Jeffries's throat. "Yes. They both are. They were killed instantly. I wrote you a letter yesterday, but..."

Suddenly the line began to crackle again, and then it went dead. Emily sat, her face ashen, holding the receiver in her hand. It's not possible, she thought. It can't be true. Just then there was a light knock at the door. When Emily didn't answer, it opened and Mrs. Travers looked in. "Emily? Did you get your call through to your mother? Emily?"

Emily looked up, her face white and drawn, her eyes staring without expression. Mrs. Travers rushed to her side. "What is it, dear? What happened?"

"She's dead," Emily said tonelessly. "She and Sam

were killed a few days ago in an accident. . . . My mother is dead."

"Oh, my God," Mrs. Travers exclaimed softly. She took Emily in her arms and held her for a few minutes. Then she went to the house phone and called Matthew. Within moments he came hurrying into the room. Emily ran to him, weeping. He swept her up into his arms and told Mrs. Travers to get some hot milk and brandy. She left the room and he carried Emily to the bed and sat down against the headboard, holding her on his lap.

"She's dead," Emily sobbed, ". . . and she never got to see me."

Matthew cradled her in his arms, murmuring words of comfort. A few minutes later Mrs. Travers returned with a tray of hot milk and brandy. She poured a cup of milk, laced it generously with the brandy, and gave it to Matthew. He held the cup to Emily's lips, and she sipped from it like a child, her body still shuddering with grief. Matthew signaled Mrs. Travers to leave, and she walked out of the room, closing the door softly behind her.

When Emily was finished, he took the cup and put it down, then held Emily until she grew quiet. "Shall I leave so you can get some rest?" he asked her.

"No, don't go yet, please." Her voice sounded woozy and her head was drooping, but she held on to him tightly.

He settled himself on the bed and she rested her head on his chest. "Stay with me," she murmured. "I don't want to be alone."

"I won't leave you, darling," he whispered. "I'll never leave you."

On the day of the parole hearing, Matthew drove Emily back to the prison. Her face was pale and drawn, and there were faint shadows under her eyes. Her hair was combed back and tied with a blue ribbon, and she was dressed in a simple skirt and blouse. She looked very young and defenseless. He glanced over at her anxiously. "Are you all right?" he asked.

"Yes, I'm fine," she replied quietly. "I was just thinking about my mother and how much this day would have meant to her." She looked over at him with a sad smile. "But I'm glad you're with me. I don't think I could get through any of this without you."

He reached out and took her hand. "In a few hours it will all be over...."

Emily grew tense as they drove onto the prison grounds. What if the board decided against her? Her record wasn't spotless; her attack on Officer Harrison, the riot in the recreation room with Lou Hook and her gang. Would they understand? As they got out of the car, she clung to Matthew's arm, trying to be calm.

Martha Kane was waiting for them in her office. When she saw Emily, she stared in astonishment, then enfolded her in a tight embrace. "You look like a different person," she said. "Matthew told me about your mother, and I'm so sorry she couldn't see how beautiful you are." Emily's eyes filled with tears and she clung to the woman. Martha patted her back and said, "If everything goes well today—and I'm sure it will—you're going to have a wonderful life."

"Thank you, Martha—thank you for everything."

"We have a few minutes before the hearing, and I promised Claudia a chance to see you. She's down the hall, in the accounting office. Why don't you say hello to her, and give Matthew and me a few minutes to talk."

Emily left them and hurried down the hall. The door to the accounting office was open, and she saw Claudia bent over several large ledgers, making notations. Emily stood in the doorway and tapped lightly on the frame. When Claudia looked up, Emily smiled and said, "Hello, Claudia—"

Claudia's hazel eyes looked at her, puzzled for a moment. Then they widened in recognition. "Emily? Oh my God! Emily!" she exclaimed. She got up from the desk and the two women rushed to embrace. "I don't believe it!" Claudia said. "You look beautiful! Oh, I'm so glad to see you!" They embraced again, laughing delightedly.

"How's Rina?" Emily asked.

"She's fine. She got out two weeks ago—now it's your turn. Martha told me the good news." She stared at Emily in amazement. "I just can't believe how wonderful you look. Oh, baby, I'm so glad you stopped by to see me." Claudia's eyes grew wet, and she fumbled in her pocket for a handkerchief. "I know you'll get the parole. And then it can all begin to happen for you, just the way you dreamed it would. What are you going to do when you leave? Do you have a job to go to?"

"No, not yet," Emily answered. She wanted to tell her about Matthew, but there wasn't time. "But I'm sure I'll be all right."

"Well, listen—I spoke to a friend of mine on the outside about you. Her name is Dolly King, and she's in the costume business. I have her card here, somewhere." Claudia went to her desk and searched in her purse. "Here it is—it's called 'The Costume House.' As soon as you get settled, give her a call."

Emily took the card. "Thank you, Claudia—and when I have an address, I'll write to you. Are you getting out soon?"

"In about two months. Oh, it will be wonderful! I'll call Rina, and if she hasn't put her black ass into bondage to some pimp, we'll all get together and have a glorious bust!"

"I'd better go now," Emily said. "It's almost time for the hearing."

Claudia gave her a big hug. "Don't worry about anything—I know you'll be released. Take care of yourself, baby, and I'll see you soon."

Emily hurried back to Martha's office, and the woman gave her a few last-minute instructions. Matthew promised to wait in the office until the hearing was over, and then Emily and Martha started for the conference room in the administration building.

The hearing took a little less than an hour. Emily answered the questions she was asked, and Martha made a statement concerning her rehabilitation through surgery. Matthew had given Emily the photographs that were taken before the operation, and these were passed around and examined. Then Martha explained that Emily's mother had died and that Dr. Matthew Sheridan had agreed to be responsible for her during the period of her parole. Several members of the board knew of Matthew and his work with other convicts, and they were visibly impressed, not only by that knowledge but by the changes they could see in Emily herself. At the end of the hearing, they whispered among themselves for a few minutes, and then Emily heard the words she had waited for.

"Parole granted."

25

EMILY WATCHED THE COASTLINE ROLL BY AS THEY drove down Pacific Coast Highway on their way back to Laguna. She felt as if she were looking at a new world. White clouds formed abstract shapes against the deep-azure sky, and the ocean rippled in slow-motion waves, making silvery caps that reflected the late afternoon sunlight in myriad flashes of color. She suddenly recalled the film *The Wizard of Oz* and thought of herself as Dorothy, opening the door of the farmhouse after the tornado and seeing a bright, Technicolored world stretching before her, inviting her to step into it. And she was a little afraid; once she took those steps, there was no turning back. But what was there to turn back to? Nora was dead, and she had no idea where Sheila was. Everything she had known was gone. Now she was free and beautiful, and a new life lay ahead of her, a life she could make completely her own.

Matthew glanced at her and saw the thoughtful expression on her face. "How does it feel to be free?" he asked.

Emily smiled wanly. "I feel relieved, excited—and a little frightened."

"Let's dispense with being frightened and concentrate on being excited."

"And what prescription does my doctor recommend for that?"

"I have a wonderful idea. I recommend that we don't stop at the clinic, but drive straight through San Diego and have dinner at the Hotel del Coronado."

Emily looked down at her clothes. "But I'm not dressed for a place like that."

"That's no problem," he said airily. "They have wonderful shops there. We'll pick something up for you, have dinner in the Crown Room, and then dance the night away in the Grand Ballroom."

"Oh, Matthew, it sounds wonderful—but I can't let you—"

"Oh, yes you can—remember, I'm responsible for you, *officially*. And I say let's celebrate!" He looked at her and smiled. "It's time you let go of the past, Emily, look forward to the future, and really start living."

His excitement was contagious. She broke into a wide smile, then started to laugh. "Yes! Let's do it! Let's make it a night to remember!"

From the moment they crossed the San Diego–Coronado bridge and she saw the Victorian splendor of the Coronado hotel, Emily felt as if she were entering an enchanted place, a fairy tale that had come to life. The five-story, four-hundred-room wood structure covered thirty-three seaside acres, and its gingerbread facade, turreted cupola roof, tall pillars, and elegant domes dominated the view for miles around.

Emily was as wide-eyed and excited as a child. Matthew led her into the ornately styled and furnished lobby with its open wrought-iron grillwork elevator, plush draperies, and marble floors. He insisted on taking rooms so they could stay overnight and have a leisurely breakfast before driving back to the clinic the next day. Then he hurried her through arcades of shops on the lower floor, buying her makeup, perfume, a dinner gown, shoes, until finally, breathless with excitement, she made him halt the lavish flow of gifts. They went to Emily's room, arms loaded with packages, and spilled everything across the bed.

Emily's face was glowing. "It's like Christmas!" she exclaimed.

"And New Year's and Valentine's Day and all the other holidays we've never shared," Matthew said happily.

Emily threw her arms around his neck and kissed him. He held her close for a moment, then said, "Our dinner reservations are for eight. You have one hour to become Cinderella at the ball. And I shall do my best to look like Prince Charming."

An hour later everything had been put away; she had showered and was dressed in a creamy yellow chiffon dinner gown with a halter neckline and a thin gold belt at the waist. It reminded her of the dress she had designed to wear at the cast party of *Cyrano*, and that made her think of Alec. That had been two years before. Two years. She had been twenty-two then. Now she was twenty-four and an entirely different person. What would Alec say if he saw her now? She pushed the thought out of her mind; tonight she didn't want to think about the past. As Matthew had said, it was time to look forward to the future, to start living.

A few minutes later, Matthew arrived to take her to dinner. He was immaculately attired in a midnight-blue suit, white dress shirt, and a grey silk tie. When he saw her, his eyes lit up. "You look glorious!" he exclaimed. He made a low bow. "I am humbled to be in the presence of such beauty."

"You look pretty beautiful yourself," Emily said, laughing delightedly. "When did you have time to get the suit?"

"While you were with that very aggressive saleswoman in the lingerie salon. They have an excellent men's shop here, and a very accommodating tailor. I shall pass your compliment to him."

"Don't you dare—keep it for yourself. You're a very handsome man."

He slipped one arm around her waist and pulled her close to him. "I was hoping that you'd notice," he said in a low, theatrical voice. "But don't give me too many compliments, or they'll turn my head." He pulled away and offered her his arm. "Shall we go dazzle them in the Crown Room?"

Emily and Matthew walked into the Crown Room and were led to their table by the maitre d'. This was the main dining room of the hotel, and featured a spectacular, arched ceiling made of natural sugar pine, damask walls that matched the carpet on the floor, and elaborate corona lighting fixtures that were world-famous. The atmosphere was heady; beautifully dressed women in sparkling jewels; elegantly attired men; gleaming crystal and silver; white-jacketed waiters hurrying about with large trays of food; and, in the background, the subdued sound of dinner music.

Emily felt like a film star making an entrance. Everyone glanced up at them as they walked by, and once they were seated, she was aware of the lingering glances of the men and the frankly curious stares of the women.

Matthew leaned close to her and whispered, "You're not wearing any jewels tonight—it's *you* they're staring at."

Emily flushed with pleasure. "And you," she countered. "You're the handsomest man in the room."

Matthew smiled, pleased. "You're right!" he agreed, and they both laughed.

Throughout dinner he was carefree and charming and attentive. Emily loved every moment and was surprised at how easily she had slipped into feeling relaxed and comfortable in this place of wealth and refinement. Being with Matthew made it possible; his own casual acceptance of the surroundings put her at ease, and she found herself behaving with a sense of style she never knew she possessed.

Later, after a superb meal accompanied by rare vintage wines, they went to the Grand Ballroom and danced to the music of a small orchestra. Enormous chandeliers hung from the ceiling, and the magnificence of the room reminded Emily of her dream while undergoing surgery. Only now, whenever she caught a glimpse of herself in the gilt-framed mirrors on the walls, it was her own face she saw, her new face, and no one else's. She looked happily up at Matthew and remembered what he had said in the dream: that as long as she was with him, she was safe.

When the orchestra began the last song of the evening, they left the ballroom and strolled along the wide, railed porch that ran the length of the hotel. They could still hear the faint sound of the music behind them when they stopped to look out at the hotel's private beach. The sand was smooth and white in the moonlight, and at the edge of the beach, they saw colorful cabanas, several small sailboats moored to the hotel dock, and beyond, the dark waters of the bay.

"There's a kind of magic about this place, isn't there," Matthew said. "It's where Prince Edward first met Wallis Simpson, and the setting must have worked its charm— he gave up a kingdom to be with her."

Emily smiled and gazed dreamily out at the soft, balmy night.

"Happy?" Matthew asked softly.

"Yes, more completely than I've ever been in my life."

She leaned back against him contentedly. He slipped his arm around her waist and brushed her hair with his lips, then leaned down to kiss the side of her throat. His hand moved up from her waist and gently cupped her breasts. A delicious sensation went through her, and she closed her eyes and pressed back against him. His lips moved over her throat to her ear, and his fingers slid inside her neckline, teasing the soft curve of flesh and finally resting on a nipple. She shuddered slightly, then turned in his arms to face him and offered him her lips. They kissed, and her mouth opened, accepting his tongue. His lips closed more fiercely over hers. She put her arms around his neck and strained against him as the kiss grew more feverish. She felt herself yielding to him in a sudden rush of desire, and her fingers slipped into his thick dark hair.

Suddenly he pulled his lips away from hers. She opened her eyes and stared at him dazedly.

"Can we go back to your room?" he asked in a husky voice.

"Yes," she answered softly, then kissed him again.

In the dim glow of light from a night-table lamp, Emily lay naked in bed, waiting for Matthew to finish undressing. The ardor he expressed a few minutes before was now somewhat subdued. He seemed almost shy, like a young man with his first woman. Still wearing a pair of white jockey briefs, he turned to her somewhat hesitantly. His body was deeply tanned, trim and muscular, with broad shoulders and narrow hips. He approached the bed and stared down at her, his large, capable hands hanging awkwardly at his sides. "You're very beautiful," he said almost sadly.

She smiled. "You're responsible for that, as you are for all the wonderful things that have happened to me since we met." When he didn't reply, she sat up, reached out to take his hand, and pulled him down to sit beside her. "What's the matter? You look so concerned."

"I am," he admitted with a deep sigh. "I've been trying not to think about it, to deny it to myself—but Emily, I'm twenty years older than you, and..."

"And you're afraid that what I'm doing now is because I'm grateful to you? You think I'm willing to make love with you because of how good you've been to me?"

He gave her a nervous smile and nodded his head. She drew him into her arms and lay back so that he was bending over her. Looking up into his eyes, she said dreamily, "You're a handsome and desirable man. Of course I'm grateful to you. But I also care for you." She moved her fingertips over his face, tracing the strong arch of his dark brows, the bridge of his nose, and the curve of his lips. She slid her arms around his back and moved her hands in a lazy caress down to his hips, her fingers pushing away the cloth of his shorts until they could rest on the flesh beneath. Her voice sank to a low murmur. "And I want you very much."

Matthew sat up, stripped off his shorts, then lay back and took her in his arms. Emily gave herself up to him with a wanton passion, and his desire flared like a storm breaking. She moaned under the fiery caresses of his hands and lips and could not suppress a gasp of surprise when he took her with a strength and virility that lifted her to heights of intense pleasure. They spiraled into a blinding explosion of sensation that left them in a delirious ecstasy. But Matthew was an insatiable lover, resting only moments before starting again, exciting her, teasing, arousing her to a frenzy until finally she begged him to take her again.

When Emily awoke late in the morning, she was startled to find that he was gone. Just as she was about to get out of bed, the door opened and he came in, carrying a tray of fresh fruit, hot coffee, toast, and an ice bucket containing a bottle of champagne. He put the tray down on the side of the bed, bent over, and gave her a warm, lingering kiss. "Good morning, darling," he said. He was dressed, freshly shaven, and smelled of soap and cologne. He sat down beside her, his eyes sparkling with excitement.

She leaned back into the pillows and smiled. "Breakfast in bed, and champagne. You'll spoil me rotten."

"That's exactly my intention," he said, chuckling. He lifted out the bottle of champagne and deftly opened it. The cork popped, and he poured each of them a glass and handed one to Emily. As she lifted it to her lips, she saw something flashing at the bottom of it. "What's this?" She dipped her finger into the champagne and pulled out a square-cut diamond ring in a platinum setting. "Matthew! What . . . ?" She looked up at him with wide, disbelieving eyes.

He put his glass down, and said, "I want you to marry

me. Will you make me the happiest man in the world and be my wife?"

"Oh, Matthew—I don't know what to say—are you sure it's what you want?"

There was an edge of tension in his voice as he replied: "Emily, I love you very much. Of that I've been sure for some time. All I'm concerned about is what you feel for me." He waited for her response, the muscles in his jaws working nervously.

Emily felt a rush of mixed emotions. She cared for Matthew but wasn't sure that she was in love with him. Yet the idea of being his wife was thrilling; he was offering her a life of wealth and luxury and his own devotion. But she couldn't help thinking about her own plans, the goals she wanted to accomplish.

Matthew sensed what was going through her mind, and said, "I won't do anything to interfere with your ambition to become a costume designer. In fact, I'll do everything I can to make it easier for you. I know a lot of people in theater and the film industry, and I could introduce you to them." He paused, then went on more urgently, "I know I'm rushing things, but I just don't want to take the chance of losing you. Forgive me for pressuring you like this, but I must know. Will you marry me?"

Emily listened to him, not so much to the words but to the emotion with which he spoke. He loved her. Although he knew who she was and what she had done and could have his pick of many beautiful and sophisticated women, he loved her. The realization was intoxicating, and whatever doubts she had about her own feelings for him were swept aside. She took the ring, slipped it on the third finger of her left hand, then held out her arms to embrace him.

As soon as they returned to the clinic, Matthew began to clear his schedule so they could be married at once. He told her that he had to attend an important international conference of plastic surgeons in Vienna that was taking place in two weeks. They could be married in a civil ceremony and honeymoon in Europe. His lawyer would contact her parole officer and take care of all the legalities so that she could leave the country. But he insisted that no one be told what they were planning.

"I've been sharing my life with a great many people for a long time," he told Emily. "This is one thing I want to share only with you."

Too happily dazed and bewildered by everything that was happening, she never questioned his desire for secrecy but was content to let him make all the decisions. Mrs. Travers was simply told that Emily had been granted her parole and that Matthew would be driving her into Los Angeles to stay with friends until she found a place of her own.

On the morning they were to leave, Matthew was hurriedly loading the trunk of his Mercedes with their luggage when Emily suddenly remembered that she had left her portfolio in his studio.

"We can have it sent up to town later," Matthew said, glancing impatiently at his watch.

"I'll just run over and get it," Emily said. "It'll only take a minute."

Before he could stop her, she started across the grounds to the carriage house. Inside, she hurried up the stairs to the loft, found the portfolio, and slipped it under her arm, then ran down the steps. As she raced across the living room, she brushed against Matthew's desk, dislodging a thick stack of papers and scattering them all over the floor. She stopped, and as she hurriedly began to pick them up, she saw a large photograph of herself with the scar. Taped to it was a piece of tracing paper with a pencil sketch on it. It was the drawing he had done before the surgery, the one he had never shown her. She smiled and began to slip the photo and sketch into her portfolio as a keepsake, then saw a second picture half covered by some papers.

Thinking it was another one of herself, she picked it up. But it wasn't a picture of her. A wave of shocked disbelief went through her as she stared at the photograph. It was a picture of a beautiful woman with long dark hair, wide eyes, and a lovely smile. She was wearing a white blouse with a ruffle at the neck, and her hair was fastened behind each ear with a pair of jeweled clips that matched the pendant around her throat. At the bottom of the picture was an inscription that read: "To my darling Matthew, from your adoring wife, Lisa."

Emily sank to her knees and held the picture in a tight grip. Lisa Sheridan looked almost exactly like her. Emily searched the details of the woman's face in the hope that the resemblance was only superficial, an illusion. But every contour and feature, even the hairstyle and makeup, made the photograph an eerie facsimile of her own new appearance. She could see that the likeness had been there to begin with—the shape of Lisa's face and eyes, the curve of her chin, even the way she smiled. Only her nose had been different from Emily's, and Matthew had corrected that. By removing the scar and reshaping her nose, he had given her the face of his dead wife.

Suddenly she heard Matthew calling from outside the house, "Emily, what are you doing? We're going to be late!" But she couldn't move from where she was kneeling on the floor or make the effort to answer him.

Then he was standing in the doorway, looking at her. He started forward and his face went pale when he saw what she was holding. "Oh, God—no!" he cried in a choked whisper.

Emily looked up at him and held out the picture. "Why did you do this to me?" she asked in a hollow voice.

"I didn't mean for you to see.... Please, let me explain how it happened," he replied weakly. He sank into a chair, his face drained of all color. He was silent for a few minutes, then he spoke, his voice ragged with emotion. "When Lisa died, I felt as if I'd lost the most precious thing in my life. Then I met you and I realized how much you looked like her. And as I got to know you and learned how alike you were in tastes and ideas, I was astonished. It seemed as if we were destined to meet, that fate had given me a chance to recapture not Lisa herself but the essence of a woman whose beauty and sweetness of nature were all I had ever wanted. . . ."

"And that's really why you brought me here," Emily said thickly. "Why you bought me the same kind of clothes that Lisa wore, gave me her jewels." Her voice rose to a shrill cry of pain and anger. "You lied to me! You tried to make believe that you loved me, that it was me you wanted. But it wasn't me you loved; it wasn't me you made love to—it was Lisa!"

Matthew's voice was bleak with despair. "Emily, please try to understand. I wanted to help you. . . ."

"Help me? No, you wanted to help yourself!" she cried. "All my life I wanted to be regarded as a person like any other, instead of being viewed as an object of pity or scorn. And I thought that was what you'd given me, a chance to create my own identity. I thought you respected me, loved me. But all you did was use me to gratify your own twisted obsession with your dead wife!"

Wrenching sobs tore from her throat and she buried her face in her hands. Matthew started out of the chair to help her. "Don't touch me!" Emily cried out. She scrambled to her feet and ran out the door blindly, not seeing where she was going, wanting only to get away from him. Moments later she found herself on a path in the thickly wooded groves behind the main house. She kept running until the woods thinned out to a grassy knoll on a cliff overlooking the sea. Still weeping bitterly, she flung herself down on the soft earth.

An hour passed, and her tears subsided. She sat up, wiped her face with her hands, and stared out at the glittery starlight dancing across the water. Out of the tumbling thoughts rushing through her mind, an understanding emerged of what had driven Matthew to do this to her. Pity began to replace anger, but she knew she couldn't stay with him. She would have to find some way to regain *herself*, to be her own person, not an imitation of the woman he had loved.

She stood up to start back for the studio when Matthew appeared in the clearing. His face was pale and his hands were clenched at his sides. They faced each other for a moment, and then he said, "I've been searching for you— I was afraid. . . ." He broke off and stared at her, his eyes filled with pleading.

"I needed to be alone, to think."

"What do you want me to do?" he asked hoarsely. "How can I make this up to you?"

"I can't stay with you," Emily began haltingly. "I think I understand why you did it, but I could never live with you. . . ."

Matthew bowed his head in resignation. "Where will you go?" he asked. "What will you do?"

"I'll go back to Los Angeles and start doing the things I planned to do before I met you. I'll take care of myself and live my own life, not the one you tried to create for me."

"But I can't just let you go like this, knowing that you hate me," he protested.

"I don't hate you, Matthew," Emily said quietly. "After all, if it hadn't been for you, I'd still be in prison and scarred. I'll always be grateful to you, but I can't be another woman for the rest of my life just to show my gratitude."

Matthew nodded his head. "I understand," he said. "Will you let me help you—just until you're able to take care of yourself?"

"I suppose I'll have to," Emily said slowly. "I'll need some money to live on until I find a job. But as soon as I do, I'll return every penny to you."

"You don't need to do that," he broke in.

"Oh yes, I do," Emily replied. "I can't allow myself to be indebted to you any further." She drew herself up and faced him proudly. "My real life—my independence has to start now."

That afternoon Emily was driven to Los Angeles by the same driver and in the same car in which she had first arrived at the clinic. The irony was not lost on her; a scant four weeks before, she had come there knowing who she was and what her hopes were for the future. Now she was leaving, with no idea of who she had become or what lay ahead. All she had with her was a small case of clothes, an envelope of cash that Matthew had handed to her without a word, and her portfolio. She sat in the back of the car, her face expressionless. As they drove out of Laguna Beach, she never once looked back, knowing that the girl she had been no longer existed.

The car entered the flow of freeway traffic moving north to the city. An hour later they were in Hollywood. Emily directed the driver to a small, cheap motel she remembered on Sunset Boulevard, and as soon as she had checked in, the car pulled away. She stood at the window and watched it disappear down the street, then turned and slowly sat down on the bed.

Hours passed and the afternoon light faded. Emily felt a strange calm fall over her, accompanied by the conviction that she had made the right decision. Twice, she realized, she had allowed herself to be swayed by romantic illusions and false promises. The need to be loved and protected by a man had made her weak, made her forget her own promises to herself. Now she knew that if she were ever going to achieve her goals, earn the success she had so long desired, she would have to create fantasies—not fall victim to them.

The room grew dark. She switched on the light and went into the bathroom to wash her face. When she looked into the mirror, she was suddenly thrown into a terrible confusion. The image of Lisa Sheridan stared back at her, and beneath it, like a fading recollection of someone she once knew, was Emily Gorden.

A surge of anger and frustration at what Matthew had done almost brought tears to her eyes. But she held them back; she was in control of her own life now and had to be strong. She would look at herself as she would a new design she was creating. Yes, that was it, she thought with rising excitement. Emily Gordon was gone, and she would erase the image of Lisa Sheridan as she would a drawing that was wrong. A change of hairstyle would help, maybe reshape the line of her eyebrows and use makeup to emphasize her cheekbones and eyes. She would start working on it tomorrow; she would begin to redesign how she looked and eventually make the face entirely her own.

Happier, but exhausted by the tumultuous events of the day, Emily got out of her clothes and slipped on a nightgown and robe. She unpacked the rest of her clothes and put them away, then reached for her purse and searched its contents until she found the two small pieces of paper she was looking for. One was the business card Claudia had given her. It read: THE COSTUME HOUSE. In smaller type, there was an address on Santa Monica Boulevard and the name Dolly King. The other piece of paper was the address Nora had given her for Sheila and Alec in Las Vegas. She stared at them for a long time, then put them back into her purse.

Too restless to sleep, she turned on the television set in the room and flipped the dial, looking for an old movie to watch. A classic MGM film called *The Women* came on and she stretched out on the bed to watch it. She and Nora had seen it many times, and Emily had never failed to be thrilled by the glamorous cast—Joan Crawford, Norma Shearer, Rosalind Russell—or the spectacular clothes that had been created for them by MGM's preeminent designer, Adrian.

As the film unfolded and Crawford made her first appearance, Emily remembered how Nora had joked about the actress's real name, Lucille LeSueur. Nora claimed it would never have gone with the famous Crawford image, and that was why she and so many other stars had changed their names: to create a new identity for their careers.

And then the thought occurred to Emily. Her name. It was her name that bound her to the past she wanted to escape. She sat up on the bed, her eyes shining with excitement. Of course! That was the answer—a new name to go with her new image, a name that would complete the redesigning of herself. And as quickly as the thought had come to her, so did the name.

Adrian, in homage to the man whose work inspired her. Adrian Gorden. No, that didn't work; it didn't have the sound she wanted, the mystery or glamour. And yet she didn't want to lose all personal connection to her new identity. A family name, perhaps. She suddenly remembered something Nora had said about her mother's maiden name, how romantic it was, like the heroine of a period novel. It was Alice Ronay.

Emily got up and went to the shoulder bag of art materials she had brought with her. She took out a sketch pad and a pencil, then curled up on the bed and wrote the name. She practiced writing it for a few minutes until it flowed in a perfect signature. Then she closed her eyes and imagined it on the credits of a film: Costumes designed by ADRIAN RONAY.

26

THE COSTUME HOUSE WAS LOCATED IN AN OLD FEDERAL-
styled brick building that had been erected in the late
twenties. The neighborhood around it was a jumble of
bars, junk shops, porno book stores, sleazy coffee shops,
and sidewalk hot dog and hamburger stands. The pavements were littered with refuse, and the street was crowded
with traffic. Emily's spirits sank a little; she had forgotten
how grimy this part of Santa Monica Boulevard was and
couldn't help wondering what kind of clientele Dolly King
catered to.

Yet, surprisingly enough, the area contained a famous
Hollywood landmark of another, more glamorous era; the
old Goldwyn Studios, now owned by Warner Brothers,
took up the length of an entire block. Emily tried to imagine how the street must have looked in its heyday, but
the image disappeared under the oppressive weight of
present-day reality.

She entered the building through a double door with
tarnished brass handles and cracking paint and found herself in a small, dusty vestibule at the bottom of a staircase.
She walls were covered by thin sheets of cheap paneling
with a wood-grain finish, and there were worn rubber stair
treads nailed across each step. She tightened her grip on
her portfolio, took a deep breath, and started up the stairs.
The second floor presented a long, wide hall with dirty
beige walls, a number of doors painted dark brown, and
a linoleum runner on the floor that she suspected had
been put down when the building was new.

A sign over one of the doors indicated The Costume House. She opened it and walked into a small, cramped room. Every corner was taken up with shelves that were stuffed with bolts of fabric. One wall contained original sketches of costumes with pieces of cloth pinned to them. A dressmaker's dummy half-draped in muslin stood near a rack of steel shelving that overflowed with boxes of yarn, buttons, beads, fringe, and ribbons. In the center of the room a short, stout woman in slacks and a workshirt was bent over a large table crowded with odd pieces of material, patterns, notebooks, several ashtrays filled with stale butts, and a paper container of Coca-Cola.

"Excuse me," Emily said nervously. "I'm looking for Dolly King."

The woman glanced up. She had short blond hair as wiry as a Brillo pad, a plain round face devoid of makeup, and a permanent frown line between her thin eyebrows. A pencil was stuck in her hair behind one ear, a long tape measure dangled around her neck, and a cigarette was clenched between her teeth, causing her to squint as she stared at Emily.

"Don't look any further," she said in a throaty, smoker's voice. "You found her."

"Oh, Miss King, hello." Emily stepped forward and held out her hand. "I'm a friend of Claudia Sherwood."

"You're Emily, right?" Dolly King shook her hand with a firm grip. "I've been expecting you to show up. I got a note from Claudia a couple of weeks ago about you. Listen, I'm right in the middle of some shit here, trying to figure out what this asshole wants." She held up a drawing that looked as if it had been done by a fifth grader. "I'd give my left tit if some of these so-called designers would only learn how to draw. I swear to Christ, I'm going to start a fund to send them all back for remedial life drawing classes! Anyway, go wait in the office across the hall. Grab a cup of coffee if there's any left in the pot, and I'll be along in a few minutes, okay?"

Emily nodded and went across the hall to the office

Dolly King had indicated. It was a large room, sparsely furnished, with an old desk, a thrift-shop sofa covered with pillows, a battered coffee table, and a floor-to-ceiling bookcase stuffed with fashion magazines, catalogues, and books on costumes. On the wall behind the desk was a cork board filled with photographs of entertainers wearing costumes that had been made by Dolly King and her staff. To Emily's surprise, many of them were well-known personalities. She felt encouraged; apparently the quality of Dolly's work attracted famous people in show business, despite the location and decor.

She found a tiny kitchen area just off the office and helped herself to some coffee from an electric pot sitting on a table. Then she went back, took a chair by the desk, and lit a cigarette. A few minutes later Dolly came in and closed the door behind her. She sat down behind the desk, picked up the phone, punched a button, and said, "Kelly? Take all the calls for a few minutes. What? Again?... Oh, Christ, spare me the details!" She banged the receiver down and groaned. "That stupid bitch! Between the last fitting and the delivery of her gown, she put on ten pounds! Christ, the woman starts eating and she inflates like a balloon!"

Dolly pulled a pack of cigarettes out of her shirt, lit one with an old Zippo lighter, and leaned back in the chair. "Okay, sweetie," she said to Emily. "Let's talk. If we're lucky, we'll get five undisturbed minutes. Claudia wrote me that you were getting out and needed a job. She said you were very talented and that you knew how to handle a machine."

Emily began explaining about the classes she had taken in college and the work she had done in prison. Then she opened her portfolio and pulled out the sketches. Dolly examined each one, nodding her head and saying, "Good, good—you can draw—" When she was finished, she closed the portfolio and leaned forward. "I like your designs. They're good. But we don't do designing here. The designers bring in their sketches and we put the costumes together. All we do is build them, not create them."

"I know that," Emily said. "But I want to learn everything I can about costume designing, including how to make them. That's why I'm here."

"It doesn't pay much, and the deadlines are frantic—that's why they come to me; I get the stuff out on time."

"I'm used to hard work. And I really need a job."

Dolly puffed on the cigarette, her round blue eyes squinting from the smoke. "How long were you in prison?" she asked bluntly.

Emily lifted her chin defiantly. "Two years. I'm out on parole."

"Okay, relax. It's really none of my business, and there won't be any more questions. If Claudia recommended you, that's good enough for me. How soon can you go to work?"

"You mean you're hiring me?" Emily exclaimed.

"I'll try you out for a few weeks," Dolly replied gruffly. "If you're good and fast, don't get drunk on the job or come in stoned, and you don't ask for a raise right away, the job is yours. Is it a deal?"

"Oh, yes! Thank you, Miss King."

"It's Dolly. Not Miss, Ms., or Mrs. I've never been any of those. Just Dolly." She stood up and came around the desk. "I'll take you on a tour of the place and introduce you to my people. It's Emily Gorden, right?"

Emily rose from her chair. "Dolly, wait—before I meet anybody, I want to ask a favor."

Dolly laughed. "Already? You haven't even started working here yet. Okay, what is it?"

"I don't want to use my real name. For a lot of reasons I'd rather not explain right now, I'd prefer no one knew me as Emily Gorden."

Dolly nodded her head sympathetically. "I understand, kid. What's past is past. Nobody has to know, and you have my word I'll never tell anybody."

Emily gave her a grateful smile. "Thank you. I really appreciate it."

"So what's the new name?"

Emily hesitated, unused to saying it aloud. "Adrian Ronay."

"Adrian? Like the designer?"

"Yes. Ronay is a family name. Do you like it?" Emily asked anxiously.

Dolly thought about it for a minute. Then she gave Emily a wide smile. "I love it—it's got class!"

She put her arm around Emily's shoulders and opened the office door. "Okay, Adrian—let's go meet the maniacs who work for me!"

A wave of excitement went through Emily as she followed Dolly out the door. She felt as if she were crossing the threshold into her future.

PART
III

27

ADRIAN RONAY.

At first she found herself caught off guard when she was addressed by her new name. But as the days slipped into weeks and the weeks into months, Emily Gorden seemed to recede into a dimly remembered past that only occasionally floated to the surface. And finally the name became as much a part of her as the new life on which she had embarked.

She found a small, furnished apartment on a residential side street a few blocks from The Costume House, and with the settlement of an insurance policy that Nora had left, she was able to buy a used car. The remainder of the money Matthew had given her was banked, to be used for emergencies only. Her salary was modest, but Dolly helped by recommending her to designers whose drawing ability left much to be desired. So, after working all day at a sewing machine, giving fittings, running errands, or chasing around the city searching for special materials, she would hurry home, make supper, then spend the rest of the evening redrawing other people's costume sketches, for which she was paid twenty-five dollars each.

She didn't mind the long hours or the extra work. It was all part of an education that she not only welcomed but enjoyed. Dolly's clients provided an opportunity to work on a variety of costumes for TV commercials, nightclub presentations, special shows at Disneyland and Magic Mountain, local opera and ballet productions, the Ice Follies, and Las Vegas club acts. Then there were the "odd" jobs that no other costume place in town handled as well as Dolly: a dozen six-foot-high Chiquita banana costumes worn by dancers in a TV commercial, cartoon animal costumes for children's shows, and a life-sized camel made of hoop wire, foam rubber, and fake fur. When an order for the "critters," as Dolly called them, came in, everyone agreed that the place looked like a surrealist zoo.

Dolly's staff consisted of five seamstresses, women of varying ages who worked to help support their families, and a young man with the improbable name of Kelly Green. He specialized in making hats and accessories, and ran errands and handled the phones when Dolly was busy. Only five feet five inches tall, Kelly had a muscular little body, a thatch of bright red hair, sparkling brown eyes that lit up his small, handsome face, and an irrepressible sense of humor. When he first met Adrian, he said, "Would you believe I'm twenty-five? I look twelve, don't I? But when I'm fifty, I'll look twenty-five—or like the oldest little boy in the world!"

Kelly's infectious humor and bubbling enthusiasm helped her through the first awkward weeks of work. And when Adrian moved into her apartment, he insisted on helping her repaint it and demanded that she replace "this tacky antediluvian furniture." They selected pieces from used furniture stores and spent several weekends refinishing them. Adrian made drapes for the windows, filled the living room windows with plants, framed some of her sketches and hung them on the walls, and added accessories from some of the boutiques in the neighborhood. When it was finished, the apartment had a quiet air of comfort and good taste combined with a designer's sense of elegance. Adrian was thrilled; this was the first home of her own she'd ever had, the beginning of her new independence and her new life.

One night after work, Kelly came over to cook spaghetti dinner for them. Adrian relaxed in the living room while he cheerfully filled the kitchen with the banging of pots and songs from *A Chorus Line*. Later, while they ate, he confided his ambitions. "I'm really a makeup artist—I learned it from my mother, who used to work in all the studios before she died. But now work is scarce—that's why I'm creating chapeaus at Dolly's. I've already done a couple of plays for some of the local theater groups, and last year I did a horror film that was shot in Canada."

"Can't you get any work in TV?" Adrian asked.

"It's not that easy. You have to know people in this town to get someplace. But I did meet a guy at a party who said he's going to produce a series of children's classics for syndication—you know, *Robin Hood* and *Treasure Island*. He told me he'd sign me on to do the makeup if I let him do me. I told him to put it in writing and I'd consider it. He wouldn't be so bad if he lost about a hundred pounds and grew some hair. Oh well, you know the old saying: 'God is a Chinese potter—there's always a flaw.'"

After dinner he scampered back into the kitchen, washed all the dishes, then said he had to leave. "I've got a hot date waiting for me at Studio One Disco. The man moves like a frightened eel and has shoulders for days. His name is Scott. Or is it Glen? Or Tom? God, there's an army of Scotts, Glens, and Toms in this town. It gets very confusing, but what's in a name? They all look alike anyway."

In the months that followed, Adrian and Kelly became close friends. They shared lunches and an occasional dinner and movie. Sometimes Dolly would join them or make dinner for them at her house. The evenings were filled with warmth and laughter, and Adrian began to think of them as a family. There was nothing else in her life but work, and she was grateful for their friendship. Matthew had discovered where she was living and had written to her several times, but she never answered his letters. As far as she was concerned, that part of her life was over. All she wanted to concentrate on was the present, and the future.

Late one night, after rushing to get out an order of Samurai costumes for a TV variety show, Kelly asked Adrian to come back to his place for coffee. "I need some company," he explained. "My producer went off to a fat farm, and Disco Dan is shaking it in San Francisco this week. Besides, I have a project to discuss with you."

"Watch out," Dolly warned, lighting a cigarette. "He'll end up telling you the boring story of his latest conquest."

"Listen, Mother Goddam," Kelly bristled. "Nobody could match the notches in *your* belt!" He turned to Adrian and said, "This woman has a thing for delivery men, do you believe? There isn't a pizza man in West Hollywood who hasn't had her. When they come to her house, they really deliver!"

Ignoring their banter, Adrian said to Kelly, "If you have any food to go with the coffee, I'm yours. I missed dinner and I'm starved."

"We'll pick up some Chinese on the way," Kelly said. He shot Dolly a fierce look. "That's food, sweetie, not men!"

A half hour later they were on the floor in Kelly's living room, happily eating out of a number of paper cartons sitting on the coffee table. Kelly's apartment was a modest one-bedroom just off Sunset Boulevard. Adrian enjoyed visiting there; it was a model of tasteful decorating and gave ample evidence of his skill as a set designer. The lightly scaled furniture and choice of warm colors in the rugs and drapes, combined with white walls and woodwork, gave the room a sophisticated and elegant ambience. A wall of framed playbills and show posters provided a colorful background for the simple furniture, and an abundance of plants near the windows added a garden touch to the clean lines of the living room. The same thoughtful choices was evident in the other rooms as well.

Adrian finished eating, lit a cigarette, and leaned up against the couch. "Okay, now that I've had some food, I feel more human. What's the project?"

"I'm doing the sets and makeup for a play, and I think I can get you the costumes," Kelly said with a wide grin.

Adrian sat up. "Do you mean it?" she asked excitedly. "What's the play? Who's doing it?"

"A little theater group over on Melrose Avenue. It's a tacky place, but they do good work and get reviewed by all the critics. The play is Noel Coward's *Fallen Angels*, and the director is terrific. Are you interested?"

"Of course I am," Adrian cried. "Did you tell him about me?"

"No, not yet. I just got the job a few days ago. We've worked together before, and I think he's a genius. I'll call him and set up an appointment for you to meet him. Just think, if he likes your designs, we could work together."

"Oh, Kelly, that would be wonderful! What's his name?"

"Paul Mallory. I'll call him first thing tomorrow." He gave her a wicked grin. "I really think you'll like him."

"Kelly, please—no matchmaking," Adrian groaned. "I don't have the time or inclination for anything right now but my work."

"Listen, sweetie, you've been hanging out with me ever since we met. Not that I mind, but it just isn't healthy! You're a gorgeous girl. Flaunt it a little, baby, flaunt it."

"Thanks, but no thanks," Adrian replied firmly.

Kelly suddenly grew serious. "You're making a big mistake if you think you're going to get ahead in this town on mere talent alone. It doesn't work that way. I'm not saying you have to fuck your way to the top, but a little teasing and a lot of promises can help make the trip easier. Remember who you're dealing with in this business. Assholes! People with little or no taste, and no brains. The directors used to be writers, the producers used to be agents, and the agents used to be starving actors. They make their deals at lunches, dinners, and in bed. They give jobs to their buddies, relatives, and girlfriends. So get your shit together and sharpen up. You want to be a success, and that doesn't come easy."

Adrian stood up and began to pace the living room,

thinking about what Kelly had said. "I guess you're right. I hadn't really thought about it that way." She stopped and looked down at him. "Thanks for straightening me out. I've always had a very idealistic attitude about my work and myself. But what you said makes sense. I have to learn how to do business, as well as be a good designer."

Kelly jumped up. "Now you're talking. And since you're in such a receptive mood for my advice, how about glitzing yourself up a little? You're a beautiful girl, but I don't think you're making the most of what you've got."

Adrian had to agree. Since starting to work for Dolly, she had had little time to spend on herself. Every waking moment had been spent learning all she could about making costumes, or doing sketches for other designers to earn extra money. She had not yet followed through on the idea of creating a new image for herself as she had planned.

"You're right," she told Kelly. "What do you suggest?"

Kelly drew himself up to his full height and peered at her face with a mad scientist gleam in his eyes. "I think it's time to unveil Kelly Green's Magical Mystery Makeup Box."

He hurried out of the room and returned a few minutes later carrying a wooden case that was the size of an overnight bag. He set it down on the coffee table and opened it slowly, as if it were a chest containing rare jewels. Hinged on two sides, it opened in the center and stood like a three-way mirror, revealing small drawers on each side and trays in the center section. He pulled open the drawers and lifted out the trays and set them down.

"Behold!" he intoned. "The treasure box of the master makeup artist! Given to me by my sainted mother, who was not *nearly* as talented as I. Within these trays and drawers lies the stuff dreams are made of—illusions, fantasies, dramas. With these little goodies I bring Shakespeare to life, and Ibsen, Shaw, and, with any luck, a dazzling Adrian Ronay!"

He began to show her the contents: various colored

makeups and bases, a variety of eyebrow pencils, translucent powders and puffs, sponges, rouge and brushes, mascara, eyeliners, different shades of lipsticks, crepe hair for moustaches and beards, a stipple sponge to create five o'clock shadow, spirit gum, silver and white hair sprays for greying hair, and assorted jars of creams and lotions.

"What's this for?" Adrian asked, picking up a plastic bottle.

"That's Latex—for creating scars. I'll show you—"

He took a piece of Kleenex, tore off a scrap, crumpled it, and held it to his face. Then he took a small sponge dipped in the Latex and dabbed it around the edges of the tissue. As soon as it was dry, he covered the entire area with a makeup base that blended with the color of his skin.

Adrian watched in morbid fascination as he peered into a magnifying mirror and quickly colored the scar with pale shades of red and brown makeup. When he was finished, he turned to her and cried, "Voila! I am disfigured!"

He gave her a leering grin and she shuddered at the lifelike welt of ridged flesh on the side of his face.

"It's dreadful," she said, her voice trembling slightly. "Take it off."

"That's easy," he replied, lifting an edge of the tissue and peeling it off. "And voila again! I am restored."

Oh, God, if only it had been that simple, Adrian thought, watching him clean off the residue with a cotton ball soaked in alcohol.

"So, whaddya say, sweetheart? Shall we make an appointment for you to spend a full evening in the Kelly Green Emporium and let the master of makeup and hairstyling have his way with you?" Kelly asked.

"It's a deal," Adrian replied.

"And let's do it before you meet Paul Mallory," Kelly added slyly.

28

ONE NIGHT, A WEEK LATER, ADRIAN HURRIED HOME from work in a state of high excitement. Kelly had made the appointment, and in a few hours she was going to meet Paul Mallory. Kelly warned her that he could be difficult and exacting, but she had done her homework and was prepared. She had read the play several times and spent evenings in the library doing research, making notes and sketches on the fashions of the period. She knew she could design the costumes for the production. Now all she had to do was convince Paul Mallory.

She stripped off her clothes and took a hot shower to relieve the aches and tensions of the day's work. Once out of the shower and dry, she slipped on a robe and blow-dried her hair, then did her makeup. When she was finished, she stared at herself, still amazed by what Kelly had accomplished.

Three nights before, she had spent the entire evening wrapped in a bath towel and sitting in his large, old-fashioned bathroom while he had restyled her hair and taught her the fine art of applying makeup. The results were spectacular. Her long dark hair had been cut to shoulder length and lightened to a shimmering ash blond that fell in full, soft waves around her face. Then he had thinned her eyebrows a little and carefully applied eyeshadow and liner to bring out the depths of her large blue eyes. When he asked about the faint scar that had been left by Matthew's surgery, she simply explained that it was the result of a childhood accident. He showed her how to cover it completely, then proceeded to accent her cheekbones with a blusher. Finally he defined the shape of her lips with a warm red lipstick and added a light touch of gloss to make them, in his words, "irresistibly kissable." The next morning when she came into the shop, Dolly and the rest of the staff did a double-take, and Dolly asked Kelly to do something with her hair, too. He refused.

Now Adrian studied herself, delighted with what she saw and with the fact that her resemblance to Lisa Sheridan no longer existed. But she couldn't help thinking of the woman in the mirror as a stranger. No, not quite a stranger; more a new acquaintance toward whom she felt somewhat distanced but not yet comfortable. Time will take care of that, she thought, smiling at herself.

Then, for a chilling moment, the image of her face with the scar appeared before her eyes like the ghost of someone she had known begging to be remembered. She shuddered and turned away from the mirror, wondering how long it would be before she forgot the scar completely. And the scars that went deeper than the skin, the scars that had been left by the awful events of the past. Would time heal them as well? Some of them, perhaps. But not the scar that Alec Darcy had left; that would never be healed until she found him.

She grew angry at herself for thinking about him on this important night and turned her attention to selecting a dress that would impress Paul Mallory. She wanted to wear something that would separate her from the jeans and sweatshirts usually worn at rehearsals, an image that would be noticed and remembered.

She finally decided on a black, tailored blouse with long sleeves, a softly pleated grey skirt with a wide belt of the same color, sheer black stockings, and black high-heeled shoes. For a touch of color, she knotted a long burnt-orange silk scarf at her throat and let the ends trail down her back. A large, black shoulder purse that would accommodate her notes and sketches completed the costume. She stepped back from the mirror to get the full effect. It was perfect—distinctive and slightly theatrical, but not flashy. Satisfied, she gathered up her notes and sketches, slipped them into her purse, and left the apartment with a brisk, determined step.

A few minutes later Adrian turned her car into Melrose Avenue and drove south for several blocks until she saw the theater called "Company of Actors." It was on a block of small shops and boutiques. Three storefront windows had been covered over with sheets of wood painted dark brown, and a tiny marquee extended over the sidewalk. On the wall next to the doorway was a framed glass case with a poster in it announcing the next production.

Adrian parked in front of the theater, a little dismayed by its shabby exterior. But even so, she reasoned to herself, their productions, especially those that had been directed by Paul Mallory, were reviewed by important critics, and Kelly had told her they attracted a large industry audience. This might be her first professional opportunity, and she was determined to make the most of it. With a feeling of confidence, she got out of the car and walked to the entrance.

Inside the front door, Adrian found herself in a small, dimly lit lobby. The only furniture was a scarred, battered-looking desk, a few straight-backed chairs, and a threadbare couch. A worn, scuffed carpet covered the floor. The walls were covered with photographs of previous productions, and newspaper reviews were pinned to a large bulletin board. Just past the desk she saw a short hallway that apparently led to the theater.

She walked down the hall to an archway covered by red drapes, pushed them aside, and stepped into a narrow space crowded with painted flats and props. Moving past them, she turned a corner and realized that she was on the stage. A few work lights were on, giving it a shadowy, dismal air. The rows of seats facing her were in darkness. She peered into the theater and called, "Hello—is anyone here?"

"Don't move!" a man's voice called sternly from the back of the theater.

Adrian froze, her eyes searching for a face to go with the voice. Suddenly a bank of lights hanging above the stage came on, bathing the area in a pale rose color.

"Ah, that's much better," the man's voice said. "You're a beautiful woman. Can you act as good as you look? What experience have you had? Tell me something about yourself, then read whatever you have prepared."

Adrian shaded her eyes with her hand and gazed into the darkened theater, looking for the owner of the voice. "I think there's been some mistake," she said. A small square of light on the back wall caught her eye. It was the window of the light booth, and behind it she could dimly make out the figure of a man. She assumed he was the stage manager, and said, "I'm not here to audition. I'm looking for Paul Mallory."

"What do you want with him?"

Adrian bristled at his abrupt tone of voice. "I'd rather discuss that with him," she replied coolly. "If he's not here, I'll come back later."

She started to leave the stage when the man called out, "Don't go! He's here—I'll get him for you. Stay where you are."

He left the window and reappeared in a doorway behind the last row of seats. As he came down the aisle and grew more visible, she saw a slim figure dressed in jeans and a denim shirt. He closed the space between them with a graceful bound onto the stage and faced her. He was about thirty, she guessed, and had a strong face with wide cheekbones, a narrow, straight nose, and square jaw. Thick rumpled brown hair fell across his wide forehead, and deep-set brown eyes stared at her from under heavy, arched eyebrows.

"So, if you're not here to read, what are you here for?" he asked.

"I told you I'd rather discuss that with Mr. Mallory. Will he be here soon?"

"He's here now."

"Then would you tell him—"

"He's here," he said, tapping himself on the chest. "I'm Paul Mallory."

"Well, why didn't you say so in the first place?" Adrian glared at him. "Or does being a director entitle you to such childish theatrics?"

He nodded solemnly. "That's right, it does. Theatrics are my curse, both publicly and privately. Publicly they often work for me, but privately I sometimes get into trouble, like now. Shall we start over?" He gave her a wide smile that revealed even, white teeth. "Hello, I'm Paul Mallory." He held out his hand.

Adrian felt her anger melt beneath the charm of his smile. She took his hand and said, "I'm Adrian Ronay. I'm a costume designer, and Kelly Green said that you would see me about doing the costumes for your new production."

Mallory dropped her hand and stepped back, a look of surprise in his eyes. "You can't be Adrian Ronay."

"Why can't I?"

"Because Kelly gave me your name and—" He fumbled in his shirt pocket and drew out a piece of paper. "Here it is—Adrian. A-D-R-I-A-N. That's a man's name; women usually spell it A-D-R-I-E-N-N-E. I was expecting one of Kelly's little friends."

"Well, I'm a woman, and one of Kelly's friends, and that's how I spell my name."

Mallory began to laugh. "One of Kelly's little jokes, I guess, not telling me you were a woman." Then a thought occurred to him and he stopped laughing. "Does the masculine way you spell your name have any—ah, other significance?"

It took Adrian a moment to understand what he was asking. "No, it doesn't," she replied, somewhat annoyed.

"Oh, I'm very relieved to hear that," he said in a low voice, his eyes sweeping over her figure.

"Mr. Mallory, I didn't come here to have an affair with you but to discuss work," Adrian said stiffly.

"What a shame," he murmured, moving closer to her. "Couldn't we do both?" he asked with an impish grin.

Adrian drew herself up and snapped, "You're right, Mr. Mallory. Theatrics are your curse. And so is being rude!"

She turned on her heel and walked swiftly out to the hallway. Mallory gave a whoop of laughter and went after her. "Wait, wait—I'm sorry! Give me another chance!" He caught up with her in the lobby and blocked her way. "Please wait. I've had a long day and I'm a little crazy tonight. I didn't mean to be rude. You've got to forgive me."

"Kelly told me you were a brilliant director and that you could be difficult. But he didn't tell me you were crazy."

Mallory smiled. "I've sworn him to secrecy. A blood oath. Will you stay?"

"Are you going to be serious?"

"You have my word. Let's sit down and you can tell me all about yourself."

Adrian allowed him to take her back into the theater. They sat down at a table on the stage and she began to talk about her work. She spoke knowledgeably about the play and the period, then showed him her sketches. He examined them closely, glanced over her notes, and looked up at her, his eyes filled with admiration.

"You've really done your homework. These sketches are wonderful, and your notes are right on target."

"Thank you. Does that mean I get the job?"

He sighed and leaned back in his chair. "I wish it did. Unfortunately, we don't have a budget for anything as elaborate as these sketches. Like many little theaters, when it comes to sets and costumes, we have to operate on a scrounge-and-make-do basis. Overhead takes most of our funds, and the rest goes into advertising."

"I can work on a limited budget."

"You'd have to work miracles with what we have. And besides, we can't afford to pay you for your time."

"I'm not asking for a salary. What were you going to do for costumes?"

"I've discussed it with the cast, and everyone has agreed to do what they can to provide their own costumes— search out thrift shops, raid family attics, find whatever they can that will work. If we keep it simple, I think we can pull it off."

Adrian struggled to hide her disappointment. She picked up her sketches and returned them to her shoulder bag. Mallory reached over and took her hand. "I'm sorry. Your costumes would have added immeasurably to the production. Kelly should have warned you. But I'm so glad you came and we had a chance to meet." He held her hand, reluctant to let her go.

Adrian was sharply aware of the warmth of his touch and quickly withdrew her hand. "Thank you. I'm sorry, too. Perhaps another time..."

"Please don't go," Mallory said softly. "Stay and watch the rehearsal. Maybe afterward we could have a drink together."

"Thanks, but I have long day ahead of me tomorrow."

Mallory looked crestfallen when she rose to leave. He followed her out to the lobby, trying to think of some way to detain her. "Adrian, I wish you'd stay," he pleaded. "I know I behaved like a fool earlier, but won't you give me a chance to make up for it?"

She was about to put him off again when she noticed a photograph on the wall of a woman in an elaborate turn-of-the-century gown. The picture had been taken on the set of a previous production.

"What play was that?" she asked.

"*Hedda Gabler*. We did it about three years ago."

"The costume is beautiful. Did you have a larger budget then?"

"No, but we did have a woman who was a terror with a sewing machine. She could whip up costumes out of scraps, reconstruct suits and dresses, even make period hats out of felt and a few pieces of ribbon. She wasn't really a designer, she just copied pictures and drawings we gave her. Unfortunately, she left town a few years ago."

Adrian faced him with a determined look in her eye. "I'm a terror with a sewing machine. And I can reconstruct clothes, make hats, and create gowns out of odds and ends. Let me work with the cast, and maybe I can produce a few of those miracles you mentioned."

A happy smile broke across Mallory's face. "Would you really be willing to do that? It's a lot of hard work—"

"I'm used to working hard. This will be a pleasure compared to some of the work I've done."

"Then you'll stay?" Mallory asked eagerly.

"Yes, of course. After the rehearsal, let me go over my notes with the cast. I can give them some guidelines about what to look for when they go hunting for clothes."

His dark eyes moved over her face like a caress. "And can we have that drink later?" he murmured. "I'd like to get to know more about you."

Adrian hesitated before answering. She remembered what Kelly had said about the necessity of using her looks to get what she wanted. But Paul Mallory had a reckless, unpredictable kind of charm that was unsettling. He might be difficult to manage. Still, he needed her to do the costumes as much as she needed him to get started professionally. And she suspected there was a great deal she could learn from him about theater.

She gave him a wary smile and said, "Yes, we can have that drink later. It will give us a chance to talk more about the play."

Mallory made a face. "That's not exactly what I had in mind."

Adrian laughed. "I know what you had in mind. But we'll have many other things to discuss. It's important for me to know what you're planning to use for sets. And what the lighting design will be, what color gels—"

"Hey, not so fast! We still have several weeks before the opening. Do you always jump into a project with all this energy?"

"Don't you, Mr. Mallory?"

He beamed and took her arm. "Call me Paul. I think we were meant for each other."

A few minutes later the actors began to arrive for the rehearsal. Adrian was introduced to the three women and three men who made up the cast: Maureen Rogers, an attractive brunette; Andrea Davis, a thin, languid blonde; Sandra Wilson, a plump, vivacious redhead; John Loring, tall and English-looking, with fair hair and blue eyes; Jason Connors, a muscular, handsome man with dark brooding features; and Michael Bailey, a stocky fellow with sandy hair and a quick smile. As Adrian had guessed, all of them were dressed in jeans and pullovers. By comparison, her own clothes appeared chic and elegant and elicited some envious looks and admiring glances from the men.

While Paul and the cast gathered on the stage to discuss the blocking of the first act, Adrian took a seat in the theater and observed each of the players closely, making notes on their clothing, height, approximate sizes, and possible figure problems. Then Paul called for a run-through of the act and she settled back to watch him work.

During the next few hours she began to understand the reason for his reputation as one of the best young directors in town. Paul had endless patience and good humor, made his suggestions quietly but firmly, listened respectfully to the ideas of the actors, and smiled good-naturedly when one of them fumbled a piece of blocking or went up in his lines. Gradually, under his sure guidance, the pace was sharpened and the high style of the play began to emerge, even though they were working on a bare stage with only minimal props.

When he wasn't on stage giving notes, Paul wandered restlessly around the theater, observing the action from every point of view. Yet, despite his intense concentration on the rehearsal, Adrian caught him glancing over at her every once in a while. She pretended not to notice and kept her attention fixed on the players. But she couldn't help being aware of every move he made; his vitality and energy seemed to fill the theater.

When the rehearsal was over, Paul called for everyone's attention and asked Adrian to come up on the stage. Notes in hand, she faced the cast. Suddenly she experienced an eerie feeling of déjà vu. She remembered the night she had first stood before the company of *Cyrano* at City College, shy and nervous, tugging anxiously at her hair to cover the scar. Then she thought of Alec, and her breath caught in her throat. She heard Paul's voice, as if from a great distance, saying, "—Adrian, don't you have some notes on the costumes for us?"

"What?" The memory fled at the sound of his voice. Quickly gaining control of herself, she smiled and said smoothly, "Sorry—I was just organizing my thoughts...."

For the next half hour she discussed in detail the costumes needed for each act and made suggestions on the style, cut, and color of the clothes they should look for. She briefly described how she intended to reconstruct them for the twenties period of the play, then finished by taking everyone's phone number and giving them her own. Since all the cast members worked during the day, it was decided that the fittings and reconstruction work would be done at Adrian's apartment on scheduled evenings.

After everyone left the theater, Paul said to her, "For a woman with so much creativity, you can be very businesslike."

"I've learned it's the only way to get things done."

"I agree. But now the business of the evening is over, and you promised to have a drink with me."

Adrian glanced away from him, uncertain. Now that they were once more alone, she felt nervous and uncomfortable. She began to make an excuse not to go with him. "Would you mind if we—?" She stopped at the look of disappointment in his eyes and thought it might be a mistake not to go with him. They'd be working closely together, and it was important that they be friends.

"Could we get something to eat, instead?" she asked. "I missed dinner, and I'm really starved."

Paul smiled with relief and took her arm. "Do you like Italian? There's a place nearby that's terrific. We can go in my car, and I'll bring you back to yours. Door-to-door service, and I'll even pay for your dinner."

"It sounds wonderful. Especially the part about you paying for dinner."

"I thought that would impress you. Oh, and there's one more thing before we go. It's something I've been thinking about all evening."

"Yes? What is it—?"

Before she could finish, Paul pulled her into his arms and kissed her hungrily. Adrian tried to pull away, but he held her tight. His lips were warm and urgent, and a shock of excitement quivered through her body. She felt his strong hands moving over her back, and the pressure of his hard thighs against her legs. A wave of sexual desire swept over her, and she suddenly found herself returning the kiss with a feverish intensity.

When he finally released her, Adrian opened her eyes dazedly. They stared at each other for a moment in silence, then Paul whispered, "Don't be angry. If I hadn't kissed you now, I don't think I would have been able to get through dinner."

Adrian took a deep breath to stop the pounding of her heart. Her legs felt weak, and her hands were trembling. She pulled herself together and said coldly, "Well, now that you've gotten it out of your system, you'll be able to enjoy your meal. I wouldn't have a director as talented as you go hungry."

An expression of dismay appeared in his eyes at the

flippancy of her remark. But he covered it with a quick smile and replied, "I was hoping you thought I was a great kisser. However, I'll accept being considered a talented director—for the moment."

After Paul locked up the theater, they got into his car and started for the restaurant. Adrian was silent, upset at the emotions he had aroused. Her lips burned from the heat of his kiss, and she could still feel the imprint of his body against hers. A terrible confusion raged within her. In one brief moment, he had awakened passions she had kept buried for months by concentrating only on her work. She glanced over at him, inwardly furious at the turmoil he had created. For a moment she wanted to tell him to take her back to her car, that she wouldn't do the play with him, that she never wanted to see him again. Then a cold, calculating logic took hold of her. She would not permit a few seconds of weakness to destroy her resolve. She would simply have to be more careful to keep him at a safe distance, be on guard against his charm—and her own reactions to him.

At the Chianti restaurant, a waiter led them to a corner booth and gave them menus. There were candles on the tables and the soft sounds of music in the background. Large framed posters of Italy hung on the walls, and the rich thick odor of Italian cooking filled the air. They ordered minestrone and mixed green salads. Adrian asked for the cannelloni; Paul, the fettuccine Alfredo and a bottle of red wine. After the waiter brought the wine and had served them, Paul raised his glass and proposed a toast: "To an exciting relationship—"

"A working relationship," she corrected him, touching her glass to his.

"Naturally," he agreed with a solemn nod. Then he grinned and said, "Tell me about yourself."

"What do you want to know?" Adrian asked cautiously.

"Everything. Where you're from, how you got into

costume designing, what other plays you've done, what kind of little girl you were, is there a special man in your life, and if there isn't, what do you think of me?"

"All that for a price of a dinner? What a demanding man you are."

"I can also be very giving." Paul's voice was suddenly serious, and his dark eyes studied her intently.

Adrian sipped her wine and made a pretense of being casual. "Why don't we just keep to the less intimate questions," she said lightly. Then she recited the personal history she had conceived to cover her past. She told him that she had been born and raised in a small town in northern California, fallen in love with the idea of being a costume designer from watching old films on TV, and studied in college, where she had done a few plays and some local theater productions.

"Then I decided to come here and seek fame and fortune," she went on. "I ended up working for Dolly King, where I met Kelly. He liked my sketches and suggested I see you. And here we are. That's my story."

"The *Reader's Digest* version," Paul said with a laugh. "There must be more, but I won't press for details now. How do you like working for Dolly? I've known her for years; she's the best costume builder in the business."

"I agree. She's taught me a great deal. Now, what about you?"

Paul talked easily about himself and his work. He was modest and witty, and Adrian found herself laughing at his anecdotes about actors with whom he had worked. She began to relax and feel less threatened by him. He explained how he supported himself by working as an actor, doing small parts on various TV shows, and occasionally working as an assistant director on low-budget films.

Observing him closely, Adrian decided he wasn't handsome; there were too many irregularities in his face. But there was strength and an open, honest quality about his features that made him attractive. And when he spoke about theater, his eyes lit up and his enthusiasm was contagious. She thought of the first time she had talked with Alec and how much bitterness he had expressed about his life. Where Alec had been all rage and self-pity, Paul was filled with determination and a positive outlook about his ambitions. It was an attitude so like her own that she felt closer to him than she wanted to.

On the way back to her car, they talked about the rehearsal schedule, and Paul asked if he could sit in on the fittings at her apartment when she started to do the costumes. She agreed, eager to have his advice and suggestions.

"I think we'll work very well together," he said as they drew up to where her car was parked.

"I'm sure we will," Adrian said briskly, preparing to get out. As she opened the door, he put his hand on her arm to stop her and said, "Does it have to be all business, Adrian? I had a wonderful time tonight—can't we do it again, have dinner, maybe catch a play and see what the competition is doing?"

"Paul, you're very nice, and I enjoyed myself, too. But for the time being, I'd really prefer if we kept it just business."

"Okay." He sighed. "But just remember that you said 'for the time being.' And I won't forget it, either." He smiled and leaned closer to her. "I'm a very tenacious man."

Adrian left him without saying anything and got into her own car. As she drove away, she glanced into the rear-view mirror and saw him still sitting in his car watching her.

29

On a Saturday afternoon, a few days after her first meeting with Paul Mallory, Adrian did something she had been putting off since her return to Los Angeles.

The night before, while sorting out some old drawings, she had come across a sketchpad that had escaped the trashing of her cell by Louise Hook. In it were the sketches she had done of Alec from memory during those first terrible months of prison. She stared at them for a long time, deliberately recalling the dreams and hopes she'd had, the love she had felt for him while doing the drawings. And how completely he had destroyed them. Not even a new face and a new identity could make her forget what she had suffered because of him. And her determination to find him was renewed.

She took one sketch, a full-face portrait that most resembled him, out of the pad, and slipped it into a folder along with the Las Vegas address that Nora had given her. She wished that she had saved the wallet-size picture he had given her, but the night of the arrest, she had slipped it out of her purse and destroyed it in order to protect him. How stupid she had been, Adrian thought grimly. But the sketch would do. If she ever got to Las Vegas, she'd take a print with her to show anyone who might have known him. In the meantime, she decided, she had to try to get more information, now.

And so, the next afternoon, Adrian got into her car and began a small odyssey into her past. She drove first to Silverlake and cruised slowly past the neighborhood in which she had lived. The streets had changed very little; the houses looked more forlorn and the lawns more unkempt. Here and there an effort had been made to revive some houses with fresh paint, and lawns had been spruced up. But they, too, seemed overwhelmed by the listlessness and slow decay around them.

She turned a corner and went down her street and stopped for a moment in front of the house in which she had grown up. It looked somehow smaller than she remembered, and other people were living there, now. Some Chicano children were playing in the front yard, and she wondered who of them was sleeping in her room. For a moment she thought of Nora and the nights they had spent together in front of the TV set, watching old movies. And she thought of Sheila. Where was she now? Where had Alec taken her? Or had he abandoned her, too?

She drove off, taking the route she had used so many times before, to Sunset Boulevard and the Skolskys' furniture store. Would Ethel still be there? For a few minutes she wondered if she would have the courage to stop, go in, and see her. Of course, Ethel wouldn't recognize her— not now. And what could she possibly say to her? How could she ever explain what she had done, and why? She was flooded with guilt and shame and almost turned the car around. But she was compelled to go on, and breathed a sigh of relief when she saw the sign hanging over the entrance had been replaced with a new one that read: THE CLOTHES MART—FINE CLOTHING AT LOW PRICES.

Ethel had sold the store. Adrian tried not to think about how she was living now, alone, without Victor. Tears welled up in her eyes, and she wiped them away angrily, concentrating on her last stop in this painful but necessary return to her former life. She continued down Sunset toward Alvarado Boulevard and turned into the street where Alex had lived. She saw the building and for a few seconds imagined him waiting for her on the front steps. Her heart pounded in her chest, and her throat went dry. She parked the car and locked it, giving a worried glance at the rowdy youths and the dangerous-looking men gathered in small groups along the trash-littered sidewalks. The street had grown shabbier and more threatening, and for a moment she was tempted to get back into her car and return to the safety of her own apartment. But she had come too far to turn back now. Almost three years too far.

Adrian took a deep breath, straightened her shoulders, and walked to the apartment house Alec had lived in. She went up the stairs to the second floor, grimacing at the odor of garbage and urine that filled the dank, dimly lit hallway. Obscene graffiti covered the walls, and she stepped carefully around piles of refuse scattered on the floor. At the door of what had once been Alec's room, she knocked and waited. No one answered, and she knocked again. Finally the door opened on a chain. A pair of fearful eyes stared at her, and a frail voice whispered, "Who is it?"

"I'm trying to get some information about someone who used to live here—a young man named Alec Darcy," Adrian said. "Can you help me?"

"Oh, no—I can't. I just moved in a few months ago. Try the woman down the hall in apartment D. She's been here for a couple of years."

The door slammed shut and Adrian heard several locks being turned. She went down the hall until she found a tarnished brass *D* on one of the doors. The door swung open after she knocked, and a frowzy woman wearing a faded, stained housecoat faced her. "What the hell do you want?" she asked roughly. "If you're selling anything, I'm not buying."

She started to close the door when Adrian said, "Wait, I'm not a saleswoman. Did you know a man who used to live here about three years ago—Alec Darcy?"

The woman held the door and stared at Adrian through bleary eyes that had once been blue. "Alec Darcy?" She suddenly gave a raucous laugh that exposed lipstick-smeared teeth. "Alec—yeah, I knew him. What about it?"

"May I talk with you for a few minutes? I'm trying to get some information about him."

"You from the cops?" the woman asked suspiciously.

"Oh, no. I—Alec and I were friends, and I've lost track of him. . . ."

The woman shrugged. "Sure, we can talk. Come in."

Adrian stepped into the apartment. It was like Alec's— one large room, with a galley kitchen and a bathroom. But this place was a shambles. Clothes were strewn over every piece of furniture; a sagging, unmade bed with faded sheets stood in one corner. Nearby was a dresser, its top crammed with old magazines, cheap plaster knickknacks, and used jars of makeup. A scarred kitchen table covered with empty take-out food cartons and dirty dishes stood near the dusty windows. The walls of the room drew Adrian's attention. They were covered with photographs of a young and beautiful blond woman. Eight-by-ten glossies crowded larger, more formal portraits, some in color. And scattered among them were magazine photos and articles, many of them fading with age. The pictures and stories were all about an actress named Evelyn Malone, and Adrian suddenly realized it was the same woman standing before her.

"Yeah, it's me," Evelyn said proudly. She drew her wrapper around her shapeless figure and touched one hand to the bleached hair that tangled around her face like an old yellow dust mop. "Back in the fifties I was at Warner Brothers. I was in a lot of those musicals with Jack Carson and Dennis Morgan. I was the girl they always dumped for Joan Leslie or Doris Day." She barked a hoarse laugh and jammed a cigarette between her carmine-red lips, searched for a match on the kitchen table, then gave it up and lit the cigarette from one of the burners on the tiny stove crowded into the gallery kitchen.

"It's a kick in the ass, isn't it, finding somebody like that—" She made a theatrical gesture to the crazy-quilt walls of pictures. "—living here, like this."

Adrian started to murmur something sympathetic, but Evelyn interrupted her. "Hey, that's life, kid." She grinned, nodding at the pictures. "I'm a walking cliché—the movie starlet who ends up a piece of trash. It's the kind of thing you see on TV movies. In fact, I just saw one last week with that old broad who used to play in all those tits-and-sand epics at Universal—Christ, I forgot her name. Well, anyway, here she was, playing an old drunk living in a dump like this, with pictures of herself like she used to be all over the walls. Jesus, I couldn't believe it!" She lifted her head with pride. "I'd never do something like that. It would be too—" She searched for the word. "—demeaning. Yeah, that's the word it would be."

Evelyn paused and took a drag on her cigarette. "But you don't want to talk about me. I'm old news," she said humorously. "Sit down, if you can find a place—just throw that stuff on the floor. Want some coffee?"

"Yes, thank you," Adrian said, settling gingerly into a chair.

Evelyn Malone went to the stove and began to heat up a pot of coffee. "So, you knew Alec?"

"Yes—we were at school together. Los Angeles City College."

"Oh, when he did that play—*Cyrano*—yeah, I saw that. He got me a ticket. Christ, he was beautiful in that show. But then, he was one of the most beautiful men I ever saw. The kid could have been a star if he hadn't been such a bastard."

She poured two cups of coffee and handed one to Adrian. "You'll have to take it black—I'm all out of cream and sugar." She pulled up a chair and sat down. "And I'm sorry the place is such a mess. I had a little party last

274

night. . . ." She gave Adrian a lewd wink. "A truck driver. God, I love truck drivers!"

Adrian smiled and sipped her coffee. Then she leaned forward and said, "I know that Alec went to Las Vegas some time ago. Has he, by any chance, kept in touch with you?"

"With me? Shit, no! I was just the old broad who lived down the hall. He used to come by once in a while, listen to all my stories about the good old days, then give me a roll in the hay, borrow some money, and leave. And I got to tell you, he was worth every penny! That kid was the best lay I've ever had. But he really was a little shit. Funny about men like that, isn't it?"

"What do you mean?" Adrian asked.

"Oh, you know—when they're that beautiful, there's always something wrong. They're either faggots or they treat women like shit. He never really hurt me—" She gave Adrian a rueful smile. "I've been hurt by the best. But he really fucked over some of his girls. I remember one in particular, a sweet little thing except that one side of her face was all scarred."

Adrian flushed and felt her nerves jump. Her hands began to shake a little, and she put the cup of coffee down to keep it from rattling. "What did he do to her?" she asked, trying to sound casual.

"Outside of screwing her silly, I'm not really sure," Evelyn replied. "I just caught a glimpse of her every once in a while. She wasn't what Alec usually brought home."

"Did he bring a lot of girls home?"

Evelyn laughed. "A parade, my dear, a parade! But the scarred girl lasted a while. She used to come by almost every night. After she went home, Alec would scoot down here, make me break out some booze, and tell me she was going to get him out of this town. That's what he really wanted—to get away from L.A. Funny thing is, he banged a couple of rich old broads, including one whose husband was a producer over at Universal—or so he said.

But every time he got his hands on some money, he gambled it away and had to start all over. I figured the little scarred girl had money, or knew where to get it. Why else would he be interested in her?"

Evelyn paused and looked at Adrian shrewdly. "Did he get you, too, baby? Is that why you're looking for him?"

"Oh, no, we just knew each other briefly," Adrian said quickly. "But I heard that he went to Las Vegas with a friend of mine. That's who I'm really looking for."

Evelyn thought for a moment, wrinkling her brow. "Blond chick, about nineteen, sexy figure? Sheila—right?"

"Yes, that's her," Adrian said, struggling to control the pounding in her chest. "Did you meet her?"

"No, but Alec told me about her. She started showing up here after he did the play. He must have dumped the scarred kid. Something happened between them, I don't know what. But Alec was pissed for a couple of weeks. Then he started seeing Sheila. One night he popped in and told me they were taking off for Las Vegas, and that's the last I saw of him. Knowing Alec, she probably didn't last very long, either. He really was just a cheap little hustler."

Adrian got to her feet, anxious to leave before Evelyn asked her any questions. "Thank you for talking to me, Miss Malone."

"No problem, honey, I enjoyed it." She laughed heartily. "I love to reminisce. If you're interested in old movies, I've got lots of stills I could show you. . . ." She looked at Adrian hopefully.

"Oh, thank you—some other time, perhaps," Adrian replied, starting for the door. There was a throbbing ache in her head, and she felt a little dizzy.

"Sure, anytime," Evelyn said cheerfully. "You know where to find me. Oh, I was so busy talking about myself, I never got your name—in case I do hear from Alec."

"I don't think he'd remember me," Adrian said hurriedly. She left Evelyn standing at the door and almost ran down the hall to the stairs.

Once she was on the street, Adrian stopped, drew a deep breath, then stumbled toward her car. She sat behind the wheel, letting ragged sobs escape her throat. The bastard! she wept to herself. A torrent of shame, humiliation, and rage swept over her as she started the car and raced down the street. Tears blinded her, and other drivers honked their horns as she weaved in and out of traffic. Somehow, she managed to get home and stumble into bed, where she let go and sobbed hysterically.

Hours later, her fury spent, she lay exhausted and dry-eyed, remembering all the details of what Evelyn Malone had told her. She went over the story again and again. Alec had lied every moment they had been together. And he had laughed with Evelyn about his treachery—with Sheila, too, probably. And the woman whose husband was the producer—that had to be Harriet Bradshaw. Had they, too, laughed about the girl with the scar who was in love with him?

Adrian sat up and hugged her knees to her chest, seeking the warmth of her own body to help shake off the chilling thoughts that plagued her. She stared blindly into space, thinking about her determination to find Alec and make him pay for what he had done. Now, fueled by what she had learned from Evelyn Malone, that resolve begun to burn more fiercely than ever. She would have to find a private investigator, she thought, with connections or offices across the country. But that would be expensive. She'd need a great deal of money before she could begin her search.

She thought about Kelly's advice and knew that she would have to do whatever was necessary to get ahead. She could start with the play she was doing for Paul Mallory. Even Paul Mallory himself. There was so much she could learn from him about the theater, and he knew a lot of people in the business, people who might come to see the play and to whom he could introduce her. She knew he was attracted to her, and if she had to, she'd use that attraction to get what she wanted. But she'd give him nothing of herself. She had made that mistake before, and she would never do it again.

30

MAUREEN ROGERS STOOD PATIENTLY IN FRONT OF A three-way mirror while Adrian made adjustments on the dress Maureen would wear in the first act. They were in the small dining room of Adrian's apartment. A few weeks before, it had been converted into a fitting room, and now it was filled with odds and ends of fabric; boxes of fringe, ribbons, and beads; a dressmaker's dummy; spools of thread and yarn; a sewing machine; and an ironing board. All the finished costumes were on a long rack, and various other articles of clothing hung on doors or were draped across the backs of chairs. Cups half filled with cold coffee and ashtrays overflowing with cigarette butts lay everywhere, and the floor was littered with scraps of cloth.

Maureen surveyed herself in the mirrors. She was an attractive young woman in her late twenties, with dark brown hair and eyes, a heart-shaped face, pouty lips, and a slim, sexy figure. Like many actresses working in the city's little theater groups, she viewed the play as a showcase for her looks and talent, and her almost neurotic concern had pushed Adrian's patience to the breaking point.

"Do you think this color is good for me?" she asked. "What about my tits? I look flat as a board in this thing."

Adrian took the last of the pins from between her lips, knelt and added them to the hem, then replied wearily, "The color is perfect, and stop worrying about your tits—it's a twenties play and women were supposed to look flat. You can show them off in the second act when you

279

wear the silk gown." She stood up and took a few steps back. "That should do it. Walk a little so we can see how it moves."

Maureen sauntered back and forth in front of the mirrors. The deep yellow dress had originally been a sheath that was one size too large for her. Adrian had shortened it so that it fell just above the knees. Then she had gathered the excess material to blouse low on the hips and added a belt at that point to hold it in place. The sleeves had been removed, and a large, floppy bow fastened at the vee of the neckline. A cloche hat made of felt and decorated with a large cloth flower, and low-heeled ankle-strap shoes, completed the costume.

"Yeah, that's okay," Maureen said grudgingly. "At least my legs look good."

"Thanks," Adrian replied with thinly disguised sarcasm. "Now let's get you out of it without pulling the pins."

"Shouldn't we wait for Paul to see it?" Maureen asked. "He's very fussy about the costumes."

Adrian tried to suppress a grin; it was no secret to anyone that Maureen had been on the make for him since the play had gone into rehearsal. She'd used every fitting he had attended as an opportunity to appear half-naked in front of him.

"He may be late," Adrian said. "And I want to get the sewing—"

Just then there was a commotion at the front door. Kelly and Paul entered the apartment, arguing noisily about the set. They were both dressed in paint-spattered jeans and sweatshirts, and Kelly's bright red hair was sprinkled with flecks of white paint.

"If Noel Coward says there's a window seat under the window, then I want to put one there," Kelly stormed.

"We don't have the room," Paul said grimly. "Besides, the piano will cover it anyway."

"I'll make the room, and we'll angle the piano!" Kelly

said furiously. "Noel Coward doesn't put a window seat in his sets without a reason!"

"Fuck Noel Coward," Paul answered wearily, throwing himself on the couch.

"He's not my type!" Kelly snapped.

Adrian called out, "Hey, you two—stop bitching and check out the dress. It's for the first act."

The two men grew quiet and Paul sat up. Maureen thrust her pelvis forward in a twenties slouch and paraded around the living room. Paul stood and circled her slowly, examing the dress from every angle. Maureen gave him a flirtatious smile and said, "So—is it okay?"

"It's great," Kelly said admiringly. "You look like a John Held drawing come to life."

Paul glanced over at Adrian, who was sitting at the sewing machine. "It's wonderful," he said to her, smiling. "The audience will exit humming the costumes."

Adrian laughed. "Okay, Maureen. Take it off and let me get to work."

Maureen strolled back to the fitting room, unhooked the back of the dress, and shimmied out of it slowly, keeping her eyes on Paul. She handed the dress to Adrian, then stood for a moment in a seductive pose, wearing only her panties and bra.

"Oh, God, there she goes again," Kelly muttered under his breath. Then he began to applaud and yelled, "Put your clothes back on, baby! I'm getting nauseous!"

Paul fell back on the couch and closed his eyes, murmuring, "Please, dear, not tonight. I have a headache."

Maureen glared at them and pulled on her jeans and a blouse. "I'm beginning to wonder which one of you is really the faggot," she said contemptuously.

"He is!" Paul and Kelly said simultaneously, pointing at each other.

"That's enough of the comedy," Adrian called out. "Get out of here, all of you. I've got work to do."

Kelly took Maureen's hand and led her to the front

door. "C'mon, sweetie, I'll buy you a drink and we can talk about our sexual frustrations."

Maureen mumbled something obscene, and then they were gone. Adrian hung the dress up on the costume rack, then turned and saw Paul watching her from the couch. "Go home, Paul. You must be exhausted from working on the set all evening." She took a gown from a hanger and spread it carefully on the ironing board. She tested the iron with her finger, then began to slowly move it back and forth over the material.

Paul swung himself off the couch and came into the fitting room. He leaned against the wall and said, "This place looks like one of Dolly's workrooms."

Adrian smiled. "I hope you remembered to give her a credit on the program. She's been so generous. Aside from all the equipment she's let me use, I've been filching goods from her shelves like a shoplifter. And, of course, she knows it."

"She gets a special thank-you at the end of the credits," Paul said. He went to the rack and looked through the costumes. "I can't get over how much you've accomplished in the last few weeks. Gowns, suits, coats, hats, lounging pajamas. The show's going to look wonderful. But you're the one who must be exhausted, working all day, then coming home to this."

"You're right," she admitted with a sigh. "I've got aches in muscles I never even knew existed."

Paul came up behind her and gently began to massage her neck and shoulders. "You should go to bed and get some rest," he murmured.

Adrian put the iron back on its stand, turned it off, and let herself sag against him wearily. "I will, as soon as I clean the place up. Oh, I forgot to tell you—I took your suggestion about the maid's uniform. Sandra came in for another fitting, earlier this evening, and now I think we've got what you want. In the second act, it will look as if she buttoned it all wrong. And her cap, too—I fixed it so it can slide to one side of her head without falling off.

Your idea was very funny; I think she'll get a lot of laughs."

"I hope you didn't tell Maureen. She thinks it's her play."

"I know. I had to fight tooth and nail to keep the neckline on her gown from plunging to her navel. We'll be lucky if her breasts don't fall out during the scene."

Paul laughed and continued to massage her shoulders. Adrian rested her head on his chest, lulled by the touch of his hands. He put his cheek against her hair and said, "We work well together, don't we?"

"Yes. And you've taught me so much. I feel more confident about my ability than I ever did."

He turned her around to face him and stared down into her eyes. "And do you feel more confident about me?" he asked.

She knew what was coming, and she was prepared for it. She reached up and tenderly brushed back an unruly lock of hair from his forehead. "Yes, I do," she answered.

Paul caught her hand and pressed his lips to the palm. "You're a very mysterious girl," he said huskily. "I still don't know you any better than I did the first night we met. I'm never quite sure what to expect from you."

Adrian smiled. "Wouldn't it be easier if we had no expectations of each other at all?" Before he could answer, she lifted her face to his and kissed him softly.

Paul drew her close to him, and the kiss deepened. Her lips parted under his, and a burning ache began inside her from the feverish caresses of his hands. She felt herself shaking as she put her arms around his neck, and quite suddenly she was frightened by her own responses. Up until that moment she had thought of Paul only as a stepping stone in the carefully organized plan to further her career. But now she was experiencing a surge of emotions that surprised and confused her. As he strained his body against hers, hungrily kissing her lips and throat, a voice within her cried out that she wasn't merely using him, that she wanted him as desperately as he wanted her. For a moment all her instincts told her to stop before anything happened to weaken her resolve and make her as vulnerable as she had once been.

But it was too late. Paul suddenly lifted her in his arms and carried her into the bedroom. In moments they were naked, and the conflict that raged inside her was forgotten. His lips moved over her breasts, kissing each nipple. He caressed the rounded curve of her hips, then moved his hand to the soft flesh of her inner thighs. Adrian gasped and gave a small moan of pleasure as his fingertips teased lightly over her, then slid into her body. She pulled his face to hers and kissed him furiously, her mouth opened wide to taste his tongue. Her hands seized his erection, and a kind of frenzy came over them, a need to be as close as possible, connected to each other so that nothing separated their flesh.

Paul shifted into a crouch between her sprawled legs, grasped her buttocks in his hands and lifted her hips. His penetration was quick and smooth, and she thrust herself forward impatiently to close the gap between them. He held her for a few seconds without moving, then began a series of long, fluid strokes that made her cry out. She gripped him with her arms and legs, fingers clamped into the flesh of his back, her lips fastened to his mouth. She was no longer thinking about anything but the swiftly rising tide of sensations that welled up from the center of her being.

As his climax approached, he strained every muscle to hold back. She began to whimper deep in her throat and he responded with his own guttural cries. Suddenly he tore his lips from hers and gave a strangled cry, his body hammering into hers as he came. Head flung back, her eyes shut tight, Adrian felt him spasm into her, and she released a deeply flowing wave within herself that seemed never-ending.

Adrian was the first to stir. She moved out of Paul's arms and sat up, brushing back her hair. The faint light of morning struggled through the windows, making the room pale and shadowy. She looked down at his sleeping figure. He had kicked off the covers and was lying sprawled on his stomach, legs spread wide, his head turned to one side of the pillow. His slim, muscular body had the relaxed look of an athlete at rest, and his face, smoothed by sleep, gave the appearance of a young boy.

For a moment she was tempted to lean down and touch him, run her fingers through his tousled brown hair and kiss him awake. Instead, she drew the covers over him, slipped out of bed, and went to shower. The stinging spray of water brought her fully awake, and she thought about what had happened the night before, the emotions he had aroused in her. It won't change anything, she told herself. I won't let it.

A few minutes later she came back into the bedroom, wearing her robe. Paul was sitting up, smiling at her sleepily. "Good morning," he said. "You look absolutely beautiful." He held his arms out to her, and she went to him. He held her close and kissed her, slipped his hand inside her robe, and stroked her breasts.

She wiggled out of his embrace with a smile and stood up. "Does bacon and eggs, toast, and coffee sound all right for breakfast? I'm afraid that's all I have."

He looked at her with a faintly puzzled expression. "Yes, that's fine," he replied slowly.

"How do you like your eggs?"

"Scrambled lightly." She started to leave the room and he called, "Adrian, wait. Is something wrong?"

She turned to him with a bright smile and answered lightly, "No, of course not. Why don't you take a shower while I get breakfast started. I put out a towel for you, and there's an extra toothbrush. I'm afraid the only razor I have is one I use for my legs, but there's a fresh blade in it, so do the best you can." She left the room without looking back at him.

When he came into the kitchen a few minutes later, he

was dressed and there was a grave expression on his face. He sat down at the table and watched her silently as she served him the bacon and eggs and poured them both a cup of coffee.

"Toast will be up in a minute," she said, sitting down across from him.

"Aren't you eating anything?"

She shook her head. "I never eat breakfast—just coffee."

He picked up a fork and stirred the eggs aimlessly. "You're being very cool this morning. Are you sorry about last night?"

"Oh, no, Paul. Not at all." She reached out and touched his arm. "It was wonderful," she said softly. Then she continued to sip her coffee.

He waited for a moment, then he said, "Adrian, I'm not sure what last night meant to you, but it wasn't just a roll in the hay for me. I'm in love with you."

Adrian's heart skipped a beat. This wasn't what she wanted to hear. She had to be careful. "Oh, Paul, you don't have to say that," she responded smoothly. "I don't need to be assured that it was anything more than what it was."

Paul's voice grew tight. "I'm not trying to reassure you. I said I'm in love with you, and I mean it. Don't you have any feelings for me at all?"

"Of course I do," she replied slowly. "But—it's just that I have so much I want to accomplish. We both do. And I don't think this is the time to get involved in a serious relationship...."

"Adrian, we both feel the same way about our careers, but that doesn't mean we can't share that ambition and care about each other at the same time. I think we could have something important together. Give me a chance—give *us* a chance."

She looked away from the pleading expression in his eyes, trying to think quickly. She didn't want to hurt him,

286

and she didn't want to lose him. Not yet, not until she had learned everything she could from him. She turned back to him, tears welling up in her eyes. "Paul, don't do this to me. You're pressuring me into something I'm not ready for."

His voice softened with concern. "Darling, I'm sorry— I didn't mean to upset you. It's just that I think you care for me, but for some reason, you won't admit it."

"Oh, yes, I do care for you. But—"

"No 'buts.' Can't we just start with 'yes, I do care,' and take it from there?"

Adrian replied hesitantly, "Only if we agree that there will be no strings for either of us. No strings, no promises, and no demands."

"You drive a hard bargain," Paul said, beginning to smile. "But it's a deal. Do you want me to cut my finger and sign the treaty we just made in blood? Or can we seal the bargain with a kiss?"

"The kiss will be sufficient," Adrian said, leaning over to him. "Now hurry and and finish your breakfast. It's late, and I have to dress and go to work."

A few minutes later she walked with him to the door. Before he left, he took her into his arms. "I'll see you tonight at the theater." He paused, then asked, "Can I come back afterward?"

"Of course you can," she replied, kissing him.

As soon as he was gone, she went back into the kitchen and poured herself another cup of coffee. Then she lit a cigarette and drew on it deeply, letting the smoke out with a ragged sigh. It will all be easier now, she thought; I've got it under control.

The play would open in a week, and she and Paul had already discussed the idea of doing another production together. And a few nights before, he had told her that Gordon Davidson, the artistic director of the Mark Taper Forum, had agreed to come to one of the previews. Paul had promised to introduce her, even saying that if Davidson liked her work, he might consider her for one of the Taper productions in the fall.

Everything was clicking into place, just as she had hoped.

31

Excitement crackled backstage on the night of the first preview. Adrian hurried back and forth between the dressing rooms, helping the cast with their costumes, Kelly raced around the set making sure that everything was in its right place, and Paul seemed to be everywhere at once, checking the lights, the sound, and giving last-minute notes to the actors. As soon as the audience began to file in and take their seats, the word went around that Gordon Davidson was out front, and everyone's nerves went raw.

"I've been trying to crack the Mark Taper for years," Andrea Davis moaned while Adrian finished repairing a break in the lace bodice of the girl's dress.

"If you don't stand still, you'll crack this dress wide open," Adrian muttered, her needle flying over the delicate material. "There, that should do it," she said, biting off the thread. "But be careful!"

Kelly burst into the dressing room carrying his makeup case, and Maureen and Sandra, who were half-naked, cursed him roundly.

"Oh, for Christ's sake, can it, you two!" he cried. "There's nothing either of you have that I haven't seen before, or ever want to see again. Now, get into your costumes so we can do makeup." He turned to Adrian. "The boys need you—John pulled the seam on his golf knickers, and Michael is having trouble with his jacket."

As Adrian turned to leave, he came up to her, his face

anxious. "Tell me the truth," he whispered. "Is the set okay?"

Adrian gave him a hug. "It will get a burst of applause as soon as the curtains go up."

"Bless you, child," he said, kissing her cheek. "Now let's see if I can make these broads look as good as your costumes." He whipped around and screamed at the girls, "Okay, you frumps—this is an English play, so let's all make English faces!"

By curtain time, everything was under control. Andrea and John took their places on the set and Sandra was in the wings, waiting for her entrance as the maid. The sound man was running a tape of Noel Coward singing his own songs, and the light man was waiting for a signal from Paul to begin turning down the house lights.

Adrian left the backstage area and slipped into the theater through a side door. She saw Paul standing at the back, waiting for the latecomers to take their seats. He had a relaxed, confident expression on his face, but Adrian knew that inside he was tense and anxious. A friend of his had told him that some producers were coming out from New York in a few weeks, and they would see the play. The success of the production could be very important to his future.

She came up to him and said, "It's going to be wonderful."

"I hope so. I'm still worried about the second act."

"Don't be. The girls were perfect at the dress rehearsal."

"That's what worries me," he said, cracking a smile. "You know the saying—a good dress and a lousy first night."

The last of the latecomers took their seats, and Paul looked up at the man in the light booth and nodded his head. The house lights dimmed, and then the theater was in total darkness. Adrian gave him a quick kiss. "Good luck," she whispered.

"To you, too, darling," he whispered back.

The stage lights came up and the curtains swept back. There was a burst of applause for Kelly's set, a gleaming art deco design in white, silver, shades of grey and black, with only Adrian's costumes to give it color. The tape of Noel Coward singing faded, and Andrea and John began their first exchange of dialogue, and the audience grew quiet and attentive.

Two hours later, the cast took their final bows to thunderous applause. A surge of friends and well-wishers poured backstage as soon as the house lights came on. Paul had brought some wine, a table was set up in the lobby, and everyone crowded around, toasting the success of the play. Adrian was introduced to Gordon Davidson, who lavished her with praise for the costumes, and Paul and Kelly were surrounded by people, shaking hands and smiling.

The crowd finally began to thin out. Adrian was backstage, hanging up the costumes and checking them for any damage. Maureen stuck her head in the door and asked, "You coming to the party Sandra is giving?"

"I'm not sure," Adrian replied. "I still have some work to do. Have you seen Paul?"

"He was out in the lobby a few minutes ago."

Maureen disappeared and Kelly came in. He rushed to take Adrian in his arms, chortling gleefully, "We did it! We did it! And you, my girl, were superb!"

"I couldn't have done it without you," Adrian said, laughing.

"Nonsense! With your talent and looks, this is only the beginning. I can see it now—you'll get rich and famous, and when somebody mentions my name, you'll say 'Kelly *who*?'"

"That's not true," Adrian said seriously. "As a matter of fact, if I do get anything out of this, I'm going to ask that you work with me. Kelly, you're incredibly talented."

"Say it again, sweetie—I could listen to that kind of talk all night!"

"Are you going to Sandra's party?"

Kelly got a shy grin on his face, and his brown eyes sparkled. "No, I've got a date with John, would you believe?"

"I'm not surprised," Adrian said with a smile. "I thought I saw some hanky-panky going on between you two during the rehearsals."

"No, dear, the hanky-panky, as you so ludicrously put it, hasn't happened yet. But it may, tonight. I tell you, that man has the eyes of a hawk, the heart of a lion, and the hands of a nurse! I really think I'm in love!" He glanced at his watch and cried, "Oh, God, I'm going to be late—he's waiting for me. I've got to go pack up my makeup case. I'll call you tomorrow, baby, and tell you all."

They hugged each other again, and then he was out the door. Adrian finished putting away the costumes and went to look for Paul. The building was empty now and suddenly very quiet. She glanced in the lobby, then walked down the hallway, stopping for a moment to look at the photographs that had been taken during the dress rehearsal. My first real professional work, she thought proudly. Some programs were lying on a nearby table, and she picked one up. Paul had given her a separate credit: *Costumes designed by ADRIAN RONAY.* She smiled and slipped it into her purse, then hurried into the theater.

Paul was sitting on the stage alone, hunched over, his hands clasped between his knees. A single worklamp cast a dim puddle of light over his solitary figure, and Adrian saw the dejection and weariness in the slump of his shoulders. She walked slowly down the aisle and up the side steps to the stage.

"It's all a bit anticlimactic now, isn't it?" she asked softly. "You must feel like an artist who's just put his signature on a finished canvas and is wondering what he's going to do next."

Paul looked up at her and smiled wanly. "You're absolutely right—that's exactly how I feel." He glanced around the stage, looking at the set with pleasure. "It was a beautiful show, wasn't it?" His eyes came back to her. "I saw you talking to Davidson. What did he have to say?"

She pulled up an ottoman and sat by him, her eyes glowing with excitement. "He told me he's thinking about doing a revival of *Mourning Becomes Electra* and asked me to read the play and submit some sketches."

"Adrian, that's wonderful news!" Paul exclaimed, taking her hands in his.

"It would never have happened if it hadn't been for you."

"Don't underestimate yourself. I haven't exactly been playing Svengali—you're a very talented woman." He stood up and pulled her into his arms. "And you've been wonderful with me this last week, putting up with all the late-night rehearsals and the changes I made in some of the costumes."

"But you were right—they didn't work—and I'm glad you made me change them." She put her arms around his neck and kissed him. "Thank you for being so patient with me and teaching me so much."

"Do I get a reward?" he asked with a wicked smile.

"Not here on the stage, you don't! But if you take me to dinner, I just may do anything you ask when we get home."

"I like the way you make deals. Shall we go to Chianti's, where we first broke a breadstick together?"

"You're so sentimental, and such a romantic," Adrian said, smiling.

He put his arm around her shoulders and they started to leave the stage. "I am sentimental. It's one of the things about me I like the most. Don't you?"

"No, I like your modesty."

An hour later, over coffee and dessert, Adrian leaned back against the booth and gazed thoughtfully at Paul.

"Are you admiring my visage, contemplating what you

will do to my body later tonight, or digesting your cannelloni?" he asked.

"None of the above," Adrian replied with a smile. "I was thinking about *Mourning Becomes Electra* and wondering what I could do to excite Davidson's interest. After all, he's had some of the best designers in town for his shows. I'm not even sure if he wasn't just being polite, asking me to submit sketches."

"Oh, he meant it. Gordon and I worked together last summer in an experimental workshop the Taper was sponsoring. He likes giving an opportunity to talented newcomers."

"I've seen stills from various productions of the play, and I caught the film version with Rosalind Russell and Kirk Douglas on the late show. But I really don't know the play that well."

"I've directed some O'Neill—*Desire under the Elms, Anna Christie*. Why don't we read it together, and I'll help you with it. I've always been fascinated with that particular play. It's melodramatic as all hell, but the complexities of the relationships, which are so Freudian, played out against the form of a Greek tragedy, give it an obsessive kind of power that few modern playwrights have dared."

As Paul continued to talk, Adrian leaned forward and listened closely, her mind registering factors and ideas like a calculator. These were the things she needed to learn, she thought. And Paul was the perfect teacher.

32

A FEW DAYS BEFORE THE OFFICIAL OPENING OF THE play, Dolly asked Adrian to come into her office to speak to someone who had just called. It was Claudia Sherwood.

"Where are you?" Adrian asked excitedly. "What are you doing?"

"I'm working at Universal. A friend of mine pulled some strings and got me a position in the controller's office. I thought I'd wait until I was all settled in before trying to find you. I'm so glad you're working with Dolly. And she told me about your new name. I think it was very wise of you; the less people in this business know about your past, the better."

"What about you? Are you safe, using your own name?"

Claudia chuckled. "In my case, it's an advantage. As far as the moguls here are concerned, juggling books and serving time because you tried to help your boss and his clients is tantamount to being a hero. Now, what about you? Dolly told me about the play and asked me to come with her on opening night. I thought I'd bring some friends with me, if that's all right with you."

"Of course it is, as long as you remember to call me Adrian."

"Adrian Ronay. It's a beautiful name, dear. And I'm sure you'll make it very famous. I can't wait to see you."

"When you do, try not to look too surprised—there's been a lot of changes since the last time we saw each other."

"As a matter of fact, I think it's best if we pretend that

we've never met. It'll be safer for you, and in a way, it will be true—I'm sure you're an entirely different person."

"Thank you, Claudia. That's very considerate. And you're right—I am a different person."

After they had hung up, Dolly came in from the kitchen, where she had been taking a coffee break. "So, it's okay if Claudia comes with me to opening night?"

"Of course it is," Adrian said. "If it hadn't been for her, I don't think I'd have gotten through serving time. And I would never have met you."

Dolly put a cigarette in her mouth and lit it, staring at Adrian with a puzzled expression. Then she said, "When Claudia called, she asked me how you were, and how you looked. I told her you looked gorgeous, how should you look? And she didn't mention it again. What was that all about? Or is it personal?"

"It's a little personal," Adrian replied slowly. "Maybe some night we'll get together, have a few drinks, and I'll tell you all about it."

"Sure, kid," Dolly said, dragging on her cigarette. "Just remember that I'm here if you need me."

"I appreciate that, Dolly, more than I can say. You've been very good to me. And I'll never be able to thank you enough for all the help with the play."

"Yeah—well, that's what it's all about with friends," Dolly replied gruffly. "Now, let's cut the schmoosing and get to work. Did you see the new batch of designs for that cockamamie rock group? They'll be lucky if they don't strangle themselves in all that Spandex!"

Kelly burst into the office with a wild look in his eyes. "Get out here, you two! The rock group just descended on us for fittings, and one of them has legs that are so long, I think his inseam starts under his chin!"

"If he's got anything else that long, he's mine," Dolly quipped as she hurried out of the office.

"His nose, baby—just his nose!" Kelly called after her.

"That's what I love about working here," Adrian said, laughing. "Such a genteel atmosphere."

She and Kelly started down the hall to the fitting rooms, and Kelly said, "So—how's it going with you and Paul?"

"None of your business," Adrian replied good-naturedly.

"That good? I knew you two were just made for each other."

Adrian gave him a playful slap. "Don't keep playing Cupid—you're liable to get an arrow up your ass."

"Oh, how kinky!" He sighed blissfully. "But seriously, as they say in our business, you do like him, don't you?"

"Yes, I like him," Adrian groaned. "Now, stuff your matchmaking and go to work!"

As the day sped by, Adrian thought about the relationship she had entered into with Paul. For the last week, after each preview performance, they had returned to her place. While she prepared late dinners, they talked about the O'Neill play and her sketches for Gordon Davidson. Paul was filled with ideas for using costumes to bring out some hidden facet of a character's personality or subconscious drive. And Adrian translated his ideas and in some instances even improved on them, in sketch after sketch. She was beginning to amass a portfolio that she was certain would capture Davidson's interest.

Paul never questioned her zeal for work. If anything, he encouraged and supported her ambitions, content in the knowledge that they were together. When they finished working, they would go to bed and make love. Adrian couldn't deny that she was enjoying being with him; he was a skillful, passionate, yet tender lover. But where Paul was convinced that they were, as Kelly had said, "made for each other," she refused to think of it as anything more than just an affair.

On the offical opening night of the play, Paul went to the theater early while Adrian stayed home to finish making a dress she had designed for the occasion. Dolly had given her the day off to shop for accessories, and Kelly had done her hair the night before. Two hours before curtain time, she put the finishing touches on the dress, then hurried to shower and do her makeup. A half hour later, she stood before the full-length mirror in her bedroom and studied the total effect.

Using Erté, the famous French designer, as a source of inspiration, she had modified the extravagance of one of his creations and used white crepe de chine and black velvet to create a dress that was at once simple, yet theatrically daring. Thin straps covered with black jets led to the plunging neckline of a closely fitted black velvet bodice that revealed her creamy shoulders and decolletage. The skirt was made up of panels of black velvet over a chemise of white crepe de chine, and the bottom of each panel was cut at an angle to make a semigeometric design. Transparent black hose and black high-heeled pumps covered in satin-finish cloth called attention to her shapely legs.

Adrian stared at herself for a few minutes, trying to remember another girl with a scarred face and a haunted expression. She searched the image in the mirror for any remaining traces of Emily Gorden or Lisa Sheridan. But all she saw was a strikingly beautiful woman with gleaming ash-blond hair, a seductive mouth, and intriguing blue eyes. A woman named Adrian Ronay.

Adrian slipped into the theater through a side entrance and remained backstage until the performance was over. Paul and Kelly were out front and didn't see her until everyone had assembled in the lobby for a first-night champagne reception. She waited a few minutes before joining them, then made a calculated entrance worthy of a star. There was a stir of curiosity as she walked through the crowd to where Paul and Kelly were talking with several people. Paul's eyes widened when he saw her. He took her aside and murmured, "You look incredibly beautiful." Then he introduced her to two men who were the critics for the Hollywood trade papers, *Variety* and the *Reporter*. Adrian graciously accepted their compliments for her costumes and chatted with them for a few minutes. They moved off, and Kelly came up to her, grinning like a proud parent.

"That's some dress, sweetie," he said. "Now you're really doing business."

"And I have you to thank for it," she replied. "You helped create this look."

"Remind me to discuss the case of Dr. Frankenstein with you some cold and wintery night," he rejoined. "Now, go work the room. The *L.A. Times* critic is over in the corner sloshing champagne. Go tell her that *shmata* she's wearing is terrific."

Adrian laughed and started across the lobby. Then she saw Dolly waving at her. Claudia was standing next to her, staring at Adrian in amazement. With them were two other people, a man and a woman. As Adrian began to make her way toward them, she suddenly stopped, too stunned to move. The woman was Harriet Bradshaw.

For a moment the room swam dizzily before her eyes and the noisy sound of conversation became hollow, echoing whispers. The years slipped away, and Adrian was once more in the store, confronted by the look of disgust on Harriet's face, the woman's braying voice complaining to Ethel Skolsky: "Aren't you worried about upsetting your customers by employing someone who is handicapped, like that girl?" Adrian instinctively put her hand to her face. Then she saw Claudia smiling at her, and moved forward slowly, struggling to regain her composure.

Dolly gave her a big hug and cried, "I'm so proud of you! Your costumes are wonderful!"

She introduced Claudia, who came forward and took Adrian's hand. "Miss Ronay, I'm delighted to meet you. You're a very talented woman. And that dress you're wearing is gorgeous. Did you design it?"

"Yes, I did, thank you," Adrian murmured, thinking that Claudia looked more striking than ever: blond, poised, and very chic in a midnight-blue dress.

Gesturing to the others, Claudia said, "These are my friends, Mr. and Mrs. Howard Bradshaw. Mrs. Bradshaw is an interior decorator, and Mr. Bradshaw is a producer at Universal Studios."

Adrian shook hands with them. Harriet Bradshaw had changed little over the years. Her pudgy figure was tightly encased in an unflattering red dress, and her blond hair was done up in a mass of silly curls. Her eyes darted greedily over Adrian's dress, and she waved her jeweled hands excitedly as she cried in her loud voice, "I just loved your costumes! I really think they are as good as anything I've seen at our major theaters, if not better. Howard was impressed, too, and it takes a lot to impress him. He said—"

"I can speak for myself, Harriet," her husband said impatiently. He was of medium height, with thinning, silver-grey hair that was artfully cut to hide a bald spot in the crown of his head. His face was strong and fleshy, with hard grey eyes, a generous nose, and thick, sensual lips. An expensively tailored, dark suit disguised his narrow shoulders and the beginnings of a paunch.

"I was very impressed with your work, Miss Ronay," he said somewhat pompously. "Have you ever done anything for television?"

"No, I haven't," Adrian replied, aware that he was examining her closely.

He reached into his inside pocket and took out a leather card case and opened it. "Here is my card," he said, handing it to her. "Give me a call sometime within the next few days. I may have a project that would interest you."

"Thank you. I'll do that," Adrian said.

Claudia took her arm. "We're all going to Ma Maison for a late dinner. Won't you join us?"

"Oh, yes, do," Harriet cried. "I'd love to talk to you about designing some clothes for me."

Adrian winced inwardly, but smiled. "Well, I'm not sure—"

"Please come with us," Howard Bradshaw said. "If Harriet doesn't take too much of your attention, we might be able to talk about my project." He gave Adrian a long, intense look. "Besides giving us the pleasure of your company, you might find it very profitable."

His implication was clear; if she didn't go with them, she might lose the opportunity. And from the way he was staring at her, she knew that business wasn't all he was thinking about.

Adrian returned his gaze with a seductive smile. "That's an irresistible invitation. I have a few people to talk to before I leave. Why don't you go ahead, and I'll meet you there?"

A satisfied expression came over his face. "Good, that's settled, then."

Dolly spoke up. "I'm afraid I can't go with you—I've got a big day tomorrow. And I brought Claudia in my car—" She looked at Adrian.

"Why don't you go with me?" Adrian said quickly. "I'll be happy to give you a lift home after dinner."

Claudia agreed, politely fielding an invitation from Harriet to go with them. Dolly and the Bradshaws left, and she said to Adrian, "I can't wait to talk to you."

"Just give me a few minutes and I'll be right back," Adrian said. She left Claudia and hurried over to Paul and quickly explained what had happened. His face darkened.

"But I made a reservation for you and Kelly and me at La Scala. We were going to celebrate together."

"I know, and I'm sorry. Please try to understand. This is very important to me. Mr. Bradshaw is a producer at Universal, and he's got a project—"

"At the moment I don't give a fuck about Mr. Bradshaw!" Paul said angrily under his breath. "This is a very important night to me, and I want to share it with you."

Adrian drew back, her face set with determination. "I have to do this, Paul. And I'm going to. Give Kelly my regrets. I think he'll understand, even if you don't!"

She turned on her heel and went back to where Claudia was waiting. "Let's get out of here," she said.

"Are you all right?"

"Yes, I'm fine." They walked to where Adrian's car was parked and got in. Furious at Paul's reaction, she took a deep breath to calm herself, then turned to Claudia and embraced her. "I'm so glad to see you again. Bless Dolly for leaving you with me. We have so much to talk about."

Claudia hugged her in return, then sat back. "We'd better get started. Howard doesn't like to be kept waiting. We can catch up when you take me home. But I must tell you that for a few seconds there, I didn't even recognize you. You look so different, and so very beautiful."

Adrian smiled to herself as they drove down Melrose Avenue toward Ma Maison. Harriet Bradshaw hadn't recognized her, either, she thought. What an odd twist of fate to have that awful woman back in her life. Then she remembered what Evelyn Malone had told her about Alec screwing some producer's wife. It had to be Harriet; she'd been so rapacious with him when they had met in the store. Her stomach churned with disgust at the thought of the two of them in bed. And now she was going to have dinner with Harriet and her husband at one of the most exclusive restaurants in town. The irony of the situation made her laugh aloud.

"What's so funny, dear?" Claudia asked.

"The vicissitudes of life." Adrian chuckled. "You and me, and everything that's happened to us, meeting in prison the way we did, and now here we are—"

"—two very elegant ladies, dining at Ma Maison," Claudia said, laughing.

"Before we get there, tell me what you know about

Howard Bradshaw. The man stripped me naked with his eyes. I felt like I was getting humped in the middle of the reception."

"Be careful of him," Claudia warned. "He's got a lot of clout at the studio. And with a wife like Harriet, you almost can't blame him for trying to fuck every girl that catches his eye. Don't let all those grand manners fool you—he used to be an agent in New York, and at heart he's a slimy little hustler. When he came out here, he got a good tailor, improved his manners, and bamboozled his way into producing. He did a couple of sit-coms that lasted more than one season, and that made him a hero to the networks. Now he's looking to improve his stature with some prestige films for television. He wants to start collecting Emmys for his mantelpiece, and I have a feeling he's going to do it. He's very shrewd, and if he's really interested in your ability as a designer, you may just end up with an award of your own. That's one of the reasons I asked him and Harriet to come to the play. I thought maybe it would help you."

Adrian gave her a grateful smile. "You're still looking after your orphans, just the way you did in prison."

Claudia laughed. "I told you that I hoped we might work together someday."

"Speaking of orphans, did you ever find Rina?" Adrian asked.

Claudia shook her head. "No, the little cat disappeared. But she was a lovely child, wasn't she?" There was a wistful note in her voice.

"Are you seeing anyone now?" Adrian asked.

Claudia sighed and brushed back her blond hair. "No, not really. A little dating, but nothing serious. Sex was never really that important to me." Her voice trailed off and she grew quiet for a few minutes. Then she asked, "And you? I saw you talking to a very attractive man who seemed upset at your leaving."

"That was Paul Mallory, the director of the play. I'll tell you about him later. . . ." Adrian pulled up to the restaurant and a parking attendant hurried toward the car. "Christ, there's nothing but Rolls Royces parked out front," she commented.

"That's right, and anything less is hidden God knows where," Claudia said.

"You've been here before?"

"Yes, and it's not my favorite place. But Howard and Harriet love it. Everybody comes here to see and be seen."

The two women were greeted with some suspicion by the maitre d'.

Claudia assumed an imperious air and told him they were expected by the Bradshaws. While he checked his guest list, Adrian saw Orson Welles rumble into the tiny bar just off the entrance, where he disappeared into a booth that was obscured from the rest of the room.

Adrian pulled at Claudia's arm to catch a glimpse of him, and Claudia said, "Yes, that's known as the Orson Welles booth. I've often wondered if he pays rents on it to make sure it's always available for him."

The maitre d' looked up from the list and gave them a superior smile, then led the way into the main room. The lack of decor surprised Adrian. "It looks like a covered patio," she whispered to Claudia. "Why is it so famous?"

"The food's good, and it has more snob appeal than visiting the pope."

Adrian spotted a number of celebrities at the tables, all talking loudly to each other. "Is the place always this noisy?" she asked.

"Usually. Just because they're rich and famous doesn't mean they have to be well-mannered."

"Did anyone ever tell you that you're cynical?"

"Everybody. It's all I have to help preserve my sanity in this town."

Howard Bradshaw stood up when they arrived at the table. Once they were seated and had ordered dinner, he shifted his chair closer to Adrian and said, "I'm so glad you decided to join us, Miss Ronay. I think you'll find what I have to tell you very interesting."

Adrian looked straight at him and smiled. "I'm sure I will, Mr. Bradshaw. But please, call me Adrian."

He leaned forward so that his shoulder touched hers. "And you must call me Howard," he replied, lowering his voice to an intimate tone.

Adrian sipped her wine, thinking that if he tried to get any closer, he'd be sitting in her lap. She glanced across the table at Harriet and caught a few words of her conversation with Claudia. She was busily describing a new house she was doing for a well-known actress, and Claudia gave every appearance that it was the most fascinating account she had ever heard.

"Did you ever read F. Scott Fitzgerald's *Tender Is the Night*?" Howard asked.

"Yes, I have," Adrian replied. "And I saw the film, with Jennifer Jones."

"Very good." Bradshaw beamed at her as if she were a student who had given the correct answer on a test. "The picture was a flop," he continued. "They couldn't handle the sexual nature of Nicole's problem as frankly as we can now. And Jason Robards was all wrong for the role of Dick Diver—too old, and not attractive enough. I had the film screened for me, and—" He paused to dramatize his announcement. "I've decided the time is right for a remake as a two- or three-part television film."

"That's a very exciting idea," Adrian said.

"Yes, I know," Bradshaw said smugly. His eyes began to glisten with visions of anticipated success. "I'm going to do it up big. I'm talking six to eight million for the budget, and everything authentic: costumes, sets, locations. It's going to be the biggest goddamned prestige show of the season. And if it's sexy enough, I know we'll get the ratings."

"Are you telling her about *Tender Is the Night*?" Harriet broke in.

Bradshaw shot her an angry look. "Yes, Harriet, I was about to—"

"Isn't it a great idea?" she cried. "Wait until you read the script! It's terrific! I told Howard on the way over, after seeing your costumes tonight—"

"Harriet, shut the fuck up!" Bradshaw barked in a hard voice.

An embarrassed silence fell over the table for a few seconds. Harriet's face flamed, and Adrian looked down at her food. Claudia stepped into the breach and said smoothly, "Are you thinking of giving Adrian a chance to submit some ideas for the costumes, Howard?"

"Yes, I am," he said grimly, glaring at his wife.

"What a marvelous opportunity," Adrian broke in. "It's such an exciting period, and the complex nature of the characters lends itself to some wonderful costume ideas."

Claudia quickly began talking to Harriet, and Bradshaw returned his attention to Adrian. "I thought you might be intersted in giving it a shot," he said.

"Oh, I would," Adrian replied eagerly. "I don't know how to thank you."

He gave her a thin, knowing smile. "I think you're very talented, and I like giving talented people a break."

Adrian suddenly felt his hand on her knee under the table. She lowered her eyes for a second, then looked up at him with a teasing smile. "Exactly what kind of a break were you thinking of, Howard?" she asked in a low tone.

His hand moved up under her skirt. She let her legs open a little, until his fingers had almost reached her panties. Then she closed them, trapping his hand between her thighs.

"Why don't we discuss that one day next week in my office?" he murmured.

She squeezed his hand with her thighs, then reached under the table and gently removed it, running her index finger across his palm. "I'll call you to set up an appointment," she said in a breathy whisper.

Claudia glanced across the table and, raising her voice a little, said, "I hate to be the one to break this up, but it really is getting late—"

Adrian gave her a grateful look, and said, "Yes, for me, too."

While Howard Bradshaw took care of the bill, the three women walked to the entrance. Adrian said to Harriet, "Thank you, Mrs. Bradshaw, for coming to see the play, and for suggesting to your husband that he give me a chance to do the costumes for his new film. I'm very grateful."

"It was my pleasure," Harriet gushed. "I think it's important for a wife to help her husband, especially in this business. Howard has so many things to deal with, getting a project like this started."

"Perhaps we can get together one afternoon and talk about clothes," Adrian said. "If you have the time, of course—I know how busy you are."

Harriet glowed with pleasure. "That would be terrific," she exclaimed. "I've been looking for someone who could design clothes for me. I hate the crap they're showing now." She reached into her purse and took out a card. "This is my office number. Give me a call, and we'll have lunch."

Howard appeared and everyone said good night. He took Adrian's hand and held it a little longer than necessary. "I look forward to discussing the script with you. I'll send you a copy by messenger, so you can read it."

"I can't wait," Adrian replied, looking into his eyes.

As soon as they were in the car, Adrian began to laugh uncontrollably. "I don't believe what just happened," she gasped. "I felt like I was doing Lauren Bacall for that lecher!"

"You were wonderful," Claudia said, joining in her laughter. "And the bit with Harriet! Very clever, my girl! You've really learned how to handle yourself."

"And I have two cards to show for it. One from the

wife, and one from the husband. Christ, it's like being in the middle of a French farce!"

"Just don't get caught in the boudoir with your skirt up and your panties down."

Adrian shivered. "God, what a thought. And especially with Howard Bradshaw. What a smarmy little man! Surely Harriet must know what's going on. Why does she put up with it?"

"Haven't you noticed? She's not very bright. And she wants to be the woman he leans over and kisses before he walks up onstage to collect his Emmy or his Oscar. A lot of wives in this business will put up with anything for that. Some of them even do a little pimping on the side, just to keep their husbands happy."

"Then she deserves everything she gets, and more," Adrian said.

"Do I detect a slightly vicious note in your voice? I've always felt a little sorry for Harriet, even though she's an awful cow. Do you know something about her I don't?"

"No, of course not. I just met her tonight," Adrian said hastily. Then, to change the subject, she asked, "Do you think Howard's offer was sincere? Or was it just a come-on?"

"A little of both, probably. Do you think you can handle the costumes for a major production?"

"I think I can handle Howard, but I must admit, I'm scared silly about getting the job. I've never done anything for television, except at Dolly's. And that's been good training, but even so . . ."

"The only difference is that you'll be in charge, you'll work harder, and you'll make a lot of money," Claudia said. "I think you can do it. And since I've been made production manager, I'll be around to help you in whatever way I can."

"Well, that's enough to take care of all my fears," Adrian said, laughing. "And Paul's done a lot of work in television—I'm sure he'll be able to give me some tips."

"Are you two seeing each other?" Claudia asked.

"We have been, but after tonight, I'm not sure—"

Claudia's apartment was in Studio City, and as they drove there, Adrian told her about Paul and how reluctant she was to get into a committed relationship with him.

"He sounds like one of the good guys, and there's damned few of them around," Claudia said. "Are you sure you're doing the right thing?"

"I'm positive," Adrian replied coldly. "All I want to devote myself to is a career."

Claudia looked at her pensively. "I can't blame you for that, after what you've been through...." She paused, then went on: "You really have changed a great deal, and not just in how you look. You're much stronger, tougher, more self-assured."

"That's good, isn't it?"

"In this business, absolutely. Just be careful not to let career become a way of life. It can squeeze all the juice out of you, and then one day you wake up and find that all you have is a career, and nothing else. That may sound like an old cliché, and very banal, but it's true, nevertheless." She laughed and patted Adrian's arm. "But don't worry about it. You have too many other things to think about at the moment. However, if I see you getting out of hand, I'll remind you."

Adrian stopped the car in front of Claudia's apartment building and turned to her. "Thank you for everything, Claudia. It was almost worth going to prison, just to make friends with you."

Claudia's eyes suddenly brightened with tears. "What a lovely thing to say." She leaned forward and kissed Adrian on the cheek. "I feel the same way, dear. Now I'd better go before we both get maudlin. Call me next week and we'll have dinner."

When Adrian got back to her apartment in West Hollywood, she found Paul sitting in his car waiting for her.

He followed her up the walk to the front door, and once they were inside, he asked, "How was dinner with the big producer?"

"Shall I make some coffee first?"

"No, just tell me what happened," he responded coldly.

She put her arms around his neck. "Don't be angry with me," she pleaded softly. "I'm sorry I couldn't be with you, but I had to take advantage of the opportunity. There must have been times when you had to do the same thing to get a job."

His eyes softened and he put his hands on her waist. "You're right. I'm being an asshole. It's just that I wanted you with me to celebrate." He kissed her softly and they moved into the living room and sat down on the couch. "So, did anything come of it?" he asked.

"I think so," Adrian said excitedly. She told him about Howard Bradshaw's offer and concluded, "He's sending me the script, and we're going to have a meeting to talk about it."

Paul looked skeptical. "Do you really think he means it? Bradshaw has the reputation of using his position to seduce little girls."

"Well, he's not going to seduce this little girl,'" Adrian said, laughing. "But I am a little scared—oh, not of him— but of the job. I've never done a show like that before, and I have so much to learn."

Paul took her in his arms. "And you want me to help you, right?"

"Oh, Paul, would you? I've learned so much from you already—you've been such a wonderful teacher...."

He drew back a little and looked down at her, his eyes warm and teasing. "Is that all I am to you? Just a mentor?"

"You know better than that," she whispered.

"I'm not sure of anything where you're concerned, except that I love you," he said huskily.

Adrian lifted her face to his and he kissed her. She pressed against him, and he pulled her onto his lap, running one hand up under her skirt. The kiss deepened, and he began to fumble with the catch on her dress. "Wait—" she mumbled. "Let me take it off. . . ."

She stood up, kicked off her shoes, and slipped out of the dress. Clad only in her pantyhose, she stood before him. "Is that better?" she asked in a throaty whisper. He nodded and reached out for her, but she brushed his hands aside. "No—let me take off your clothes."

Kneeling, she removed his shoes and socks while he shrugged out of his jacket and tie. She took off his shirt and pressed her lips to his chest, lightly flicking her tongue over his nipples. Then she loosened his belt and he lifted his hips so she could take off his pants. He leaned back and she knelt between his legs and pressed her face to his thighs, moving her lips over him until she reached the bulge at his crotch covered by his jockey shorts. He gasped softly as the heat of her mouth enflamed him. She pulled him to his feet and slowly tugged the shorts down, freeing his erection. He watched, mesmerized, as her arms encircled his thighs. Her hands played teasingly over his buttocks while she ran her lips and tongue delicately over his swollen member. His body shuddered and his legs began to buckle. "Adrian, wait—" he groaned.

She let go of him and lay back on the floor, wriggling slowly out of her pantyhose. When she was naked, she held her arms out to him and whispered, "Now—now let's celebrate."

Sometime during the night they moved into her bedroom. But when Paul awoke in the morning, he was alone. He found Adrian at her drawing board in the living room, deeply engrossed in preparing sketches for Howard Bradshaw.

33

THE REVIEWS OF THE PLAY APPEARED AND THEY WERE unanimous in praise for everyone involved. Adrian was singled out by the critics and acclaimed for her costumes. Paul presented her with a leather-bound scrapbook in which he had mounted all the clippings, with her notices circled in red, and Kelly sent her flowers with a note that read, "I told you all you had to do was flaunt it!" and was signed, "Dr. Frankenstein." Claudia sent her a silver charm bracelet with a little angel on it signifying the play—*Fallen Angels*—and said she would add a charm for every play and film Adrian did until it was filled.

The play settled in for what appeared to be a long run, and Adrian continued to work at Dolly's and spend her evenings with Paul. She submitted her sketches for *Mourning Becomes Electra* to Gordon Davidson, who praised them and said that if the revival went into the fall season at the Taper, they would discuss the possibility of her doing the costumes. At first she was disappointed that it wasn't going to happen right away. Paul cautioned her that it was the nature of the business to have shows reach the preproduction phase and then, for one reason or another, be shelved.

Then she received the script of *Tender Is the Night* from Howard Bradshaw and her spirits soared. Although Paul had begun to work as an assistant director on a low-budget independent film, they spent many nights together studying the script and discussing key scenes for which she designed costumes. Sometimes, long after he had fallen asleep, she was still at her drawing table, refining and polishing her sketches. Once she was confident that they were ready, she called Howard Bradshaw and made an appointment to see him.

Adrian pulled into the parking lot at Universal Studios and hurried into the lobby of the black tower office building where she was checked in and given a visitor's pass by a security guard. At the fourteenth floor, she stepped off the elevator and turned left into a large reception area. An attractive young woman sitting at a desk looked up and gave her a bright, artificial smile.

"I'm Adrian Ronay, and I have an appointment with Howard Bradshaw," Adrian said.

"Oh, yes—he's expecting you." She had the soothing voice of an airline stewardess. "I'll take you to his office."

Adrian followed her and was ushered into a large suite with floor-to-ceiling windows that offered a panoramic view of the San Fernando Valley. The receptionist said, "Mr. Bradshaw had to step out for a few minutes. May I bring you some coffee while you're waiting?"

"No, thank you," Adrian murmured, a little awed by the size and rich furnishings of the office.

The young woman nodded, glided silently out the door, and closed it. Adrian put her portfolio down on a side table and looked around at the elegantly framed steel engravings hanging on the paneled walls, a large built-in bookcase filled with red leather-bound editions of classics, and the fine pieces of antique furniture. Then she saw something that brought a momentary chill. It was the Sheraton mahogany display cabinet that Harriet had bought from the Skolskys' the day Alec had walked into her life. For a few seconds the entire scene replayed itself before her eyes, and she found herself feeling a little faint. She sat down in a deep leather easy chair and nervously lit a cigarette, trying to erase the moment from her mind. A few minutes later, Howard Bradshaw walked in and she rose to greet him.

"Adrian, it's good to see you again," he said with a wide smile. He took both her hands and held her at arm's length, his eyes moving swiftly over her figure. "You look absolutely wonderful."

She had purposely dressed in a severely tailored, dark blue suit and a pale rose-colored blouse, hoping to effect a businesslike appearance. Howard stepped closer, still holding her hands, and said in a lowered tone, "I've been thinking about you a lot since we met."

"And I've been thinking a lot about you," Adrian said smoothly, taking her hands from his and walking over to the side table to get her portfolio. "As a matter of fact, I've been thinking about you every night—while I was working on my sketches."

Howard's face fell a little; then he smiled and said, "Ah, yes—the sketches. I'm anxious to see them." He went to his desk, pressed the button on the intercom, and told his secretary to hold all his calls. Adrian opened the portfolio, spread the drawings out, and began to explain some of her ideas. He listened, nodding vaguely and pretending to examine the designs, but his eyes kept shifting to her face and the neckline of her blouse. Adrian encouraged him a little by unbuttoning her jacket and leaning forward to reveal the swell of her breasts. You old fool, she thought, this routine went to the grave with Darryl Zanuck!

Howard finished looking at the sketches and sat back in his chair. "They're wonderful, my dear, as I knew they would be," he said expansively.

Adrian took a breath, then plunged ahead and asked, "Does that mean I get the job?"

"Well, it's not as simple as that," Howard said slowly. "We're talking about a major film for network television. It is absolutely essential that we have someone experienced, someone whose work has been recognized by the industry to design the costumes for a project as important as this. So—taking all that into consideration, we've signed Anthony Trent, whose work I'm sure you know."

He paused at the look of dismay on her face, then went on: "But I can talk to Anthony about putting you on as his assistant, if you're interested. And I could also help you get into the Costume Designers' Guild. As I'm sure you know, you can't work in television or films without being a member." He gave her a crafty smile. "It could be a marvelous opportunity for you, being the assistant to an award-winning designer like Anthony."

"Yes, it would," Adrian replied automatically. Her mind was racing: this wasn't what she'd hoped for, but even so, the chance to work with Anthony Trent was a major step forward in her career. And she needed Bradshaw to help get her into the Designers' Guild. She could see him watching her with a sly look in his eyes, waiting for her decision. For the moment he knew that he held all the trump cards. But only for the moment, she decided.

"How soon could I meet Mr. Trent?" she asked.

Bradshaw made a vague gesture. "In a few days, I'm sure. In the meantime, perhaps we could have dinner together?" He gave her a meaningful look.

The question hung in the air for a few moments. Now he's thrown the ball to me, Adrian thought. If I don't come across, he won't come across. But if I'm not careful, he could ruin me. There has to be a way to outsmart this old bastard and get what I want without screwing him for it.

She reached across the desk and took his hand. "Howard, I'd be so grateful for the chance to work on such an important project...." She caressed his hand with her fingertips. "But I'm sure that Mr. Trent has worked with many other people he's considering for this job. If only I had the assurance that he was really interested in my work, I'd be so much more grateful...." Her voice sank to a low, intimate whisper. "Then we could have dinner at my place, one night. Just the two of us—and celebrate."

"Is that a promise?" Howard asked in a thick voice.

"Of course," Adrian answered easily. "After all, if I

get the job, you and I will be working together and seeing each other almost every day." She withdrew her hand and sat back, giving him a smile that was filled with promise. "How could I face you if I didn't keep my word?"

Howard picked up the phone and asked his secretary to get Anthony Trent on the line.

Anthony Trent's office was in a large bungalow near the wardrobe department. In previous incarnations it had been the dressing room of many famous stars. Now it reflected the somewhat eclectic taste of the celebrated designer. Howard and Adrian entered the white frame house and walked into a sitting room that was wildly decorated in a mix of modern and antique furniture, heavy white nubby linen drapes on the windows, and a thick, white plush carpet covering the floor. One wall was covered by studio photographs of well-known actresses wearing clothes that Trent had designed for their films, while another was splashed with a collection of abstract paintings and watercolors by renowned modern artists. Behind a Spanish-styled desk in the corner was a wall of framed awards, plaques, and certificates of honor that Trent had collected over the years, and on a shelf just below them stood his three Academy Award Oscars. In the rest of the room every table surface was covered with objets d'art ranging from African sculptures and Delft from Holland, to Chinese vases and jade from Japan.

Trent was sitting in a brocaded chair that barely contained his wide, corpulent figure. He was wearing a black fish-net sweater styled like a smock to cover his large belly, beige linen slacks, and white espadrilles. A too-handsome young man in skin-tight Levi's and a green polo shirt was standing at a small bar, mixing drinks.

"Ah, Howard, do come in, come in," Trent called out without rising. His voice quivered between a tenor and a falsetto, and he had a heavy, theatrical English accent. "And you've brought your little friend yourself. How very gallant of you. Delightful to meet you, Miss Ronay. Do sit down; be comfortable. Would you like a drink?" His round blue eyes darted to the young man. "Perry, make them one of those lime concoctions of yours; they're absolutely delicious. Oh, dear—I'm forgetting my manners. Howard, Miss Ronay, this is Perry DiMarco, a very talented sketch artist who's been working with me."

Adrian nodded to the young man and turned back to Trent. "It's a great pleasure to meet you, Mr. Trent. I've admired your work since I was a little girl."

Trent's eyes went icy. "Oh, dear, that makes me feel older than God. But thank you, my dear. And which of my films did you *admire* the most?" he asked, deliberately mimicking her use of the word "admire" with undisguised sarcasm.

Adrian realized at once that he was angry about seeing her. She glanced at Howard and saw him staring furiously at Trent. Something was going on between them, and she was in the middle of it. She gave the designer a warm smile and said, "Oh, Mr. Trent, there were so many: *Scarlet Woman*, *Three on a Honeymoon*, *Careless*, *The King's Mistress*, *Shadow Over*—"

"Enough, my dear!" Trent cried petulantly. "You've obviously had a misspent youth in front of the telly watching the Late Show." He looked over at the young man and barked, "Perry, do bring me a drink!"

DiMarco crossed the room carrying a tray and handed one to Trent, then offered drinks to Howard and Adrian. Howard took one, but Adrian shook her head. He put the tray down on a coffee table made of glass and bamboo wound with leather thongs, and retreated to a seat next to Anthony Trent. He sat down, his muscular legs spread wide, and draped one tanned arm casually around the back of the Englishman's chair.

Trent took a healthy gulp of the drink, then looked at Adrian with some disdain. "I understand that you are a designer, Miss Ronay, and you've brought me some sketches to look at."

Adrian opened her portfolio and handed Trent the

drawings. He put the drink down and began to look through them. His eyes widened slightly and grew bright. "Oh, I see they're for *Tender Is the Night*—did you send her a script, Howard?" he asked with feigned innocence.

"Yes, I did," Howard replied tightly.

"How very thoughtful of you," Trent murmured, shuffling through the sketches. He held one up for Perry to look at. "They're very pretty, aren't they?"

"They're okay," the boy mumbled.

Adrian watched Trent closely. Even though he was apparently just glancing at her designs, she could see that he was giving them an intense scrutiny. When he was finished, he handed them back to her with a false smile of encouragement.

"You have a nice little talent, my dear. Your sketches are charming. Thank you so much for letting me see them."

There was a note of finality in his voice; the interview was over. Adrian looked up at Howard, waiting for him to say something. He gave her quick smile of assurance and walked over to Perry. "Would you mind leaving us alone for a few minutes?" he said quietly.

It was more a command than a request. The young man looked quickly at Trent, who was glaring stonily at Howard. The designer finally nodded his head and Perry got to his feet. "I'll go up to wardrobe and see if that shipment of fabric has come in," he said, throwing Adrian a sulky look. "Nice to meet you," he said to her, and left the room.

As soon as he was gone, Howard said to Adrian, "Would you mind waiting outside, please?"

"No, of course not," Adrian replied, getting to her feet. She turned to Anthony Trent and said politely, "Thank you for seeing me. It's been a great privilege meeting you."

He forced a smile and nodded his head, making his chins wobble. "You're very welcome, Miss Ronay. And good luck."

She walked out of the bungalow into the bright glare of the afternoon sun but left the door slightly ajar. Looking around to see if anyone was close by, she stood near the door, straining to hear what Howard and Trent were saying. At first there was only a low murmur of voices. Then Howard's rose angrily. "I want her on this picture, Tony. Do you understand? Not your boy—my girl!"

"How dare you!" Trent bristled. "Perry is very talented! I've been training him myself!"

Howard's voice turned ugly. "You've been training him, and he's been *shtupping* your fat ass! Well, as far as I'm concerned, that's okay. You can keep him on the payroll to serve you drinks and let you play with his dick. But Adrian goes in as your assistant designer. Is that clear?"

Adrian noticed several people coming up the street. She stepped away from the door and lit a cigarette, trying to look nonchalant. A few minutes later Howard came out of the bungalow. He took her arm and they started back toward his office.

"He didn't want me, did he?" she said.

"Of course he did," Howard replied calmly. "As a matter of fact, he asked to keep your sketches for a while, so he could study them later, when he has more time."

She looked at him, incredulous. "You mean I've got the job?"

"Of course. You'll start working with him next Monday. In the meantime, I'll see to it you become a member of the Designers' Guild." He looked at her, his grey eyes hard and businesslike. "I always keep my promises."

His meaning was clear; now it was up to her to keep her promise. "Give me a few days to get my schedule cleared up, and I'll call you," Adrian said in a low voice. She glanced at her watch and uttered a groan. "Speaking of schedules, I've got to get back to Dolly's. Oh, I can't wait to tell everyone how wonderful you've been! Howard, I'm so grateful."

"You'd better be," he answered with a rough laugh,

putting his arm around her waist and flattening his hand on her hip.

"Walk me to my car," she said huskily.

In the parking lot, she opened the door and got in behind the wheel. Howard stood inside the opened door and looked around to see if anyone was watching. Then he took Adrian's hand and placed it on his crotch, putting her fingers firmly around his member. She stroked him for a few seconds and felt him get hard. She looked up at him with a teasing smile. "Lean down and kiss me good-bye before we end up doing something indecent in the Universal Studios parking lot."

"It wouldn't be the first time." He laughed, bending down to her.

As he came closer, she shut her eyes, steeling herself for the touch of his lips. He bent her head back a little and covered her mouth with his. She felt his hand reaching to touch her breasts and caught it, moving it up to cup her cheek. His tongue was insistent and she opened her lips just a little. Then she pulled away from him and said in a breathless voice, "I really must go now. I'll call you as soon as I can. I promise." She handed him her portfolio to give to Trent. "Thank you again," she whispered.

He stepped away so she could close the door and pull out. She turned back to wave to him, then drove off in a hurry, entering the flow of traffic onto the Hollywood Freeway. Once out of sight of the studio, she began to laugh. She had done it! Assistant designer on a major film! A feeling of elation and power rose up in her, and her hands on the wheel trembled with excitement. But she knew she still had to be careful; Anthony Trent was a bastard and would try to make her life miserable. That didn't matter, however—she had Howard in her corner. And she knew exactly what to do to keep him there.

To celebrate her new job, Paul took Adrian to dinner at Le Dôme on Sunset Boulevard. Afterward, he suggested they drive out to Malibu Beach. He found a turnout on Pacific Coast Highway and parked the car. They sat in silence for a few minutes, watching the lights twinkle along the curving shoreline and the dark waters of the ocean pound against the beach.

Adrian said finally, "It was a lovely dinner, Paul. Thank you."

He smiled and took her hand. "You know what they say—success doesn't mean anything unless you have someone to share it with."

Adrian sensed the direction he was moving in and began to feel a little uneasy. "I'm not sure that's true," she said lightly. "It means a great deal to me, whether I share it or not." She hadn't meant to sound so flippant, but the damage was done.

Paul gave her a hurt look. "Well, I'm still very proud of you. And, taking nothing away from your personal accomplishment, I'm glad I was some help to you, in my own small way."

She heard the slightly bitter edge in his voice and lifted his hand to her cheek in a gesture of apology. "I'm sorry, Paul. I didn't mean to sound so arrogant. You know how much I appreciate everything you've done for me and taught me. I couldn't have gotten this far so quickly without you."

He slipped an arm around her shoulders and sighed deeply. "You're very frustrating," he muttered, absently stroking her hair. "I never know what's going on in your mind."

"Do you find me mysterious?" she asked, grinning up at him.

"Mystifying would be more like it." Then his voice grew serious. "Adrian, what the hell are we all about? I mean, are we lovers, or what? We've been seeing each other for almost six months. We work together, sleep together, share our ambitions and hopes, but I still don't know what that amounts to where you're concerned. All

I know is that I love you, and I think you love me. But I'm never quite sure. I guess I'm really just an old-fashioned man, and I want some kind of commitment...."

Adrian was silent for a few seconds, her mind filled with conflicting urges. Then she began hesitantly, "I can't give you one—not right now. My work is so important to me, more than I can express. But you know I care for you. Can't we just go on like we have?"

Even to her, the words sounded weak and unconvincing. In truth, she was beginning to find herself torn between her growing feelings for Paul and her burning desire to achieve success. And the more she considered the future, the less possible it seemed that she could have both.

"I'm not sure if we can go on this way," he replied wearily. He got out of the car and went to stand by the guard rail at the edge of the embankment, staring moodily at the waves breaking against the shore.

Adrian followed him. "Paul, don't be angry," she pleaded, touching his arm. "I really do care for you, but—"

"I know—your career comes first," he said flatly. "Christ, we sound like a TV movie. Amazing, isn't it, how life imitates art—if you can call that crap art."

"But that's just the point," Adrian said. "I do think of my work as art, and I can't think about anything else, or anyone else, until I've accomplished what I want."

He gave her a piercing look, made more intense by the shadows thrown across his face in the moonlight. "Fame, wealth, success—power? Is that what you want?"

"Don't you?" she challenged him. "Isn't that why you're working your ass off, so you, too, can make what we laughingly call the big time?"

He threw his hands up in a gesture of defeat. "I can't argue with that. Of course I do." He swung around and took her in his arms. "But I want us to do it as a team. Together. Adrian, listen to me," he went on urgently. "I had some good news today, too. I met with a producer from New York who came out here last week and saw *Fallen Angels*. He offered me a chance to direct a play off-Broadway. He's very excited about it, and there's already talk of taking it uptown."

"Paul, that's wonderful!" she exclaimed.

"There's more. He was very enthusiastic about your work, and I asked him if you could do the costumes, and he went for the idea."

"But, Paul, I can't leave now—"

"It will be several months before the play goes on, enough time for you to finish your work on the film and then come to New York. In the the meantime I could find an apartment so we could live together. Adrian, it would be so wonderful, being in New York, working on a play together. . . ."

She pulled away from him. "Paul, I can't do that—not now or in a few months. I'm just getting established here. What if the play flopped? You could come back here and work; people know you here. But I'd have to start all over. I can't take the risk."

They stared at each other, silent for a long few minutes. Then Paul gave her a mirthless smile. "We've just fallen into a common Hollywood syndrome: being separated by our careers."

"When do you have to leave?" she asked in a small voice.

"This weekend. Frank—the producer—wants me to meet with the playwright and discuss some revisions. And I have to look for a place to live."

"How long will you be gone?"

"That depends on the play. Just a few months, maybe. Or longer, if it's a success."

Adrian grew silent, suddenly realizing the impact of his news. Paul had come to play an important part in her life. More important, perhaps, than she was willing to admit. At the same time, she couldn't help feeling a surge of relief. It would be easier to get started in her new job without him around to confuse her emotionally.

"Maybe being apart for a while will do us both good," he said quietly.

Adrian nodded her head slowly. Then, feeling guilty for what she was thinking, she said, "Oh, Paul, I will miss you. Terribly." Tears glistened in her eyes and she began to cry. He gathered her into his arms and she buried her head in his chest, feeling momentarily bereft. "Will you write to me? Call me?" she asked.

He tilted her face up, wiped away the tears, and kissed her gently. "Of course I will."

"And I promise to think about us while you're gone," she said fervently.

Paul gave her a disbelieving smile. "You don't have to make any promises. Just remember one thing."

"What?"

"I love you."

34

Two weeks later Adrian made an urgent call to Claudia and asked to meet her for lunch.

"I can steal an hour from my busy schedule," Claudia said. "How 'bout the Commissary at one o'clock?"

"No, I don't want to chance being overheard—all the production people eat lunch there. Meet me at that French restaurant—Robaire's—down the street."

"Sounds serious," Claudia said.

"It is," Adrian replied cryptically, and hung up.

A few hours later they met inside the restaurant. After the maitre d' had seated them at a table, Claudia asked, "You look pretty grim. Isn't being Trent's assistant designer working out?"

"Assistant designer? Flunky is more like it," Adrian fumed. "He has me running all over town for fabrics, shoes, jewelry, and whatever other errands he can think of to keep me out of his sight. I'm doing all the research, and when we have fittings, I do all the work while he sits on his fat ass and drinks and gossips with the actors. If I offer any suggestions, he dismisses them out of hand."

"I'm not surprised, considering how he felt about Howard getting you the job. What did you expect?"

"I didn't expect him to steal my designs!" Adrian cried angrily. "He must have copied my sketches before he gave back my portfolio. He's modified at least a dozen of my designs—badly, I might add—and now he's claiming them as his own. It's no wonder; he drinks like a fish and can barely get through the day, much less do any real designing. Not even the director knows what's going on."

"Have you told Howard about this?"

"Not yet. I've been using every trick known to woman-kind to keep him at bay, and he's not happy about it. Besides, I wanted to talk to you first." She looked at Claudia desperately. "There must be a way to stop Trent. I can't just let him work me over like this!"

A concerned expression came over Claudia's face. "I don't think you're the only one who's getting screwed on this production." She signaled the waiter for the check. "Let's go—we'll discuss this in my office. I have some expenses I want you to look at."

As soon as they were in Claudia's office, she pulled out a sheaf of papers and handed them to Adrian. "Trent sent me these memos for a batch of costumes that were made at Dolly's."

"Yes, I know about them. I delivered the designs and fabrics myself. They were dresses for Laura Sydney, who's playing the role of Nicole."

"Well, the costs seemed a little high to me, but when I mentioned it to Howard, he simply brushed aside my doubts and okayed them. Take a look and tell me what you think."

Adrian thumbed through the papers, her eyes widening with surprise. "Yes, these are high. They must be three times what Dolly usually charges."

"Are you sure of that?"

"There's a simple way to find out." Adrian reached for the phone and called Dolly, asked her about the charges for the dresses, then hung up. "I was right. Dolly only charged Trent a third of these figures."

Claudia went into her file and pulled out another batch of papers. "Take a look at these. They're requisitions from Trent for his expenses: fabrics, hand-made shoes, beading work, dying and screen painting, and other services."

Adrian examined the sheets carefully. "I've worked with most of these people, and none of them charge this much," she declared.

"They were all submitted to Howard for his approval, and he signed them all." Claudia sat down at her desk and drummed her fingers nervously. "It's just as I suspected. Trent is marking up all the bills and pocketing the difference. It's not an unusual procedure; everybody in town does the same thing when they can. But Howard is okaying all these extravagant costs...." She gave Adrian a significant look.

"You mean you think he's in on it?"

"It wouldn't surprise me. With all the money involved in a project as large as this, it would be a simple way to skim some off the top."

"But you're the production manager," Adrian said. "Isn't there something you can do?"

"I'm not sure, but I think so." Claudia explained that the film was a coproduction of Universal and an independent company called Zenith Films that was headed by a former studio executive named Irving Green. "He was one of my former employer's clients—one of the people I helped cover up for. Getting me this job was his way of saying thank you. And he wanted someone whom he could trust working on the budget."

Claudia went on, telling Adrian how Irv Green and Howard Bradshaw had made two TV films together, and although it was not widely known in the industry, the men quietly detested each other. Irv was a hardworking, unpretentious man who deplored Howard's extravagant life-style and arrogant manner. But Howard had a track record with the networks, and Irv felt compelled to work with him until his own company was firmly established.

"What it all comes down to," Claudia said, "is that Trent and possibly Howard are ripping off Zenith Films. Trent has his own company—Seven Veils, Inc.—and he gets all the bills. Then he sends me memos of expenses, Howard okays them, and I issue a check to Trent's company from Zenith. When the production begins to go over budget—and at this rate it will—Irv will have to answer to Universal."

"Can't you tell him about this?" Adrian asked.

"I could, but it's a difficult thing to prove. There's so much paperwork involved. If Howard were confronted, he could always claim he was ignorant of Trent's actions. And for all I know, Howard may be doing the same thing with other production people. He could even be marking up the bills without them knowing about it."

"Does that mean there's nothing we can do?"

Claudia gazed at her thoughtfully before replying, "I have an idea that just might solve our problems. In fact, if it works, we just might be able to get both Trent and Howard off the film. And if that happens, you could have a clear shot at being the head designer on the project."

Adrian's eyes gleamed at the prospect. "What's your idea?" she asked eagerly.

"Claudia, I still don't understand what this is all about," Irv Green said as he followed Claudia out of the elevator and down the hall to Howard Bradshaw's office. He was a small, dapper man with bushy grey hair and worry frowns creased across his forehead. Now, as he questioned her, they grew deeper than ever.

"Please trust me, Irv," she replied. "You've been a good friend to me, and I just don't want to see you get hurt."

"Hurt? By whom? Who wants to hurt me?"

"Just do as I ask, and in a few minutes you'll understand the whole thing."

They approached the young woman sitting at a desk outside Howard's office. She looked up at them and smiled. "Hello, Mr. Green, Miss Sherwood. Shall I buzz Mr. Bradshaw and tell him you're here? He's in a meeting right now with Mr. Trent and Miss Ronay, but—"

"No, don't bother, Sherry," Claudia said. "We can wait." She glanced at Irv and he caught her signal.

"Sherry, why don't you take a coffee break," he told the girl. "Miss Sherwood and I have something to discuss."

The secretary looked hesitant, and Claudia said, "If there are any calls, I'll take them until you get back."

Sherry took her purse out of the bottom drawer of the desk and stood up. "Thanks, I'll be back in a few minutes."

"Don't hurry," Claudia said, sitting down behind the desk.

As soon as Sherry was out of sight, Claudia flipped on the intercom and breathed a small sigh of relief; Adrian had managed to do the same inside Howard's office. She and Irv could clearly hear the voices raised in argument.

"I really didn't mind being treated like an errand boy," Adrian was saying. "But I was shocked to learn that Mr. Trent was modifying my designs and claiming them as his own!" She sounded tearful and helpless.

"That's an insulting lie!" Trent screeched. "It's positively absurd nonsense!" His voice was shaking, his words slurred; he had been drinking all afternoon.

"I think we should consider this carefully, Tony," Howard said sternly. "Adrian showed me the designs in question, and I have to admit, it appears that you borrowed them from the sketches in her portfolio."

"I don't need the doodles of an amateur in order to do my job!" Trent exploded. "I've been at the top of this business for thirty years!"

Howard said in an admonishing tone, "We're not talking about your reputation; we're asking why you copied Adrian's sketches."

"How dare you even suggest that!" Trent cried, outraged. "She's the one that's profiting from the experience of working with me. I've had assistants beg me to use their ideas, just for the chance to see their work on the screen!"

"While you claimed all the credit," Adrian said bitterly.

"Why, you little bitch!" Trent cried. "And you'll probably use my name all over town to hustle some other producer into giving you a job!"

"We're not here to insult Adrian," Howard warned.

"Then I suggest we stop all this shit and get back to work," Trent said as if he were delivering an ultimatum. "I don't have to justify myself to you, Howard. After all, we've been doing business together for a long time," he added meaningfully.

The two men stared at each other for a few seconds, then Howard said to Adrian, "I've never known Anthony to steal from other designers. And if he says that his assistants have offered him their ideas without credit, I believe him. Perhaps he should have made that clear to you before this misunderstanding took place. After all, this is your first job on a major film, and you have a great deal to learn. I'm sure we can work out all these problems and get back to business as usual."

Adrian began to panic. Howard was clearly siding with Trent and warning her to behave. The spineless bastard was obviously not going to jeopardize his business arrangement with the designer just for her. She saw Trent grinning at her triumphantly and realized she'd have to talk fast.

"Is it business as usual for the head designer to steal from the budget, as well as from his assistants?"

Her words caught both men by surprise. Trent's smile faded, and his hands shook, spilling the drink he was holding.

Howard came up to her with a grim look on his face. "What are you talking about?" he asked quietly.

Adrian backed away from him and began to pace around the desk to make sure that everything she was going to say could be heard over the open intercom. "Mr. Trent's company is charging Zenith Films three times the actual expenses he pays to his suppliers. I happened to see some of his memos concerning the work done by Dolly King and was astonished. I called her to check the figures, and she told me how much she really charged. Mr. Trent is pocketing the difference."

Before Howard could reply, Trent began a laugh that rose to a high-pitched giggle. "My dear girl," he gasped, "are you on a crusade to clean up this dirty corrupt industry single-handedly? How very brave!"

"Then you don't deny it?" Adrian shot back.

"Deny what? Putting a few extra crumbs on my plate?" He made a languid gesture with one of his pudgy hands. "I pay my suppliers what they want and charge the company what I *need*. It's common practice—" He narrowed his eye and gave her a look filled with venom. "As common as fucking your way into a job."

Adrian ignored his insult and turned to Howard. "He admits that he's stealing from Zenith!"

Howard's face was pale, his voice weak and hesitant. "It isn't a matter of stealing, Adrian...."

"You've turned to the wrong person for help, Miss Ronay," Trent said, taking a deep gulp from his glass. "Mr. Bradshaw is completely aware of what's going on." He laughed drunkenly. "Howard approves all my expenses, don't you, Howard?" He waggled a finger at Bradshaw with a giddy smile. "He's such a naughty boy. He knows all sorts of tricks to keep *additional* pennies rolling in. And he's well taken care of for his efforts." Trent nodded and winked at Adrian. "We have an agreement."

"Tony, I think you've said enough!" Howard declared, glaring at him.

In the outer office, Irv Green switched off the intercom and looked at Claudia. "I think I've heard enough."

Claudia put her hand on his arm. "I'm sorry, Irv. But Adrian and I thought you should know what's going on."

They left the reception area and headed for the elevators. "Thank you, Claudia. And thank Miss Ronay for me," Irv said.

"Is there anything else I can do?" Claudia asked.

"Yes. Collect all of Anthony Trent's expense memos and verify the real charges from his suppliers. And do the same with anyone else in production who may have been involved with Howard's scheme. I'll take care of the rest myself."

* * *

A week later, a story appeared in the Hollywood trade papers announcing that Howard Bradshaw was being replaced as producer of *Tender Is the Night* because of artistic differences with its executive producer, Irving Green. The article also reported that costume designer Anthony Trent had been released from his contract at his own request and that Adrian Ronay had been signed to take over in his place.

Adrian plunged into work, quickly picking up the slack left by Anthony Trent. She took over an office in the wardrobe department and organized a staff. Every scene in the script was broken down, and there were daily conferences with the writer and the director, who had also been signed to produce the film. A schedule was made up for fittings, and Dolly and her staff were assigned to make the costumes. At Adrian's suggestion, Kelly was brought in to do the makeup. Within weeks, everyone in the company was talking about her efficiency and the brilliance of her designs.

Finally, the *Tender Is the Night* company, including Adrian and Kelly, was ready to leave for France, where the principal shooting would take place. That same week, Paul's play opened off-Broadway. A few days before she left, Adrian sent Paul a note and two dozen roses to wish him luck. Kelly came into her office and heard her giving instructions to the florist.

"Why don't we make a stopover in New York and see the play?" Kelly suggested.

"I can't take the time," Adrian said. "There's going to be a lot of work to do in Paris, and then I have to fly to Switzerland to see the locations for the sanitorium sequence."

Kelly raised a questioning eyebrow. "Are you afraid to see him? Did something happen between you two?"

"Nothing happened," Adrian replied curtly. "I just don't have the time. You know how tight the schedule is, and I still don't have that scene in the jazz club finished."

"Okay, okay," Kelly said soothingly. "I just thought I'd ask."

"Sorry, I didn't mean to snap your head off. It's just that I want everything I do in this film to be right."

"That doesn't mean you have to make yourself crazy." Kelly grinned at her. "Stop worrying. You're doing a terrific job. The whole company is already putting down money that you're going to win the Emmy."

Adrian threw her hands up in mock despair and groaned. "That's all I needed to hear! Now *you're* making me crazy!"

Six months later, on a fine clear night, Adrian, accompanied by Irv Green, Claudia, and Kelly, alighted from a hired limousine in front of the Pasadena Civic Auditorium. Here the Academy of Television Arts and Sciences was going to present the technical awards. Later in the week, when the Emmy show was televised to the nation, segments of the evening's program would be shown and the winners announced.

As soon as they were inside and seated, the ceremonies started with an orchestral fanfare. Then the main business of the evening began: categories were explained, the nominees were announced, and the winners were called to the stage to receive their awards.

Adrian's heart was beating wildly with excitement. Kelly sat next to her, and she gripped his hand tightly as a line of beautiful girls began a fashion parade across the stage. They were dressed in a rich array of costumes created by some of the finest designers in the business. When a group appeared in the gowns from *Tender Is the Night*, there was a burst of applause. Kelly leaned over and whispered in Adrian's ear, "You're breaking every bone in my hand. I'll never dance again."

"I'll pay all the hospital bills," Adrian muttered, swallowing hard as the names of the nominees were announced. There was a moment of silence while the envelope was opened. And then her name was read.

"I knew it!" Kelly yelled. Claudia reached over to kiss

her, and Irv Green helped her to her feet. Adrian floated down the aisle, propelled by the sound of applause. As she ascended the steps and walked across the stage, a sense of complete happiness and fulfillment surged through her, washing away all memories of the pain and anguish she had gone through to reach this moment in her life.

PART
IV

35

ADRIAN BECAME ONE OF THE MOST SOUGHT-AFTER designers in Hollywood. She did two more films for Irv Green and created a sensation with her daring and innovative costumes for Gordon Davidson's production of *Mourning Becomes Electra*, for which she won the Los Angeles Critics' Award.

In order to associate herself and her work with the legendary glamour of Hollywood, Adrian moved into a suite at the Chateau Maront, the famous residence hotel that overlooked Sunset Boulevard and was a romantic landmark of elegant living; Gable, Garbo, Monroe, Errol Flynn, and many other stars had lived there.

The dizzying whirl of fame accelerated when she hired a publicity firm to capitalize on her success. A campaign was launched to make her name a household word, and soon she was romantically linked in print with some of the industry's most famous actors, producers, and directors. She was the guest of honor at a charity event that featured a fashion show of her costumes, and whenever she attended a premiere or a gala, her picture appeared in the society pages.

But despite all the acclaim and success she had achieved, Adrian couldn't forget the vow she had made to herself in prison. Now that she could afford it, she employed a firm of private investigators and gave them the sketch she had done of Alec while serving time, and the address in Las Vegas that Nora had given to her.

Late one night, after attending a star-studded tribute to Bette Davis, Adrian came into her apartment and heard the phone ringing. It was her private line, used only by those people she chose to give the number. She dropped her coat on a chair, kicked off her shoes, and answered the phone. It was Jerry Gilroy, the head of the investigating firm.

"Sorry to call so late, Miss Ronay. But my man just got back from Las Vegas, and you said to contact you immediately if we had anything."

Adrian sat down and lit a cigarette. "What did he find out?" she asked.

"Well, to be brief, Mr. Darcy worked for a short time booking entertainment for one of the smaller hotels on the strip. He got heavily involved in gambling and lost the job. Then he did some drug dealing, and for a while he ran a call-girl operation. We couldn't get much on his wife. We're not even sure he was married. Apparently he was quite a ladies' man, and was always surrounded by a number of women."

Of course he was, Adrian thought to herself grimly, remembering Alec's extraordinary handsomeness and charm. "Did you find out where he is now?" she asked.

"There were some rumors that he made a connection with the syndicate, but we couldn't verify them. The town really clams up on that subject. Anyway, he left Vegas very suddenly about four years ago. A woman did go with him, but we don't know who she was. There was one lead that he might have gone to Chicago, but it was pretty vague. Do you want us to follow up on it?"

"Couldn't you learn any more about the girl he came to Vegas with?" Adrian asked impatiently.

"No, I'm sorry. We couldn't. He appeared to be traveling alone, but that could have just been a cover to allow him to operate more freely." Gilroy paused, then asked, "Do you want us to go on looking for him? Shall we follow up the Chicago lead?"

Adrian hesitated. "I'm not sure. Send me a bill for the

expenses you've incurred so far, and I'll get back to you."

She put the receiver down and leaned back against the chair, closing her eyes. Gambling, drugs, and a call-girl ring, she thought. And what about Sheila? Where was she? Where had Alec abandoned her?

Even now, despite all her good fortune, the thought of him still brought a taste of bile in her throat, an anger that churned in her stomach. A new face and a new life had not been able to erase the memory of how he had betrayed her.

She got up and went to the bar in the corner of the living room, mixed a drink, then carried it out to the terrace. Leaning against the balustrade, she gazed down at the brightly lit, gaudy fling of the Sunset Strip. Beyond, the wide stretch of the city touched the edge of the night sky. But she was not comforted by the fact that she was here, living the kind of life she had dreamed of, surrounded by luxury and success. It had all been achieved for a purpose. And that purpose had not yet been fulfilled.

Leaving the terrace, she went back to the phone and called Jerry Gilroy. "Follow up that lead you had on Chicago," she told him. "I want you to keep looking for Alec Darcy until you find him."

"You look a little tired," Claudia said to Adrian. They were having lunch in the garden patio restaurant of the Rodeo Drive Hotel.

"I've been on a crazy schedule. In the last three months, I finished two films."

"Perhaps it's time you took a vacation and got away from tinsel town for a while."

"I suppose you're right," Adrian sighed. "But I really love the work."

"Yes, but all work and no play—have you been getting out, having any fun?"

Adrian gave her a wry smile. "If you mean men, the answer is an emphatic no."

"Gee, and I thought you were getting laid every night

of the week," Claudia kidded her. "Every time I read the columns, you're cuddling with some new, gorgeous man."

"Don't believe what you read. That's just my publicist working overtime. Oh, there's been one or two that were fun for a few dates, but nothing serious. It's mostly business, for them and me. I'm someone to be seen with now, and every actor in town looking for some free publicity has called. It's like going out with a chorus line of narcissists—I have to work like hell to look prettier than they do."

"Ah, Hollywood," Claudia laughed. "What about Paul? Have you kept in touch with him?"

"No, not really," Adrian replied quietly. "A few letters. He called once, after I got the Emmy. But that was almost a year and a half ago." She fell silent for a few minutes. "He asked me to marry him when he called, and I turned him down."

"How did he take it?" Claudia asked softly.

"He was angry, hurt. I can't blame him. . . ." She paused to light a cigarette. "I must admit, there are times when I miss him, but—"

"Do you want some advice? Or should I keep my mouth shut?" Claudia asked.

Adrian smiled and patted her hand. "You're a good friend. Keep your mouth shut. Let's just have lunch and then go shopping in every expensive store on Rodeo Drive."

One morning a few weeks later, Adrian received a phone call from Sam Phillips, asking her to meet with him to discuss a new project in which he was involved. She was immediately intrigued. Phillips was a well-known *wunderkind* in the record industry and in the last few years had added further luster to his reputation by heavily investing in films and several hit Broadway shows. Adrian had met him at a dinner in his honor and had been impressed by his lack of pretense and his good humor. She agreed to see him at his office the following afternoon.

Sam Phillips's company, Gemini Records, occupied the entire top floor of a new office building on Rodeo Drive, just off Wilshire Boulevard. Adrian stepped off the elevator into a gleaming high-tech foyer that reflected Phillips's taste and energy. The stark white walls were hung with colorful photorealist paintings, and contemporary black and white furniture was arranged around glass and chrome tables.

The receptionist sitting behind a black, lacquered desk was on the phone, making notes, and trying to ignore several men with attaché cases who were standing around looking impatient. Adrian saw that she was wearing one of the latest Melrose Avenue new-wave dresses, a fashion style that reminded her of Beverly Hills wives trying to resemble their fourteen-year-old daughters.

"Can I help you?" the receptionist asked, putting down the receiver.

"I'm Adrian Ronay. I have an appointment with Mr. Phillips."

The girl nodded and buzzed Phillips's secretary, much to the irritation of the men who were waiting. Another young woman, with long legs and the plastic beauty of a fashion model, appeared a few minutes later. She led Adrian down a long corridor whose walls were covered with gold and platinum records, the emblems of success in the record industry.

Sam Phillips was already on his feet, his hand extended in greeting when Adrian entered his office. A short, wiry, compact man in his early forties, he was casually dressed in loafers, slacks, and a sports coat. Tinted aviator glasses dominated his small, square face, and his thinning, black hair had been carefully styled to disguise a receding hairline. He moved gracefully across the deep, white carpet and took her hand.

"Adrian, it's good to see you again," he said in a voice that was pure New York–ese. "Ya look gorgeous. How 'bout a cup of coffee or a glass of wine?"

"No, thanks, Sam," Adrian replied, sitting down in a

white leather chair and glancing around the room. Like the foyer, it was done in a stark, modern design, with only a shelf of Grammy Awards and a couple of elegantly framed film and show posters to indicate Sam's accomplishments.

Phillips sat down behind a massive glass and chrome desk and gave her a winning smile. "I saw a screening the other night of *Starburst*, and I gotta tell you, the costumes you designed are sensational. Come Academy Award time, and you're gonna be up there on the stage picking up your Oscar."

"Thank you, Sam. From your lips to God's ears," Adrian said, laughing.

"Yes sir, you're the hottest designer in the business, and that's why I wanted to talk with you. I got a project that's right up your alley."

"A new film?" Adrian asked.

"Nope. A new show that's going to be the biggest thing on Broadway since *Dreamgirls*. I'm tellin' you it's got everything—a great book, a score that will make Sondheim leave the country, and an opportunity for a costume designer that guarantees a Tony."

"But, Sam, I've never done a Broadway musical—"

"Yeah, well, it's time you did, and I want it to be mine. The costumes will be crucial to the show's success." He pushed a thick manuscript across the desk to her and started to declaim as if he were delivering a press release. "It's a musical comedy-drama based on the life of Rudolph Valentino. From the immigrant Italian boy to the tango dancer in New York. Then Hollywood in the Roaring Twenties, fame, his love affair with Rambova, the scandal about his being a fag, his tour of the country, and his untimely death, which shocked and bereaved thousands of women all over the world. I tell you, the show is dynamite! We're calling it *Rudy!*"

Adrian picked up the script. "Sam, that's a wonderful idea for a show."

He sat back with a smile of satisfaction. "So—you interested?"

"You'd better believe I'm interested," Adrian said. "But of course, only if the money is good," she added, looking at him directly.

"Trust me. The money's good. And the budget's even better," Sam said smugly. "Just say the word, and I'll have my secretary bring in the contract."

"Can I have a couple of days to read the script before I give you my answer?"

"There's no time. I'm leaving for New York day after tomorrow, and I want you to come with me. We can talk about the script on the plane. I've booked a suite at the Plaza for you, and your salary starts as soon as you sign on the dotted line. And if you need an advance to cover any expenses, name your figure."

"You don't fool around, do you?"

"I know you can give me what I want. I could've gotten Theoni Aldredge or Florence Klotz, but I wanted you. And when I want something, I don't fool around."

"I like the way you think, Sam," Adrian said, lighting a cigarette. She sat back and smiled. "When I want something, I don't fool around, either. Tell your secretary to bring in the contract—and a cup of coffee. I'm going to be here for a while, reading it. And don't tell me there's not enough time."

Sam gave her a big grin. "Adrian, it's a pleasure doing business with you."

The plane landed at Kennedy Airport in the early evening. A chauffeured Mercedes limousine was waiting for them. As the powerful car smoothly negotiated traffic into Manhattan, Adrian stared out the window like an enraptured child.

"Your first time in New York?" Sam questioned.

"Yes," she replied, gazing in awe at her first glimpse of the world-famous skyline.

343

"You may never want to go back to L.A." Sam chuckled. "This is really my home. I like a place where you have to fight the weather. All that fucking sun in Hollywood has sautéed everybody's brains. They're so laid back, they're dead. Here, it's a struggle just to keep up with the cabbies!"

By the time they arrived at the Grand Army entrance to the Plaza, it was seven o'clock. The spring night was alive with people hurrying along the brightly lit streets and the noise of traffic, and the air was filled with a scent of new grass and flowers blooming in Central Park. Across from the hotel, the Pulitzer fountain was bathed in light, and nearby stood a group of vendors selling hot dogs, shishkebob, and hot pretzels.

The chauffeur followed Adrian and Sam up the steps to the entrance of the hotel with their luggage, where a bellboy took over. Sam dismissed the driver and they went into the lobby. They walked past the Palm Court, where people were dining to the music of a small chamber group, and got into an elevator.

"I asked a few people up to have some drinks," Sam said. "You're not too tired, are you? It's just the producer, set designer, director, and choreogorapher. They were anxious to meet you—they're the guys you'll be working closely with for the next couple of months."

"No, I'm not tired at all," Adrian replied. "I think I could use some fresh makeup, though."

"Don't worry about it. You look great, like you belong here." He grinned.

They got off the elevator and the bellboy led them down a long corridor to the suite Sam had reserved. They entered a small foyer and Adrian saw several men gathered in a spacious sitting room.

"Ah, the West Coast has arrived!" one of them called out.

Sam began to introduce Adrian around: Milo James, the set designer, was a tall, thin, intense young man with owlish eyes and frizzy blond hair; Terry Ambler, lithe and dark, with a cheerful, friendly smile, was the choreographer; John Hill, a heavyset man with greying hair and worried brown eyes, was the producer. The last man, who was standing at the bar with his back to them, turned around and came across the room with a hesitant smile on his face.

"And this is our director—" Sam started to say.

"Adrian and I are old friends," he interrupted. "We knew each other when."

It was Paul Mallory.

36

A FEW HOURS LATER, ADRIAN AND PAUL WERE SITTING at a table in Maxim's, a dinner club on Madison Avenue that replicated the Belle Epoque style of a Paris nightclub. The interior was a lavish array of mirrors and chandeliers, deep maroon carpeting, accents of alabaster and brass, and murals of lush gardens. In the background, a small group of musicians played familiar waltzes.

Adrian's eyes sparkled with delight as she looked around. "Paul, this is so exciting, being with you on my first night in New York. And this place is so beautiful!"

"I thought it would appeal to you," he said. "Are you sure you're not too tired from the flight for all this?"

"Oh, no. I'm much too excited to be tired." She sipped some wine and stared at him over the rim of the glass. "I'm so proud of you. Three hit plays in a row. And you look wonderful. You wear your success very well."

Paul smiled, his face shining with pleasure. "So do you," he replied huskily. "I can't tell you how it feels, just to be with you again."

"Sam should have told me you were going to direct. He never even mentioned your name when he told me about the show."

"I asked him not to. I wanted to surprise you, and—" His voice dropped a little. "—I guess I was afraid that if you knew, you might not..."

They were silent for a few minutes. Then Adrian said slowly, "I wasn't very nice to you the last time we spoke, and I'm sorry. But that would never have stopped me from working with you." She looked at him almost shyly. "In fact, your being here really makes everything perfect."

Paul beamed. He took her hand and leaned across the table, his deep brown eyes gazing at her intently. "Adrian, I still feel the same way about you. Perhaps I shouldn't bring it up so soon. I don't want to do or say anything that will make you uncomfortable, but maybe, now that some time has passed and we've both accomplished what we set out to do, we could—"

"Start over?" Adrian curled her fingers around his. "I think I'd like that, Paul. I think I'd like that very much."

They had a week before getting to work on the show, and Paul insisted on showing Adrian the town. She wanted to see the museums, and they went to the Metropolitan, the Frick, the Guggenheim, and the Whitney. They took the elevator to the top of the Empire State Building, and a trip on the Staten Island Ferry. They had lunch in Windows on the World, and dinner at The Four Seasons. For one whole day, Paul patiently trotted behind her through Bergdorf's, Henri Bendel's, B. Altman's, Macy's, and Bloomingdale's. They wandered through Tiffany's and Cartier's and joined a crowd of tourists to gape at the wonders of Trump Towers.

Paul led her through the narrow streets of Greenwich Village, with its many art galleries, coffee houses, old buildings that had witnessed history, and bustling bars and restaurants. They walked under the arch in Washington Square at dusk, and had a three-o'clock-in-the-morning breakfast in the Empire Diner. Adrian demanded to be taken to an automat, and they slipped nickles, dimes, and quarters into the slots of the sole surviving one at the corner of Forty-second and Third Avenue. One leisurely afternoon was taken up strolling through the famous shopping bazaar on Orchard Street in the Lower East Side.

Late one afternoon, after tramping through the art galleries and shops on Madison Avenue, Adrian finally declared that she was too exhausted to take another step. "This city is more overwhelming than I believed possible," she said weakly. "It's like the line in that old song: 'The great big city's a wondrous toy...!'"

Paul hailed a taxi and they collapsed in the back seat. "There's one more place I want you to see," he said. "The Chelsea Hotel."

Adrian groaned. "Paul, I can't move. I've got to get some rest or I'll wind up in the hospital and never get to do the show."

"But you've got to see the Chelsea," he protested. "Some of the most famous people in the world have lived there: Dylan Thomas, Eugene O'Neill, Jane Fonda, Thomas Wolfe. It's a haven for artists, dancers, painters. Even rock stars like Sid Vicious lived there."

"Sounds like the east coast Chateau Marmont," Adrian said.

"No, the Chateau Marmont is the west coast Chelsea," Paul quipped. "We'll just stop by for a few minutes. I have a friend who lives there."

The cab pulled up in front of the building and they went into the lobby, where the walls were hung with paintings by many of the famous residents. In the elevator, Paul said, "I love this place; it's a real cultural landmark. And my friend got lucky when he moved in—he has a place on the top floor, with a roof garden and a great view of the city."

"Does he have a bed I can collapse on?" Adrian muttered as they got out.

Paul smiled and led her down a hallway to a door. When no one answered his knock, he took out a key, explaining, "My friend gave me an extra key so I could stop by whenever I wanted."

They stepped into a small foyer that led to a high-ceilinged, spacious room with creamy yellow walls divided by white-wood wainscotting and carved moldings. Deep, soft rugs covered the floors, and the furnishings were a mix of antique tables and cabinets and modern chairs and sofas. Sunlight streamed through leaded-glass French doors that led to a large roof-garden, where elegant white wicker and wrought-iron furniture stood among a large grouping of leafy plants. The room had an ambience of elegance and serenity that provided a soothing balm of relief after the noise and bustle of the city streets.

"Do you like it?" Paul asked eagerly. "It even has a working fireplace. And at night, when the city lights up, you feel as if you own it."

"It's simply beautiful, Paul," she exclaimed, wandering around the room. She stopped before a wall filled with prints and sketches and saw a group of drawings that had been set off to one side by themselves. They were costume sketches she had done for *Fallen Angeles*.

"How did these get here?" she asked in surprise.

"I put them there," Paul replied. "This is my place. I live here."

Adrian burst out laughing. "Why didn't you tell me? Why all the build-up?"

"Remember me? Theatrics are my curse," Paul answered with a smile. "I've spent the last year decorating and fixing it up, thinking you might see it someday. If you look closely, you'll see there's enough room here for two. . . ."

He took her hand and led her through a large dining room, a kitchen, and a master-bedroom suite complete with dressing room and bath. "And there's still one more room," he said, guiding her to a side door and opening it. They walked into a large, airy studio with a skylight, teak-stained floors, built-in bookcases, and a wall of glass that offered a panoramic view of the city.

"Oh, Paul, this is marvelous!" Adrian said excitedly. "I've always dreamed of having a studio like this!"

"I was hoping you'd say that." He came up to her and took her into his arms. "Adrian, being with you these last few days, the fun we've had together—I don't want it to stop. Please, don't make it stop. . . ." He bent and kissed her, softly at first, then more passionately.

349

A deep warmth flooded through her, a sense of being wanted and needed that she hadn't felt for some time. She returned Paul's kiss, straining her body against his. He pulled away and looked at her, his dark eyes anxious. "Did you say something about wanting to collapse in bed?" he asked in a ragged voice.

She put her arms around his neck and slipped her fingers into his thick brown hair, pulling his face down to hers. "Oh, yes—" she whispered against his lips.

They made love as if it were the first time, tender and unrestrained, filled with passion and an eagerness that rekindled the warmth and familiarity they had known. As the last, dim glow of twilight faded and night shadows crept across the room, they moved together in a sensual, dreamy languor that slowly rose to an intense and thrilling ecstasy. Paul's lean, hard body worked against hers, and Adrian gave herself up to him, crying out with pleasure until they finally reached a moment of almost unbearable rapture.

Adrian stood by the bedroom windows and stared out at the city. The towering buildings that thrust into the sky were alive with lights, and the streets below were teeming with traffic, criss-crossing one another in a myriad spectrum of lights. It was an awesome sight, at once inspiring and intimidating. She had conquered Hollywood, but now she was faced with a new and greater challenge that would take all her talent and courage.

She heard Paul stir and turned to look at him. He was sprawled across the bed, head thrown back, arms outflung. His hair was disheveled and fell across his forehead in dark curls, and his face looked smooth and calm, like that of a little boy whose childish worries all disappear the moment he falls asleep. He's so relaxed, she thought, suddenly irritated. And then she realized why she was annoyed; Paul's open, easygoing temperament was like an unspoken reprimand to her. He had achieved success without becoming tough and manipulative, and Adrian couldn't help resenting it. All her life she'd had to conceal her true feelings—about being scarred, about her love for Alec, to protect herself in prison; and in business, to advance her career.

How could Paul ever understand what she had gone through? He had always been accepted for who he was, not how he appeared. He'd never had to use subterfuge or guile to get what he wanted. She looked away, sadly reflecting that Paul possessed the one thing her beauty and success had not provided: the freedom to be yourself.

She saw her image in the windowpane, vague and misty against the dark silhouette of the city. My face, she thought. Once it was destroyed by accident, then remade by Matthew Sheridan. And now it's called Adrian Ronay. But it's not me.

Paul opened his eyes and looked up at her. "Hello," he mumbled sleepily, sitting up against the pillows. "What a beautiful sight you are."

Adrian ran her fingers through her hair. "You're still dreaming. I must look like a wreck."

"You never look anything but wonderful to me." He held out his arms. "Come to me, you vision, and let me see if you're real."

Adrian smiled and went to him. "Oh, I'm real, all right," she replied, almost laughing at the irony of the words. She curled up in his arms and took one of his hands, lightly biting his fingers. "I'm real, and I'm hungry."

"So am I," he murmured, leaning down to capture her lips. His tongue slipped into her mouth, and she clung to him, feeling a renewed tug of desire. They moved down on the bed and he began to caress her breasts, teasing the nipples with his lips.

"Again?" she asked as he bent over her. "My God, you're insatiable!"

"Only with you," he murmured. "Only with you."

351

37

A FEW DAYS LATER, WORK ON THE SHOW BEGAN IN earnest. The company moved into a rehearsal hall in the Carnegie Building on Fifty-seventh Street, and Adrian worked with Paul; the set designer, Milo James; and Terry Ambler, the choreographer. The script was broken down for all the costume changes, and there were meetings, conferences, arguments, and compromises. Then her sketches were shown to the producer, John Hill, who worried them all into a frenzy.

Adrian declared vehemently, "John, if *all* the costumes are glitzy, then the musical numbers won't have any real impact! The everyday scenes in Rudy's life should look real, with the actors wearing clothes that are authentic for the period. Believe me—they'll be wonderful, and the audience will love them, but they can't be as glorified as the big numbers or the film sequences. Otherwise there's no contrast."

"Adrian is right," Paul said. "If we overload the show, it will get boring."

"Audiences pay fifty dollars for a ticket," John snapped. "And the scalpers get a hundred. The people have a right to see something that will make their eyes pop!"

The arguments raged back and forth until Sam Phillips intervened. He studied Adrian's sketches, talked quietly with Milo, Paul, and Terry, then took John out for a long lunch at the Russian Tea Room, where they served some of John's favorite foods. When they came back, the producer was all smiles, and everyone heaved a sigh of relief.

"You're the Henry Kissinger of Broadway," Adrian

said to Sam admiringly. "No wonder everything you've been involved in has been such a success."

Sam gave her a smile. "John has an image of himself as Max Fabian—remember him?—the dyspeptic producer in *All About Eve*? If John isn't worrying and questioning everything and everybody, he doesn't feel he's doing his job."

"And what image do you have of yourself?"

Sam's smile grew mischievous. "I've always thought of myself as a swashbuckling adventurer who overcomes all opposition to get what he wants. Like Errol Flynn."

Adrian burst into laughter. "Sam, I knew there was a reason we got along so well—we have a lot in common."

The costumes were built in a loft on Fifty-fourth Street by a woman who reminded Adrian of Dolly King. Her name was Maxine Klein, and everybody called her Maxie. Short and pudgy, with a raspy voice, china-blue eyes, and flaming red hair that was a hiding place for pencils, eyeglasses, and an extra cigarette, she commanded her staff of seamstresses like a general preparing for battle. A curt nod and a brusque "Terrific!" meant approval. But if she looked at a finished gown and growled, "I need a cup of coffee," the gown was taken apart and done over.

Adrian began to learn from Maxie the tricks of costuming a Broadway show. Together they went all over town, selecting fabrics, beads, feathers, sequins, furs, jewelry, shoes, stockings, gloves, and wigs. Maxie haggled over coats, cried with delight at finding some perfect material, and groaned and cursed when there was a conflict of schedules among the suppliers. Then it was back to the loft, where Adrian had a small office. Maxie's staff was a hardworking, tough bunch of women who had been costuming shows for years. Adrian quickly won their respect with her knowledge of workroom procedures and her ability to solve the various figure problems they encountered.

When the dancers and bit players came in for fittings,

the place became chaotic. "What'll we do with her?" one of the women asked Adrian about a hippy actress. "Her ass is big enough to feed half the starving people in China."

"Do a cross-over band on the bodice in red satin," Adrian replied, sketching quickly. "And repeat it around her waist. Then give her a full, black skirt edged in bangles. That will take the attention away from her hips."

A male dancer stood by, looking bored, as two other women took his measurements for a tight-fitting Flamenco suit. "He's got legs like a racehorse," one of them muttered to Adrian. "And that isn't all he's got like a horse."

"Sew a cup into his pants," Adrian advised, laughing.

"He'll never fit into a cup—maybe I should try a soup plate."

Maxie shooed them back to their sewing machines, grumbling, "Everybody's a comedian. But they get the work done on time," she added gruffly.

Adrian handed her a cup of coffee, took one for herself, and lit a cigarette. "They're terrific to work with. They really know what they're doing."

"Yeah, they do. And I'll tell you somethin' kid—you're the best designer we've had come in here in a long time."

Adrian smiled. "Thanks, Maxie—that means a lot to me."

Maxie pulled a cigarette from behind her ear and lit it, drawing deeply. "I think you're going to be around New York for a long time."

"You know, I think you're right."

The company moved into the Majestic Theater for a month of rehearsals before the out-of-town opening in Boston. The days flew by in a hectic succession of rehearsal calls, production meetings, last-minute changes, and long hours of coping with an infinite number of emergencies. Tempers flared, quarrels broke out, dancers complained about the tempos, actors swore at their dressers. Paul worked onstage, soothing the cast and shaping the

354

show, while Adrian worked backstage with the wardrobe crew and made dressing-room alterations.

Some nights she would return to her suite at the Plaza in a state of collapse. On other nights, she and Paul would join the production staff and some of the stars of the show at Sardi's for dinner and a continuous exchange of arguments and ideas laced with anecdotes that brought roars of laughter. Afterward, she would return with Paul to his apartment in the Chelsea. While he sat at his desk, poring over notes, she would go into the studio, where they had set up some equipment for her, and sit quietly at the drawing table, creating new designs for the changes that had been made. Later, when they had finished working, they would have a nightcap together, sitting on the roof garden above the roar of the city. Then they would go to bed and make love.

As in every show, gossip circulated throughout the company about the members of the cast who were falling in love, having affairs, or just sleeping together. But where Adrian and Paul were concerned, there was a respectful silence. They were simply accepted as a couple, almost as if they were married. Paul was too busy to take much notice, but Adrian was aware of how they were viewed, and sometimes it made her a little uneasy.

One night they skipped going out with the others and went back to the Chelsea. Paul sent out for a delicatessen dinner, and they relaxed in the living room before the fireplace, relishing the solitude. For a while they chatted quietly about the show, and Paul said, "How do you feel about the idea of moving in with me?"

Adrian looked up at him. "You want me to give up my suite at the Plaza and live here in sin with you?" she deadpanned.

"You're right. It's a lousy idea. Let's get married, instead."

"You call that a proposal?" Adrian asked, imitating Maxie's rasping voice.

"Goddammit, will you stop kidding! I love you. I've loved you for a long time—I think since the first night we met. And I want you to be my wife. I want that more than anything else in the world."

Adrian was silent for a few minutes. Then she replied gravely, "I think I want it, too."

"Is that a yes?" Paul asked tensely.

Adrian stared at him for a long time, suddenly remembering something Claudia had said to her. *"He sounds like one of the good guys, and there's damned few of them around."*

"Adrian, is that a yes?" Paul asked once more.

"Paul," she began slowly. "I think I really love you, but I don't think I'm ready to commit myself completely to you. At least, not to the point of moving in here and living with you. Maybe that sounds foolish, even old-fashioned, but it has nothing to do with that. It's just that I've worked so hard to be independent—I'm not quite ready to give it up yet."

But even as she spoke, she knew she wasn't telling him the whole truth. She had been hurt before, and was afraid; that was the truth. How could she give him the kind of love he expected and deserved? The past still hovered over her life like a shadow, and she wasn't sure she could find the courage to tell him who she really was, or what she had been.

"I understand your need for independence," Paul said quietly. "It's one of the many things about you that I love. And you don't have to move in with me—at least, not right away. But I'm old-fashioned enough to want some assurance, some indication from you that we have something very special between us." He gave her a shy, hesitant smile. "A kind of commitment, if you wish, that's binding, but not a ball and chain."

I have to begin to trust him, Adrian thought, and eventually I may be able to trust myself. She leaned over and kissed him gently. Then she said, "You can go shopping for an engagment ring tomorrow."

He broke into a wide, excited smile. "I don't have to. Stay where you are."

He hurried out of the room and returned with a small black box in his hand. It was from Cartier's. Adrian opened it and saw a large, square-cut diamond in a platinum setting. Tears began to gather in her eyes as she took it out. "How long have you had this?" she asked, her voice breaking.

"Since the first week you were here. I remembered you admiring it that afternoon we were shopping, and went back the next day to get it."

"Oh, Paul—" She began to cry as she slipped the ring on her finger.

He gathered her into his arms. "Now it's official," he whispered.

Before they left for Boston, Adrian made one last telephone call to Jerry Gilroy.

"We didn't learn much in Chicago, Miss Ronay," the investigator said. "Mr. Darcy was there for a while, and we're pretty certain he was working with the syndicate. We think he may have left the country, but we're not sure. Every time we got a lead, it was a dead end. He really knows how to cover his tracks."

"Was there a woman with him in Chicago?" Adrian asked.

Gilroy chuckled. "A harem would be more like it. Mostly one-night stands, though. We managed to get to a few of them, but as soon as we started to ask questions, they clammed up. We could keep trying, if you want us to."

"No, that won't be necessary," Adrian said. "You can close my account. How much do I owe you?" He named a figure, and Adrian said, "I'll send you a check. Thank you, Mr. Gilroy."

She hung up and sat back in the chair. Is this where it ends? she wondered. Searching for Alec was like pursuing a phantom, and all she had to show for it was some vague information that had no real value. Once more he had outwitted her. There was no point in going on, she decided. She had her work, and she had Paul, who wanted to give her his love. It was time she learned how to accept and enjoy the happiness she was being offered, without looking back, or letting the past interfere. In time, perhaps, she'd even be strong enough to tell Paul the truth about herself.

Adrian began to make out a check to Gilroy, writing slowly, as if performing a ceremony that would close and lock the door on a part of her life that was over. But hours later, while she was sleeping, she had a nightmare and suddenly awoke in a cold sweat, hearing the hollow, mocking sound of Alec's laughter.

38

THE FIRST PREVIEW PERFORMANCE OF *RUDY!* IN Boston exceeded everyone's expectations. The audience applauded the sets and atmospheric lighting and the complex and rousing dance routines. There were many show-stopping numbers, but the one that drew a thunderous ovation was the recreation of the famous tango scene from *The Four Horsemen of the Apocalypse*. The silent film was projected on a large screen at the back of the stage and accompanied by the sound of a tinny piano. The cast, wearing facsimilies of the costumes from the screen, repeated the actions in a smoky blue light, on a small set that duplicated the one in the film. Then the orchestra softly took over from the piano, the film began to fade, and the lights came up. At the same time, the set seemed to enlarge, and suddenly the entire stage was filled with dancers in a dazzling array of gowns, all moving in a sinuous, seductive tango.

The final scene of Valentino's death and the riots that ensued while his body lay in state were played out against newsreel films of the event, with the dancers simulating the frenzy of mourners in a furious number that brought the show to a rousing conclusion.

The audience stood and cheered, and the cast took repeated curtain calls. Then, as a final grace note to the evening, the stage lights dimmed and a young woman appeared carrying a single red rose. Dressed in a stunning creation of black crepe, satin, and veils, she walked slowly to the center of the stage and knelt before a final image of Valentino on the screen while the orchestra softly reprised the songs of the show. The house went wild.

Sam Phillips had reserved the hotel dining room for a celebration dinner. By midnight it was noisy with drunken sounds of revelry. The investors who had come up from New York for the preview were congratulating one another, the cast was drinking and singing, and Sam was wreathed in smiles, waving a glass of champagne and shouting, "It's a fucking hit!"

He came up to where Adrian was sitting with Paul, Milo, Terry, and John and hugged each of them. Then he sat down and, in his typical fashion, began to talk business.

"We'll cut a cast album as soon as possible, a two-record album with photographs and Adrian's sketches of the costumes. I'll set interviews for *People*, *Life*, and *New York Magazine*, and take a half-page ad in the *Times* to announce the opening. Adrian, I want to use your sketch of the couple doing the tango as the logo of the show. And I want to make up a display case of your best sketches for the lobby of the theater." He took a breath, gulped some champagne, and went on: "I'll get *Esquire* and *GQ* to do profiles on Paul, Milo, and John, and all the fashion mags to interview Adrian. I want her designs to be seen and talked about all over the country."

"Do you ever slow down?" Terry asked.

"Not when I've got a hot show on my hands. I'm going to hype *Rudy!* into a box-office landslide!" He filled his glass again and stood up to make a toast. "You all did a terrific job, and I'll take bets right now that everyone of you is going to walk off with a Tony!"

They all gave him a round of applause, and Adrian cried, "Sam, I like your style!"

"How 'bout my style," Paul whispered in her ear.

"Your style is sensational," Adrian whispered back. "There are some things you can do that I don't think even Sam can."

"Shall we get out of here and do a little celebrating by ourselves?"

"My very thought," Adrian murmured.

A few weeks after the show opened in New York to critical acclaim and sold-out houses, Adrian learned that she had been nominated for an Academy Award for the film *Starburst*. Sam had his publicity people redouble their efforts, and she appeared on the "Today" show and "Good Morning America." The magazine interviews he'd promised appeared, and there was an in-depth story about her in the *Sunday Times*. Paul, too, was profiled in numerous articles, and wherever they went, they were greeted as the most accomplished and glamorous couple in the New York theater world.

A number of wealthy young women and society matrons approached Adrian to design gowns for them. But Sam had a better idea.

"Why don't you modify your theatrical designs for public wear and put out your own line?"

"You mean start my own business?"

"Sure. I'll bankroll you to begin with. As soon as word gets out, you'll have investors breaking down your door. Be your own boss, sweetheart—it's the only way to go. Get a staff together, find a place in Manhattan, give it a fancy name, like 'The House of Ronay,' and remember to keep a controlling interest. Never let the bankers get you—they're worse than lawyers."

Adrian was dazed by the idea. That night she discussed it with Paul. He agreed with Sam's idea, then laughed. "That crafty shark—I know what he has in mind."

"What do you mean?"

He went to his desk and came back with a thick manuscript. "Sam sent this by messenger a couple of days ago. He asked me not to say anything to you about it until I'd read it and decided if it was good."

Adrian took it from him and read the title on the cover. "*The Great Ziegfeld*—is he kidding? A Ziegfeld show?"

"He's not kidding, and it's a terrific idea. Sam's no fool. He knows there's an audience of women out there who are panting for shows like this, shows filled with music, dancing, romance, drama, and gorgeous costumes designed by you-know-who. If you get a line of clothes going all over the country, there'll be even more of a reason for them to want to see the show, especially when it goes on the road. And if *Rudy!* picks up a couple of Tonys and you win the Oscar, he'll have enough big guns to get more investors than he needs for *The Great Ziegfeld*."

Adrian fell back against the couch and began to laugh. "My God, we'll all be rich as Creosus! And to think you and I started out in that tacky theater on Melrose Avenue, with me remaking thrift-shop clothes and you building your own sets!"

Then she suddenly grew serious. "Do you really think I have a chance of winning an Oscar, or the Tony?"

"Listen—by the time Sam gets through, you'll probably get the Congressional Medal of Honor!"

A few days later before the Academy Awards show, Adrian flew to Los Angeles. Kelly and Claudia met her at the airport. "Oh, it's so good to see you both!" she cried, hugging them.

"I thought Paul was coming with you," Claudia said.

"He couldn't make it. He's tied up in meetings on the new show."

"You look fantastic!" Kelly exclaimed.

"It's true, dear," Claudia chimed in. "You have that New York sheen that women out here struggle to achieve and never get. Going to the Big Apple was the best move you ever made."

"I think it's time you two also took a bite out of the Big Apple," Adrian said. At their puzzled expression, she laughed. "Let's get to the hotel. We have a lot to talk about."

In a poolside cottage at the Bel Air Hotel, Adrian

explained Sam's idea of starting her own business. "I can't do it alone— I don't know anything about running a business. And if Sam gets the financing for the new show, I won't have time. I'll be too busy designing costumes." She looked at Kelly and grinned. "And I'll need a master makeup artist. Does the Magical Mystery Makeup Box travel?"

They stared at her, incredulous. "Are you asking us to come to New York to work with you?" Claudia asked.

"I told both of you that if I ever made it, I wanted you right there alongside me. Well . . . ?"

"Yes!" they chorused joyfully.

The next day Paul and Sam unexpectedly flew in from New York to be with Adrian at the Academy Awards ceremonies. The following night the three of them drove to the Dorothy Chandler Pavilion of the Music Center in downtown Los Angeles. Huge crowds had gathered to cheer the hundreds of stars attending the event. TV crews were everywhere and newscasters were interviewing the celebrities as they made their way into the auditorium.

"God, I thought I was nervous about the Emmys, but this is terrifying," Adrian said as they took their seats.

Sam patted her hand confidently. "You're a cinch to win, sweetie. Trust me."

The theater was filled to overflowing with the most famous names in the industry. Many people with whom Adrian had made friends stopped to greet her and wish her good luck. Several actresses were wearing gowns that Adrian had designed, but none of them looked as resplendent as she did. She had chosen to wear a simply cut white chiffon gown with a layered skirt that was lightly sprinkled with sequins. Over it she wore a bright-red cloak with full, puffed sleeves and a high, stand-up collar.

"You look like a fairy-tale princess," Paul whispered.

"Thank you, darling. This is a fairy-tale night for me, whether I win or not."

The houses lights dimmed, the orchestra struck up the

overture of themes from the nominated films, and the show was underway. The atmosphere was charged with tension as the different categories and nominees were announced.

As the proceedings continued, Adrian's mind drifted to thoughts of the events in her life and the people she had known who had brought her to this extraordinary moment. She knew that Dolly King was with Claudia and Kelly at the hotel, waiting to join them later, but there were so many others who might be watching the show on television who had no idea of the part they had played in her success. Mr. Bradley, her design teacher, Matthew Sheridan, Martha Kane, and Rina. Adrian wondered if Anthony Trent was watching, and Howard and Harriet Bradshaw. She suddenly wished her mother were there to share all the excitement and glory; Nora, whose enthusiasm for old movies had started all of this. And then she thought of Alec and Sheila; were they watching tonight?

Suddenly she was shaken out of her reverie by a shout from Sam. Paul was kissing her and shouting, "You won! You won!"

Adrian got to her feet in a daze. Sam helped her slip off the cloak, and she glided down the aisle in a glare of lights, hearing the music and applause, and underneath it all, the voice of her father, whose last words to her had been, "Hold on, sweetheart, hold on!"

As she mounted the steps to the stage, her eyes swimming with tears, she said to herself softly, "I held on, Daddy. I held on."

39

Soon after Claudia and Kelly had arrived in New York and were settled in, they began the task of setting up Adrian's business. Claudia took over the management and handled all the paperwork, while Adrian and Kelly took Sam's advice and began to look for a place they could convert into The House of Ronay. Maxie put them on to an art gallery on Fifty-seventh Street that was going out of business. It was the top floor of an old building, with enough space for workrooms, offices, dressing rooms, and a large showroom for fashion shows. Sam negotiated with the corporation that owned it, and got a lease, and Kelly began to supervise the remodeling.

In the meantime, Paul was working on the book of the Ziegfeld show with the writer. Terry Ambler, and Milo James had been signed for the production, but John Hill had already made another commitment, and Sam decided to take over the producing chores himself. *Rudy!* had been running for over seven months and was still a hot-ticket show, and he was confident that he'd have no trouble selling *The Great Ziegfeld* to potential investors.

Adrian spent most of her time with Maxie and her staff, preparing the first line of her clothes. Finally, one night in late fall, The House of Ronay had its premiere showing. The event was covered by fashion magazines and newspapers, television reporters, and their crews. A catering service had been employed for the evening, and a long banquet table was covered with imported delicacies, gleaming cut glass, and silver. Waiters made their way through the crowded room, serving drinks to the elite of New York society, buyers from Saks, Neiman-Marcus, I. Magnin's and other fine stores, and celebrities of the stage and screen.

Standing at the bar, Paul, Kelly, and Sam watched proudly as the brilliant evening progressed into a breathtaking fashion show. A stage had been set up at the front of the room; the models appeared from behind plush black velvet curtains and sauntered down the runway, bringing murmurs of approval and applause. At the end of the show, the curtains swept aside dramatically to reveal each model standing inside an enormous gilt frame, like living works of art. The applause started, then grew in volume as Adrian made her first appearance of the evening wearing the last gown of the show. It was a black satin evening dress with a beaded flowers-and-butterflies motif and featured a bias-cut, clinging skirt that flared to a wide ruffle of black chiffon. The audience stood, applauding loudly as she came to the front of the stage and made a deep bow.

Claudia, who had been backstage, came hurrying up to Paul and Kelly, breathless with excitement. "How did it look out there?"

"Fantastic!" Kelly exclaimed. "I thought that yenta from *Women's Wear Daily* would have herself. Or at the very least the man sitting next to her."

Paul was all smiles. "What a night! Adrian was radiant."

Sam edged in beside Claudia and said, "But the big question is—"

"You don't have to ask, Sam," Claudia said. "The orders are pouring in! In a few months, the most exclusive stores in the country will be carrying Adrian's designs."

"That's what I wanted to hear," he said gleefully. "I love art, but money buys happiness."

"Isn't he adorable?" Kelly said. "Such depth, such soul. Why can't I find a man who thinks like Sam and looks like Paul Newman?"

"Because you're too short," Paul wisecracked.

Sam finished his drink, set the glass down on the bar, and ran a hand over his thinning hair. "I've got to leave—all these gorgeous women have made me very horny."

"Do you want me to introduce you to some of the models?" Claudia asked.

"No, thank you," he replied politely. "I've fucked all of them."

Before leaving, he took Paul aside and said, "Kiss Adrian for me; tell her the show was great. And I want to see the two of you in my office tomorrow morning. We've got a few problems with *Ziegfeld*, and I'm going to need your help."

"What problems?" Paul asked.

Sam grinned and shook his head. "Tomorrow. And don't worry. It's nothing I can't handle."

"So, that's the story," Sam said to Adrian and Paul the next morning. He leaned back in his chair and smiled ruefully. "Money's tight, and *Ziegfeld* is an expensive show."

"What are you going to do?" Paul asked. "How can we help?"

"Much as I hate the idea, I'm going to throw a few backers' auditions. You know, have some of the big boys from out of town up to my place, give 'em a taste of New York glitz. Wine 'em, dine 'em, play the best songs from the show, tell them about the book, and show them some of Adrian's designs. Surround them with pretty girls and drown them in good whiskey to ease those checkbooks out of their pockets. Will you help?"

"Of course, anything you say," Paul answered.

"What can I do?" Adrian asked.

"Be my hostess. Dazzle them with your charm, talk about your awards, whatever it takes. . . . Just make 'em cough up the bread."

Adrian laughed. "Okay, Sam. I'll be the most elegant B-girl in New York."

* * *

The taxi pulled up in front of an elegant condominium complex on Park Avenue. While Paul paid the driver, Adrian checked her makeup. "Do I look all right?" she asked as they walked up to the entrance.

"You'll give every man in the place a hard-on and make their wives jealous as hell."

Adrian smiled grimly. "I'm getting a little tired of these backers' auditions and how crude some rich men can be. It's amazing how they can have so much money and so little style. And their wives! The less said about them, the better."

"That's where we come in—to dazzle them with style. You charm the big oafs, and I'll do soft-shoe and snappy patter with the ladies."

The security guard in the lobby checked them in, and they entered the elevator. "This makes the sixth one we've done," Adrian sighed. "Christ, I hope it's the last."

"Sam thinks it may be. He's invited some businessmen from Florida and a couple from Texas. Just plain folks with oil wells in their backyards who want a taste of the big time."

They got off the elevator at Sam's penthouse and were greeted by a maid, who took their coats. "Keep smiling," Paul whispered as they went down the steps into a living room the size of a basketball court. It was a spectacular showplace, designed to impress Sam's business associates and his never-ending procession of women. A gleaming concert grand piano stood at right angles to a wall of glass that overlooked the city. Fine paintings hung on the walls, Aubusson rugs stretched across a highly polished, teak floor, and the sofas were from Directional. From the moment she had seen it, Adrian thought the place looked more like a set designer's concept than someone's apartment.

A small crowd had already gathered, and waiters were serving drinks while maids went about with trays of canapés. Sam went over to greet them with a worried look on his face. "One of the guys I've been waiting for hasn't shown up yet, and the crowd is beginning to get a little restless." He took Adrian's arm and led her into the room. "I've got a hotel magnate from Florida who wants to meet you," Sam said, gesturing to an overdressed, beefy-looking man who was ogling the legs of one of the dancers in the show.

"Oh, God, I wish he'd stayed in Florida," Adrian wailed softly.

An hour went by. Adrian and Paul circulated among the guests, chatting with them about the show. Sam had made up a display of Adrian's costume designs on one wall, and several women gathered around to look at them while Adrian discussed her work, adding a little sales pitch for her line of clothes. Every once in a while, she'd glance up and see Sam and Paul conferring with a group of men with furrowed brows and thoughtful expressions on their faces. Despite the informal appearance of the party, everyone was there to do business, and an undercurrent of big-money talk buzzed through the room, keeping the mood tense.

Adrian joined Sam and Paul at the bar. "Sam, I think it's time the kids did some entertaining," she said. "The party's beginning to slow down. Has the man you've been waiting for arrived yet?"

Sam frowned. "No, he should have been here two hours ago. I'll get the music started; he may show up soon."

The composer of the score sat down at the piano, and several singers and dancers prepared to do some of the songs in the show. Everyone quieted down and the music began. Adrian and Paul remained standing at the bar. She looked over at the wall of glass behind the piano and saw a soft reflection of the room: the fine furnishings and paintings, the guests in their evening clothes, and finally, herself next to Paul. How beautiful it all looks, she thought, an enchanting image of everything she had been striving for: wealth and fame. Success.

A movement at the front door caught her eye. Sam was greeting a late arrival. The man he was waiting for, she thought, lifting a drink to her lips. Then she stopped, her hand frozen in mid-air. The man had his back to her, but there was something about the shape of his head, the set of his shoulders, that made her breath catch in her throat. He turned around to enter the room, and Adrian felt the blood drain from her face.

It was Alec Darcy.

Shock bolted through her body like a charge of electricity, and for a moment she thought she would faint. Her mind protested that it wasn't possible, that it couldn't be Alec. But there was no mistaking the thick black wavy hair, darkly lashed green eyes, the arrogant stride of his body. She made an effort to move and turned to the bar, blindly searching for her drink. She gulped it down quickly, head back, eyes shut. But when she opened them, she saw his reflection in the mirrored wall behind the bar. Everything else in the room seemed blurred and indistinct except for his face. She shuddered and felt a cold sweat break out on her forehead. She couldn't stop watching him, like a terrified victim unable to look away from her murderer. He was glancing casually around the room, and then his eyes came to rest on her.

Adrian panicked. He was staring at her in the mirror. He recognized her! No, he couldn't possibly, could he? She quickly glanced at her own image for reassurance. Could he see beneath this carefully created facade? Could he see Emily Gorden?

A torrent of fear swept over her. She had to leave, get away before they met! But wait—wasn't this what she had dreamed of, worked for, planned for? This was the moment that had sustained her all these years; she couldn't leave now. She had to get control of herself. She had to face him!

Adrian turned slowly back to the room and slipped her arm through Paul's. He patted her hand, absorbed in the songs that were being performed, completely unaware of what was happening. She drew a deep breath. Her fear began to dissipate, and an old but not forgotten anger took its place, coursing through her like a shot of adrenaline. She examined Alec coldly. Time had not diminished his handsomeness; if anything, it had added a sheen of finesse and style to his virile beauty. And his impact on women was still as immediate and visible as the first day she had met him. The investors' wives were giving him lingering glances, and a few of the girls waiting to perform stared at him frankly, their eyes betraying an eagerness to meet him.

Finally the performance was over. Everyone stood and applauded, and Sam began to introduce Alec to his guests. Adrian waited, unconsciously gripping Paul's arm more tightly, her heart beating wildly.

Then she and Alec were face to face.

Sam made the introduction, "Adrian, Paul, I want you to meet Alec Darcy. He represents a group of financers who've expressed an interest in the show. Mr. Darcy was kind enough to join our little party tonight to hear the score and discuss business."

Alec smiled and shook Paul's hand. Then he turned to Adrian. She looked directly at him, searching his face for any sign of recognition. "Good evening, Mr. Darcy," she said, managing a cool, indifferent tone. "Thank you for coming."

"The pleasure is mine, Miss Ronay," he murmured, taking her hand.

Adrian's flesh burned at his touch. She studied him, waiting for some indication—a knowing smile, a gleam in his eyes—that would betray the fact that he knew her. But there was nothing. She was a stranger to him.

Alec said to Paul, "I've been out of the country the last few years and missed seeing the plays you've directed. But I did catch a performance of *Rudy!* a few nights ago and enjoyed it very much. Particularly"—he looked at Adrian—"the costumes. They were breathtaking. You have an extraordinary talent, Adrian—may I call you Adrian?" He gave her an insolent smile, and his eyes swept over her in a bluntly sexual appraisal. "In fact," he went on, "I've never met a designer whose beauty was the equal of her creations, until now."

"And have you known many designers?" Adrian asked boldly.

"As a matter of fact, yes. The company I represent has financed a number of shows, particularly in Europe. But the Europeans don't hold a candle to Americans when it comes to musical comedies. I think that form of theater is native to this country, like Dixieland jazz, don't you?"

Adrian murmured agreement, thinking: His acting has improved. He's eloquent, well-tailored, and completely at ease. He's finally found a role that suits him. She suddenly remembered what Gilroy had told her, that Alec had made a connection with the syndicate. That's who he was representing, and that's why Sam was so anxious to have him here; with syndicate backing he'd have no trouble putting on the show. And Alec was the front man. The role suited him—a high-class gangster.

Alec began to talk with Paul, and she nervously fumbled in her evening purse for a cigarette and put it between her lips. Without breaking his flow of dialogue, Alec reached into his jacket, came out with a lighter, and flicked it for her. She lit the cigarette and glanced up at him. The tiny flame made gold specs dance in his green eyes. He was looking at her with an expression that recalled a moment in the back booth of a dingy coffee shop when he had whispered, "Am I sexy?"

Her composure started to crumble, and she said to Paul, "It's getting late, and I have a full day tomorrow—"

"Yes, you're right," Paul agreed. "I'll get our coats."

Before she could stop him, he went off, leaving her alone with Alec. "I'm sorry you have to leave so soon," he said. "I was hoping we might have more time to get to know each other."

Adrian gave him a thin smile and looked around anxiously for Paul. Alec moved closer to her. "I think you're one of the most beautiful women I've ever seen," he said in a low voice "May I call you tomorrow?"

Adrian felt a wild, hysterical laugh threaten to burst from her lips. She edged away from him and replied stiffly, "I don't think Paul would like that, Mr. Darcy. And neither would I. You might do better with one of the dancers."

Just then Paul returned and slipped her coat around her shoulders. Alec nodded good night to Paul and took Adrian's hand. He held it firmly, an amused smile playing at the corners of his lips. "Good night, Adrian. It's been a great pleasure meeting you. I'm sure we'll be seeing a lot of each other."

Adrian took her hand from his and she and Paul walked out of the room. As they stood waiting for the elevator, she stared straight ahead, afraid to look back. She could feel Alec's eyes watching her.

Out on the street, Paul hailed a cab. "Do you want to come back to my place?" he asked as they got in.

"Not tonight, dear. I'm very tired."

"Me, too," Paul said, sighing deeply. "The whole evening was like a sales convention. I began to feel like Willy Loman—'Keep a shine on your shoes and a smile on your lips.'"

Adrian remained silent.

"What did you think of Darcy?" Paul asked.

"Not much," Adrian replied. "He reminded me of some of the actors my publicists arranged for me to go out with—smooth, too-handsome hustlers."

"Darcy has a lot more going for him. Needless to say, the *company* he represents has connections with the syndicate. Apparently Darcy has had some show business background, and Sam told me that for the last few years, he's guided their investments in theater, both here and abroad."

So she'd been right, Adrian thought; he was a front man for the syndicate. "Have you heard anything else about him?" she asked cautiously.

"Just some gossip from one of the investors' wives.

Some French actress was supposed to have committed suicide when Darcy left her for another woman. A mysterious boating accident, the police said, but others claimed it wasn't an accident." He laughed and added, "He probably got tired of her, and when she started to cause trouble, he 'had her taken care of'—as they used to say in the old Bogart movies."

Adrian shivered, and Paul asked, "Are you okay? You look a little pale."

"Just tired. The evening seemed very long."

They were quiet for a few minutes, then Paul said abruptly, "Adrian, let's get married. Don't you think we've put it off long enough? Let's take off, drive to Maryland, find a Justice of the Peace, and make it legal."

Oh, Paul, not now, she begged silently, please not now. Aloud, she said, "We can't just take off; we both have so much to do. Besides, I want a real wedding and a honeymoon in some exotic place."

"It could be months before we find that much time," he grumbled.

"Darling, please let's not discuss it now," she pleaded. "Let's wait and see how Sam makes out with the financing. Maybe there'll be a couple of weeks before we get into the show."

"If there is, can we do it then?" he persisted.

She couldn't help laughing. "You're like a little boy begging for Christmas to come early."

"That's because you're everything I want for Christmas," he said, drawing her close and kissing her.

The cab drew up to the Plaza, and with a feeling of relief, Adrian got out. "Don't bother to come up with me," she told Paul. "I want to go straight to bed. I'll call you in the morning."

She hurried up the steps and into the lobby, making an effort to hold herself together until she got to her room. As soon as she had closed and locked the door, she began to tremble. She went into the bedroom and flung herself across the bed, giving way to a series of long, shuddering gasps. Her body shook convulsively, and she wept uncontrollably, releasing all her pent-up feelings.

Finally, she was spent and grew quiet. She lay still for a long time, then sat up and wiped her tear-stained face. She could still see Alec's eyes mocking her, his confident smile challenging her.

She drew back the drapes and stared out the windows. In a few hours it would be dawn. The streets were almost empty, and the city was quiet, resting like a tired animal pausing for breath before once more taking up the chase. Adrian gazed out at the skyline. The monolithic buildings of Manhattan rose up around her like an army of stone and glass centurions. But she took little comfort from their towering strength. Somewhere, behind a window in one of those buildings, perhaps only a few blocks away, was the man who had cast an inescapable cloud over her life. And now he had materialized out of the past, more seductive than ever, flaunting the rewards of his deceits.

And Sheila; where was she? Adrian wondered. Did he even know? Probably not. Dumped along the way, like all the other women he had known and used. And now he had made it very clear that he wanted her. No—not *her*. It was Adrian Ronay he wanted.

But Emily Gorden still had a score to settle with him.

40

A FEW DAYS LATER ADRIAN LEARNED THAT SAM HAD received all the additional financing he needed to mount the show. It had come from the men Alec represented. She also learned that there was a provision in the contract Alec had made with Sam that he was to be involved in every phase of the production.

"I've been through this before, with other major investors," Sam told her. "It's just an excuse to hang around and lay the chorus girls. As soon as he's had all the nooky he can handle, he'll leave us alone and forget the thrill of show biz."

But Adrian knew better. He was using his power to be near her. He really hadn't changed, she thought. He was going to pursue Adrian Ronay just as he had Emily Gorden. For different reasons, of course, but with the same intent—to get what he wanted. But this time it wouldn't be that easy. She had acquired power of her own and had learned how to use it.

Much to Paul's dismay, production meetings for *The Great Ziegfeld* were scheduled to start immediately. But Adrian was relieved; now she had a legitimate excuse to put off their wedding—until after the show had opened. And it gave her time to deal with Alec. She was determined to hurt him in every possible way she could.

Alec began to attend all the staff meetings and became a familiar presence at the cast auditions. He sat in on all the production meetings, and whenever there was a break, he insisted on taking everyone out for lunch or dinner and picking up the check. Adrian was constantly aware that he was watching every move she made, and steeled herself to be polite to him. When he finally approached her with an invitation to dine with him, she was cordial but aloof in her refusal.

As the days went by, he grew more persistent, and she began making excuses to avoid being alone with him. Once, when he was particularly insistent that they have lunch together—"to discuss the show," he told her—she agreed, and then met him with Paul, Kelly, and Milo in tow.

One evening she was sitting in the back of the rehearsal hall, making some notes while Paul was working with the actors, when she sensed that Alec was behind her. She turned to find him peering over her shoulder.

"Why don't you stop trying to avoid me?" he whispered with a taunting smile. "I'm beginning to think you don't like me."

"And you just might be right," she said with contempt in her voice. Then she got up and walked away.

Adrian was completely aware of the effect of her indifference to him. Rather than putting Alec off, it only whetted his appetite, increased his fascination for her. Alec was used to having women pursue him, and her disdain was a challenge to his vanity. Even though she dreaded every moment she was in his presence, she couldn't help feeling exhilarated by the power she had over him. Alec had the ego of an actor, sensitive and easily bruised; it was his Achilles' heel. And she could plunge a knife into it.

One afternoon, Adrian hurried to the Palace Theater, where Terry Ambler was holding an audition for dancers. She slipped inside and found Kelly sitting in the darkened theater. She took the seat beside him and lit a cigarette.

"How's it going?" she asked.

"Beautiful, just beautiful," he murmured dreamily.

She smiled. "Which chorus boy are you taken with?"

"The tall blond in the blue tights, on the end."

"Do you really think blonds have more fun, Mr. Green?" she asked like an inquiring reporter.

"They do when they're with me." Kelly chuckled.

They watched Terry take the dancers through a routine. Adrian made some notes on her clipboard, then stubbed out her cigarette and lit another one.

Kelly glanced over at her with raised eyebrows. "Are we chain-smoking these days?"

"We are," Adrian muttered.

"Do drugs and drink come next?"

"If we're lucky."

"Is it premenstrual blues, or has Paul taken to beating you?"

"None of your business."

Kelly sat up, a serious expression on his face. "Every time you say that, I know something's wrong. What is it? Darcy getting on your nerves?"

Adrian looked at him, startled. "What made you ask that?"

"I've been watching you. Every time he makes an appearance, you either turn into the Ice Queen, or you put on a very phony act. What's going on? Is he trying to beat Paul's time, as we used to say in high school?"

"What do you think of him?" Adrian asked, ignoring his question.

"If he were gay and came on to me, I'd probably get on a plane and fly back to L.A."

"Why?"

Kelly made a dramatic gesture with his hands and answered in a quivering imitation of Katharine Hepburn, "Because I'm sure he'd break my heart!" In his own voice, he said, "Darcy looks like trouble. Beneath that silky facade, I think he's ruthless. Now tell Poppa what he's been doing to our little Nell."

"Sometimes you amaze me," Adrian murmured.

"You're not answering my question. Has he been hitting on you?"

"Not really—but he does make me uneasy," she admitted. "As you've so voyeuristically observed, he's always watching me."

"Of course he is! The man is seething with lust, and you won't give him a tumble. But just wait—soon he'll be sending you little gifts: a tasteful brooch from Cartier's, a diamond and ruby necklace from Van Cleef and Arpel's, a tiny Titian, the deed to an elegant little town house, to which he'll have an extra key—"

"I think you're describing your fantasy, not Alec Darcy," Adrian said, laughing. "But tell me, Dr. Frankenstein, what do you think I should do?"

"My advice is to wait until he sends all the gifts. Then keep them and break his heart. He looks like a man who deserves to have his heart broken."

"I couldn't agree with you more," Adrian said softly.

Slowly, like an actress working her way into a complex role, Adrian began to alter her manner toward Alec. She became more cordial, almost friendly. But whenever he responded too eagerly, she drew back, leaving him confused and irritated. She would flirt with him, tease him with a sidelong glance, then look away quickly, as if afraid he had seen her. She deliberately wore provocative clothes to excite him, and sometimes at rehearsals she made a point of taking the seat next to his. Once he casually put his arm across the back of her chair and let his hand rest on her shoulder. Flinching inwardly, she glanced over at him and smiled, letting her eyes lock with his in a warm, melting expression. And all the time she kept thinking: I detest you, you son of a bitch. He leaned close and was about to say something, when she suddenly got up and went to talk to Paul, leaving Alec with barely concealed anger and frustration.

* * *

The pressure of designing the costumes, working with Maxie, then rushing to a meeting or rehearsal where Alec was always waiting began to take its toll. She was thankful that Paul was too busy to notice her frayed nerves and irritability. But Claudia saw the strain she was under. One afternoon, while they were going over some papers in the office at The House of Ronay, she said, "You've been very jumpy the last couple of weeks. Is something wrong?"

"No, just the usual," Adrian replied. "*Ziegfeld* is not an easy show to costume, and all this"—she gestured to the desk covered with receipts and shipping orders—"is a lot to take care of."

"Bullshit," Claudia said bluntly. "You're at your best working under pressure, and I think the staff and I are handling the business very well."

"I didn't mean to imply that you weren't!" Adrian snapped. Then she quickly apologized. "I'm sorry—it's just nerves...."

"I already know that," Claudia said gently. "But I don't know why. Can't I help?"

God, I wish you could, Adrian thought desperately. But I can't bring you into this; I've got to handle it alone. She gave Claudia a grateful smile and replied, "You can help by ignoring me. I haven't been sleeping well lately—probably too much coffee late at night."

There was a light tap at the door, and a secretary came in carrying a long florist's box. "These just arrived for you, Miss Ronay," she said.

"Thank you, Andrea."

The girl left and Adrian opened the box to find three dozen roses and a note from Alec that read: "Stop teasing me—I *must* see you alone."

"From Paul?" Claudia asked.

"No, they're not," Adrian admitted slowly. "They're from one of the investors in the show."

Claudia raised an eyebrow. "Oh...?"

"It doesn't mean anything, just a thoughtful gesture."

She tore up the card and threw it in the wastebasket.

"Three dozen roses is a pretty romantic 'thoughtful gesture,'" Claudia said kiddingly.

"Don't be ridiculous," Adrian replied, trying to sound unconcerned.

"Adrian, I'm surprised that half the men in New York haven't hit on you already. And they would, if you weren't attached at the hip to Paul."

"Well, it's a good thing I am. Half the men in New York are schmucks, and I don't give a damn about the other half. Now, let's get back to work."

For the next few hours, she tried to concentrate on business. But all she could think about was Alec, excited by the idea that she was beginning to unnerve him.

When Adrian left the office later that afternoon, she saw Alec waiting for her in the lobby of the building. He was at the newsstand by the door, looking through some magazines. Although he usually dressed in conservative, three-piece suits, today he was wearing a thick brown pullover sweater that strained across his broad shoulders, and beige linen slacks that had been tailored to cling to his muscular legs. His hair was mussed from the breezy fall weather, and there were high spots of color on his cheeks, giving him a boyish look.

Adrian's heart lurched at the sight of him; for a moment she remembered the first time she had seen him walk into the Skolskys' store, looking more beautiful than any man she'd ever dreamed of.

Several young women walked past and turned to stare at him. He flashed them an engaging grin, then looked up and saw Adrian and waved, smiling broadly. She stiffened her back and walked slowly toward him.

"Hello there," he said. "May I offer you a lift to wherever you're going? My car is outside."

She forced a polite tone. "No, thank you, Mr. Darcy. I'd prefer to walk." She went out onto the street in a brisk stride.

Alec fell into step behind her. "Don't you think it's time you called me Alec? I thought we were becoming friends—and after all, we are working together."

"We're not working together, Mr. Darcy," Adrian said. "You're involvement in the show is just financial, not creative."

Alec's face grew flushed. "That may be, but I could make some valuable suggestions about the show, given half a chance. I've had some experience in the theater— I used to be an actor."

Adrian stopped and turned to face him. "You were an actor?" she asked, feigning surprise. "Where? What did you do? Television—films?"

Her abrupt questions took him by surprise and he began to stammer. "Well—I did do some TV, nothing important, of course, and I did some work on the stage...."

Adrian's smile was condescending. "Mr. Darcy, why don't you leave it to the professionals? Oh, and by the way, thank you for the roses. I gave them to my secretary, and she was so pleased. Now I really must run—see you soon."

An angry scowl came over Alec's face, but before he could reply, Adrian turned on her heel and walked off.

A few weeks later the company started to rehearse in the Palace Theater before the out-of-town previews in Philadelphia. Adrian had been working around the clock with Maxie and her staff and had seen little of Alec. But always at the back of her mind was the sure knowledge that he was around, somewhere, waiting for her. The thought pleased her. She wasn't through with him—yet; they still had a long way to go.

One night there was a first run-through with full orchestra, and everybody was on edge. Adrian and Kelly were backstage, working on the makeup and with the wardrobe people. Dancers were limbering up in front of mirrors, singers vocalized scales, prop men hurried by with their arms full, calling, "Comin' through!" and stage technicians were checking the lights and sound.

Onstage, Paul was giving last-minute directions to the cast, and Terry Ambler worked with a team of dancers doing a specialty number. Milo James was going over the set for the first act, and the composer of the score was checking cuts with the conductor while the musicians made notations on their sheet music. Finally, it was time to begin. The house lights dimmed, the theater fell silent, and the orchestra struck up the overture.

During one of the scene changes, Adrian slipped quietly into the theater and took a seat in the back to make notes. One of the stars of the show, Ella Korvin, who was playing the role of Anna Held, was about to do the famous telephone scene that had won Luise Rainer an Academy Award. Adrian settled into her seat, happy to get away from the chaos backstage for a few minutes. The theater was dark and cavernous, musty with age and traditions. These were the moments she liked best, sitting alone in the dark, watching the show unfold before her. When it opens, she thought, I'll have two shows running simultaneously on Broadway; the ticket sales for *Rudy!* were still going strong. She felt a sense of accomplishment and smiled to herself. Then the stage lights came up on a lavish boudoir set, and Ella Korvin made her entrance.

Adrian was watching her closely, and jotting down notes about her gown when someone quietly took the seat beside her. It was Alec. She glanced at him, momentarily startled by his sudden appearance, and drew a quick, shaky breath. Then she managed a smile and said, "It's going very well, isn't it?"

"I don't think so," he replied.

"Oh? Why not?"

"I'm not talking about the show. I'm referring to you and me."

Her heart began to race. "You and me? I don't know what you mean."

"I think you do. The other day on the street you made me feel like a piece of shit. Why? What's your problem? You know how I feel about you, and I was beginning to think you felt the same way. What kind of game are you playing with me, anyway?"

There was a dangerous edge in his tone. Adrian tried to think quickly; she'd struck a nerve, and now she had to do something to keep him hooked, keep him squirming. She looked up at him with a pleading expression.

"Don't be angry with me," she said softly. "The truth is—I think I do feel the same way about you, and . . . it frightens me." She paused and swallowed hard. "You're one of the most exciting men I've ever met."

Alec smiled, his confidence restored. "I knew you felt something for me. I could tell that first night we met at Sam's place."

Adrian nodded, thinking: You egotistical bastard. "Yes, I did," she whispered. "And I loved your roses—it was such a sweet, thoughtful gesture. I hated giving them away. But what else could I do? After all, I'm engaged to Paul."

Alec put his arm around her shoulders and stroked the side of her neck with his fingertips. She stiffened at his touch, and her body went cold.

"All I think about is you," he said huskily. His eyes looked shadowy through the thick fringe of lashes, and his lips were blood-red. "I've never known anybody like you or wanted any woman as much as I want you."

Adrian felt a little panicky. It's going too fast, she thought; I've got to be careful. "You'll have to give me time," she begged in a soft voice. "I don't want to do anything to hurt Paul."

"Sure, I understand," Alec said soothingly. "But don't take too long. I'm a very impatient man." There was a hint of threat in his words that made her tremble. He mistook it for the effect he was having on her and touched her knee, insinuated his fingers under her skirt. His hand began to move up the inside of her thighs.

Adrian pulled away from him. "Stop it!" she hissed. "Someone might see us!" She stood up suddenly, reeling a little, and fled down the aisle to an exit that led backstage.

She hurried into the restroom and locked herself in a stall, shaking and nauseated. Her body was like ice, but her flesh burned where Alec had touched her. She leaned against the wall to steady herself and heard one of the girls come in to use the facilities. Adrian waited until she had left before unlocking the door and stepping out. At the sink, she ran cold water over her wrists and splashed a little on her face. Then she reached for a paper towel to pat it dry, staring at herself in the mirror.

I can't break down like this, she told herself. I've got him right where I want him. She kept staring at herself, taking courage from what she saw: a beautiful, successful woman who had overcome great odds to get where she was. She had carved a life for herself out of the misery Alec had caused, and she was going to keep that life the way she wanted it. She had nothing to fear from Alec, she decided; there was nothing he could do to hurt her.

But there was still a great deal she could do to hurt him.

41

Adrian BEGAN TO CARRY OUT A CAREFULLY PLANNED scenario to torment Alec. First she let him take her to lunch, then an occasional dinner, making sure they went to some out-of-the-way place where they were not apt to run into anyone they knew. She let him do most of the talking, guardedly watching and listening to everything he said. He was eager to impress her and spent money lavishly, ordering expensive meals and leaving enormous tips for the waiters. He made a great show of enthusiasm about her career, and she began to realize that he saw in her something he had never been able to attain—a distinctive place in society. She was accomplished and respected, and being with her gave him a kind of reflected glory. Adrian relished the idea. He had cast her into the role of someone priceless, almost unobtainable, and she knew that the more contemptuous of him she was, the more he would want her.

Every time they were together, she studied him intently, gauging the effect she was having on him. Alec used every means at his command to win her over; he was charming, witty, and attentive. But she was armored against him, amused by his efforts. You're like a trained dog, she thought, performing all your tricks to please me. Adrian Ronay might have been swept off her feet by you, but Emily Gorden knows better; she remembers every calculated move you made, every lie you told.

Despite all her efforts to keep it a secret from Paul and the company, gossip about Adrian and Alec started to circulate and finally reached Paul's ears. One evening, after a long and arduous rehearsal, they went back to her suite at the Plaza and he confronted her with what he had heard.

"Yes, we've been out to lunch or dinner a few times," she admitted, trying to sound nonchalant. "You know I've gone way over budget on the costumes, and he does represent the major investors in the show. So, I didn't think it would do any harm to be nice to Mr. Darcy."

"I heard that you've been seeing him almost every night," Paul said with an edge of anger in his voice.

"That's just company gossip," Adrian replied casually.

Paul looked at her with narrowed eyes. "I'm not so sure," he said tightly. "Usually, where there's smoke, there's fire."

"I can't believe you actually said that!" Adrian said sharply. "I thought you trusted me!"

"Maybe I've been too trusting!" Paul snapped.

Adrian felt herself sliding into irrational anger and tried to stop the argument. "Paul, we're both tired. I don't think we should discuss this now."

"When should we discuss it?" he exploded. "For the last few months I've been waiting patiently for you to set a date for our wedding, and now you and Darcy have suddenly become the talk of the company! What the hell does it mean? Do you think I'm just going to stand around while you make a fool of me?"

"I don't have to make a fool of you—you're doing a splendid job of that all by yourself!" Adrian cried.

Paul glared at her. "You're right. I've been making a fool of myself about you for a long time. Too long!" He turned on his heel and started for the door.

"Paul, wait!" Adrian called. "This is silly—"

Without looking back at her, he replied, "Not to me, it isn't!" Then he slammed out of the suite.

Adrian stood shaking with anger and frustration, cursing herself for letting the argument get out of hand. She should never have agreed to talk to him tonight, when they were both so tired. For a moment she was tempted to go after him. But then she realized it wouldn't do any good to make up with him just yet. Oh, God, Paul, she thought miserably. I've hurt you so much. But I can't stop what I'm doing—not yet. Not until I've finished with Alec.

A few nights later, she and Alec were leaving a small club in the Village, where they had been having drinks and listening to jazz. As they got into his chauffeured Rolls, he said to her, "Why don't we stop at my place for a nightcap before I take you home?"

She had been anticipating this moment and had prepared for it. That night she had purposely worn her sexiest dress; a sleeveless, clinging white silk with a plunging neckline and a slim skirt that revealed every move of her body. Alec had not been able to take his eyes off her all evening.

Adrian waited a few seconds before answering him. "That's a lovely idea," she said. "I've been curious about where you lived."

"It's a showplace," he said proudly. "I know you'll love it." He moved close to her and put a possessive hand on her thigh. She smiled and covered it with her own, twining her fingers through his.

The car drew up to a townhouse on Sutton Place. Alec dismissed the driver and they went in. He took her from room to room, boasting about the things he'd bought in Europe or had imported from the Orient. Adrian thought it was the most expensively furnished yet tasteless place she had ever seen. Alec's idea of the rich life, she mused dryly, was vulgarity and ostentation.

They went up a wide, curving staircase to the second floor, where he flung open a pair of double-doors to the master suite. "This is my favorite room in the whole house," he said huskily, taking her hand. "I've waited a long time for you to see it."

They stepped in, and Adrian almost laughed aloud. It was like something out of *Playboy* magazine. Soft, indirect lighting cast an amber glow over the large room. Thick, plush carpeting covered the floor, and the paneled walls were hung with erotic prints and paintings. The furniture was all modern: glass and plastic tables, soft white chairs and black cabinets. A white rug lay in front of an ornately carved fireplace, and nearby stood an art deco bar with black and white leather stools. The dominating piece in the room was a large, circular bed with a headboard dotted with rows of buttons and switches. Alec explained that they controlled the lights, TV, and stereo. The ceiling over the bed was mirrored, as was one long wall of closet doors. Through an arched doorway, she saw a room with gleaming tile and a marble, sunken tub.

While Adrian wandered slowly around the room, Alec knelt to light the fire. Then he assumed a master-of-the-house pose by the mantelpiece and asked, "Well, how do you like it?"

"It's incredible," Adrian answered truthfully.

He smiled and slipped off his jacket, then loosened his tie. "It's a room to have fun in," he said, holding his arms out to her.

Adrian remained standing where she was, taunting him with a seductive smile. "Yes, it is," she replied softly. Then she said in a soft, caressing voice, "Take off all your clothes. I want to see you naked."

Alec smiled with anticipation and began to strip. "Slowly," Adrian said in a half-whisper. "Slowly ..."

As she watched him, she was suddenly transported back in time to the dressing room behind the stage at Los Angeles City College, where she had first seen him naked. He continued to take off his clothes, and another image came to her mind, that of a frightened, scarred girl in a shabby room, lying nude on the bed, watching him with trembling excitement. How desperately she had loved him, desired him. She remembered all the dreams and hopes he'd inspired in her. And then she saw herself in prison, being beaten into unconsciousness while screaming out her pain at his betrayal.

Alec had dropped his clothes on the floor and stood clad only in a pair of brief nylon shorts. The bright, rosy firelight flickered and moved over his muscular body. His eyes were burning with undisguised passion, and his shadowed face had a rapacious, feral look. He hooked his thumbs into the waistband of his shorts to pull them down.

"No, don't," she said in a choked whisper. "Let me...."

She dropped her coat on the bed and moved toward him, swaying in a provocative, sensuous glide. Alec's lips parted slightly, his breath came in short gasps. When she was close to him, he started to reach for her.

"No, don't move," she murmured, pushing his hands away.

He dropped his arms to his sides and closed his eyes at the first touch of her hands on his chest. She trailed her fingertips across the smooth, tawny flesh, playing lightly with his nipples. He trembled, and she saw his erection straining against the thin cloth of his briefs. Her hands fluttered down to his waist, and around his hips to caress his buttocks. He threw his head back and a moan of pleasure escaped his lips. She pressed herself against him, slowly grinding her pelvis, and a tremor shot through his body. He reached for her once more.

"No, don't," she cautioned him, pulling away a little. "I want to do it all."

Moving one hand up between his thighs, she lightly cupped his balls. Then she slid her fingers inside his shorts and pulled them down to the middle of his legs, freeing him. "You're so big," she whispered, stroking him lovingly.

"Oh, Christ," he groaned. "Please, let me touch you, let me have you."

"Not yet," she replied in a low voice, pulling away from him. "And not ever."

Suddenly she turned and ran swiftly across the room, picked up her coat and started for the door. Alec stood rooted in place, his face a mask of shock. "What are you doing?" he gasped. "Where the hell are you going?"

"I'm going home, Mr. Darcy. I've decided I don't want you," Adrian calmly replied, opening the door.

"You fucking bitch!" Alec started after her and almost fell, hampered by the shorts trapping his legs. Furiously, he pulled them up and began to run, but she was already down the stairs and in the foyer, releasing the catch on the front door.

"You can't do this to me!" he shouted. "You cock teaser! You can't leave me like this!"

"Oh, yes I can!" she cried triumphantly, and slammed the door behind her.

When she got back to her suite, Adrian found a message that Paul had called and wanted to talk to her. For the last week they had avoided each other at rehearsals, but the few times she had glimpsed his face had made her heart ache; he'd looked so pale and hollow-eyed, so unhappy.

Despite the lateness of the hour, she dialed his number quickly, desperately needing to see him, be with him.

His voice was fuzzy with sleep when he answered. "Adrian? Why are you calling so late? Are you all right? Is anything wrong?"

"Paul, I need to see you. I've been so miserable these last few days. May I come over now? Please?"

"Get in a cab right away," he answered happily. "Oh, darling, I'm so glad you called...."

Adrian rushed to change out of her gown, then left the hotel. A few minutes later she knocked at Paul's door. He opened it and swept her into his arms. They clung to each other, apologizing and kissing until finally Paul picked her up and carried her to bed.

Alec did not put in an appearance at any of the meetings or rehearsals for the next few days. Adrian felt an exhilarating sense of victory. She had ridiculed and humiliated him, reduced him to a groveling schoolboy. She had plunged a knife into his ego, his vanity, and had shamed him. It was a moment she would cherish forever. All the rage and hatred she had felt for him over the years had abated. She would never forgive him for what he had done to her, but she no longer had to despise him. She finally realized how pathetic he was, and how foolish she had been to keep herself from completely enjoying the happiness she had worked so hard to achieve. A glorious life lay before her, doing the kind of work she loved, and having Paul alongside to share it with her. And one day, when the time was right, she would tell him the truth and free herself at last from the past.

Alec finally showed up at the theater for one of the last dress rehearsals of the show. When he saw Adrian, he looked at her as if nothing had happened between them. But during a moment when they were alone, he said under his breath, "I'm not finished with you, Adrian. Not yet."

"Don't sulk, Mr. Darcy," she replied. "It's very unattractive in a grown man."

He gave her a quick, hard smile and walked off.

Later that evening, after the performance was over and Paul had given his notes to the cast, he and Adrian prepared to leave the theater with Ella Korvin and Christopher Bruce, who was playing the role of Flo Ziegfeld. They were going to join Kelly, Milo, and Terry, who had gone on ahead to get a table at Charlie's, a small restaurant in the theater district.

"Why don't we invite Mr. Darcy to come with us?" Adrian suggested, wanting to lay the gossip about them to rest once and for all.

"Oh, that's a good idea," Ella Korvin agreed quickly. A devilish gleam sparkled in her eyes. "Now, if I can just get him to stop mooning over Adrian long enough to notice me...."

"Hey, is he still after my girl?" Paul asked kiddingly.

"She's just teasing," Adrian laughed, putting her arm around him.

Christopher Bruce, a floridly handsome middle-aged man who affected a somewhat theatrical manner, gave Ella an amused glance. "Ella always blames another woman if a man doesn't pay enough attention to her. You must overcome feeling so insecure, my dear."

Ella's bitchy temper flared. "I'd feel a lot more secure about this show if you'd learn your lines!" she snapped.

"I could, if only you would stop improvising yours," he replied mildly.

Just then, Alec came up to them and nodded to everyone. "The show looks great, Paul; I think it's going to be a real winner. And Ella, you were wonderful. You, too, Chris."

"Oh, Gawd, I thought I was just awful," the actress moaned. "But thank you anyway, Mr. Darcy." She smiled at him flirtatiously. "I think you are a very patient man, sitting through all our dreary rehearsals."

"They weren't dreary at all," Alec replied gallantly, casting a glance at Adrian. "I've enjoyed watching the whole production take shape, and being with all of you."

Adrian smiled. "How very kind of you to say that, Mr. Darcy. We were about to go to Charlie's for something to eat. Won't you join us?"

"I'd like that very much," he responded quietly. "But don't you think it's time you all called me Alec? Mr. Darcy was my father."

Ella trilled a musical laugh and took his arm. "Alec— that's a lovely name. It suits you. But let's hurry. I'm starved."

When they walked into the restaurant, a young actor working as the host recognized them and took them to the table where Kelly, Milo, and Terry were waiting. He engaged Paul in conversation about the forthcoming show and at the same time managed to reel off his list of credits. Alec took advantage of the situation and sat down next to Adrian. She pretended not to notice and studied the menu. Kelly, who was sitting on the other side of her, leaned close and whispered in her ear, "Did you break his heart yet?" She couldn't suppress a giggle, and covered it by asking the waiter to get her a drink.

During dinner, everyone talked about the dress rehearsal, and comments rapidly shot back and forth across the table. Mishaps were recounted with great relish, followed by gales of laughter. Alec casually put his arm around the back of Adrian's chair. She did her best to ignore him, aware that Ella Korvin was watching them with a malicious little smile.

Suddenly Adrian had the feeling that someone else was watching them. Her eyes were drawn across the room to the slender figure of a young woman who was standing at the bar. The restaurant was dimly lighted, and it was difficult to see her clearly, but Adrian knew that the woman's gaze was fixed on her.

She looked away to answer a question from Terry Ambler, but even as they spoke, she could feel the woman's eyes boring into her with an unnerving intensity. When she glanced back, she saw the woman hadn't moved and was still staring at her.

Then the woman abruptly left the bar and started toward them, moving unsteadily across the room. She's drunk, Adrian thought uneasily. Ella noticed her approaching.

Alec looked up and his face went pale. He moved his arm away from Adrian's chair and started to get up, half rising from his seat. But the young woman was already at the table, and he sank back, going crimson with embarrassment and anger.

"What are you doing here?" he asked her through clenched teeth.

She looked down at him with a mocking smile. Heavy makeup couldn't disguise the dark circles under her eyes, and the sunken hollows of her cheeks gave her the appearance of being ill. Her blond hair was bleached almost white and had a stiff, unnatural look. Her dress was obviously expensive, and the jewelry she wore was real, but there was a calculating expression in her eyes, a languid sexuality in the slouch of her thin body that suggested a high-class hooker plying her trade.

"I've been looking for you, lover," she answered Alec in a whiskey-sodden voice. "I went to the theater, and one of the stagehands said you were here."

She looked around the table, her head nodding drunkenly. "Aren't you going to introduce me to your friends?" she demanded. "Especially her—" she jerked her head at Adrian—"I was hoping she'd be here."

Adrian sat paralyzed, staring at the woman in shock. Beneath the garish makeup there was still evidence of a once-lovely young girl whose features she would never forget.

It was her sister, Sheila.

Alec stood up and grabbed Sheila's arm. "You're drunk," he said thickly. "I'll take you home."

She yanked away from him and cried, "Not until you've introduced me!" She glared at everyone around the table. "I'm his wife! Or didn't you know he had a wife?" She swung back to Alec, eyes livid, her voice rising shrilly. "Introduce me, you bastard!"

Alec's face was white with rage. "Stop it! You're making a scene!"

"You're goddamned right I am," Sheila said loudly. "Why shouldn't I? Leaving me alone all the time to run after some new bitch!" She suddenly leaned across the table and thrust her face close to Adrian. "It's you, isn't it? You're the new pussy he's after!"

Adrian sat horrified, unable to move or speak. Alec furiously pulled Sheila up and slapped her hard. Her cheek flamed with the imprint of his hand and a trickle of blood ran from her lips. She began to cry and collapsed in his arms, pressing her face against his chest.

"Sorry about this," Alec said stiffly. "She has a drinking problem." Keeping a tight grip on her, he led Sheila out of the restaurant.

A shocked silence had fallen over the table. Finally, Ella said, "Well, that explains why he's been at all the rehearsals. Poor darling, having a drunken slut like that for a wife—"

Christopher Bruce laid a restraining hand on her arm. "Ella, my dear, why don't you shut up? We don't need a coda to the little drama we've just witnessed."

She pushed his hand away, flaring angrily. "Don't be silly! The whole town will probably be reading about it in the columns tomorrow!"

Adrian was still reeling from shock. She took Paul's hand and said, "I'd like to leave now."

She told Paul that she wanted to be alone, and he took her back to the Plaza. In the cab, she rested her head against his chest and closed her eyes. But she couldn't get the image of Sheila's tortured face out of her mind.

42

ADRIAN SPENT THE LONG HOURS OF THE NIGHT AGO-nizing over what had happened. She paced the floor rest-lessly, trying to think what to do. For years she had been positive that Sheila cared nothing for her, that she had known about the robbery, had even helped Alec plan it. But now she wondered if her sister had simply been his dupe, so bewitched by his charm, taken in by his lies, that she would do anything he told her.

Hadn't she herself done the same thing? Adrian remembered with shame her willingness to do whatever he had asked, make any sacrifice he had demanded. If things had worked out differently, it might have been she, not Sheila, making that scene in the restaurant.

As the night wore on, Adrian became convinced that she had to do something to help her sister, get her away from Alec. But how could she, without revealing herself? Where could she find the strength to face her own sister without telling her who she really was? But she had to do something to help Sheila—she'd never forget the bru-tal expression on Alec's face when he had slapped her.

The following afternoon Adrian called the stage man-ager and got Alec's unlisted phone number. She discov-ered that there were two numbers—one for a residence on Sutton Place, the other an apartment on Park Avenue. So, he kept the Sutton Place town house for himself, Adrian thought, where he could entertain his women.

She dialed the Park Avenue number and waited, praying that he wasn't there, that Sheila was alone. The phone rang several times, and finally a woman answered.

"Darcy residence." It was the maid.

"Is Mrs. Darcy there?" Adrian asked.

"Who's calling please?"

Adrian hesitated; what if Alec was there? She had to chance it. "Adrian Ronay," she said.

"Just a minute...."

There was silence for a few minutes, and Adrian held her breath. Then the maid came back on the line. "I'm sorry. Mrs. Darcy can't come to the phone."

"Please tell her it's very important."

Adrian heard a murmur of conversation in the background, then Sheila took the call. "What the hell do you want?" she asked brusquely.

"Mrs. Darcy, I've got to talk to you."

"I don't want to talk to you," came the snappish reply.

"Please, it's very important. Won't you see me for just a few minutes?"

Sheila was silent for a moment, then she said, "All right. I've got some shopping to do—where shall we meet?"

"Would you come to my apartment?" Adrian asked quickly. "I'm at the Plaza, and we could be alone here."

"Yeah, all right. I'll be there around two."

"Yes, that's fine. I'll see you at two."

When the buzzer sounded, Adrian went to the door, her heart thudding painfully. She fixed a smile on her face and let Sheila in.

"Thank you for coming, Mrs. Darcy," she said, taking her sister into the living room.

Sheila made no reply. She appeared sober, but a little unsteady. Her hair had been hastily brushed and was limp, and her face had an unhealthy pallor, except for a slash of lipstick. There was a bruise on her temple that she had tried to cover with makeup. Alec hit her, Adrian thought, wincing.

"Would you like some coffee?" Adrian asked.

"I'd prefer a drink," Sheila answered bluntly. "Scotch, if you have it."

Adrian brought her the drink and Sheila downed it quickly. She sat down on the couch and Adrian pulled up a chair to face her. Sheila opened her purse and took out a gold cigarette case. She offered Adrian one, took one herself, then lit them both with a matching gold lighter. Drawing deeply, she sat back and stared at Adrian suspiciously. "Okay, why am I here?" she asked in a belligerent tone of voice.

Adrian looked at her, thinking how much she had changed. And yet, in some ways she was still the same girl: her wild and beautiful kid sister. The arrogance was still there, the defensive nonchalance, and the petulant manner that men had found so irresistible. But the years with Alec had left their mark. She looked worn, used, and she couldn't disguise the slight tremor of her hands or the fearful, anxious expression in her eyes.

Adrian took a deep breath and began to answer her question cautiously. "I wanted to talk about last night—to set your mind at rest about me and your husband. Nothing has been going on between us. I swear. I'm very much in love with Paul Mallory, and we're going to get married."

Sheila made an ugly sound that was a laugh. "You think Alec gives a shit about that? He gets what he wants: husbands, boyfriends, lovers don't stand in his way. He doesn't give a damn about other people's feelings. Including mine," she added bitterly, stubbing out her cigarette and lighting another one. She held up her empty glass. "How 'bout another drink?" At Adrian's concerned expression, she smiled. "Don't worry—it takes a lot more than two scotches to get me drunk." She paused and giggled. "Drunk was last night—me at my worst. Sorry about that. And listen, I may not show it, but I appreciate your wanting to see me and tell me about you and Mallory."

Adrian got her another drink and brought it back. "I'm glad you understand. I just didn't want you to think I was having anything to do with your husband."

"Women don't have anything to *do* with Alec," she said ruefully. "He just takes them over and fucks them over. It's the way he is, the way he's always been."

Adrian sensed her sister's need to talk and tried to draw her out about the life she'd had with Alec. Sheila was reluctant at first, unused to confiding in anyone, and suspicious of Adrian. But the whiskey loosened her tongue and her inhibitions, and gradually Adrian won her confidence. She said nothing about the circumstances under which she had met Alec, but told a rambling, ugly story of being manipulated and deceived.

Adrian had to put it together in bits and pieces; Sheila shied away from talking about some things, and others she merely alluded to. Finally, Sheila began to cry softly, recounting how Alec had made her sleep with some of the businessmen he'd been involved with, how he had betrayed her with other women and even made her work as a whore to keep them going when they were broke. The list of indignities tumbled from her lips, wrenching at Adrian's heart.

"Why didn't you leave him?" she asked.

Sheila wiped her tear-stained face and gave Adrian a crooked smile. "Would you believe I thought he needed me? Every time I threatened to leave, he got crazy, like a kid afraid to be alone in the dark. He'd say, 'Don't leave me, baby—I need you. All those other women, they don't mean anything to me; they're just pussy, that's all. But you really care about me; you understand me.'"

Adrian remembered hearing those same words, and believing them.

Sheila sighed and lit another cigarette. "So—I stayed with him. What the hell, I guess I loved him. . . ."

"Do you love him now?" Adrian asked quietly.

Sheila looked away from her, gazing into space, her brow furrowed as if she were searching for an answer.

When she looked back, there was an expression of pleading in her eyes. "Can I trust you? Really trust you? You won't tell anybody what I've been saying?"

"Of course I won't," Adrian replied. She leaned forward and took Sheila's hands. "You can trust me. I promise you can."

"I believe you. I don't know why—I've never trusted other women, but I like you. And I have to trust somebody—" Her voice began to break. "Because I'm scared. I'm scared to death." The words caught in her throat, and she gripped Adrian's hands tightly.

"What is it? What are you afraid of?"

"Alec," she whispered. "I'm afraid of Alec. He's getting meaner to me all the time." She touched the bruise on her temple. "He didn't use to hit me," she said in a small voice, like a bewildered little girl. She looked at Adrian anxiously. "You know he's in the syndicate?" Adrian nodded. "They like him," Sheila went on. "He told me they have big plans for him, that they think he's got the style and class they need in their business." She paused, then lowered her voice. "But I don't think they like me. I don't think they want me around...."

"What do you mean?"

"We had a couple of guys over for dinner one night, and I got a little tight. When they were leaving, I overheard one of them tell Alec to get rid of me—and that I was just a lush, that I was in his way...."

"But if you got a divorce, it might be the best thing for you," Adrian said.

"What the hell would I do?" Sheila cried. "I don't know anything. I can't do anything except whore! I've always depended on Alec!" Fresh tears came to her eyes and she began to sob.

Adrian moved quickly to Sheila's side and took her in her arms. "Don't cry, Sheila, don't cry," she crooned softly, rocking her. "I'll help you...."

Sheila clung to her for a few minutes. When she had quieted down, Adrian let her go, and Sheila looked at her with a puzzled expression. "I don't understand why you're being so nice to me," she said. "And you called me Sheila— I don't remember telling you my first name. And I know Alec didn't; he never tells anyone about me."

Adrian was afraid to speak. Enraged at how Alec had victimized her sister, and torn by pity for her, she wanted to cry out, I'm your sister! I'm Emily!

Sheila stared at her questioningly. "Do we know each other? Did we meet someplace—Vegas? Chicago? I don't know why, but ever since I walked in, I thought there was something familiar about you."

Adrian hesitated; did she dare tell Sheila who she was? Could she take that risk? Finally, she made up her mind. She went to the bar, got another glass, and came back with the bottle of Scotch. "I've got something to tell you, Sheila. And I think we're both going to need a drink. My name isn't Adrian Ronay...."

"What do you mean? Who are you?"

Adrian's eyes filled with tears. "Oh, Sheila, baby— I'm Emily! Your sister! My real name is Emily Gorden—"

"You can't be!" Sheila exclaimed. "I mean—Emily was in prison—she was scarred. I don't believe you!"

Adrian began to weep. "It's true, Sheila." She caught her breath and said in a rush, "We lived in Silverlake, and Mom was a beautician. I worked at the Skolskys' antique store and studied design in college at night. You were going with a boy named Mike, and one night Mom found you together, stoned and necking in your room, remember?"

"Oh, my God," Sheila whispered.

The two sisters fell into each other's arms for a long, sobbing embrace. They clung to each other, laughing and crying, and Adrian felt the years of painful memories and separation wash away in their tears. Quiet, finally, they held each other's hands while Adrian told her everything that had happened.

Sheila sat in stunned silence until Adrian was finished. Then she cried out, "Oh, Em—I didn't know anything about the robbery. I swear I didn't! Alec began to see me after we met that night at the play. He never told me about you! When you were arrested, I thought your story was true, that you wanted the money for an operation. I didn't even know you were seeing Alec. You've got to believe me!"

Sheila's voice rang with tearful sincerity, and Adrian held her close, saying, "I believe you, Sheila. I really do. Knowing what we do now, about Alec, it's easy to understand how he took advantage of the situation. But that's all in the past. We have to talk about what's going to happen now. You've got to leave him."

"But, Em—what'll I do? Where will I go? I'm afraid of him; look what he did to both of us!"

"I know," Adrian said grimly. "He's a ruthless bastard, but I think I know a way to get back at him for everything he's done. Will you trust me and do as I say?"

"Yes, I think so—" Sheila said, her voice quivering.

"Good. The first thing is to get you away from him. I need some time to figure everything out, but I don't want you to worry—I'll take care of you. If Alec starts any trouble, I'll get the best lawyer in town. You know more about his criminal activities than anyone else; if he gets rough, so will we. The only thing you have to remember is not to say a word about me. As long as he doesn't know who I am, we're safe. I have enough money to set you up in a place of your own, and then later, I can get you a job somewhere. I have business contacts all over the country."

"Em, do you really think we can do it?" Sheila asked hopefully.

"I know we can," she replied with conviction. "You'd better go now; it's getting late. Can you come back tomorrow? The company is going to Philadelphia for the out-of-town opening, but I can beg off and be here. We have so much to talk about."

"Yes, I'll come back," Sheila said eagerly. "Oh, Emily, I still can't believe it! You're beautiful now—and successful. Mom would have been so proud of you. Wouldn't she be happy if she could see us together like this?"

"I know she would. Sheila, I'm so glad we've found each other!"

Adrian hugged her sister tightly. "Be here at seven o'clock tomorrow night. By then I'll have cleared my schedule, and we can make some plans."

"Yes, tomorrow night at seven," Sheila repeated. "I'll be here."

The company was scheduled to leave for Philadelphia the next morning. Adrian called Paul, not trusting herself to see him in person. He reluctantly accepted her excuse that she needed some time to work with Claudia on business for The House of Ronay and couldn't be with him for the opening.

"It should only take a few days," she told him. "As soon as I'm finished, I'll join you. I know it's rather sudden, darling," she said hurriedly, "but things have been piling up at the office. And besides, a little vacation from each other will do us good. Think how much fun we'll have when we see each other again."

"What happens if there's an emergency backstage?" he asked.

"My assistants can handle it—I've already called them, and they're prepared for anything."

For the rest of the evening, Adrian tried to organize a plan to help Sheila. She knew that they would have to be careful; once Alec discovered that she was gone, he might make trouble. If it came to the worst, she would call Sam Phillips for help; he had powerful lawyers who could advise her. She checked her calendar; Sam had been on the West Coast for the last couple of weeks, but he was due back in town in a few days.

Adrian felt a little uneasy; with the exception of Claudia, there was no one really close to her she could turn to for help if she ran into any trouble. But it shouldn't be that difficult, she reassured herself. She would simply get Sheila out of town as quickly as possible, see to it that she had enough money, and later help her sister arrange a quiet divorce.

With any luck, Alec would never know about her part in the scheme.

43

THE FOLLOWING EVENING, AT EXACTLY SEVEN O'CLOCK, there was a knock on the door. Adrian hurried to let Sheila in. But it wasn't her sister.

It was Alec.

He gave her a cheery smile and walked past her into the room. "I heard you didn't go out of town with the show, and I thought you might be ill. So I dropped by to see how you are."

Panic streaked through her. Sheila would be here any minute; she had to get rid of him!

"That was very considerate of you, but I'm not ill. And I'd prefer to be alone. Thank you for coming by—"

"I'll just stay for a few minutes," Alec said, taking off his coat.

"I'd rather you didn't," she said flatly. "We have nothing to say to each other."

Alec dropped his coat on a chair and calmly sat down. "I think we have a lot to talk about—*Emily*."

Adrian felt as if the blood had suddenly been drained from her body. Her knees began to buckle, and she moved blindly to a chair, almost stumbling as she sat down.

"How did you find out?" she asked in a choked whisper. "Did you beat it out of Sheila? If you hurt her, I swear I'll—"

"No, no, I didn't touch Sheila," he replied, laughing. "I had no idea who you were; she told me all about you on her own." He leaned forward, peering at her. "Christ, it's really incredible. I would never have guessed in a million years."

"You must have found out that she came to see me—that I was going to help her get away from you," Adrian cried. "She swore she wouldn't tell you!"

Alec sat back grinning, enjoying the moment hugely. He wagged a finger at her and said, "Blood is *not* thicker than water, Emily—not where Sheila is concerned."

"I don't believe you! She wouldn't tell you like that, not after the way you've abused her!"

Alec threw his head back and laughed. "Cross my heart and hope to die, Em—I didn't touch her. What you don't seem to understand is that Sheila loves me. Oh, sure, we've had our little tiffs now and again, but doesn't every couple?" He paused to light a cigarette, taking pleasure in Adrian's confusion and anger. Then he went on: "After she left you yesterday, she began to think about it—to the extent that Sheila can think about anything. I mean, after all, it was quite a shock—poor, scarred little Emily, now a wealthy, famous, and beautiful woman. More beautiful, even, than she had been—" He shook his head sadly. "Isn't it a shame the way Sheila's lost her looks?" He sighed deeply before going on. "Anyway, she thought about you, and the little romance we'd had when we were kids. Funny, isn't it, how things turned out? When we met, you were a poor, frightened girl trying to hide her face from the world, and I was just a hustler looking for a way out. And look at us, now—"

Adrian couldn't stand his maddening performance a moment longer. "Alec, stop it!" she cried. "Get to the point and then get out!"

"Get out?" he repeated mockingly. "No, I'm not getting out—not yet." He smiled at her and continued. "Well, she began to think about us—that is, Adrian Ronay and me. She knew we'd been seeing each other, and she began to worry about why you were so anxious to help her get away from me—"

"But she told me she hated you, that she wanted to leave you—"

"Logic has never been one of Sheila's strong points, has it? And she's a very jealous woman, always has been. So, despite everything she told you about her life with me..." He paused and grinned. "Most of which is true, by the way—she decided that you still wanted me. And she got very angry, and when Sheila gets angry, her brains go out the window. I guess she thought if I knew who you really were, it would turn me off, that I wouldn't want you anymore."

"You mean she didn't believe what I told her about me and Paul?"

"Not a word."

Adrian stood up and said firmly, "Well, you can go back and tell her it's true. I'm going to marry Paul in a few weeks."

"Oh, no, you're not," he said softly. Then, more menacingly, "You're not going to marry Paul at all. I won't let you."

"Don't be ridiculous!" Adrian stormed. "You can't threaten me!"

"Sure I can," he said smoothly. "I know who you are, and what you did. I know all about your lurid past."

"If you think telling Paul about me will make any difference to him, you're mistaken. He loves me; he'll understand. So you can forget all your cheap gangster theatrics and get out! As for Sheila, she's welcome to you—you deserve each other!"

Alec suddenly got up and lunged across the room to Adrian, grabbing her upper arms tightly. "I've had enough of your shit!" he said harshly. "We're going to play by my rules, not yours!"

The suddenness of his move took her by surprise and frightened her. She stared at him coldly, trying to brazen it out. "Don't play the tough guy with me, Alec; it doesn't work."

"You'll see just how tough I can be," he muttered. "I

haven't forgotten what you did to me the other night."

"You deserved it!" Adrian taunted him. "It was small enough revenge for all the hell you put me through!"

"You might have saved yourself if you had told them about me. Why didn't you? Come on, Emily, tell me the truth. Why did you cover for me? Why didn't you tell the police that I planned the robbery, that you were stealing the money for me?" He tightened his grip, digging his fingers into her arms.

"Stop it—you're hurting me!"

"Tell me, Em—why didn't you give me away?" he demanded. "Say it, goddamn you, or I'll break your arms!"

"Because I loved you!" she cried out. "I believed every lie you told me!"

He pulled her against him roughly and looked down at her with a triumphant smile. "That's what I wanted to hear, baby. You did all that because you loved me, and you still do. I saw it in your eyes, the other night when you were playing with me—"

"No, I despise you!" Adrian shouted, struggling to free herself.

"The hell you do!" He fastened his lips on hers in a bruising kiss. Adrian fought against him with all her strength. His arms tightened around her, and she felt his tongue forcing her mouth open. She bit down hard, catching the soft flesh of his lower lip between her teeth.

Alec reared back in pain. "You bitch!" he shouted, striking her violently across the face. Before she could recover, he hit her again. "We're going to finish what you started the other night!"

Adrian's eyes filled with tears and she tasted blood in her mouth. She got one hand free and tried to claw at his face, but he grabbed her arms, twisting them back cruelly, and forced her to her knees. A sick sensation came up in her throat and she swallowed hard, crying, "No, Alec—don't!"

He pushed her down on the floor and began to tear at her clothes. Shaking with terror, she begged him to stop.

He clamped a hand across her mouth; he was breathing hard, his mouth twisted in an ugly sneer, his eyes glittering.

"Relax, Emily, and enjoy it like you used to...."

Robbed of her strength by fear and shock, she lay helpless, powerless to fight him. Holding her down with one arm across her chest, Alec kicked off his shoes and tore off his pants and shorts. Then he ripped off his shirt and flung himself down on top of her. At the touch of his naked flesh against hers, a shock vibrated through her body. He took his hand away from her mouth and kissed her, licking away the trickle of blood from where he had hit her. She steeled herself against the touch of his lips, the dizzying, familiar heat of his body.

"It's almost like old times, isn't it?" he whispered.

"Alec, don't do this to me," she begged. "It won't change anything—it won't make any difference."

"Yes it will," he murmured.

Holding her down with the weight of his body, he began to stroke her throat and breasts. His lips followed his hands, his tongue licking her skin, exciting her nipples. Adrian shut her eyes, willing herself to resist, not to respond. Alec deliberately teased his fingers over her stomach and hips. He shifted his legs and rubbed his body against hers in a slow, provocative motion. She felt his erection pressing against her thighs and tensed, trying to make herself rigid, unyielding.

"Remember, Em?" he whispered in her ear. "When we were so hot to fuck we couldn't wait to get at each other?"

"It was a lie!" she said, clenching her teeth. "It was all a lie!"

"The fucking wasn't a lie, Emily," he said. "I loved every minute of it, and so did you. And you're going to love it now...."

A surge of strength swept through her and she flung a hand into his face, trying to shove him away. He grabbed both her wrists in one hand and held them down against the floor over her head. "Don't fight me, Em—" he crooned, pressing his body to hers and grinding his hips in a lazy, sensuous motion. He moved his free hand down to the juncture of her thighs and forced them open, playing his fingertips over her.

Despite her efforts to remain unmoved, Adrian felt her resistance beginning to break down, as if her flesh were betraying her. Alec sensed that she was weakening and used all his skill to excite her. His lips fastened on hers in a hungry, demanding kiss. He worked his fingers inside her in a gentle, teasing caress until she began to quiver in response. Helpless before the onslaught of emotions he was arousing, her legs fell weakly apart. Alec took his lips from hers and gave a brutish laugh. Then he plunged himself into her in one hard shove. She gasped and in a blinding rush lost all sense of herself. Adrian Ronay seemed only an illusion; she was Emily now, in the arms of the first man she had ever loved. All pretenses fell away and she lifted herself to him, locking her body around his.

Alec moved slowly at first, then more quickly, hammering into her and whispering her name—Emily—over and over, like an incantation. The sound began to echo in her mind, and a strange and terrible impression took hold of her. She began to imagine that the flesh on the left side of her face was tightening, shriveling up into a ridged welt of scar tissue. She could almost feel it tugging at the corner of her eye and pulling her lips down into a grimace. She felt trapped in a vortex of conflicting emotions and wanted to scream her fury at him for doing this to her. But at that moment, Alec brought her to a powerful climax, and her rage gave way to ecstasy.

Adrian opened her eyes.

She was lying in bed, and Alec was beside her, sleeping. She remembered with shame what had happened. After the first time, he had carried her into the bedroom and made love to her again and again. She stared into the darkness feeling numbed and degraded, too exhausted to think. The digital clock by her bed blinked and caught her eye. It was almost ten o'clock. In another hour or so, Paul would be calling from Philadelphia to tell her about the opening-night performance.

Paul.

She didn't dare let herself think about him right now. She started to get up, but her body felt like a raw wound, and she lay still for a few minutes, gathering her strength. She couldn't bring herself to even glance at Alec, but remained motionless, trying to imagine that he wasn't there.

Finally, she got out of bed, went into the bathroom, and ran a hot shower. Standing under the scalding spray, she prayed it would wash away all traces of what had happened, cleanse her body and her mind. But she couldn't vanquish her overwhelming sense of shame and guilt.

I can't let him do this to me, she told herself furiously. I can't let him ruin everything I've worked so hard to achieve. She needed rage to fight him, and she deliberately made herself remember the torment she had gone through because of him: the ghastly moments of her arrest and conviction, the harrowing months, years she had spent in prison. A fierce, implacable anger began to grow within her, and she thought: I will never let him hurt me again.

She got out of the shower, slipped into a soft terry robe, and went to the mirror. Her face was pale and there were dark circles under her eyes. Her lips were bruised, swollen, and her hair was disheveled. She took a brush to her hair, giving it vigorous strokes until it gleamed. Then she opened her makeup kit and slowly began to do her face. With each touch of base, liner, lipstick, and powder, she felt somewhat restored, and gave herself a hard smile of satisfaction as she saw Adrian Ronay begin to reemerge.

A few minutes later she returned to the bedroom. Alec wasn't there. She walked into the living room, wildy hoping for a moment that he had gone. But she found him sitting at the bar, having a brandy. He was dressed, and looked relaxed, confident.

Before he could speak to her, she stiffened her back and said coldly, "Now that you've evened the score, get out."

Alec gave her an easy smile. "I'm not ready to leave yet. Now that we've enjoyed ourselves, we have some business to discuss."

"What are you talking about? What business?"

"Your business, Em—The House of Ronay. I got a rundown on it a couple of months ago, just after we met at Sam's place. You've been doing very well; contracts with the leading department stores and some of the most exclusive shops in the country, more orders coming in every month, and I heard that you were thinking of opening a branch in Europe—Paris, isn't it?"

"What does that have to do with you?"

His smile faded into a hard, level stare. "It's very simple. I want you to turn over your controlling interest in the business to me. I have quite a few companies working for me right now, and yours would make a very prestigious addition."

She looked at him, dumbfounded. "Are you crazy? I'll do no such thing!"

"Oh, yes, you will," Alec replied curtly.

Adrian responded with eyes blazing. "If you want to reveal my past, go ahead! More famous people than I have survived much worse scandals. Nothing you can say or do will hurt my career. If anything, the publicity would probably help sell more clothes!"

Alec stared at her thoughtfully for a moment. Then he put down his drink and stood up. "Don't underestimate me," he said softly. "I've come a long way from seducing little girls into robbing stores. For the past couple of months you've been playing with me like I was some high-school kid, and I let you—that is, I let Adrian Ronay tease the shit out of me. But that's all over. I want your company, and I intend to have it."

Adrian's lips tightened into a thin smile. "Alec, I've come a long way, too. I don't intend to give you anything."

His green eyes turned hard as stone. "I'm going to have everything I want—including you. Oh, not like tonight; that was great fun, but it wasn't enough. You're going to marry me. You've got everything I want—beauty, style, class. I never had that with Sheila, or any of the other women I've known. And there have been a lot. But none as exciting as you."

She stood staring at him, speechless, while he picked up his coat and started for the door.

"There's nothing you can do to frighten me, Alec," she said, following him. "You were a liar and a cheat when I first knew you, and you still are."

He opened the door and turned to face her. There was a dangerous expression on his face that made her take a step back.

"As I said before—don't underestimate me. I can hurt you in more ways than you'd think possible."

He turned his back on her and walked out the door, closing it softly behind him.

Adrian's first thought was to call Sam Phillips on the coast. He was a man with powerful friends—she would tell him about Alec's threats, even confide in him about her past, if she had to.... No, she couldn't do that, not yet. Sam depended on Alec's investors in order to open the show in New York. If she said anything now, that might be jeopardized.

She lit a cigarette and paced nervously for a few minutes, then went to the bar and mixed herself a drink. She had to keep her wits about her, she told herself. Alec was bluffing, dramatizing himself to get back at her. Making her submit to him wasn't enough to soothe his bruised ego; he wanted to intimidate her, frighten her. Well, she wouldn't let him. If he made a single move against her, she'd fight him with everything she had. Even if she had to make public her past, and his part in it.

44

THE SOUND OF THE PHONE JARRED HER AWAKE. ADRIAN looked at the clock and saw that it was almost four in the morning. She remembered lying down to wait for Paul's call; she must have fallen asleep. The phone rang again and she picked it up, answering groggily, "Paul—is that you?"

"Yes, dear..."

"What happened? Why are you calling so late?"

"Adrian—there's been an accident."

"Oh, darling! Are you hurt?"

"No, it's not me—it's Kelly. He's at Jefferson Hospital," Paul replied tersely. "It looks pretty serious—he's in intensive care."

"My God! What happened?"

"We're still not sure. He just regained consciousness a few minutes ago, and the police are trying to get a statement. Can you get down here right away? You can rent a car and be here in about three hours."

"Of course I will," she said. "Paul, what happened to him?"

"I've got to go—his doctor just came out of the room. When you get here, come to Emergency—I'll be waiting."

"I'll get there as quickly as I can."

Adrian called the front desk and asked them to get her a car immediately. She threw on some clothes, wrapped a scarf about her hair, and pulled on a coat. Her heart was pounding, and she was gripped by a feeling of dread.

* * *

Adrian raced the car along the New Jersey Turnpike. All her concerns about Alec had fled with Paul's call. She concentrated on the driving, thinking only about Kelly. By dawn she was on the Pennsylvania Turnpike, just a few miles outside Philadelphia. Night had given way to a grey, oppressive day. A leaden sky hung low over the countryside, and the autumn foliage on both sides of the highway looked like old wallpaper, their colors worn and faded.

The downtown streets of the city were coming to life as she drove into the parking lot of the large red-brick building that was Jefferson Hospital. A biting chill in the air cut through her clothes as she hurried toward the entrance marked EMERGENCY. Paul was in the corridor, waiting for her. His face was ashen and gaunt, his eyes darkly circled from lack of sleep.

Adrian rushed into his arms. He held her close for a few minutes, then led her into the waiting room where they sat down.

"What happened?" she asked anxiously.

"Well—we gave a terrific performance of the show," Paul began. "We decided to go out for a late dinner. Kelly was still packing up his makeup box, so we went on ahead to get a table. He was the last one to leave the theater. We were all waiting for him, and when he didn't show up, I thought maybe he had decided to hit some of the bars instead. After dinner, I went back to the hotel and found a cop waiting for me. He brought me here, and—" He paused and took a deep breath before going on. "Kelly had been found in an alley behind some warehouse. He'd been beaten and..." His voice began to crack. "He was stuffed into one of those big trash cans."

"Oh, God!" Adrian cried, taking Paul in her arms and holding him. "Have they found out who did it?"

Paul straightened up and rubbed his hand over his face. "No, not yet. When Kelly regained consciousness, he couldn't say anything—his jaw had been broken, and his teeth smashed...." He stared at her, hollow-eyed. "I don't think he's going to make it, Adrian...."

She began to cry. "Do you think they'll let me see him?"

Paul took her arm and they went down the hallway to the room marked Intensive Care. Terry Ambler, Milo James, and a group of dancers and actors from the show were huddled together. Ella Korvin was leaning against the wall, being comforted by Christopher Bruce.

A doctor emerged from the room. He looked around the group and asked, "Is Mr. Mallory here?"

Paul and Adrian went up to him. "I'm Paul Mallory," he said. "And this is Adrian Ronay."

"I'm Dr. Lang," he said, shaking hands with them. "Does Mr. Green have any family?"

"No," Paul replied. "We're all the family he has.... How is he?"

Dr. Lang shook his head gravely. "I'm sorry—we did all we could. He lost a lot of blood, and we couldn't stop the internal bleeding. Whoever did it really worked him over. There was nothing we could do to save him."

"Oh, Christ," Paul moaned softly. Adrian buried her head against his chest, weeping. A cry went up from the group and several of the girls began to sob.

A tired-looking man with a lined face and short, thinning grey hair entered the corridor and came up to Dr. Lang. He gave him a questioning look, and the doctor shook his head and said, "We lost him." He turned to Paul and Adrian and introduced the man. "This is Lieutenant Parker; he's with Homicide."

"Have your men learned anything?" Paul asked.

The lieutenant looked over at the grieving actors, then at Paul and Adrian. "You two close friends of Mr. Green?" he asked.

"Yes, we are," Paul answered. "He had no family."

"I'd like to talk with you for a few minutes," Parker said.

"You can use my office," Dr. Lang offered. "It's just down the hall."

Paul went over to Terry and Milo. "Take everybody back to the hotel and get some rest," he said quietly. "We have a show to do tonight."

As the group began to leave, he went back to Adrian and they followed the lieutenant into Dr. Lang's office. The police officer closed the door, and Paul and Adrian sat down. She wiped her eyes with a handkerchief, then clutched Paul's hand.

Lieutenant Parker took out a crumpled pack of cigarettes, freed one, and put it between his lips, but didn't light it. "I'm trying to cut down," he explained gruffly. He sat down on the edge of the desk and said, "Mr. Green was gay, wasn't he?"

"Yes, he was," Adrian replied. "Why do you ask?"

"I wasn't asking—just confirming," Parker replied. "I think this is a gay killing. We've had a couple in the last year or so, and Mr. Green sustained certain injuries that indicate that this is one of them. Did he make a habit of picking up rough trade? You know—men off the streets?"

"Not as far as I know," Adrian said. "Kelly never said anything to me about street pick-ups. He didn't even go to bars very often."

"What kind of injuries did he have to make you think that, Lieutenant?" Paul asked cautiously.

The officer cast a quick glance at Adrian. She saw his reluctance to answer Paul's question and said, "You can tell us. . . . What were the injuries?"

Parker drew a deep breath and replied, "He was pretty badly mutilated. Whoever did it castrated him and shoved a broken wine bottle into his anus. And wrote the word 'faggot' on his chest in his own blood."

Adrian fainted.

Later that afternoon, Adrian and Paul met Lieutenant Parker at police headquarters, where they answered more questions and signed statements. Before they left, an officer brought a large, plastic bag into Parker's office and gave it to him.

The lieutenant opened the bag. "We found this in the alley near Mr. Green's body. Can you identify it?"

Fresh tears filled Adrian's eyes. "That's his makeup case," she said, her voice breaking. "His mother gave it to him. He used it whenever he did a show. He never left it in the theater, but always took it with him. He called it his good-luck charm." She began to cry and Paul put his arms around her.

"We dusted it for prints, but only found Mr. Green's. He must have dropped it when he was attacked."

"May I have it?" Adrian asked.

"Well..." Parker hesitated. "We really should hold on to it...."

"Oh, please—it would mean so much to me," she begged.

Parker put the case back into the plastic bag and handed it to her. "I'm sorry about all this. From what everybody has told me, your friend was quite a guy."

"He was the best," Paul said.

A few minutes later they left the building and got into Adrian's car. Paul said, "I have to get to the theater— we're doing a run-through before tonight's performance. Do you want to wait for me at the hotel?"

"No, I really should get back to New York...."

"Are you sure? You shouldn't be alone—"

"Please, darling—I'd rather. I couldn't bear to be around everybody right now. Will you be all right without me?"

"Not really. But I understand how you feel. Will you call me as soon as you get back? You look so tired—I'm worried about you."

"I'll be okay."

They drove to the theater. Before he got out of the car, she clung to him. "I love you very much, Paul. More than I can say."

He kissed her hands and her lips, then waited on the curb until she drove away.

* * *

Dazed with grief, Adrian took her time driving back to New York. It was twilight, and a scattering of dark clouds moved across the fading sky. A light rain began to fall, and she turned on the windshield wipers. In the distance the rolling hills and meadows began to disappear into a fine, silvery mist. A wind came up, and tree branches bowed before it, lowering their limbs mournfully. It seemed to her as if the earth itself were sharing her sorrow.

It was a little after nine o'clock in the evening when Adrian arrived at the Plaza. She went into the lobby, carrying Kelly's case, and checked in at the desk for messages. The clerk told her there were no calls and handed her an envelope that he said had been delivered by a messenger. She asked him to see that the car was returned to the rental agency, then took the elevator to her suite. Once inside, she put the case down on a chair, shrugged out of her coat, and went to make some coffee. Then she sat down at the desk and opened the envelope. A small gold key fell out. And the note was from Alec Darcy.

Emily,
Sorry about your friend, but now you know I mean what I say. I had to go to Florida for a few days, but I'll be back Sunday night at nine o'clock. The key is to my place on Sutton. I want you to be there waiting for me.

Adrian stared at the words in disbelief. She read the first line of the note again: "Sorry about your friend, but now you know I mean what I say."

Sorry about your friend . . .

An uncontrollable shuddering took hold of her. The room began to blur and swim dizzily, and she held the letter tightly, almost tearing it.

Kelly! He had murdered Kelly!

A sharp pain gripped at the pit of her stomach like a fist and she opened her mouth to scream. But no sound issued from her lips, only a raw, hoarse gasp.

Now you know I mean what I say....

The words repeated themselves over and over, tearing at her brain. Nausea bubbled up in her throat. She dropped the letter and ran to the bathroom, where she fell to her knees and spewed out her revulsion. When she was finished, she sank weakly to the floor and pressed her face against the cold tiles.

Alec had done it. He had ordered Kelly's execution. Not a madman roaming the dark streets looking for a victim to provide a release for his psychotic hatred.

Alec. Handsome, wealthy, and more terrifyingly powerful than she had realized. Behind the cloak of ill-gotten respectability, he had murdered with the same cold-blooded intent as a deranged killer. She was wrong; he was no better than the madman roaming the streets. He *was* the madman.

She reached up, grasped the side of the tub, and pulled herself to her feet. Staggering a little, she made her way blindly back to the desk and stared down at the letter and the key. She wouldn't let him get away with it, she thought, and her hand moved to the phone to call Lieutenant Parker in Philadelphia. But her fingers hovered over the receiver as another, more chilling thought came to her. She had no proof that Alec had done anything; only a typewritten note that was unsigned. And even if they could trace Kelly's murder back to him, how long would it take? And what other horrors would he commit in the meantime?

Adrian fell back into the chair, still staring at the letter. *Now you know I mean what I say*, he had written. The awful words scattered across her mind like a hail of bullets. Suddenly she remembered the opening night of *Cyrano* and heard his voice echoing back over the years: *"There's nothing like it, that feeling of power. It's what everybody wants—to make the world dance on your string. And someday I intend to have it."*

Now he intended to have her and everything she had worked for. And he would stop at nothing to get what he wanted. Kelly's death had simply been a warning. If she didn't acquiesce to his demands, Sheila might be next; poor, foolish Sheila, who was ruled by her emotions. It would be so easy—a drunken fall from the windows of their penthouse. And he would calmly say it was an accident.

Or Paul! A terrible vision flashed across her mind of a car swerving out of nowhere to hit him in the street, leaving him crushed, dead.

A deep and burning hatred began to consume her like a fever. She couldn't let that happen. She couldn't let Alec go on destroying her life and the lives of those she loved. She looked across the room at Kelly's makeup case sitting on the chair where she had put it. The Magical Mystery Makeup Box. She stared at it for a long time and finally knew what she had to do.

She turned back to her desk and glanced at the calendar. It was Friday. Alec would be back in New York Sunday night. That only gave her two days. But it was all the time she needed.

45

Early the next morning, Adrian called Claudia to tell her about Kelly. "The police think it's a gay killing," she said.

"Oh, God, how awful!" Claudia said, shocked. "Are you all right? Why didn't you call me when you got in last night? I'll come right over—"

"No, don't," Adrian said. "I'm all right, really I am. I just want to be alone for a while. Please don't come over. I don't want to see anyone right now."

Claudia was crying. "Are you sure, dear?" she asked, catching her breath.

"I'm positive," Adrian said calmly. "And don't try to call me. I'm going to have the desk take all my calls so that I don't have to speak to any reporters. As soon as I'm feeling all right, I'll call you. But for the time being, I really want to be alone."

Later that afternoon, Adrian left the hotel wearing slacks, a sweater, and a coat. A scarf was tied around her head, and large dark glasses covered her eyes. She walked a few blocks from the hotel and then hailed a cab and told the driver to take her into Lower Manhattan. The cabbie weaved in and out of traffic, blowing the horn and cursing other drivers. It was a bright, sunny day and the sidewalks were thronged with people. Golden shafts of sunlight fell over the city like a benediction, giving the streets a charged, festive air. But Adrian felt none of the excitement. She sat in the back of the cab, quietly waiting to reach her destination.

Soon they were cruising along in the Bowery, a shabby, grimy area filled with decaying, old buildings whose dark doorways and moldy halls hid the secrets of lives crushed by despair. Adrian saw a shop she wanted to go in and asked the cabbie to wait for her. Her transaction only took a few minutes, and then she directed the driver to take her to one of Maxie Klein's suppliers. She didn't mind being recognized and greeted by name; she had done business there many times before, and what she took with her when she left would not particularly be remembered as anything out of the ordinary.

She made one more stop at a neighborhood dress shop on Lexington Avenue. When she was finished there, she returned to the hotel in another cab.

That night, she called Paul to reassure him that she was all right. He told her that the police had started a manhunt all over the city for Kelly's murderer. Adrian made no reply. The search might go on for months in Philadelphia, she thought to herself. But tomorrow night, in New York, it would be over.

She told Paul about the desk taking her calls and said she would get in touch with him again, late Sunday night after the show was over and he was back at his hotel. She told him not to worry about her and that she loved him.

46

Sunday afternoon, Adrian dressed in the same clothes she had worn the day before, packed a small bag, and left the Plaza by the service stairs so that no one would see her. She headed west on Fifty-seventh Street until she reached Broadway. There she turned left and walked down on the broad thoroughfare. Near the corner of Forty-eighth Street, she found what she was looking for.

Layers of old paint were flaking off the frame of the door, and the single word "Hotel" lettered on the inset window was scratched and faded, almost obscured by streaks of dust. Inside the door, a staircase led to a landing where a Puerto Rican youth sat behind a check-in counter, watching a movie on a small, black-and-white television set.

Adrian signed something indecipherable in the register and paid in advance for one night. The boy looked away from the TV set long enough to take the money and hand her a key. He jerked a thumb at a door down the hall, then went back to watching the movie. He had barely glanced at her.

The room had flaking, scarred walls, a narrow cot of a bed and a dirt-encrusted bathroom. It was every nightmare she'd ever had about being back in her prison cell. She put the bag down on the bed and glanced at the dust-layered mirror over an ancient dresser standing against the wall. Then she went into the bathroom, took a handful of toilet paper, dampened it, and came back. It took her a long time to clean the mirror, but finally she was able to see a clear reflection of herself. Satisfied, she opened the bag, unpacked it, and began to prepare for her meeting with Alec.

47

AT SIX O'CLOCK, ADRIAN LEFT THE HOTEL. IT WAS DUSK, and along the street lights were coming on, blazing a colorful invitation to bars, coffee shops, cheap restaurants, and a porno movie house featuring blatant posters of naked men and women in the throes of sexual excitement. She walked a block before flagging down a cab and told the driver to take her to Sutton Place.

She got out a few blocks away from Alec's town house and walked the rest of the way. At the front door, she took the gold key out of her purse and let herself in. She stood in the foyer for a moment; the rooms filled with tasteless, expensive furniture were dark. She found a light switch at the foot of the stairs, turned it on, and went up to the master suite on the second floor. On the panel of switches over the circular bed, she located the one controlling the lights and fumbled with it until the room was dimly lit. A glance at her watch told her it was six-thirty. She walked to the windows, parted the drapes a little so she could see the street, and waited.

A few minutes after seven, Adrian saw Alec's car drive up to the front of the house. He got out, said something to his chauffeur, then started for the front steps as the car drove off. Adrian stepped away from the window and held her breath. She heard the front door open and close. Alec called out, "Emily?"

"I'm up here."

As he started up the steps, she walked swiftly to the dressing room and closed the door.

Alec came into the room and said, "Where are you?"

"In the dressing room," she replied. "Why don't you get comfortable and mix some drinks? I'll be out in a minute."

Alec took off his coat and jacket, loosened his tie, and went to the bar. "I couldn't wait to get home," he said gaily. "Couldn't wait to see you again, baby." He went to the bar and set up two glasses. "Champagne?" he asked. "To celebrate?"

"Yes..."

Alec opened a small freezer, filled a bucket with ice cubes, and set it on the bar. He took a bottle from a rack, worked it into the ice bucket, then went to the fireplace and lit the gas to start a fire.

Adrian waited behind the door, wondering if he would say anything about what he had done, if he would even mention Kelly. No—he was behaving as if nothing had happened. In a way she was glad; it would make what she had to do that much easier.

"Hey, how long are you going to be?" Alec called, sitting down at the bar. "I'm getting very lonely out here."

"I'm coming." Adrian opened the door of the dressing room and slowly began to walk toward him.

"I'll open the champagne," he started to say, then saw that she had stopped halfway across the room. "What's the matter? Why are you—" His face went pale and he gasped at her. "What the hell are you doing?"

The woman who stood before him, arms at her sides, was wearing a cheap cotton dress and low-heeled shoes. Long, dark brown hair fell to her shoulders, and a fringe of bangs covered her temple. On the left side of her face there was a jagged red scar that ran from her temple down to the bottom of her jaw. The welted scar tissue pulled at the corner of her left eye and tugged one side of her mouth into a grimace.

"Here I am," she said quietly. "Just the way you want me."

"Emily, for Christ's sake!"

"That's right. I'm Emily." She raised her right arm. A revolver was clutched in her hand. "Amazing what you can do with makeup, isn't it? I used Kelly's makeup box to recreate myself, just as you once knew me. In a way, he's helping me to avenge his death." She paused, then said tonelessly, "You murdered him. And now you're going to die for it."

Sweat broke out on Alec's face. "I didn't kill him," he protested. "I just made a phone call. I said I wanted him roughed up a little—not killed!"

"It comes to the same thing."

Alec began to plead. "Em—don't do this. . . . You won't get away with it—one shot and the whole street will hear it."

"No they won't. See?" She lifted the gun slightly. "There's a silencer on it. I tried to think of everything—" She gave a low, mirthless laugh. "All those old movies I watched taught me something. I bought this at a pawnshop in the Bowery—no papers, no permit, no questions."

"Someone must have seen you coming here," he cried. "They'll remember you!"

"They'll remember a girl with a scarred face and cheap clothes. They'll describe Emily Gorden, not Adrian Ronay. She's in seclusion at the Plaza mourning the death of her closest friend."

Suddenly Sheila's voice said from the doorway, "So that's why I couldn't reach you." She walked into the room, giving no sign of emotion.

Alec looked at his wife, stunned. "How did you get in? How did you know about this place?"

"I've known about it since you moved in," Sheila said calmly. "And I have a key. I stole yours and made a duplicate. You taught me that trick in Vegas—remember?"

Without taking her eyes off Alec, Adrian said, "How did you know I was here?"

"I didn't. But when I couldn't contact you at the hotel, I thought you might be."

Alec said hoarsely, "Sheila, get the gun away from her. She's crazy! She wants to kill me!"

"I know—I've been listening at the door," she replied. "I heard all of it."

Alec stared at her wild-eyed. "Get the gun!"

Sheila ignored him and went up to Adrian. She looked at her sister and exclaimed softly, "Jesus! Oh, Em—I'd forgotten you looked like that...."

Adrian stared straight ahead, her eyes fixed on Alec. "Don't try to stop me, Sheila—"

Alec began to plead. "Baby, take the gun! Please!"

Sheila swung around and faced him. "You were going to dump me for her, weren't you? Maybe get rid of me the way you got rid of her friend?"

"No, Sheila, I swear!"

"Sure you were. I know I'm not very bright, but it didn't take me long to figure out how stupid I'd been to tell you about her. I practically threw you into her arms, didn't I?" She glanced at Adrian. "You know what's funny about all this, Em? Even when we were kids, when you really had the scar, I was envious of you. Oh, sure—I had all the looks, but you had brains and ambition. You were going to do something with your life. And then you met this piece of shit—"

Alec began to babble. "Baby, please, I'll do anything you say—I'll make it all up to you. I swear I will! You know you're the only one—"

"And when he was finished with you," Sheila went on, "he ran away with me and made me just as rotten as he is."

She moved close to Adrian and put her hand on the gun. "I can't let you do this, Em—"

"Sheila, get out of my way," Adrian said tensely. "I don't want to hurt you."

"Of course you don't," she said gently. "And you don't want to hurt yourself, or Paul, either." Her fingers closed around the gun. "Let go, Emily," she said softly. "You could never kill Alec. You're not that tough."

Adrian felt something inside her give way, like a fragile piece of cloth being torn. Tears filled her eyes, and she let Sheila take the gun.

Alec fell weakly against the bar, grinning with relief. Then he held out his hand. "Better give that to me before somebody get's hurt—"

"Sure, lover," Sheila said. And then she fired.

There was a soft, popping sound. Alec's eyes filled with surprise as a red stain began to spread across the front of his white shirt. He lurched toward Sheila, reaching for the gun, and she fired again. He threw himself on her and grabbed her wrist, twisted her arm. Sheila screamed and they grappled with each other. Alec got the gun away from her and she struck at him with her fists. There were two more quick pops from the gun, and suddenly they were both still, clutched in an awkward embrace.

Adrian stared at them in shock. She tried to move but her legs felt leaden, heavy, as if they were being sucked into a swamp with each step.

Alec gave a terrible, raw gasp and began to slide to the floor, leaving a smear of blood on the front of Sheila's dress. He slipped to his knees, the gun in one hand, the other clutching at her skirt. He looked up at her and tried to say something and a gush of blood spilled from his lips. Then he sank to the floor and was still.

Sheila stared down at him, her face chalk white, then slowly raised her eyes to Adrian and whimpered, "Emily—" She began to double over.

Adrian forced herself to move, and caught Sheila before she fell, easing her down onto the floor. Sheila's eyes were open, the lids fluttering rapidly. "Don't move," Adrian cried. "I'll call the police...."

"No," Sheila whispered. Her hand clutched wildly at

431

the air, and Adrian took it, held it tightly. Sheila turned her head slightly to look at Alec. "Is he dead?"

"Yes," Adrian wept. She put her arm under Sheila's shoulders and lay next to her, their faces close together.

"Em—I'm sorry," Sheila said. The words came out in short, wheezing breaths. "I'm sorry about everything. . . ."

"Baby, don't talk—let me call someone, a doctor—"

"Not worth it. Too late, anyway . . ." Sheila's eyes began to cloud over. "Get out of here, Em—no one will ever know. . . ."

"I can't leave you—"

"Yes, you can—you must. . . . God, he was really beautiful, wasn't he?"

She squeezed Adrian's hand tightly, then turned and flung her arm out to Alec, her hand falling against his arm.

48

ADRIAN MOVED THROUGH THE STREETS LIKE A SLEEP-
walker. Images of Alec and Sheila lying dead on the floor
wavered before her eyes like flash photos, all white glare
and blurred faces. Somehow she managed to get back to
the hotel on Broadway. In the bathroom, she took off the
wig, peeled away the makeup-covered tissues that had
been the scar, and washed her face. Then she packed
Kelly's makeup case and her dress, put on her slacks,
sweater, and coat, and left the hotel.

She walked back to the Plaza, slipped in a side door
and took the service stairs to her suite. Once inside, she
closed and locked the door, put the bag down and staggered into the bedroom, where she fell across the bed,
exhausted. For a long time she lay very still. Then she
began to cry, her fist clenched into her mouth like a lost
and frightened child. Time seemed to stop while she wept,
as if her tears were washing away all the pain and anguish
of the past and the horror that had just taken place.

Hours later she stood by the window, looking out at
the city. It seemed to her a vast, dark territory concealing
the secrets that remain at the center of people's lives. But
not her life, not any longer. She felt she had been given
a new understanding of the differences between her two
identities. Adrian Ronay had fed her ambition on dreams
of revenge. But Emily Gorden had not been capable of
realizing that revenge; it was not in her character. Despite

everything she'd had to do as Adrian, the virtues of Emily had survived.

She glanced at her watch; it was almost midnight, and she had promised Paul that she would call him. She went to the phone and dialed his hotel in Philadelphia. While she waited for the operator to ring his room, she glanced up at her reflection in the mirror and smiled. There was no trace of Emily Gorden. Now she could finally accept the fact that the face of Adrian Ronay belonged to the world.

And she realized at last that it also belonged to her.